**Praise for Iris Johansen
and Her Acclaimed Trilogy . . .**

EVE

"Johansen launches a trilogy that takes the reader on an action-packed journey filled with killers and heroes, leaving readers on tenterhooks." —*Booklist*

"Gripping . . . Johansen deftly baits the hook for the next volume." —*Publishers Weekly*

"The suspense and action will entertain all, even those new to the series."

—*Library Journal* (starred review)

"Johansen's stories keep getting better with each installment. You will find yourself drawn to Eve and caring about what happens to her."

—*Night Owl Reviews* (Top Pick)

"A superb kickoff . . . an excellent presentation to this fantastic series that is a one-sitting read."

—*Reader to Reader Reviews*

"Read *Eve* and be hooked." —*RT Book Reviews*

QUINN

"The pulse-pounding pace will leave readers breathlessly anticipating the final installment."

—*Publishers Weekly* (starred review)

TAKING EVE

IRIS JOHANSEN

St. Martin's Paperbacks

This is a work of fiction. All of the characters, organizations, and events portrayed in this novel are either products of the author's imagination or are used fictitiously.

Published in the United States by St. Martin's Paperbacks, an imprint of St. Martin's Publishing Group

TAKING EVE

Copyright © 2013 by Johansen Publishing LLLP.
Excerpt from *Hunting Eve* copyright © 2013 by Johansen Publishing LLLP.

For information, address St. Martin's Publishing Group, 120 Broadway, New York, NY 10271.

www.stmartins.com

Library of Congress Catalog Card Number: 2013002635

ISBN: 978-1-250-83285-6

Our books may be purchased in bulk for promotional, educational, or business use. Please contact your local bookseller or the Macmillan Corporate and Premium Sales Department at 1-800-221-7945, ext. 5442, or by email at MacmillanSpecialMarkets@macmillan.com.

Printed in the United States of America

St. Martin's Press hardcover edition / April 2013
St. Martin's Paperbacks edition / October 2013

10 9 8 7 6 5 4 3 2 1

CHAPTER

1

He was ready.

Jim Doane drew a deep breath as he locked the front door of the small cedar house behind him. All the searching and planning was at an end, and now it was time to put the plan into action.

Soon, Kevin. I know it's been a long time, but I had to be sure before I moved forward. Everything has to be in place.

He threw his suitcase into the trunk of the car, then carried his metal toolbox and shoved it onto the passenger seat. Then he climbed into the driver's seat and started the car.

"Doane, wait." His neighbor Ralph Hodder was running toward him across the postage stamp–sized lawn that separated their houses. "Did you think you were going to get away before I saw you?" He was breathing heavily as he stopped beside Doane's car. He was overweight, and even the short run had robbed him of breath. "No way, man."

"Yeah?" He tensed, then deliberately forced himself to relax. Hodder was no threat. He was overreacting. "Do you need something, Ralph?"

"Yeah, I need to thank you. My son said that you were going to be gone for quite a while, and I just wanted you to know I'd keep an eye on your place." He clapped him on the shoulder. "We'll miss you. You've been a good friend to Matt, a real role model, and Leah and I appreciate it. Raising a teenage kid is always a headache, but having you next door, helping him work on that old car, and letting him talk to you has made it easier."

"No problem. Matt's a fine boy, and I was glad to help. In the end, the most precious things we have are our children."

"You're right there." His smile faded. "Matt said you were leaving because you had family trouble. I hope that everything will be okay."

"It will be fine. But it may take a little while, so I'm grateful that you're going to watch the place." He'd better pretend to be concerned. It wouldn't do to let Hodder know he'd been tempted to burn the place to the ground. "I'll call you now and then and check on it if that's all right."

"We'll be glad to hear from you. I'll have Matt cut your grass until you get back." He stepped back from the car. "You've been a great neighbor, Doane. I'll try to be one, too. Thanks for being good to my son."

"Take care of that boy," Doane said as he backed

down the driveway. "You never realize how much you love them until you lose them. Believe me, I know."

But that wasn't true; he had known how much he had loved his son from the moment he had been born. It hadn't taken loss to drive that truth home. His Kevin had been extraordinary in every way, and being his father had dominated his life.

Until that bastard had taken away his son.

He controlled the flare of rage that went through him. He could not afford anger now that the game had begun. Everything must go according to plan. All the sorrow and rage must be put away until he had the weapon he needed to satisfy it.

He checked his GPS, which was already set for Atlanta, Georgia, and pulled out his address book. He hesitated, then carefully looked around him before he reached over and unfastened the large tool chest on the passenger seat and flipped open the lid.

He needed to share this first moment of the journey with his son. They had both waited far too long. He drew back the velvet cover he had draped over the silk nest he had built in the interior of the tool chest. "We're on our way, Kevin. I'm keeping my promise."

The empty eyeholes of the burned and blackened skull gazed up at him.

Pain shot through him. After all these years, you would have thought he'd become accustomed to the horror, but there were still moments like this when it hit home. He remembered what a handsome boy Kevin had been and his sweet smile and the way he . . . Tears stung his eyes. He reached out and deliberately touched the skull. "Forgive me. I still love you. I'll always love you." His gaze lifted to the photo of the woman taped to the lid of the tool chest. "She'll give you back to me the way you were." His lips tightened. "And then she'll give us the son of a bitch who did this to you." He gave one last look at the skull before he closed the lid. "She can do it all, Kevin. We'll see that she makes it happen."

He reached forward to the GPS and typed in Eve Duncan's address.

Darkness! Smothering. No breath! Can't breathe.

"Hey, wake up." Joe's lips brushed Eve's as he cuddled her closer in the bed. "Nightmare alert."

Her eyes flew open, and she stared up at him. Joe. Smiling. Safety. She immediately relaxed and drew a deep breath. "I'm awake. Sorry."

"Nothing to be sorry about. You were just panting as if someone were trying to smother you." He stood up. "I thought you should wake up and get back to the real world."

Smothering. Yes, she vaguely remembered that sensation. Darkness closing in and something, someone, fighting to keep the smothering suffocation away from her. "I'm duly grateful." She sat up in bed. "Not a pleasant dream." She tilted her head. "You're already dressed. Are you going in to the precinct this morning? I thought you had a plane to catch. That Miami court case."

"Later today. Paperwork this morning." He pulled her from bed. "Come on. Have coffee with me before I leave."

"Gladly. I definitely don't want to go back to sleep." She grabbed her robe and followed him out of the bedroom. "And I have to work on Ryan's reconstruction anyway. I made a lot of headway last night, and I might finish today." She passed the worktable and dais where the little boy's skull was placed, waiting for the final forensic sculpting. "It's going well."

"They all go well." He handed her a cup of coffee. "They wouldn't dare do anything else. You're the best, aren't you?"

"One of the best." She took the coffee and went out on the porch. The early-morning sunlight was shimmering on the lake, and the air was cool and clear. "And they do not all go well. Sometimes things seem to get in the way. Why are you being so complimentary?"

"What can I say? I'm just a man." He chuckled as he sat down in the swing and pulled her into his arms. "I'm encouraging you to have good thoughts while I'm gone so that I can look forward to one hell of a homecoming celebration."

"You're only going to be gone two days," she said dryly. "I'll hardly have time to miss you."

"You really know how to hurt a guy."

"I'll miss you," she whispered as she cuddled closer. Moments like this were precious. They had been together for so many years, and yet the love kept deepening with the passing of time. "Maybe. Who knows? I might have another nightmare." She gave him a quick kiss. "You're my hero."

"It was that bad?"

She wished she hadn't mentioned that dream even as a joke. Joe was always fighting to keep her safe, but who could fight against a nightmare? But it was a nightmare that was still with her. She couldn't seem to shake it.

"It was . . . like a battle. I was being smothered, and someone was trying to stop it. But they couldn't do it, and I wasn't sure I could either." She sat up from the swing. "But you came to the rescue, and everything turned out fine. So let's forget it." She finished her coffee and pulled him to his feet. "Now you get to work, and so will I. If you get back in time, maybe we'll have lunch together before you have to go to the airport."

"I'll get back in time." He ran down the steps. "I just wish I could be here when Jane arrives. I'll be flying out when she's flying in."

Jane, their adopted daughter, would be sorry, too. She was an artist who had been temporarily living in London because her work had taken off at light speed in Europe, and she needed to be available for gallery shows. She had called Eve a month ago and said that enough was enough, and she was coming home to the people she loved. Joe seldom was called out of town, and Jane would be disappointed not to see both of them at the airport. "She'll still be here when you get back."

"But I know you were looking forward to family time. We haven't been together in a long time." He frowned. "It's not as if we're the typical normal family. I hate like hell to disappoint you."

"You're not disappointing me. You're doing what you have to do. It's your job. What family is normal except on the sitcoms?" She smiled as she shook her head. "And today they all create their own definition of normal. And what was normal about our families when we were growing up? You were a rich boy whose parents stuck you in snooty boarding schools. I was a slum kid with a mother who never even knew who my father was and was high on drugs all through my childhood. I'd say by comparison we're doing pretty damn well. We all love each other and guard each other and give each other freedom. That's awesome, Joe."

He smiled back at her. "I guess it is. Thanks for reminding me."

"You're welcome. I just have to keep an eye on your penchant for trying to make everything perfect. Perfect can be boring." She watched him open the car door. "Maybe we'll have a barbecue the night you fly in."

He lifted a wicked brow. "That's not the celebration I had in mind."

"So much for family time." She chuckled. "You'll enjoy that one, too. Why not have—Joe?"

He was standing ramrod straight, his head lifted, looking out at the lake, the smile completely gone.

"Joe, what's wrong?"

He jerked his gaze back to her. "Nothing. Just a—I don't know." He opened the car door. "I'll be back in a few hours."

She watched the car go down the road and around the curve before she slowly turned and went in the house. Those last few minutes had made her uneasy, and it was difficult to dismiss them.

But she would dismiss them. It was time to forget nightmares and unexplained uneasiness. The sun was shining, and she had to get on with her life. It was a good life, with purpose and people she loved. That was what was important. She moved quickly back to the bedroom to dress and get ready to work on Ryan.

VANCOUVER, CANADA

"Venable phoned," Howard Stang said when Lee Zander walked into the house after his gym work-out. "He called on my cell. He wasn't happy when he couldn't reach you. He should know by now that you change your phones every week or so."

"Venable is always unhappy when things don't go like clockwork. That's his CIA mind-set. He takes it as a personal insult." Zander dropped down in the chair in front of the fire. "Did he say what he wanted?"

"For you to call him back." He grimaced. "Venable doesn't confide in me. Not that I'd want him to. I prefer to stay out of the CIA's sphere of influence."

"So do I."

"It's not the same. I'm intimidated, and you just choose to avoid." Stang studied Zander as he watched him reach for his phone. Lee Zander was a tall, muscular man with white hair cropped short and a bone structure that was both craggy and bold. His brown eyes were sunk deep in his tan face beneath a slash of dark brows. Stang had no idea how old he was . . . fifties? Sixties? It didn't matter. He appeared ageless, and he had seen Zander take down men who must have been half his age. He kept that powerful body exercised and his mind razor-sharp. Stang could not imagine Zander being influenced or intimidated by anyone, even a power player like Venable. Stang had been working for him for the last three years as his personal assistant and accountant, and he had never lost his respect . . . or his fear . . . of Zander. At times, he wondered why he stayed with him when the comfort level was always being jeopardized by the uncertainty of how Zander would respond to any given situation. But those moments were rare; when he subdued the panic, he knew exactly why he stayed with him. He'd made a decision years ago when he'd sworn on his brother's grave that he'd never leave Zander until the day he died. "Venable sounded urgent."

"He never calls me unless it's urgent." He gazed at him as he punched in the number. "I'll probably need to talk to you after I finish with him."

"Why?" Stang unconsciously tensed. "Is something wrong? Did I—"

"Why do you always think that something is wrong?" His lips twisted. "You're brilliant. Everything you touch turns to gold. You give me choices."

"Then what do you—"

"Venable?" Zander held up his hand and gestured for Stang to go out on the terrace. "What's the problem?"

Stang had already reached the French doors and was opening them. It was standard operating procedure. Zander never permitted him to be in the room when he was dealing with anyone. For his part, he wanted no part of knowing anything about Zander's lethal business. It could either make him an accessory or a danger to Zander or his client. Neither prospect was appealing.

He strolled over to the balcony and gazed out at the

mountains. It was a glorious view from this magnificent house. Stay out of hearing range and just stand here and wait for Zander to finish with Venable and get to him.

And hope to hell he hadn't screwed up.

"You took your time about calling me back," Venable growled. "Or was it that Stang took his time about telling you I called?"

"I was working out in the gym. He has orders not to disturb me unless he knows that it's important."

"And he was too scared to make a mistake. I don't know why he stays with you. He's smart as a whip and makes you richer than you deserve to be. He could be one of the fair-haired boys on Wall Street if he walked away."

"It's complicated. We have a history. I don't think Stang can decide whether or not to slip arsenic into my brandy. I'm curious to see if he whips up enough courage to do it. You did impress him enough that he told me the minute I walked into the house." He paused. "But evidently it wasn't that urgent if you're choosing to growl at me instead of telling me what the matter is. I'll give you two minutes, then I'll—"

"Doane has taken off."

Zander's hand tightened on the phone. "Really? When?"

"He left Goldfork, Colorado, at seven this morning according to his neighbor."

"According to his neighbor?" Zander's tone was icy. "Weren't you supposed to have him under surveillance? Wasn't that our agreement?"

"We've been watching him for five years. Naturally, you tend to relax when there's been no change in the status quo in that time."

"Bullshit."

"Okay, our agent screwed up."

"Yes, he did. Do you have any idea where he was going?"

"He said family emergency."

"He has no family. He's coming after me."

"You don't know that. He has no idea that it was you who did the killing."

"Doane is obsessed, and he's had five years to hunt for answers. I would have found those answers long ago. I'd bet he's only been waiting for his chance."

"What are you going to do?"

"What do you think? We had a deal. I told you I'd leave Doane alone as long as it was safe for me. You screwed up. I'm not going to wait around for him to come knocking on my door. I'll get rid of him in the most convenient and safe way for me."

"Let us try to find him first."

"No. I trusted you once. It was a mistake. I won't do it again."

Venable muttered a curse. "You cold son of a bitch. What kind of monster are you?"

"You know what kind of monster. You've used me on occasion . . . when the game was rich enough." He paused. "The world is overrun with monsters. I'm just the one who doesn't make excuses."

"Two days. Give me two days. I'm having an agent break into his house and see if he can find the disk or a way to trace him."

"I don't give a damn about the disk. Give it up. Why does it matter to you if he lives or dies?"

"I made a promise. This isn't only about you. I do give a damn about the disk and several lives that are more important than yours. After all these years of keeping him contained, I'm not going to let Doane ruin everything for us." He added sarcastically, "I know that sounds bizarre to you that anyone would care to keep his word."

"Why? I always keep my word," Zander said. "I told you exactly what would happen if you lost track of Doane."

"Two days."

Zander thought about it. It would take him one day to wind up things here, and now that he was alerted, he could afford to give Venable the time he wanted. "Two days. But I want to know what your agent finds out. If you don't gather Doane in, I'll be right on top of him. No second chance." He paused. "And find out if he knows about Eve Duncan."

"There's been no sign that he's even been looking for her."

"But then you've obviously been taking Doane for granted all these years. How would you know if he's gone after her?"

Silence. "And would you care?"

"You know me better than that. I just have to know which way the bastard is going to dodge." He hung up and headed for the desk across the room.

He was surprised he'd had to nudge Venable to explore the Eve Duncan possibility. The CIA agent not only knew Duncan but liked her. Perhaps he was rejecting the idea because he did care about her and didn't want to accept the blame for turning Doane loose on her. Foolish. You couldn't ever allow feelings to interfere if you wanted to stay alive.

He opened the drawer of the desk, drew out the folder he always kept handy, and flipped it open. Eve Duncan's photo and dossier were front and center. The dossier was short and concise. Duncan was illegitimate and raised in the slums of Atlanta, Georgia. She'd been raised by a mother who hadn't known or cared who Eve's father could be and who'd been hooked on drugs for most of Eve's childhood. That hadn't stopped Eve from becoming one of the foremost forensic sculptors in the world and in demand by every law-enforcement authority in the U.S. Her career had been motivated by the kidnapping and murder of her daughter, Bonnie, when the child was only seven years old. She had only recently discovered the child's body and the person responsible for her abduction and death.

And Zander could see in her face the pain and endurance that had been the result of that agonizing search. Eve Duncan was not a beautiful woman, but her features were interesting, and her hazel eyes gazed out of the photo with directness and boldness as if to challenge the world.

But she did not have to fight that world alone. She might be queen of her particular world, but she had two knights who were always on guard.

He had placed two other photos and brief dossiers on either side of Eve Duncan's. Joe Quinn, her lover, whose square face and tea-colored eyes reflected both strength and intelligence, and Jane MacGuire, Eve's adopted daughter, who was far more beautiful than Eve and reputedly just as strong. It was always Zander's procedure to surround the target with the paths to get to them so that he could study the possibilities. In this case, Quinn and MacGuire could be either the guardians to protect Eve Duncan or Doane's means to the end.

If Doane had searched deep enough to find Eve Duncan.

There was a possibility he was wrong, and Doane hadn't made the connection. He might be coming directly to him. Oh well, it was possible he would know as soon as Venable got into Doane's house and looked around. If Doane was on the move, he must have a plan, and he might deliberately leave clues to taunt him. No one could say Doane was entirely sane, but then neither was he. Madness was all in the eye of the beholder.

He stared thoughtfully at the glimpse of mountains he could see beyond the French doors. It would be a long time before he'd see those mountains again. Perhaps never. The Doane problem might make it unsafe for him to chance staying here any longer. He had a twinge of regret before he shrugged it off. He had been here too long anyway. It would only have been a matter of weeks or months before it was time for him to move on. Doane's flit had only escalated the action. He had a keen sense of self-preservation, and it was never safe for him to forget who and what he was. He had only stayed alive this long by recognizing that he was always a target. Someday, he would grow tired and no longer care, but that day had not yet come.

He got to his feet and moved toward the door. "Stang.

Pack up all the records and destroy the computers. Move the money to the alternate bank accounts. I want it done by the end of the day. I'm leaving Canada."

"What?" Stang whirled to face him. "What's wrong?"

"Nothing. It's just time I faded away . . . and cut all ties. Do it."

Stang opened his lips to protest, then closed them again. "Yes, sir. Whatever you say." He left the library.

Zander strolled back to the desk as the door closed behind Stang. He looked down at the faces on the dossiers. The premonition was growing stronger by the moment that Doane might have probed deep enough to reveal a possible vulnerability in Eve Duncan.

No proof.

But he would have been a dead man a dozen times over if he had relied on proof instead of instinct.

Joe Quinn and Jane MacGuire. They were the guardians at the gates of the castle that was Eve Duncan. Strong and competent guardians. Joe Quinn was particularly formidable, a detective with the Atlanta Police Department, ex-SEAL, ex-FBI. Totally devoted to Eve. Jane MacGuire was an up-and-coming artist, but she had been trained by Joe Quinn, and she, too, was devoted to Eve, who was more best friend than parent to her. She had been a street kid until she was ten years old, and she and Eve had found each other. The reports on her were that her ingrained toughness was still present and had become a force with which to be reckoned since she had left college.

Yes, Quinn and MacGuire should be able to keep Eve Duncan safe.

As long as those guardians at the gates stayed close, alert, and on guard.

LAKE COTTAGE

ATLANTA, GEORGIA

"I'll be back in two days." Joe brought Eve close and kissed her, hard. "I have to testify tomorrow afternoon in Miami, a cross-examination the next morning, then I'm out of there. I promise."

"Maybe." Eve made a face. "How many times have you been tripped up by lawyers? They might bring in another witness and put you on hold." She kissed him again and stepped back. He was frowning, and she had sensed an edginess since he'd walked into the cottage for lunch. "It's okay, Joe. It's not as if I won't have company. You know that Jane will be flying in from London tonight."

"Yeah, I know. It makes me feel better but I should—"

"You should do exactly what you're doing. Jane and I can handle everything here on the home front. I'll miss you like crazy, but I know better than to fight the system. And I don't like drug dealers. I want Martinez to be put away for a long time."

"Me, too. We've been working on pinning this drug deal on him for two years. And hopefully he'll run into a rival drug king in jail who will stick a knife in him and save the prison system trouble and money," Joe said grimly. "What time does Jane come in?"

"Eight." She opened the door and walked out with him on to the porch. "And she says this is going to be

a long, long visit, so you won't miss her. We'll both
meet your plane when you come back." She kissed him
again. "So hurry and get through with Martinez, dammit."

He started down the stairs, then stopped and turned
back to look at her. "I don't want to do this."

She frowned. "Joe, you're being weird. What's
wrong?"

He shook his head. "I don't know. I just don't want
to leave you."

"And that's all?"

He shrugged. "I had a call from Venable about an
hour ago."

"And?"

"Nothing. He said that he heard about the Martinez
case and was glad that we were going to nail the bastard at last."

"Did he have something to do with the case?"

"He's CIA. Not DEA. Marginally, perhaps. Nothing
direct."

"So why did he call?"

"That's what I'm asking myself. After he finished
talking about the Martinez case, he asked about me and
you and Jane. It was more like a casual social call." He
added grimly, "And Venable is never either casual or
social. He always has a reason."

"But this time it appears to have more to do with you
and Martinez than me. So why be worried about me?
Venable may be showing up at the courthouse down at
Miami."

"I doubt it. It sounded . . . like an excuse. I may call
him back."

"Joe."

"Okay, I'm going. Since you're obviously trying to get rid of me."

"Because it's your job." She smiled. "And you'd only get in my way. I've got to try to finish Ryan's reconstruction before I go pick up Jane. Heaven knows, I won't have time once she gets here. She's already set up visits with half her friends from school, and it seems I'm included in those plans."

"Of course you are. You're her best friend."

"Yeah." She smiled brilliantly. "Nice, isn't it?"

"When it doesn't get in the way of your work."

"I can live with it. She can be pretty obsessive about her own work. She jokes about being a starving artist, but she'd never be anything else. It's usually a good balance." She watched him walk down the steps. "Are you sure you don't want me to take you to the airport?"

"No, I'm meeting the captain at the precinct, and she's giving me a final briefing. I'll leave the car at the airport." He grinned. "But I'll still expect my two favorite women to meet that plane. I'll get someone to pick up the car."

"We'll be there." She watched him get into the jeep. "Call me when you get settled."

He nodded as he started the car. "I'll probably be able to talk to Jane by that time. It will—" He broke off, his expression suddenly serious. "Be careful."

"Joe . . ." She shook her head. "You're the one taking a trip to face the big bad drug mogul. Jane and I are going to stay here and catch up on what we've missed."

"Yeah, I know." He started to back out of the driveway. "Just . . . be careful."

"Right." She watched him drive down the road until he went around the bend. She didn't want to let him go. She had made fun of his unusual concern, but neither of them ever took the love between them for granted. Maybe he sensed something wrong, something that would endanger that bond. You couldn't live your life worrying because you felt things weren't right. That wouldn't be logical or smart. Yet you couldn't ignore those feelings either.

She shivered suddenly and turned to go back into the house. Had Joe's uneasiness been contagious, or was she feeling that same sense of something . . . not right?

Forget it. She had work to do.

She strode over to the dais, where her current reconstruction was displayed.

"We have to finish you right away, Ryan. Jane is coming," she murmured. She always gave her skulls a name so that she could maintain a connection that would help her with the reconstruction. Her hands moved gently, sculpting, smoothing. She felt the same calming closeness as she usually did when working at bringing these lost ones back to the world that had abandoned them. It was as if their souls were trying to reach her, tell her, help her. "No disrespect. We did the big work last night and this morning. Just a little tidying up, then I'll add the eyes . . ."

She had no idea who this little boy, who had been sent to her by the Bloomington Police Department, actually was. She estimated he was nine years old. He had been unearthed in a grave in a construction site, and no one had been able to offer a clue to his identity.

Hopefully, once the photos were taken of the completed reconstruction, he would be identified.

And so would his murderer.

Ryan would go home.

And hopefully the person who had shoved him into that grave would go straight to hell.

"Brown eyes, Ryan . . ." She always used brown because they were more common than lighter shades. She carefully put the glass eyes into the orbits. "What a handsome little boy you are . . ."

BIRMINGHAM, ALABAMA

"We're getting close, Kevin," Doane murmured, turning on his lights as he got on the freeway. "The next state. I'll have to stop once we're over the border and steal a license plate. Venable will know that I've left Colorado by now. It wouldn't be smart to let him know where we're heading, would it? You'd have probably changed the plate before now. And once we reach the lake cottage, I'll definitely have to change cars. Or maybe a truck . . . You were always better at this than I was." He turned on his computer on the seat beside him. "But I'm trying, Kevin. I worked it all out. I won't let you down." He typed in a quick e-mail to Blick on the computer. "In place?"

No answer.

Doane could feel a trace of panic surge through him. "It will be okay, Kevin. It takes time. Blick won't let us down. We've been planning this for months. I've told him exactly what to do."

His computer suddenly pinged. Blick.

"In place."

Relief flooded Doane. "You see, I told you. He's steady. He'll do the job," he murmured as he got on the freeway. "I just have to keep him from killing her . . ."

LAKE COTTAGE

Eve glanced at the clock across the room—6:10 P.M.

Time to shower and head for the airport.

She wiped the clay from her hands on the cloth she kept on the worktable beside the reconstruction. "Okay, Ryan. That's as good as I can do. No, as good as *we* can do. You helped a lot." Coffee, first. She hadn't had anything to eat or drink since lunch, and she didn't know how long it would be before Jane got out of Customs.

She popped in a Southern Pecan K-cup in her Keurig. She didn't need anything stronger, and she liked the smell of the brew. These single-cup coffee-makers were a miracle on par with—

Her cell phone rang. Jane.

"Don't tell me your flight got in early. I haven't left the cottage yet."

"No, I'm in San Juan."

Eve stiffened with shock. "What?"

"I know. I meant to call you earlier, but there was an emergency, and I had to arrange to leave London. I got a lift on a private jet."

"Why on earth?"

"Toby. My dog's sick, Eve." Her voice was shaking. "The vet in London didn't know what was wrong. Toby's just getting weaker and weaker. The vet can't pin it down, and nothing he's tried has helped. None of the tests are conclusive. He suggested I put him to sleep. I told him to go to hell."

"I can see you doing that." Toby was Jane's beloved pet, half-dog, half-wolf, and totally endearing. Eve had taken care of Toby herself when Jane had been unable to have her dog with her, and she loved him almost as much as Jane did. "Couldn't you go to another vet?"

"Eldridge is the best. He's just giving up too easily. I won't give up. So we practically smuggled Toby out of London to avoid all the red tape and took off."

"Toby's not a young dog any longer, Jane," she said gently. "You've had him since you were just a kid yourself."

"That doesn't mean he shouldn't have his chance." Jane paused. "We're on our way to Summer Island. I'm taking him to Sarah Logan. I just hope he's alive when I get there."

"You're taking him to the island? Did you call Sarah?"

"Yes, she said that she couldn't promise miracles, but they have some terrific vets and a few extraordinary consultants who might be able to help." She added, "Miracles. You know me, Eve. I'm not one to trust in miracles, and I had a hard time believing that the experimental research center Sarah and her husband set up on that island could be all that she promised it to be."

"Sarah always tells the truth."

"But dogs that are able to heal and extend life to an undetermined span? That's pretty hard to swallow."

"Sarah had trouble herself until she saw the effects on her golden retriever, Monty. She said he acts like a five-year-old, and he's Toby's father."

"I don't care about any sudden rejuvenation. I only want to keep Toby alive and with me for a little while longer. If Sarah's started a clinic on that island, it's got to be a great one."

"And you're willing to close your eyes to what doesn't strike you as reasonable and let Toby have his chance."

"I love him. And Toby's so full of love. Dogs like him should live forever." She cleared her throat. "Do you know that Sarah said that they call the dogs that they have on the island the dogs of summer? She said that dogs should always live in the summer of life. Toby is heading toward his winter, but he's not there yet. Maybe I can hold him back."

"Maybe you can. Do you need me? I'll hop on a plane and be there tomorrow."

"No, we're just refueling and checking our flight plan. I want to get Toby to the island as soon as possible. The island is only a tiny speck in the middle of the Caribbean, and you'd have to fly private, too."

"And your point is?"

"That I can handle this myself. With any luck, Toby and I will be at the lake house in no time."

"I hope so." She had a sudden thought. "You said *we* smuggled. Who helped you get Toby out of the country?"

Silence. "Seth Caleb."

Eve's hand tightened on the phone. "And?"

"Nothing. No pound of flesh. He just showed up after I'd had the bad news from the vet and offered his services."

"Just out of the blue. I'm wondering how he so conveniently found out about Toby. Knowing Seth Caleb, that makes me very uneasy."

"But you're always uneasy around Caleb. You've been that way since the day you met him."

"And realized he . . . wasn't like other people. For God's sake, Jane. I watched him kill a man by controlling the blood flow to his heart."

"The medical examiner never confirmed that happened. And Caleb saved Joe, didn't he?"

"Yes, but he . . . I don't like him around you."

"You're talking as if he's some kind of vampire. He's no such thing. He just has a kind of . . . talent."

"And you find him fascinating."

"So do you."

"Yes." She couldn't deny it. "But it's like watching a cobra weave back and forth."

Jane chuckled. "There's nothing snakelike about Seth. He's more in the panther line. Yes, if I ever do a sketch of him, I'd make him a black panther."

"But you're trusting that panther to take your Toby to safety." There was no use arguing with her. Eve had watched Seth Caleb's effect on Jane, and it was both complicated and reckless. Most of the time, Jane realized how dangerous he could be to her and kept him at a distance. In the end, Jane would have to deal with him in her own way.

And if that deal did not turn out happily, Eve would have to go after Caleb and take care of him herself.

"Call me as soon as you reach the island and meet Sarah. I'll be worried until I know about our Toby."

"It will be all right." Jane's voice had a note of desperation. "It has to be fine. I won't have it any other way. I'll bring him to you. Bye, Eve. I love you." She hung up.

Eve slowly pressed the disconnect. Lord, she wanted to be there with Jane. Toby was very important to her, and this might be a tragic ending for her old friend. Jane had grown up on the streets and in foster homes and had never allowed herself to trust anyone but Eve and Joe. The closest she had come was that zany half-wolf who had bounded into their hearts and lives and stayed there.

Until now.

Maybe it would be okay. Unlike Jane, Eve did believe in miracles. They weren't always on the horizon, but there was a balance between horror and wonder. Miracles as well as disasters could happen. Sometimes it seemed impossible when you faced the tragedy of little boys like Ryan, but she had to believe because of Bonnie.

Bonnie, who had been taken from her in the most horrible way possible, kidnapped and dying when she was only seven. Yet she had been permitted to come back to comfort Eve and help her through life. Eve had first thought she was a dream, and only after years had she admitted that Bonnie was a spirit and accepted her presence in her life.

Accepted her with joy and gratitude.

Yes, there were miracles in this world.

Maybe Ryan would be someone's miracle. "I hope so, Ryan." She turned and picked up her cup of coffee. "I guess there's no hurry about drinking this. Jane may be a few days. I'll go out on the porch and sit down and enjoy the sunset."

But the sun was already down when she went out on the porch. The dusk had fallen, and the lake looked silver-cold.

She shivered and took a sip of coffee.

It didn't warm her.

She felt suddenly very alone. No Joe. No Jane.

She was being ridiculous. It wasn't as if she hadn't been alone before. So what if the only entity she had to talk with at the moment was the skull of a dead child?

She turned quickly and went back into the house and slammed the door and locked it. "I'm heading for a long, hot shower, Ryan. Then I'll come out and pack you in your FedEx box to be picked up tomorrow. Joe should be calling soon, and I'll have to tell him about poor Toby. I'm sorry Jane won't get a chance to see you. She's an artist, and she might have made a wonderful sketch of you that could have led to everyone's knowing who you are. But we'll get there anyway . . ."

CHAPTER

2

"The plane's ready."

Jane turned to see Seth Caleb coming toward her across the tarmac. His silver-threaded dark hair was ruffled by the wind, and he was dressed in jeans and a leather flight jacket; he should have looked casual, even unobtrusive. But Caleb never appeared unobtrusive no matter what he wore. He was always high-impact. His high cheekbones and deep-set dark eyes drew the attention and kept it focused. He radiated magnetism and charisma that was impossible to ignore. "Good. Did you check on Toby?"

"Resting quietly." He glanced at her phone. "How did Eve take the news? She loves Toby, too, doesn't she?"

"Of course. She would have jumped on the next plane if I'd asked her. I told her to stay home, that I'd bring Toby to her." Her hands clenched into fists at her sides. "And that's what I'll do. Just get me to that island."

"Another hour and fifteen minutes," Caleb said quietly. "But if the security on the island is as strict as you've told me, you'd better give Sarah Logan a call and tell her we're on our way."

"I will." She climbed the steps of the Gulfstream jet. "I told Sarah that I'd be coming; I just didn't tell her who was bringing me."

His brows lifted. "But you told Eve, I assume? What did she say? Did she ask any questions? I can't see her being comfortable with my having you in my clutches."

"Don't be absurd. I'm not in your clutches."

"Only if you choose to be," he said softly. "I promised you that a long time ago. But you're understandably wary of me. I try to keep my word, but I have moments when the control slips."

Jane had seen moments when that had happened, and it had frightened . . . and excited her. Neither response was wise to accept or encourage. Which was the reason she tried to keep her distance from Caleb. She had not seen him for almost a year before he had shown up in her apartment yesterday. "Stop this bullshit," she said curtly. "I don't want to deal with it right now. The only thing I want to think about is Toby."

His smile faded. "I'll back off. I know it's not the time. I told you I slip occasionally. In spite of Eve's suspicions about my wicked motives, I actually want to help you and Toby. I like your dog."

She believed him. However, that didn't mean that it was the entire truth. Seth Caleb had so many intricate facets to his character that he was like a juggler whose balls in the air could be pure gold or deepest ebony. "And I love him." She fought to keep her voice steady.

"Eve thought your sudden arrival on my doorstep was too convenient. I agree with her."

"But you didn't question me."

"I didn't care. You said you'd do anything I wanted to help Toby. You're rich, you don't care about dodging the law if it suits you, I could trust you if I handled you right. I didn't have the money to rent a private jet myself." She added baldly, "I needed you."

"A circumstance much to be desired." His tone was light. "So it was important that I continue it."

"But now I'm going to ask you the question Eve would want me to ask. How did you know about Toby? I haven't seen you in months."

"I do hate to lose touch with people I care about."

"Does that mean you've been watching me?"

"In a very safe, distant manner. How could I just walk away from you? You're a very special woman, Jane. I know you find the thought of a relationship with me a little intimidating."

"No way. Don't flatter yourself."

He smiled faintly. "You do, you know. I'm very encouraged by it. A little uncertainty can be intriguing. Don't worry; I haven't been lurking in the shadows. I've just been . . . waiting." He stopped beside the stretcher where Toby lay and stroked the dog's golden white muzzle. Toby's tail wagged, but he didn't open his eyes. "His spirit is still strong. He's not going to leave you soon. I'll get him there in time, Jane."

"You'd better." She knelt to stroke Toby. "I'm here, boy," she said to him softly. "I'm taking you to see Monty and Maggie and some other dogs who may become your friends. You stay with me. Okay?"

Toby whimpered and tried to turn so that she could rub his belly.

"Buckle up, Jane." Caleb went down the aisle toward the cockpit.

"I will." Jane laid her cheek on Toby for a brief instant, then slipped into the seat across the aisle and fastened her seat belt. "Trust me, boy. We'll get through this together."

"I don't like it," Joe said flatly when Eve finished speaking. "When will Jane be able to get there?"

"As soon as she can," Eve said. "How do I know? Jane doesn't have any idea what's wrong with Toby or if he can be cured. She'll let me know."

Silence. "Maybe I'll be able to leave after the testimony tomorrow. I could take the night coach out."

"Not likely. Since when did court cases ever go the way you want them to go? You'll have to stay for that cross-examination. Stop worrying about me, Joe."

"I don't like leaving you alone."

"I'm fine."

"Keep your phone by your bed, your gun on the nightstand, and be sure to put the alarm on."

"The alarm is already on. I can take care of myself. Stop worrying. Now go to bed and get to sleep."

Another silence. "Maybe you're right. Logic is on your side. I don't have any reason to go off the rails."

"Absolutely right."

"To hell with being right. I'm going to call and have a patrol car make a couple swings by the cottage tonight and tomorrow."

"And what would the captain say? Personal business."

"I'll pay someone off duty. Stop arguing."

She chuckled. "You're impossible."

"I love you. Don't go for any strolls. Don't open the door without knowing who's on the other side."

"I have to call FedEx and send Ryan off to Bloomington."

"Send him with one of the cops I arrange to do a pass by. As soon as I set up who it will be, I'll call you and leave his name and cell-phone number. And I'll call you first thing tomorrow morning."

"Relax, Joe." She paused. "You're spooking me. I'll be careful. When you get back, we'll laugh about this."

"Maybe. At the moment, I'm not amused." He was silent. "Phone me when you hear more about Toby. I love that old guy."

"Me, too. Jane's not sure that she believes in miracles, but she's hoping for one tonight. I'll call as soon as I hear. I love you, Joe." She hung up.

Joe was definitely overreacting. As an independent woman, she should feel a little insulted that he was being overprotective.

She was not insulted. When you loved someone, your instinct was to fight and cling to them against all odds . . . and logic.

And, as Joe said, to hell with being right or logical. Joe's instincts had been honed in the most extreme classroom in the world when he was with the SEALs. He was not often wrong.

She would put her gun on the nightstand tonight.

"We have company." Caleb was glancing out the window as he left the cockpit. "And they look serious. I don't think they're the kindly vets you were expecting."

"I told you to expect security. But there's a van pulling up." Jane frowned at the attractive, dark-haired young woman getting out of the vehicle. "That's not Sarah Logan."

"Let's just hope that she has some authority." He threw open the door, and the steps emerged. "Stay with Toby. Let me check it out."

Before she could protest, he was down the steps and crossing the tarmac.

But the dark-haired woman was striding toward the plane and obviously giving orders to the two armed security guards who had gotten out of their jeep.

She pushed by Caleb and ran up the steps. "Jane MacGuire. I'm Dr. Devon Brady. Sarah got an emergency call from her husband right after she talked to you. She had to leave and go back to California. She asked me to take care of Toby." She turned and yelled at the security men. "Come up and take this stretcher."

"Wait a minute." Jane had been expecting Sarah, and this was going too fast. She instinctively stood defensively in front of Toby. "What are your qualifications? How do I know you're any better than that vet I left in London?"

"I have authority to run this facility. And you don't know if I'm as good as that vet in London. I don't know either. But I'm very good, and I care." She looked Jane in the eye. "And we have a few rabbits in the hat here that they don't have anywhere else. We might be able to pull one out for your Toby. Let me try. Your friend, Sarah, trusts me. That should count for something."

"It counts for a hell of a lot." She reached into her briefcase, pulled out a folder, and handed it to Devon Brady. "Here are his medical records." She slowly moved from in front of the dog. "Toby's breathing is shallower than when we left London." She added unsteadily, "I'm scared, Dr. Brady."

"Devon. I know you're scared." She was gesturing to the two security men who had entered the plane. "Take him to the lab. I've set up the tests." She handed Jane a set of car keys. "I'll go with your Toby and do an initial exam on the road. You and your pilot can follow in the security jeep." She pushed by Caleb again as she ran back down the steps. "I'll see you at the lab."

"I'm feeling very unimportant and definitely brushed aside," Caleb said ruefully as he fell into step with Jane as she started toward the jeep. "So much for taking care of the opposition. I take it you trust her?"

"Maybe. I think so. I don't have much choice. Sarah is very smart, and anyone she hired would have to be exceptional."

"Really? What do you know about this place?"

"I told you, it's an experimental facility. It's already been confirmed by several scientific studies that dogs have certain healing properties. That's why they permit dogs to be taken to critically ill patients in hospitals. It's not only psychological, though some critics claim that's all it is. Well, Sarah became involved with a group that discovered that some dogs have a heightened ability in that area."

"Why?"

She shrugged. "It's a mystery. That's why they started this experimental colony. Sarah says that they have a few theories, but they have to have cast-iron proof."

"And those theories?"

"I didn't ask her, and I don't know if she'd tell me if I did. She's very protective of her dogs."

"But you've known her for years."

"And she knows I've been skeptical. I have to have proof." She started the jeep. "It's my nature."

"But you're here now." He smiled faintly. "An atheist in a foxhole?"

"I'm not an atheist, but I admit this is a terribly deep foxhole." She blinked away the moisture in her eyes so that she could see the taillights ahead of her. "Did you know that Monty, Toby's sire, was a search-and-rescue dog? He knew all about foxholes and earthquakes and mudslides. He saved my life once when I was a kid. He was the first dog I ever knew and cared about. Sarah knew I loved him, but he would never have left her. So she gave me his first pup, Toby."

"A half-wolf? Not exactly a tame animal to give a little girl."

"Toby has the heart of a golden. He was zany and a little clumsy and easily distracted, so he would never have made a rescue dog." She cleared her throat. "But so much love. I've never known any creature that was so loving. Talk about healing? Just the love he gave could make my sadness and pain go away." She swallowed. "There's a building up ahead. That must be the lab."

"Yes." Caleb reached out and covered her hand resting on the steering wheel. "It will be all right. We'll make it all right."

"We don't have much to say about it." She pulled to a stop in front of the rambling one-story building. "Right now it's up to that vet and God."

LAKE COTTAGE
ATLANTA, GEORGIA

Thunder . . .

It was raining hard, Eve realized as she turned over in bed to look at the clock.

One-forty in the morning.

She had drifted off to sleep about midnight, but it had been a restless slumber. The thunder must have woke her.

Go back to sleep.

She lay there for ten minutes, then sat up and swung her feet to the floor.

Get a glass of water and try again.

She stood at the bedroom window and watched the rain hitting against the windowpane as she drank the water. She always loved the sound of the rain on the roof and the lake. It was wild and yet strangely comforting. Usually, she went out on the porch and sat with the veil of rain surrounding her.

Not tonight.

This was good enough and she—

Headlights speared the darkness.

She tensed.

A car was coming down the lake road.

She set the glass down and stepped closer to the window.

Lightning flashed.

She released the breath she'd been holding.

Foolish. It was the patrol car Joe had set up to cruise by the cottage.

Poor guy, he probably hadn't counted on driving through this awful rain. She'd have to find out with whom Joe had made the arrangement and make it up to him. But even if it wasn't necessary, the sight of that patrol car did give her a feeling of comfort.

She went back to the bed and crawled under the covers. Jane must have arrived at the island, but Eve hadn't heard from her yet. She hoped that was good and not bad for Toby. She remembered how Toby had tried to crawl up on Jane's bed during a thunderstorm when he was a puppy. How many times had Eve come into Jane's room to see them curled up together? She had always turned a blind eye. She had just been glad Jane had formed an attachment that could not hurt her and only be healthy. She'd always been so alone . . .

Get well, Toby. God, don't let her lose him yet.

She had gone back to bed, Doane thought as he took the earphone out of his ear. It was clear Eve Duncan was restless from the movements he had heard in the cottage.

Why not? A woman who dealt with the dead would naturally be highly sensitive.

Do you feel me out here, Eve?

Or are you worried about your Jane? She had talked to Jane MacGuire a few hours ago, and the affection between them was very obvious. Affection and a protective bond that was as clear as sunlight. He had been right to take measures to remove Jane MacGuire.

He had enough problems with trying to avoid that patrol car that was making rounds. He had thought Venable was responsible for that before he'd monitored the call between Joe Quinn and Eve earlier. Of course, Venable could still have done something to trigger Quinn's concern.

"Difficulties, Kevin," he whispered. She's not as alone and fragile as I thought. I expected it to be easier. I planned it so well. Just the way we did when you were alive.

He looked up at the window of Eve's bedroom. The rain was striking the sheet of glass between them. She didn't realize how vulnerable she was as she lay in that bed.

Not yet.

Sleep well, Eve. I'll get back to you.

I have things to do.

Jane straightened as Devon Brady came into the small waiting room at the lab facility. It had been over an hour since the vet had taken Toby into the examination room and told them she'd get back with a report as soon as she could. "Is he okay? What can you do for him?"

"No, he's not okay," Devon said gently. "He's failing. I think you know that's true."

"Don't tell me that. Tell me what you can do for him. I didn't bring him all this way to have you tell me he's going to die. What's wrong with him? With all these instruments and research files, surely you know more than that doctor in London."

"It could be several things, but it doesn't fit in any one slot. Respiratory failure, but for what reason? His lungs look fine and so do—" She broke off. "I know you don't want to hear details and guesses."

"No, I want you to tell me how you're going to cure him," she whispered. "You can find a way, right?"

"Maybe. But first I have to find out what it is we have to cure."

"Then do it."

"I intend to make every effort. I've called in a consultant to help me, but I had to get your permission." She checked her watch. "She should be here in another five minutes. I had to call and roust her out of bed."

"Why didn't you have her here when we came from the airfield?" Caleb asked.

"I didn't know I'd need her. I had your vet's records, and I trust myself in most cases. I thought I'd be able to make a diagnosis." She shrugged. "And you have enough to deal with right now. I didn't want to upset you unless it was necessary."

"Why should I be any more upset than I am right now?" Jane asked.

"You didn't trust me. Margaret is not very professional-appearing. You have to know that she—"

"I hurried as quick as I could. Where is he, Devon?"

Jane turned at the question to see a woman coming in the door. No, not a woman, she looked more like a young girl of not over nineteen or twenty. Her thin body was dressed in jeans and a loose white shirt, and her pale brown hair was shoulder length and glowed under the lights. Everything about her glowed, Jane thought absently. She was tanned a golden brown, with a sprinkling of freckles dusting her nose. Even her bare feet were tanned in the leather thongs.

"He's in the lab," Devon said. "I had my assistant take him off the table and lay him on the floor for you."

"Good. I'll go right in." She started for the door. "You should have called me before you—"

"Wait, Margaret," Devon gestured to Jane. "You have to get permission. This is Jane MacGuire. Margaret Douglas. Margaret's going to try to help your Toby."

"What?" Jane stared in disbelief. "This is your consultant? I thought she was a tech."

"Because I look so young?" Margaret wrinkled her nose. "I'm almost twenty."

"A great age," Caleb said.

She gave him a brilliant smile. "Old enough." She turned back to Jane. "I can't take much time to try to convince you I can help your Toby. Devon says he's going downhill." Her expression was suddenly grave. "So you'll have to trust me. Will you do that?"

"Why should I?"

"Because I'll treat your Toby with as much love and

care as you give him." She was holding Jane's gaze. "And I can sometimes help."

"Only sometimes? That's not good enough for me to—"

"Please," Margaret said softly.

Radiance, warmth, blue eyes glowing with life and gentleness. Jane found she couldn't look away from that face. She suddenly felt as if she was a part of the light that seemed to envelop the girl. She could feel the anxiety and edginess ebbing away from her.

What the hell.

She said jerkily, "You can go look at Toby, but I don't want you doing anything without a vet's okay."

"I won't." She gave that luminous smile again and moved toward the door. "You don't mind if I have Monty with me, do you? He might help." She didn't wait for an answer but raised her voice. "Monty, come."

Shock. The golden retriever that bounded through the doorway at her call was so familiar to Jane. Familiar, yet not familiar.

Monty acts like a five-year-old now, Sarah had told her.

Jane had not really believed her. Monty was years older than his pup, Toby. She couldn't imagine that he could be this spry when her Toby was arthritic and slow and had lost that wonderful vim and vigor. Yet here he was, and Jane could swear he looked no older than when she had first seen him all those years ago, when she had been a child of ten.

"Okay if I use him?" Margaret was looking at Jane. "Sometimes, I can't do it alone."

"Do what?" Jane instinctively started toward Monty. "Monty? Do you remember me?"

The golden retriever gave a low woof, and his tail wagged, but he turned and trotted toward Margaret.

"He remembers you," Margaret said quietly. "He'll greet you later; now he has a job to do."

Margaret and the golden disappeared into the exam room.

"What the hell is happening?" Jane asked Devon in bewilderment. "Why do you think she can help?"

"Because she's done it before," Devon said. "And I have to know what's wrong with Toby before he can be treated."

"And she can tell you?"

"Maybe. If Toby knows why he's sick."

"If Toby knows . . ." She stared at her in disbelief. "Are you saying what I think you are?"

"Interesting." Caleb gave a low whistle. "You're not going to like this, Jane." He tilted his head. "A dog whisperer, Dr. Brady? That young girl can talk to dogs?"

"Anyone can talk to dogs." Devon made a face. "She seems to get answers. And not only dogs; she has an affinity with most animals."

"Get her away from Toby," Jane said tightly. "I won't have his time wasted with someone who thinks she's a voodoo priestess."

"Did she really strike you that way?" Devon asked.

"No, she's appealing as hell, the girl next door, everyone's best friend, but that doesn't mean that she can help my Toby."

"It doesn't mean that she can't," Devon said. "I can see why you're suspicious. Do you think I wasn't? When she showed up on the island, my first reaction was to throw her into the ocean. We always knew that the research might attract weirdos, and she seemed a prime example."

"How did she even manage to get on the island with all your security?" Caleb asked. "I can see a plane's being surrounded as soon as the landing gear hit the ground."

"She didn't come by plane. She moored her speedboat on the other side of the island and hiked through the rain forest until she got to the hospital."

"And where did the speedboat come from?" Caleb asked. "There's not another island anywhere near here."

"She said that her friend had a schooner and dropped her off."

"And who is this friend?"

"She said that he wouldn't want anyone to know who he was or that he'd gone out of his way to bring her near here."

"A smuggler?" Caleb was thinking about it. "Or maybe he was—"

"Stop it." Jane was tired of speculation. "I don't care who he was. But it should have raised red flags that would keep you from welcoming her here."

"It did." Devon shrugged. "But she asked for a chance to work with the dogs, and she convinced me that she could help take care of them." She held up her hand. "She just took a job as kennel help. She didn't claim any special abilities."

"That came later?" Caleb asked.

Devon nodded. "I could tell you the stories, but all you need to know is that Margaret is fairly amazing. She still works with the dogs, but I occasionally call her if I need her."

"I can't believe you'd trust her," Jane said.

"Yes, you can," Devon said. "Everyone trusts Margaret. You let her go in and look at Toby, didn't you?"

"But that's before I—" She headed for the exam-room door. "I'm going to see what she's doing to him."

"Go ahead. She won't mind," Devon said. "Just let her keep on working with him."

"I don't care if she'd mind or—" Jane stopped as she opened the door.

Margaret was on the floor holding Toby in her arms as he was stretched over her lap. Monty was lying quietly beside them, so close he was touching Toby.

She looked up at Jane in the doorway and shook her head. "Not yet. Soon." She was gently stroking Toby's neck. "Soon . . ."

Jane stiffened. What did she mean? Was Toby fading?

"No," Devon said behind her. "No danger. She'd tell you if it were near."

Toby's eyes were open, and he was licking Margaret's hand.

"Shh, rest." Margaret was hugging him, holding him closer. "You don't have to show me."

Love.

Jane could almost see the love bonding Margaret and Toby together as a visible force.

"Satisfied?" Devon asked quietly.

Jane nodded jerkily and backed out of the room. "How long?"

"She said soon." Devon strode toward the cabinet across the room. "Coffee?"

Jane shook her head. "I don't want anything. I just want to *know*. I'm feeling so damn helpless."

"Join the club." She poured coffee into a Styrofoam cup. "It's my worst nightmare. That's why I let Margaret talk me into using her the first time she came and asked me to let her try to find out what was making my greyhound sick."

"And did she do it?"

"Yes." She sipped the coffee. "But it took two more cases before I stopped telling myself that it was coincidence or luck." Her lips twisted. "I still use science first; and then whatever works."

"And Margaret Douglas usually works?" Caleb's gaze was narrowed on Devon's face. "But you're still scared and shaky."

She shrugged. "I like to be in control. Control doesn't seem to be a factor when Margaret is involved. I can't be sure if she's even in control of what's going on. She told me once it was just nature. I'd be happier if there was—"

"We have about four hours." Margaret was standing in the doorway. "You'll have to flush out Toby's entire system and replace the blood."

Devon frowned. "Flush out the system?"

"It's poison," Margaret said soberly. "Slow-acting but it's had time to take hold and is probably attacking some of his organs. Get rid of it."

"Poison?" Jane repeated. "No way. He had toxicology tests in London."

"And I gave him a couple when I brought him in," Devon said.

"He's not had any stomach issues," Jane said. "And I'm super careful of what he eats."

"Poison," Margaret said again. "By injection in the ruff of his neck. You can probably find evidence if you look for it, Devon. But I wouldn't take the time. We don't have much left. I called Jeff, your assistant, and told him to get back out of bed and get here fast. Flush Toby out and give him a general antidote and antibiotic."

"You're sure it's poison?" Devon asked.

"Toby's sure. He remembers." Her lips tightened grimly. "Whoever did it leaned down, petted him, then gave him the injection."

"That's crazy," Jane said. "I'd know if—" She stopped. Arguing wasn't going to do any good. "Even if she's right, this seems like a radical treatment, Devon."

"Not as radical as it sounds."

"Is it dangerous?"

"Everything is dangerous in Toby's state." She put her cup down and headed for the exam room. "But doing nothing is the most dangerous of all."

"Could it be poison?"

"A very sophisticated one, nothing simple. Or we would have been able to detect it."

"It's poison," Margaret said again. "Get that ugly stuff out of him, Devon." She turned to Jane. "You go with her. If he starts to slip, Toby will want to come back to you."

"I'm not even sure I'm going to let—" She met Margaret's gaze, and the memory of the sight of her with Toby in her arms surged back to her. So much love, so much caring, and that same glow of caring was staring out of the blue eyes gazing steadily into her own. "Is he going to—" She didn't want to hear the answer. She turned on her heel and started after Devon. "He's going to live, dammit. And I'm going to believe that somehow you know what you're talking about. If you're a phony, and this hurts Toby, I'm going to come after you." She glanced at Devon as she passed her. "Now tell me what to do to help him. She said we only have four hours."

CHAPTER

3

Someone had followed him, Doane realized, as he gazed down at the tracks.

The man had stood in the shadows and watched Doane as he'd disposed of the car. Then he had slipped away.

Did the fool think he hadn't been aware of him? Kevin had taught him the art of hide-and-seek in the most dangerous game.

This one probably was one of Venable's men.

So what did he do? What action to take. Ignore or pursue?

The answer came to him immediately.

Why, do what Kevin would do, of course.

He moved silently through the woods.

Three hours later, Jane came out of the exam room and sank down on the leather couch.

"How is it going?" Caleb asked as he handed her a cup of coffee. "Anything I can do?"

She shook her head. "Nothing anyone can do right now that's not being done. This process could last for the next six or eight hours." She rubbed her eyes. "They kicked me out. They said he might need me later, when he rouses, but not now."

"Then I'm sure you'll be there for him. You've gone to extraordinary lengths so far." He studied her. "And they may have kicked you out, but they can't stop you thinking about him."

"How could I not think about him?"

"By talking, not brooding." He sat down in the chair across from her. "Talk to me, Jane. You care a great deal for Toby, don't you?"

"Yes." She took a drink of coffee. "You probably don't understand. Some people love animals, some people tolerate them, and some people don't know why we go to so much trouble for them."

"And you think I'm trailing in the rear." He grimaced. "Why doesn't that surprise me?"

"Well?"

He was silent for a long moment. "I've never had a pet I loved. Affection isn't . . . easy for me. Passion, on the other hand, is no problem at all. I admire animals, I find them interesting, but I guess I may be too close to being an animal myself to accept a relationship like that." He smiled. "I still have moments of savagery if you'll recall."

She did recall. Their history together had been filled with isolated incidents that had sometimes frightened her. She had a sudden memory of his throwing the body of a man who had been attacking them down at her feet. His eyes had been as wild as the primitive action itself. She considered herself civilized, but those moments of fear of him had not lasted long. Was that due to his cleverness and magnetism, which made those moments fade so quickly? Or was it that he was a constant puzzle that her curiosity was trying to force her to solve?

His lips turned up at the corners as he read her expression. "Oh, yes, you remember. We're nothing alike, but, then, we don't have to be. It tends to make our relationship more interesting." His gaze went to the examination room. "And my heart may not be as soft as yours, but I don't like the helpless being targeted. Your Toby was no threat to anyone. Why would anyone want to poison your dog?"

"I still can't believe anyone would." She paused. "But Devon Brady did take a look at the skin beneath the hair on his neck while they were setting up the IV. There was a tiny place that could have been from a shot." She frowned. "And I was trying to think how it could even have happened. Toby is always with me when I'm home at the apartment. When I have to be gone for a day, I check him into Nedra Carlisle's Dog Day Care. He likes being with other dogs. They have slides and pools and trainers to play with the dogs."

His brows rose. "Day care?"

She gave him a cool glance. "Don't go there."

"I'm not. It's just a new concept for me. When was the last time he was at this day care?"

"A week ago."

"And Toby became ill?"

"Five days ago."

"Slow-acting poison. It could have been given at this day care."

"Nedra and her people are totally trustworthy, or I wouldn't have sent Toby there."

"But what about the other owners who bring their dogs there? What do you know about them?"

Nothing. But it hadn't seemed necessary that she know anything except about the people who ran the place. She supposed it would have been easy for one of the clients to go up to Toby and pet him . . . and then administer the poison. Easy and totally evil.

"Why?" she whispered.

"Revenge? Have you antagonized anyone lately who might want to get back at you?"

She shook her head. "I'm an artist. And you know I keep pretty much to myself."

"Yes, but that doesn't stop trouble from swirling around you, does it?" He was silent, thinking. "How long has it been since you've seen Eve and Joe?"

"Several months." She frowned. "You're suggesting someone poisoned Toby because they want to hurt Eve or Joe?" She shook her head. "That's really reaching."

"Probably. I'm just trying to put together a logical scenario."

"It doesn't have to be logical. It could be some sicko."

"Who used a very sophisticated poison and waited until you put the dog in that fancy day care to do it. Which means that he knew your schedule."

"Then why not target me and not my Toby?"

"I don't know. Let me think about it." He smiled. "It will give me something to do while you're busy saving your Toby."

"I'm not saving him. Devon Brady is saving him, that dog-whisperer person is saving him. I'm just standing by in case I'm needed." She rubbed her temple. "I wish I could be the one to be able to help him. I feel helpless."

"Have you called Eve yet?"

"No, I don't want to call until I have something positive to tell her."

"So she'll think that the fact that you ran the risk of involving me will have been worth it."

"No." She shrugged. "Partly."

He was looking around the office. "This research facility is quite a setup. How long have you known about it?"

"Over a year. Sarah told Eve and me when they were setting it up. She invited me to bring Toby down here and let him be studied with the rest of the dogs. They wanted to look at the increased possibility of the accelerated healing gift being transmitted genetically. After all, Toby is Monty's son."

"But you didn't go."

"I'm a hardheaded realist. It was a little over the top. I wasn't quite sure I believed any of it, even coming from Sarah." She grimaced. "But I guess I did. Here I am." She glanced at him. "And so are you," she said jerkily. "I guess I should thank you. I haven't been very gracious."

"Because you know how self-serving I am and that I wouldn't do anything that I didn't believe would reward me amply." He reached in her briefcase and took out her computer. "In your case, I'm hoping for extravagantly. You know that I've been trying to inveigle my way into your bed since the moment I saw you." He handed her the computer. "Send an e-mail to that daycare place and ask if someone other than the staff had anything to do with Toby on the day you left him. Do they have security cameras?"

"Of course."

"Why did I ask? See if they'll check the cameras and send you a photo of anyone suspicious."

"I don't want to do this now."

"I know, but it will keep you busy. I'd do it myself, but it's better if you send it." He got up and headed for the front entrance. "Besides, I want to make a couple calls and have a friend do a little checking on a few other things for me."

Why not, she thought as she flipped open the computer. He was right. It would keep her occupied. But when she finished sending the e-mail, she was going back into that examination room to Toby whether they wanted her or not.

It might be a total waste of time. Caleb's theory was all guesswork anyway.

But it was keen, analytical guesswork and far better than she could do in her present state.

Send the e-mail. Try to keep her mind off Toby, lying in there fighting for his life.

And what she wanted to do to the son of a bitch who had put him there.

LAKE COTTAGE

Darkness. smothering . . . no breath. No breath.

Eve jerked upright in bed, her breath coming in swift, harsh pants.

Just another nightmare.

And no Joe to hold her and make the fear go away.

Joe . . .

She shook her head as much in impatience as to clear it of the remnants of that stupid nightmare. Was she a child to have to have someone to cling to and pat her on the back and tell her everything was all right? It was probably the storm and the edginess that seemed to be assaulting Joe that had caused that nightmare to return.

Forget it. Think of something else. Something that had nothing to do with that smothering feeling of—

Jane.

Love flowed over Eve, and the nightmare receded. She relaxed, then she stiffened again.

No call yet from Jane.

Eve turned over in bed after glancing at the clock. Stop worrying. It probably only meant that they were working hard to save Toby and hadn't had time to call. It was easy to tell herself that she should stop worrying, she thought ruefully. Not so easy to comply. She couldn't bear the idea of Jane's being hurt if she lost Toby.

Strange how tough, wary Jane had always been vulnerable to dogs when she'd been so guarded with people. Perhaps not so strange when you realized that she had spent most of her life in foster homes and on the street. Eve would never have met her if Jane hadn't been targeted by a man Eve thought had also killed her Bonnie. Jane had been ten years old then and smart, independent, and defiant. In the fight to keep her alive, somehow they had come together.

And it had been a golden retriever, Monty, Toby's father, who had caused the breakthrough that Eve thanked God for every day of her life. Monty, Sarah Logan's search-and-rescue dog, had been ill, and Jane had been working slavishly to get him well. The memory of that last night flowed back to Eve as if it was yesterday.

"Eve."

She was surprised to see Jane, small, straight, a child of ten with all the presence of a grown woman, standing in the doorway of the study. "Hi. How's Monty?"

"I don't know." She shrugged. "Okay, I guess. I'm hungry. You want me to make you a sandwich, too?"

Something was wrong. She was too indifferent. Why had she left Monty's side? "Sure. I'd like that."

"You don't have to come with me. I'll bring it here for you." She disappeared down the hall.

Was she worried about Monty? Was she scared? It was always difficult to know what Jane was feeling. But she was reaching out, and it was important that Eve be there for her.

She dropped down on the couch and rubbed her eyes and kept them closed for a moment. Too many things to think about.

"You asleep?"

Jane stood before her, holding a tray.

"No, just resting my eyes. I didn't get much sleep last night."

Jane set the tray on the coffee table. "I brought my sandwich, too, but I guess you don't feel like company."

It was Jane who never admitted the need for companionship. "I was just thinking I was a little lonely. Sit down."

Jane curled up at the far end of the couch.

"Aren't you going to eat?" Eve asked.

"Yeah, sure." She picked up her sandwich and nibbled at it. "You're lonely a lot, aren't you?"

"It happens."

"But you've got your mother and Joe and Mr. Logan."

"That's true." She took a bite of her sandwich. "Are you lonely sometimes, Jane?"

She lifted her chin. "No, of course not."

"I just wondered. Sometimes loneliness creeps up on you."

"Not me."

Try another road. "I'm surprised you're not with Monty. I'm sure he needs you."

A silence. "He doesn't need me. Sarah said I was helping, but she's the only one he needs. He barely knows I'm there."

Ah, there was the pain. "I'm sure he does."

Jane shook her head. "He's Sarah's dog. He belongs

to her." She didn't look at Eve. *"I wanted him to be-long to me. I thought if I loved him enough, he'd love me more than Sarah."* She added defiantly, *"I wanted to take him away from Sarah."*

"I see."

"Aren't you going to tell me how bad that is?"

"No."

"It . . . was bad. I like Sarah. But I love Monty. I wanted him to belong to me." Her hands balled into fists. *"I wanted something to belong to me."*

"He does belong to you. He just belongs to Sarah more. It's natural. He's a search-and-rescue dog. She was first in his life."

"Like Bonnie was first in yours?"

Shock rippled through her. *"I thought we were talking about Monty. How did we get to Bonnie?"*

"She belonged to you. That's why you're helping me, isn't it? It's because the man who wants to kill me could be the one who killed Bonnie. It's for Bonnie, not me."

"Bonnie's dead, Jane."

"But she still belongs to you. She's still first." She took a bite of her sandwich. *"Not that I care. Why should I care? It's nothing to me. I just thought it was funny."*

My God, her eyes were glistening with tears. *"Jane."*

"I don't care. I really don't care."

"Well, I do." She slid across the couch and pulled Jane into her arms. *"I'm helping you because you're a very special person, and that's the only reason."*

Jane's body was ramrod straight in her arms. *"And you like me?"*

"Yes." She had forgotten how small and dear a

child's body felt. She wanted to keep her there forever.
"I like you very much."

"I . . . like you too." Jane slowly relaxed against her.
"It's okay, I know I can't be first. But maybe we can
be friends. You don't belong to anyone like Monty
does. I'd like to—" Jane stopped awkwardly.

"Maybe we can," Eve said. Jane was breaking her
heart. So defensive. So resistant. And yet so in need.
"I don't see why not, do you?"

"No." Jane lay still against her for a moment, then
pushed her away. "Okay, that's settled." She jumped
up and hurried to the door. "I'm going to get Monty
some food. And then I'm going to bed." The moment
of softness was clearly over. Now Jane was eager to
escape a situation that made her uneasy.

Well, wasn't Eve equally uneasy? The past few mo-
ments had been as awkward for her as for Jane. She
hadn't believed she was ready to love anyone after
Bonnie had been taken, but suddenly it was here in
this child who was as complicated and wary as Eve
herself. They were quite a pair, she thought ruefully.
"I thought you said Monty didn't need you."

"Well, he needs to eat. Sarah would have to leave
him to get food, and that would make him sad." She
added before leaving the room, "He can't help it if he
doesn't love me best."

Adjustments, compromises, and acceptance. Jane's
life had never been anything else, and she was afraid
to ask for anything more. But there had been a break-
through tonight and Jane was beginning to admit that
she did need someone and Eve had been chosen to fill
the void.

Thank God.

*But Jane wasn't the only one to make compromises,
Eve thought with sudden amusement. She was playing
second fiddle to a golden retriever.*

*That was okay, too. They had a long way to go, but
the promise of something beautiful and precious was
beckoning for both of them . . .*

Sarah had given Jane one of Monty's first pups, and
she had called him Toby. By that time, Eve and Joe
had adopted Jane. What had started out awkward and
tentative had become a bond that couldn't be broken.
Zany Toby had become part of the family though not
the watchdog Joe wanted for the property. He was far
too loving.

She could use a watchdog right now, Eve thought
dryly. Or just a friendly body to cuddle and ward off
the chill she was feeling. Those memories of the past
had been warm and sweet, but they were in stark con-
trast to the storm raging outside.

She put her arm under her head as she stared out at
the rain. Think of Jane and the life they'd made together.

Close out the storm.

Close out the nightmare.

Call me, Jane.

"I'm staying," Jane said belligerently to Devon as
she went back into the examination room an hour later.
"I won't get in your way, but I'm not leaving him again."

"It's okay." Devon was checking the IV. "I didn't

think I'd be able to keep you out for long. I was just at a point where I wasn't sure which way it was going to go." She smiled at Jane over her shoulder. "Now I do. He's going to make it."

Jane's knees felt suddenly weak. "He's going to live?"

"He's getting stronger with every IV." She stroked Toby's head. "Aren't you, boy? Margaret was right. We just had to get it all out of you."

"Poison? What kind?"

She shook her head. "I'll have to send a blood sample to the lab in San Juan. It will be a few days before I hear. I'll be lucky if it's that soon since the usual toxicology tests came out negative. Thank God we had Margaret."

Jane came over to the table and gazed down at Toby. He was going to live. Sweet, loving, crazy Toby. "Thank God," she said hoarsely. "Where is Margaret? Did you kick her out, too?"

"No, she took Monty out that back door as soon as she realized that Toby was going to make it. I sent my assistant back to his bed, too. The big push is over now. Margaret said that she'd be back as soon as she dropped Monty off at the main house."

"I want to thank her."

"You'll get your chance. She wants to see you." She looked at Toby. "She's very upset about what happened to Toby."

"So am I." She moved toward the rear door Devon had indicated. "Where's this main house?"

"About a mile down the road." She smiled. "But there are security people there, too. Tell them to call me when they stop you."

"I will." She opened the door and went out into the courtyard that led to a dirt path. She had just started down the lanternlit path to the main house when she saw Margaret coming toward her. "I was going to see you." She stopped in the center of the path. "I wanted to thank you."

"You should have gotten him here sooner. He almost died, you know." She stared her in the eye. "And what did you do to make someone want to hurt him?"

"I have no idea." Jane was a little shocked by the sudden attack. Margaret had been so gentle and full of warmth since the moment she had appeared at the hospital. "I'm trying to find out who did it. I don't know that either."

"Then you have to find out," Margaret said soberly. "It could happen again. Cowards usually prey on the helpless when they're too scared to go after a person they want to hurt. Animals are often targeted."

"I'm not exactly threatening," Jane said dryly. "So that kills that theory."

Margaret studied her. "Not obviously threatening. But I think you could be intimidating if you had cause. You were very protective of Toby." She paused. "And the man you're with could make someone afraid. Maybe it was because of him."

"I agree that Seth Caleb is in a class by himself in that department. But he only came on the scene after Toby got sick."

"Really? There could still be—" She shrugged. "He makes me . . . uneasy."

"Why?"

She hesitated. "Maybe it's the blood thing."

Jane's eyes widened. "What?"

"There's something about blood whenever I look at him. I see it. I *feel* it. It's strong."

Jane felt stunned. She hadn't expected that answer. She certainly hadn't dreamed Margaret would be able to sense that strangeness about Caleb. Blood . . . Most people were aware of his strength and magnetism but made no connection to anything more bizarre. He managed to keep it hidden . . . unless he chose to unleash it. "Listen, you're supposed to be some kind of dog whisperer or something. Are you saying that you can read people, too?"

"For Pete's sake, no." She made a face. "I have enough trouble without that to worry about. But sometimes I get impressions. It's usually when a person is closer to—when their instincts are like—"

"A bit closer to the wild?" Jane supplied.

"Yeah, I guess," she said. "Anyway, Caleb is radiating something that worries me. I think I'd better go and talk to him."

"No," Jane said sharply. The idea of Margaret's confronting Caleb about anything personal was both amusing and chilling. "Stay away from him. This isn't your business, Margaret."

"Yes, it is." She added simply, "Because after tonight, Toby is my friend, and no one hurts my friends." She started down the path. "And I don't like that blood. I've never felt that kind of—"

"He didn't hurt Toby."

"I'll find out." She smiled back over her shoulder. "Just as soon as I ask Caleb a few questions, then—"

"Wait." She was so damn stubborn, Jane thought

in exasperation. "I can tell you about the blood you're sensing if that's what's worrying you. You don't have to ask him. That's not a good idea."

Margaret stopped and turned to face her. "You think he'll hurt me?"

"I didn't say that. It might be awkward."

"But you're not sure Caleb won't hurt me." She was staring curiously at her. "You're not entirely sure of anything about him, are you?"

"I know he wouldn't hurt Toby."

Margaret just looked at her.

"Look, he's a little like you." Margaret was still staring skeptically at her, and Jane knew she'd have to try to elaborate. "He has a kind of talent. He can control the flow of blood in people around him."

"How?"

"I don't know. He can just do it. It's a gift passed down through his family. I could ask the same of you."

She shook her head. "No one in my family was able to do what I do. I don't think they ever tried." She thought about it. "Flow of blood . . . that could be bad or good."

"Yes."

"But you've seen the bad."

Shrewd Margaret. So young, so shrewd.

"I've never seen him hurt anyone that didn't deserve it."

"Perhaps he didn't let you see it. You said he inherited the talent from his family. Families teach their young. What do you know about them?"

"Nothing." Caleb never talked about his home or his

relations. "He lives in Scotland most of the year. He has a place in Italy. Haven't I told you enough?"

"No, you're skirting around trying to not tell me something. I think I should talk to him."

"He doesn't like to discuss—" She drew a deep breath. Just tell her and put that curiosity to rest. "He comes from a very ancient family originating in a village in Italy. Back in medieval times, they were known as the Ridondo family, and there were all kinds of stories in their village about their supposed dark powers. Not pleasant stories."

Margaret started to chuckle. "Vampires?"

"Don't be ridiculous. Caleb is *not* a vampire."

"Though that could be where the vampire legends originated." Margaret was looking intrigued. "How cool."

"Not cool at all."

"Yes, it is. I wonder how that blood thing works."

"Don't ask him," Jane said dryly. "He might show you."

"But you just said he was no danger."

"Is that what I said? I believe I said he was no danger to Toby."

Her face was lit with eagerness. "You know, I've always been curious about vampire bats. I've never been able to merge with them. They're too single-minded."

"Merge? Is that what you do?"

"Sort of," Margaret said vaguely. "It's difficult to explain."

"Like Seth Caleb. I'm asking you to take my word for it that he had nothing to do with hurting Toby and not start questioning him."

She was silent a moment. "I'll take your word. And I won't question him . . . anytime soon." She added brusquely, "But if he has nothing to do with it, then all this has to be about you." Her tone was no longer amused or speculative. "Find out who did it and keep him from doing it to Toby or some other dog." She put up her hand as Jane opened her lips to speak. "I can't talk any more now. I have to get back to Toby." She started back up the path toward the hospital. "I just had to tell you what you have to do. You say you're grateful to me. Prove it. Keep Toby safe from that ugly man."

"Was he ugly? How do you know?" Her brows rose quizzically. "Did Toby tell you?"

"No, Toby thinks all humans are beautiful. But he doesn't know about ugly souls." She stopped at the door and looked back at Jane. "You'll do this for me?"

"No," she said quietly. "I'll do it for me and for Toby."

"Good." Margaret's face lit with a luminous smile. "That's how it should be." The harsh bulb above her surrounded her with a glow that should have been stark and unflattering but somehow wasn't. She looked soft and young and appealing, as if even that unkind glare couldn't alter that essential effect. "Why don't you come in and stay with Toby and me? He's still under sedation, but I think he'd like to have you with him."

"Think? You don't know?"

"Of course not. He's out cold." Margaret giggled, and suddenly she looked more like sixteen than twenty. "You're making fun of me." She opened the door and stepped aside for Jane to enter. "Because I make you a little uncomfortable, and you don't know how to treat me. You half believe I helped Toby, but you're not quite sure. Devon was like that for a long time."

Close. Except how could Jane be uncomfortable with the kid in leather sandals and jeans who could accept being the butt of jokes and suspicion and giggle about it? "How do you want me to treat you?"

"As a friend." Margaret's voice was wistful. "That would be nice. The other trainers and techs like me, but they think I'm kind of strange."

"You are strange." Jane smiled. "But I know a lot of strange people, and it doesn't get in the way. We could work through it if you don't mind me asking you questions. I'm very curious."

"Sure." She grinned. "I don't have to answer all of them. I probably won't. Everyone deserves their privacy." She added impishly, "Even Seth Caleb." She turned to Devon as she came into the room. "You go rest and get a cup of coffee. Jane and I will watch over Toby. I'll call you if I see him doing anything that worries me. You know you can trust me."

"I'll take you up on that." Devon wearily rubbed the back of her neck. "Thirty minutes. No more." She headed for the door to the waiting room. "And yes, I can trust you."

"See?" Margaret murmured as the door closed behind Devon. "No one knows more than Devon how strange I am, but she still thinks I'm okay." She went over to Toby and stroked his head. "And this one agrees with her."

Jane was beginning to see that Margaret was a strange and somehow wonderful mixture of strength and vulnerability. She was beginning to wonder what experiences had created that unique blend. "I can see that he does." She smiled and tapped her own breast with her index finger. "This one agrees with her, too."

LAKE COTTAGE
ATLANTA, GEORGIA

A banging on the door.

Eve was abruptly jarred from sleep.

What the hell?

She sat upright in bed and looked at the clock.

Don't open the door.

Joe's words came back to her even as she swung her feet to the floor.

But what if it was the policeman who had been cruising the area?

The banging increased in volume.

One way to find out. She checked her phone and retrieved the telephone number for the policeman Joe had hired. Ron Hughes. She dialed quickly.

He answered on the first ring. "Hughes. Is everything okay, Ms. Duncan?"

"You tell me. Is it you that's been banging on my door?"

"Hell, no. I'm about six miles from your place making the circle from the highway. I'll be right there. Don't answer the door." He hung up.

And she had no intention of opening that door. But she wasn't going to cower in this bedroom, either. There was desperation, maybe even violence, in the force with which those blows were being struck against the front door. If it was desperation, it could be that someone had had an accident in this torrential rain and needed help. If it was violence, she wanted that violence to have a face she recognized. The person on the porch might very well take off when he saw the patrol car coming down the road. For good or ill, she had to know who it was out there.

No problem. The two picture windows on either side of the door had drapes that she could pull a little aside so that she could see who was standing in front of the door. She thrust her feet into slippers, shrugged on her robe, grabbed her gun from the bedside table, and left the bedroom. The next moment, she had reached the front door.

The banging continued.

She moved to the far right side of the door and carefully drew the red drapes the tiniest bit away from the window.

She stiffened with shock.

The next moment she was at the front door, turning off the alarm.

She thrust her gun in her robe pocket and threw the door open.

"Stop that banging. What are you doing here?"

"You need me," Ben Hudson said simply. "So I came, Eve. May I come in? I'm all wet."

"For heaven's sake, of course you have to come in." She took his arm and pulled him into the cottage. "Just look at you." She grabbed a dish towel from the kitchen cabinet and handed it to him. "You look like you've been swimming in the lake."

"Do I?" He smiled his warm sweet smile as he wiped

his face. "I guess so. After all, it's all just lots of water." He dried his sandy hair until it stood up in spiky tendrils. "But kind of different."

She shook her head as she gazed at him. Here he was on her doorstep smiling at her as if he had just dropped in to say hello. Wide-set blue eyes stared at her from beneath that ridiculously spiked hair, and he was obviously pondering the difference between lake and rainwater. He was the same calm, sweet, slow boy she had grown to know all those months ago when he had helped Joe and her find Bonnie's body. The counselors at the charity camp where he worked had told her he was twenty years old but had the mental capacity of a child of ten. She had never been sure that was true. He was indeed special, but that uniqueness seemed far beyond the easy pigeonhole where they wanted to put him. When she had first seen him, his joyous smile had reminded her of Bonnie's. It still did. She wanted to hold him, take care of him, shake him for wandering outside in this storm.

"Sit down. I'll get you some hot chocolate."

He shook his head. "No, I have to go back outside. I just wanted to make sure you were okay."

She was already at the counter putting in a chocolate K-cup under the drink dispenser. "So you decided to bang down my door and make sure."

He nodded gravely. "I thought that would be the right thing to do. I had to be sure. She said Joe wasn't with you."

She stiffened as her hand closed on the cup of chocolate. "She?"

"I had a dream last night. She said that I had to try to help you."

She. He had to mean the dream had been about Bonnie. Bonnie had reached out to Ben in the past in dreams. Perhaps she recognized and bonded to his clear, simple soul, which was so like that of the child she had been when she had been alive. The fact that Bonnie had chosen to come to this boy made Ben all the more close to Eve.

She crossed the room and handed him the cup, and said very carefully, "Let's go slowly. You had a dream about Bonnie?"

"Sort of." He frowned. "It was more about you. She said she couldn't get through to you. She said the darkness was holding her back."

"Darkness?"

"Bad darkness. She said it was coming toward you, and I had to try to help."

"Because Joe wasn't going to be here?" She felt a sudden chill. "Were you at the vocational camp when you had this dream?"

He nodded. "She came almost as soon as I went to sleep. So I started out right away."

"All the way from the camp in south Georgia? You don't drive."

"I woke up Kenny. He brought me. He's a counselor, too, and sharing my tent right now. But he was afraid his Honda would get stuck in the mud and wouldn't bring me past the highway and I had to walk." He made a face. "I think he was kind of mad at me for waking him up. But it was nice of him to bring me, wasn't it?"

"It would have been even nicer if he'd gone the extra couple miles," she said dryly. But it didn't surprise her that he'd been able to persuade this Kenny to drive over a hundred miles when Ben had asked him. Ben was special, and everyone he touched seemed to realize that. "You've got to get out of those clothes. I don't suppose you brought anything with you?"

Ben shook his head.

"Then I'll get something of Joe's for you to wear." She started to turn, then saw a spear of headlights outside the window. "That's the patrol car. I almost forgot he was coming." She headed for the front door. "Stay here. I'll talk to the officer."

But Ben was at the door before her. "No, I have to be with you."

She looked at him in exasperation. "Ben . . ."

He shook his head. He wasn't going to be persuaded.

She drew back the drape and glanced out the window and saw the uniformed officer coming up the porch stairs. She opened the door before he had a chance to knock. "I'm sorry, Officer Hughes. I didn't have time to call you. It was a false alarm. It was only my friend at the door."

"At this hour?" He was looking beyond her at Ben. "May I come in for a moment?"

It was clear he wanted to check Ben out and make sure she wasn't being coerced. Why not? It would be the quickest way to reassure him. No one would believe Ben would be a threat once they'd spoken to him. She opened the door wider. "Of course."

"Thanks. I'll only be a minute." He showed her

his ID as he came into the house. "Detective Quinn wouldn't like it unless I did everything by the book." He looked at Ben. "Your name?"

"Ben. Ben Hudson."

"And your purpose here?"

"To help Eve." He smiled. "Like you. Right?"

"Right." Officer Hughes smiled back at him. It was hard not to smile at Ben. "But from now on call her and tell her you're coming. It will save all of us a lot of trouble. You don't want to scare her." He turned back to Eve. "I'll be on my way. If you need me, just call. I'll be on duty for another two hours, and I think Detective Quinn has arranged for Pete Dolanelli to take over."

"Thank you for being so prompt." She went with him to the door. "I hope it's the last time I'll have to call you."

"So do I." He grinned. "But it broke up the duty a bit. Monotony is always best, but it gets boring." He started down the steps and looked back over his shoulder and lowered his voice. "No offense, ma'am, but I'd rather you rely on me or Dolanelli. Mr. Hudson seems like a nice guy, but there's no . . . edge."

"You're absolutely right," Eve said. "Ben has no edge at all. But he's very loyal and has a good heart. When I need edge, I'll definitely call you." She went back in the house, locked the door behind her, and turned back to Ben. "You see, I have that very nice and competent policeman to protect me. I don't need you, Ben. Go back to the camp."

He shook his head. "I have to stay with you."

She nodded. She hadn't thought that she'd be able to

convince him. "I'll go and get Joe's clothes. The bathroom is the first door on your left. Why don't you take
a hot shower?"

He shook his head. "I'll only get cold and wet again
when I go back outside."

"Outside? Why should you go outside again? You
want to protect me? Do it from the living-room couch."

"I just wanted to make sure that the cottage is safe.
That Officer Hughes is in a car. I'll be able to see more
if I move around on foot."

"Ben, there's no solid proof that I'm even in danger. It's all fog and mirrors." She met his eyes. "And
dreams. And that dream of yours was very vague."

"Because of the darkness," he said gravely. "But it
wasn't vague that Bonnie sent me here. She wanted me
to come."

"And park yourself out in the rain?"

"Maybe the rain will stop."

"And maybe it won't." She gazed at him for another
moment and turned on her heel. She wasn't making
a dent in that solemn determination. "I'll get those
clothes. Do you have a cell phone?"

"Yes, but I keep doing things to it that make it go
wonky."

"Well, don't do anything tonight, dammit. I want you
to call me every hour, and I want to be able to reach
you."

He smiled. "Yes, Eve."

"And I'm going to give you Joe's slicker, and I want
you to keep beneath the trees and out of the rain as
much as possible."

"Yes, Eve."

"And if you see something you don't like, then call me, and I'll call Officer Hughes. Don't try to deal with it yourself."

His smile widened. "Yes, Eve."

"And stop saying that and grinning at me. I mean it."

"I know you do. But it's hard not to smile. You're worried about me, and that means that you like me. That makes me happy."

She felt a melting within her. "Of course I like you. I've always liked you, Ben. Don't you know that?"

He shook his head. "I thought it was because I helped you with Bonnie. It was okay that it was all about her, but it's nice that you like me, too."

She went back and gave him a quick hug. "Don't you ever say that again. Bonnie was the beginning, but you're very special to Joe and me on your own. Because you're who you are." She turned and strode toward the bedroom. "So you have to take care of yourself and don't do anything foolish."

"Some people think I am a fool, Eve," he said quietly.

"Then they're stupid. Are you different? Yes. But we're all different, and we just have to accept each other. Finish that chocolate and dry your hair."

"Yes, Eve."

"Now you're making fun of me."

"I think I am." He thought about it. "Do you mind?"

"No. Just don't make a habit of it." She slammed the door behind her.

Dammit, she didn't want Ben to go out there.

But he had said that Bonnie had told him to come here. Surely she wouldn't have sent him if she'd thought there was any danger. Or would she? Bonnie had shown that she wasn't above weighing her choices as to whom she wanted to protect. She loved Eve as much as Eve loved her. Eve would always be first where Bonnie was concerned. From the moment she had given birth to Bonnie, Eve had realized her little girl was very special, and they would always have a bond that would last forever. But forever had lasted only seven short years when Bonnie had been kidnapped and died. Eve couldn't bear the agony of living without her and had been spiraling downward to follow her through that final door when she had started to dream of Bonnie. It wasn't until years later that she would admit to herself that she believed Bonnie was no dream but a spirit who had come to show her that forever was still possible if they were patient and didn't break the rules. It had been difficult because Eve always had been hardheaded and practical, and ghosts were not acceptable in her vision of life . . . and death. But those visits from Bonnie were so real, so right, that she had gradually realized that Bonnie was alive for her no matter what anyone else thought.

And when she was searching for Bonnie's body to bring her home, she had come across Ben, who was as special in his way as Bonnie. Somehow, it had hardly surprised her that he, too, dreamed about Bonnie. Nor that he loved her as much as Eve did.

No, that wasn't true. No one could love her that much.

Good God, was she a little jealous that Bonnie had come to Ben and not to her?

She said the darkness around you was holding her back.

So Bonnie had sent Ben to try to keep Eve safe.

And now Eve had to find a way to keep Ben safe.

The rain was lessening, Doane noticed. That was too bad. The rain was his friend right now.

"It will still be fine, Kevin." He looked down at the skull in the chest beside him on the seat of the truck as he pulled out his earphone. "I'll just have to make a few adjustments here. I kind of thought Venable might send that man who was watching us at the lake. But I wasn't expecting Ben Hudson to show up. Fate seems to be putting obstacles in our path. But you always said the victory was sweeter if it wasn't easy." He opened his computer. "Everything has to be ready to go like clockwork when I put it in motion. Let's check on Blick."

Text or Skype?

No, he wanted to see Blick's face, make certain that there was no hesitance or lies. He trusted the man as much as he trusted anyone. He had been Kevin's friend and worshipped him. Besides, he liked money. Between the two, he had a chance that he wouldn't betray him. Or that he wouldn't move too soon and trigger a response that would make it difficult for Doane to initiate his plans for Eve Duncan. Blick had never had Kevin's coolness and was prone to panic. He had to keep him calm and on track.

He pressed the button and waited for Blick to pick up the line on Summer Island.

"Is everything okay?" Blick's face was tense as he picked up the line. "Have you done it?"

"Not yet. There are problems. I'll work them out. MacGuire's attention is still focused on the dog?"

"Yeah, the doctors seem to be busy. I don't know what's going on."

"You don't have to know. Just keep her there and away from here. That's your job. You understand?"

"I heard you."

"Good. Then do it." He hung up.

CHAPTER

4

"How's he doing?" Caleb asked, as Jane came out of the examination room.

"Good. Very good." She smiled brilliantly. "Devon doesn't think there's any internal organ damage from the poison. That means that once we get the poison totally out of his system, he has a chance for total recovery." She looked at the computer on his lap. "That's my laptop. What are you doing with it?"

"Nothing criminal. That's not saying I couldn't have made you a cybervictim if I'd chosen. It was ridiculously easy to access anything I wanted to see." His brows lifted. "And your password? Eve/Joe. It took me all of three minutes to decide what you'd use."

"So? It's not as if I really cared. Nothing is top secret on my computer. Technology is not my life." She added, "Though you might have asked permission if you wanted to use it."

"You weren't around, and I have a tendency to be

impatient. I didn't go into your Facebook account or anything. I was just checking your e-mail to see if you got an answer from that Nedra woman at your luxury pup day-care center."

"And did I?"

"Yes." He turned the computer around. "Shocked disbelief. And then abject apologies. When they checked, they found their cameras caught this man with Toby." He paused. "Syringe in hand."

"What?" The next moment, she'd snatched the computer from him. One glance, and she could see it was true. It was taken in the outdoor play area, and the short, stocky man with curly, red hair had his back to the camera, and she couldn't see his features. But she could see that he was standing over Toby and she could see the syringe he was slipping back into the pocket of his jacket. For an instant she could feel the rage run hot before she got it under control. "The son of a bitch. Who is he? Did Nedra know? Everyone has to check in at the front desk."

"She said his name is Herbert Connors. He'd brought a boxer to the day-care center three times before that day. He said he was dropping the dog off for his next-door neighbor at his flat. She says he appeared to be a nice man and was very friendly with all the dogs. She can't believe he would do something like this."

"Well, he did." Her hands tightened on the laptop. "And she'd better check out the other dogs he had contact with."

"That was her first thought. She said she'd get on the phone immediately with all her clients and see if any other dogs are sick." Caleb tilted his head. "But somehow I don't think she's going to find any. I think that Toby was the only target."

Her gaze flew to his face. "And why do you think that?"

"She said Herbert Connors hadn't been back since that day he'd evidently given Toby the poison. I think he'd gone the other three times to set it up. He was waiting for you to drop off Toby so that he could finish his job."

"For God's sake, you're making it sound like some diabolic scheme instead of a vicious crazy preying on a helpless animal."

"Haven't you noticed?" He smiled faintly. "I tend to think on diabolic lines."

"True. But you're very clever, and sometimes you're right. So tell me what you're thinking."

"That you're a target. That this Herbert Connors used Toby to nudge you in the direction he wanted you to go." He paused. "And he wanted you to leave London and come here to Summer Island."

"You're crazy. How would he even know about Summer Island?"

"I'm sure there are several messages from Sarah Logan in your e-mail. If he tapped it, he could put together a way to lure you out of London to take Toby to the island if it was an emergency."

She stared at him incredulously. "You believe he found a way to get access to my computer?"

"You probably made it easy for him. To use your own words, technology is not your life." His forehead wrinkled thoughtfully. "It wouldn't surprise me if he also found a way to bug your apartment."

"You're really reaching. This is getting more and more complicated . . . and absurd. If he got into my apartment, why not poison Toby while he was there."

"Because he wanted information and a way to move you out of London, not just to hurt the dog."

"I was already moving. I was planning on visiting Eve and Joe," she said. "So there goes your motive for the scenario."

"Maybe not. At any rate, I put a few wheels in motion to start verifying. For one thing I'm running a check on Herbert Connors. Though I doubt that's really his name." He stood up and headed for the front entrance. "But I do need to think about it. Let's get some air."

"Caleb, what—" He was already out the door. She closed the computer and hurried after him.

The air was soft and fragrant, and a breeze brought a hint of salt from the sea she could not see. It must be close to dawn, but night was still clinging stubbornly.

"The sea is just over that hill," Caleb said. "I went out and reconnoitered the area earlier."

"You're lucky you didn't get shot by a security guard."

He only smiled.

No, he wouldn't be worried about guards. She had seen him in action, and he was truly intimidating. He was not only a hunter but had the instincts and skill of a jungle cat. "Reconnoitered? That's a military term."

He nodded. "But this is far from an armed camp. Margaret Douglas was able to get on the island with very little problem. The airspace is probably secure, but it's not as if there are constant patrols along the beaches."

She gazed at him quizzically. "And are we expecting a D-Day assault?"

"No, one man would be enough," he said quietly. "One gun."

"Caleb."

He shrugged. "What can I say? I'm a suspicious bastard. I don't like the way this is playing out. Whoever gave that poison to Toby went to a good deal of thought and trouble."

"If you're right."

A brilliant smile lit his face. "But I usually am, Jane."

"Arrogant bastard." She was finding it hard not to smile in return. That wicked magnetism always disarmed her when it should have put up red flags. "And what other wheels did you put in motion to verify that?"

"I made a call and asked one of my associates to burgle your apartment and see if there were any bugs."

"What? I could have just called and gotten permission from the landlord."

"It was just as easy my way. And I was in control."

"By all means, that's of the utmost importance," she said dryly.

"It is to me." His head lifted, and he looked out into the trees. "Control can mean the difference between life and death. It's something I've always had trouble with. But you know that, don't you?"

"Yes."

He looked away from the trees to her face. "But I've done extraordinarily well with you. You've been a great temptation, and I've managed to be almost civilized."

"Almost."

"That's all you can expect from me." His smile deepened. "I'm hoping you'll learn to appreciate the fact that I could be so much worse . . . or better. Depending on how you look at it."

She looked away from him. "I'm not looking at anything that doesn't concern Toby right now."

"And quite right. Sorry. One thing seems to lead to another." He chuckled. "And selfish bastard that I am, it usually ends up back with me. How peculiar." He shrugged. "I can wait."

"For me to jump into bed with you?" She looked him directly in the eye. "It's not going to happen, Caleb."

He smiled. "It will, you know. I'm working with a handicap, but I can deal with it."

"What handicap?"

"Well, actually there are several. The most important is who I am and who you are. You have a problem with trust, and no one can say that I'm the steadiest man in the universe."

She made a rude sound. "You're as volatile as a runaway comet."

"Comets usually have a general direction. They can occasionally be deterred, but only by a major force. I have my course set."

"Prepare to be deterred." His smile never changed, and she continued impatiently, "Why me, Caleb? You said yourself that we're not a good match."

"We could be a fantastic match, just not in the ordinary sense. Why you?" He tilted his head, gazing at her appraisingly. "Besides the fact that you're beautiful and intelligent and make me hot just looking at you?"

"I'm not that unusual. I'm sure there are other women who have that same effect on you."

"Lust is definitely a part of my makeup but there are degrees." He added softly, "And you shoot up and break all the gauges, Jane."

Heat. Breathlessness. Electricity.

She pulled her gaze away. "You'll get over it."

"I'm not sure. Because there's something else. I don't know quite what it is, but it holds me. Sometimes I get a glimpse, but then it's gone. I can't let you go until I find out what I'm losing."

"I don't want to get involved with you, Caleb."

"I know. Because you think I'm not safe." His eyes were suddenly glittering with recklessness. "You're right, I'm not safe. You'd have to watch me all the time. But I'd make it entertaining for you."

"I'm not that starved for entertainment."

"I could make you think you were starved. That would make the satisfaction all the more delicious." He was studying her face. "But I'm going to have to move very slowly. As I said, I've never seen anyone more wary of making a commitment. Even one of a purely sexual nature. You couldn't even make one with Trevor, could you?"

She stiffened. "Trevor? Why are we suddenly talking about Trevor?"

He smiled crookedly. "Because I think a lot about Mark Trevor. I did a little checking when I found myself becoming . . . drawn to you. I wanted to know with just what I had to contend. The only man who has been important to you was Mark Trevor. He was your lover for a number of years. I was very glad to find out that you'd cast him out of your life."

"I didn't cast him out. We just agreed that we weren't right for each other."

"I'd bet that you were the one who made the decision. Did he get too close?"

"Stop trying to pry into my business, Caleb. I don't want to talk about Trevor."

"Right." He held up his hands. "Neither do I. I just wanted to see your reaction."

"And?"

"Guarded but not overly emotional. It's a response I can handle," he said. "Now I'm going to skip out of the line of fire and concentrate on your dog and your situation here since that's all you want from me at present: I've probably disturbed you. Why don't you forget me for a while and go back inside to your Toby. I think I'll stay out here a bit and commune with nature."

"Good. But I'm not going to run along because you tell me to do it." He did disturb her. She couldn't remember a time when he hadn't. That disquiet was always present, burning low, and she had become almost accustomed to it. Yet she had to admit that she was relieved that he had taken a step back. "I'm not going anywhere until I get you back on track and tell me why you were sure enough that you were right to have someone burgle my apartment. I can almost hear that brain of yours clicking away. You gave me a scenario, now fill it in. Why would anyone go to all that trouble to make sure that I would come here to Summer Island?"

He didn't speak for a moment, then said slowly, "Maybe it wasn't that he wanted you to come to Summer Island. Maybe it was that he didn't want you to go home to Eve."

She froze. "What are you saying?"

"Coincidences. I always have problems with coincidences. You were planning to go home to visit Eve and Joe. Then suddenly your dog became very ill, and you had to cancel your trip to Eve and bring Toby here. Coincidence?"

"Why would anyone want to stop me from going to see Eve?"

"Inconvenient?"

"Caleb."

"How do I know? It's all just a product of my suspicious mind."

But that product was beginning to scare the hell out of her. "It's too . . . Why?"

"We'll have to find out, won't we?"

"No, we won't," she said harshly. "Because it's not true. Nothing is wrong with Eve. None of this is going to touch her."

"I scared you," he said. "You asked, Jane."

Yes, she had asked. But she hadn't thought he would say anything that would involve Eve. "It's all supposition."

"I never claimed anything else."

She drew a shaky breath. "I know." She pulled out her phone. "But I think I'll call Eve anyway. I promised I'd call her about Toby."

He smiled. "That's right you did."

She dialed quickly.

Answer, Eve.

One ring.

Two rings.

Eve picked up on the third ring. "Jane?"

Jane felt heady with relief. "Yes. Did I wake you?"

"No, I was awake. I've had trouble sleeping tonight. How's Toby?"

"Better. He's going to live, Eve."

"Thank God. What was wrong with him?"

"Poison."

"What?"

"I know, it's crazy. Some bastard poisoned him."

"Who?

"I don't know yet. The whole thing's beyond any kind of sanity." She paused. "How are you? Is everything all right there?"

"I'm fine. Don't worry about me. Take care of Toby."

"If you're fine, then why are you having trouble sleeping?"

"I should have known that you'd pick up on that. Ben Hudson dropped by unexpectedly."

"Really? Why? You haven't seen him since you found Bonnie, have you?"

"No." She changed the subject. "How long before Toby will be well enough for you to bring him here?"

"I'm hoping only a day or two. He's getting wonderful help here on the island."

"Let me know as soon as you know for sure. Now I'm going to call Joe and tell him the good news about Toby. Or maybe not. It's still the middle of the night, and he has to be in court tomorrow. I'll phone him first thing in the morning." Her voice was suddenly tense. "And I may decide not to wait until you come to me.

Maybe I'll hop a plane and check on you and Toby myself. Take care of yourself." Eve hung up.

Jane slowly pressed the disconnect.

"Okay?" Caleb asked.

She nodded. "She said she was fine."

"But you don't believe her?"

"Sure I do." She was frowning. "But she said something about coming down here to check on Toby and
me. And she got off the phone too soon."

"So?"

"She didn't want me to ask questions. That bothered
me. And what is Ben Hudson doing at the cottage?"

"I might be able to help you if I knew who Ben Hudson was. Is he a threat?"

She shook her head. "No way. It's just odd that he
should turn up tonight." She turned and started for the
door. "I'm going to ask Devon Brady how soon I can
transport Toby."

"And if you don't get the answer you want?"

She hadn't known that the answer had already formed
in her mind. "I need to get to Eve. I think something is
going on with her. I'll just wait until I'm sure Toby's
stabilized. He may already be there." She was thinking
quickly. "And then I may turn him over to Margaret until I can come back. She'd take good care of him."

He looked at her in surprise. "You'd trust her with
your precious Toby? You just met her."

"I'd trust her." She met his gaze. "Will you take me
to Eve?"

"That goes without saying." He bowed mockingly.
"I'm at your service. Why else would I be here?"

"I don't know. I can never quite figure you out, Caleb."

"But you're willing to use me. Maybe you even actually trust me a little. Wouldn't that be interesting?" He gestured with a little shooing motion. "Run along and make your arrangements about Toby. Oh, that's right, you don't like me to give you orders."

"No, I don't."

"Then I'll just gas up the plane and have it ready to go if you decide that's your best option."

"Thanks, Caleb," she said absently. "Of course it all depends on Toby . . ."

"No, it depends on Jane MacGuire." She heard him chuckle as he turned away. "You've made up your mind, and you'd find a way to save your Toby and fly to Eve's rescue no matter what the obstacles."

"Maybe." She opened the door. "But Eve said she doesn't need rescuing."

"And you hope she's telling the truth."

"Eve never lies to me. I just don't like the poison. I don't like having to come here instead of going straight to the lake cottage. I don't like the way she shunted me off that call." She said over her shoulder, "So I'm going to go and ask her in person why she did it."

"I'll be back soon, boy." Jane's hand gently stroked Toby's head. He was still under sedation and didn't move. But she hoped somehow he might be able to understand her. "We made it through, Toby. We've been together so long and it looks like God wants us to stick together for a while longer." Her voice was unsteady.

"Isn't that great?" She put her cheek on his ruff. He was so soft and silky. "I love you," she whispered. "I wouldn't leave you if I didn't have to do it. But Devon says you're doing fine, and you're out of danger. I'm not so sure about Eve. You'll understand, you love Eve, too."

"Devon says you're leaving."

Jane straightened and turned to see Margaret standing in the doorway. "Yes, I'm glad you're here. I wanted to see you before I left. Devon says that it will take a day or two before Toby will be well enough to travel." She gave Toby a final pat. "I'll be back in a few days. Will you take care of him for me?"

Margaret nodded. "I told you that he belonged to me, too, now." She looked down at Toby. "He'll be well soon. He has a strong heart. I'll put him with Monty and Maggie and that will help." She smiled. "After all, they're his parents. It's right that they're together now." Her smile faded. "You wouldn't leave Toby if it wasn't important. Did you find out who tried to kill him?"

"No." She shook her head. "Maybe. I just know I have to get to Eve. She adopted me when I was a kid, and I'm uneasy that this may have something to do with her."

"Why?"

She shrugged. "I don't know. I'm trying to put the pieces together. I was going to see Eve when all this began. She could be the key."

"You're worried about her."

"I love her," she said simply. "She's the most important person in my life."

"That's . . . nice," Margaret's voice was wistful. "But it's kind of dangerous, too."

"What?"

"All your eggs in one basket . . ." Margaret said vaguely. "You have too much to lose. It's safer not to narrow down the field." She tilted her head. "I'd think that you'd be afraid of doing that. It doesn't seem your style."

Jane gazed at her in surprise. Margaret and she had spent less than a few hours together and exchanged little conversation. How had Margaret realized that Jane had problems with trust? It should have made her feel uneasy to be so easily read, but somehow it didn't. "Sometimes you can't help yourself. People come into your life, and you know that you can't let them leave again even if there's a chance that they'll hurt you. Haven't you found that, Margaret?"

"Yes, but I try to keep them at a distance . . . like you, Jane."

Jane shook her head. "I've never seen anyone more open to people than you are."

Margaret suddenly chuckled. "I said I try, I didn't say I succeed. I know what's good for me, I just dive in anyway." She gave Toby a pat. "Like Toby here. He'd rather take a chance than close himself away from people who might show him affection. That's why we have to protect him."

"And who protects you, Margaret?"

"Oh, I have a whole army who take care of that." She grinned. "And now Toby is enlisted into that army. We understand each other, we belong to the same club. He wouldn't let anything happen to me."

"If you have to rely on Toby, then you're in bad

shape," Jane said dryly. "Being a guard dog isn't his long suit, as you've already noted."

"Everyone protects those they care about." Margaret met her gaze. "Toby would die for you."

"He almost did," Jane said. "There was no reason for that bastard to hurt him. It had to be something to do with me."

"Or your Eve?"

Jane nodded jerkily. "Or Eve. Thank you for taking care of Toby until I get back."

"Yes," she said gravely. "I'll keep him safe. Though he doesn't really need me. You don't have to worry about him. I can feel the strength coming back to him. In a few days, he'll be fine."

"Thank you." She gave Margaret an impulsive hug and stepped back quickly. "I'd appreciate it if you'd let me call you and check on him."

"Devon could give you better medical details."

"She's wonderful," Jane said. "But I want to talk to you."

"Then call me." Margaret smiled. "Though you may be one of those people I have to be wary about. What the hell. Life would be boring without taking a few chances. I'll give you my cell number before you get on the plane." She turned away from Toby. "Are you ready? I told Devon I'd take you to the airfield. She said Caleb was already there."

"Yes, I've already said good-bye to Devon." She bent down and gave Toby another quick hug. "Get well quick, Toby. That's an order." She hurried out of the office after Margaret.

But Margaret was standing by the van, her head lifted, her gaze on the trees.

Jane stopped short. "Margaret?"

"Get in the van."

Jane got into the passenger seat. "Is something wrong?"

"Maybe." She got into the driver's seat. "Someone's been out there in the forest, watching."

Jane tensed. "Who?"

Margaret shook her head. "I don't know. It could have been someone from the village. But they're not usually curious about anything that happens at the research center. They accept us now."

"How do you know that there was someone out there?"

She was silent a moment before she said reluctantly, "The birds."

Jane's brows rose. "The birds told you?"

"No, I just felt it. And stop looking at me like that. Dammit, I didn't want to answer that question. I know it sounds crazy." The headlights of the van pierced the darkness as Margaret drove down the rough dirt road. "Look, I'm not a Dr. Doolittle. I can just sometimes sense things that are connected to nature or animals. I don't know why. It just happens. Sometimes I can get pictures or memories, but it's usually from animals with a higher degree of intelligence." She made a face. "I have real problems with birds."

"I . . . see."

"And stop being tactful. You don't see anything."

"True. So explain. How do you *feel* it?"

She shrugged. "A disturbance. Something that's not

normal. But most birds forget so quickly that you only get an immediate impression." She made a face. "But someone was there, and they didn't like it. That's all I know. It's just as well you're getting on that plane."

Jane smiled. "Since the birds don't like me?" Then the smile faded. "I'm not really making fun of you. I just don't understand, so it's easier to laugh. But I'm not laughing at how you helped my Toby. I'm very grateful."

"Then find out who hurt him. That's all I want from you." A few minutes later, she pulled into the airfield and stopped beside one of the three hangars. "Nice plane. Sleek, powerful." She watched Seth Caleb come down the steps of the plane. "A little like him."

"Yes." Jane jumped out of the van and went toward Caleb. "Are we ready for takeoff?"

He nodded. "I was just about to call you." He looked at Margaret. "What's wrong with her?"

Jane looked back to see Margaret coming toward them. The girl's expression was tense.

Jane tried to smile. "Birds?"

Margaret shook her head, her gaze on the third hangar. "Get on the plane, Jane."

"What's wrong now?"

Margaret whirled to Caleb. "Get her on the plane."

Caleb took Jane's elbow. "Let's do what she says. She seems to want you out of here. My instincts say that we should listen to her." He was nudging Jane toward the plane. "Good-bye, Margaret."

"Good-bye." But Margaret was following closely behind them. "You have very good instincts, Caleb." She was still gazing at the third hangar. "I thought you would the moment I saw you. But maybe not good enough to—Down! Rifle!"

"What?" Jane glanced at the hangar and caught a glimpse of long metal cylinder emerge from the darkness of the hangar.

A rifle aiming in their direction.

"Down!" Margaret cried again as she ran toward Jane.

But Margaret was directly behind her, Jane realized. Any bullet would have to go through her to reach Jane.

"You get down, dammit!" Jane turned, pulled away from Caleb, and tackled Margaret to the ground.

She didn't even hear the shot.

She only felt the pain.

And then even that pain was lost in the darkness.

LAKE COTTAGE
5:40 A.M.

Dawn.

The rain had almost stopped, but the dark clouds made the gradually lightening sky retain its gloom, Eve thought.

Still, she was glad to have the night over. The two hours since Ben had left seemed more like years. She'd get dressed, then call Ben and make him come back to the cottage for breakfast. Then she'd phone FedEx and arrange the pickup for the reconstruction. She wanted it out of her hands because she was almost certain that she wasn't going to twiddle her thumbs here when she was so disturbed about what had happened to Toby. She would go to Summer Island and try to find out what was—

Her cell phone rang.

Joe.

"You're up early. I was going to call you. I've been thinking and I've decided I need to go to—"

"Jane's been shot."

Shock. She couldn't breathe. "What?"

"I just got a call from Seth Caleb on Summer Island. He thought the news would come better from me."

"She's dead?"

"No," he said quickly. "God, I'm messing this up. I'm scared to death, and I'm not handling this right. So much for me being the right person to tell you. She's not dead, but they don't know how bad it is. It just happened and they've taken her to the—"

"Who shot her?"

"Caleb didn't know. It was a sniper shooting from a hangar at the airfield. Caleb couldn't leave Jane to go after him." He added grimly, "But you can bet he'll be on his trail the minute it's safe for him to do it."

She didn't care about that bastard right now. All she wanted to know was that Jane was going to live. "What kind of wound?"

"The bullet entered the back and exited the upper shoulder." He paused. "She's losing a lot of blood. They took her back to the veterinary research center for treatment."

"Why not the village hospital?"

"No hospital on the island. Just a resident doctor and

clinic. Caleb said something about Margaret's saying that she'd get better first aid at the animal hospital at the center."

"Who the hell is Margaret?"

"I don't know. Someone who evidently has no faith in the village medical facility."

"Then get Jane on a plane back to the States."

"Caleb will do that as soon as he thinks she's stable. I told you, she's losing a lot of blood."

"I'm so scared, Joe," she whispered. That was an understatement. She was terrified. "I just talked to her a few hours ago. How could this happen?"

"We'll find out. I'm not going to wait for Caleb to bring her back to us. I'm on my way to the airport now. I've rented a plane to take me to Summer Island."

"Good." She drew a shaky breath. "You're closer to her down there in Miami and will be able to get to her sooner. Don't wait for me. One of us has to be there for her right away. I'm heading for the airport here as soon as I hang up. It may be easier for you to arrange a plane to the island for me out of Miami. Though I hate like hell to have to change planes. I'll call you when I get to the airport and let you know if I have a problem arranging a nonstop out of there."

"Right. And I'll make a few calls before I take off. I'll call headquarters, and maybe the captain can pull a few strings to get you out of there." He added, "Though she's not going to be pleased I'm skipping out on that trial. Screw it. If they let the bastard off, I'll go after him again." He paused. "It's going to be okay, Eve."

"Maybe." She closed her eyes. "She told me that

Toby was poisoned, Joe. Who would poison a sweet dog like Toby? Who would shoot our Jane?"

"We'll find out." His voice was suddenly harsh. "Dammit, I can feel your—I want to be there for you."

"Be there for Jane." She cleared her throat. "I've got to go, Joe. I've got to tell Ben that I'm leaving and ask him to give the reconstruction to the FedEx man."

"Ben?"

"Ben Hudson. He showed up last night after I went to bed."

"Why?"

"He said he'd had a dream, and he wanted to be with me." She said unsteadily, "It's almost funny, isn't it? All those premonitions that were plaguing you. Everyone seemed to be so worried about me when it wasn't about me at all. It was about Jane. We should have been worried about Jane." She had to get off the phone before she broke down. "I'll call you when I get to the airport." She hung up.

She drew a deep breath and turned toward the bedroom.

Get a grip. Throw some clothes into an overnight bag and get out of here. She called Ben.

He answered on the second ring. "Do you need me?"

"No, but Jane needs me. I have to go to her. Where are you?"

"About a mile or so down the road, just inside the woods."

"Come to the cottage. I have something I want you to do."

"Right away, Eve." He hung up.

At least she wouldn't have to worry about Ben in

those dark, wet woods any longer, she thought as she quickly packed her bag and set the FedEx box by the front door.

She checked her watch. Almost fifteen minutes had passed since her call to Ben. Shouldn't he be here? He was young and strong and when he said right away, it meant full speed ahead.

Stop worrying. He'll be here soon.

But she needed to get to the airport, and she couldn't sit here twiddling her thumbs. She'd meet him on the road and tell him about the FedEx. In two minutes, she was in the car and driving down the driveway toward the road.

It was starting to rain again, dammit. She hit the windshield wipers and headlights, her eyes straining for a glimpse of Ben. He was wearing Joe's yellow slicker. He should be easy to spot as he walked toward her.

But she almost missed him.

Because he was not walking toward her. He was crumpled on the ground at the side of the road.

"Ben!"

She stomped on the brakes and jumped out of the car.

Then she was kneeling beside him, her knees sinking into the rivulets of mud and water. The yellow slicker was also streaked with smears of mud.

Mud, not blood. But he was so damn still.

Eve pushed the hood of the slicker back away from his face.

And then she saw the blood. His face was white in the pale morning light, and there was a deep, long gash over his left eye.

"Ben," she whispered.

"Don't you worry. I don't think he's dead. I'll take care of him."

Her head jerked to the side, and she saw a gray-haired man in a green camouflage slicker just behind her. His old red pickup truck was parked at the curve of the road with headlights blazing. He was gazing at Ben with concern as he came toward them.

She tensed warily and her hand reached in her pocket and closed on her gun. He could just be one of the neighboring farmers who used the lake road to cut across to the highway. He didn't seem to be a threat. As he drew closer, she relaxed a little more.

A seamed and weathered face, blue eyes that had creases at the corners.

And she had never seen a more kindly expression.

"Why, he's just a kid. Who is he? Your brother?" He fell to his knees beside her. "That looks like a bad cut. Maybe we'd better get him to the hospital." He took out his phone. "I'll call 911." He was dialing even as he reached out to grasp Eve's shoulder in sympathy. "We'll get him help right away."

She instinctively flinched away from him. "Who are you?"

"Just someone who wants to help. My farm is down the road from your property. I believe in being a Good Samaritan. We all have to help each other." His smile was as gentle as his expression. "My name is Doane." He extended his hand. "What's yours?"

"Eve Duncan." She turned back to Ben. "Finish making that call. I don't like the way he's breathing."

"Really?" He leaned forward over Ben and his hand

fell on her shoulder as he tried to get closer. "I think he may be—"

She didn't hear the end of the sentence.

She didn't feel the pinprick on her upper back.

But she slumped forward over Ben's body a second later.

CHAPTER

5

R elax." Rex Nelker, the pilot Joe had hired to
take him to Summer Island, glanced at him as
the Learjet lifted off the Miami runway. "We're moving as fast as we can. We should have good weather
all the way to the island. I'll have you there in an hour
or so."

"I'll relax when you tell me we're landing." But
Joe knew that Nelker was right. Everything had gone
as smoothly and quickly as possible for a last-minute
departure. He had practically been able to step on the
plane minutes after he arrived at Miami International.
But that didn't keep him from being on edge. He hadn't
heard back from Seth Caleb after that first phone call.
For all he knew, Jane could be dead.

Don't be negative. It would tear the heart out of him.

He'd assume the best until he found out differently.
He couldn't bear the alternative.

And neither could Eve. He loved Jane, but she was

not only Eve's adopted daughter, she was her best friend. She and Jane had come together when Jane was a street kid, and they had found ways to bond in many, many ways. It would tear Eve to pieces if anything happened to Jane.

So don't borrow trouble. Do the job and make things as easy for Eve as possible. He'd made a few calls just before he got on the Learjet and arranged a private flight for Eve out of Atlanta. She'd be arriving at Summer Island only an hour after he landed.

He just hoped it wouldn't be too late.

Everyone seemed to be so worried about me when it wasn't about me at all. It was about Jane. We should have been worried about Jane.

He stiffened.

It was about Jane.

But was it all about Jane?

Eve had said she'd call him when she reached Atlanta International.

No call.

Don't panic.

She hadn't had more than forty minutes to pack and get to the airport.

He reached for his cell phone and dialed Eve.

No answer.

Shit. He should at least get a voice mail.

Unless her phone was turned off.

Eve would never turn her phone off in an emergency like this. She'd be afraid not to be able to get word about Jane.

We should have been worried about Jane.

But they should also have been worried about Eve.

The swirling puzzle pieces were taking form, becoming clear.

Every instinct had made Joe reluctant to leave Eve. The only thing that had made him feel safe was that Jane would be with her.

But Jane had not come.

Ben had a dream.

And Ben's dreams were always about Bonnie.

Perhaps Bonnie was having some ghostly trepidations, too? He had only recently come to believe that Bonnie actually was an entity and not a figment of Eve's imagination. He was hardheaded and a complete realist, but sometimes a knockout vision could change everything. He had to accept that if Bonnie was Eve's hallucination, she was also his. Now it appeared Bonnie was somehow involved with all this.

And Jane's being shot would make Eve forget everything but getting to her daughter.

She would be vulnerable.

"Something wrong, man?" Nelker said.

"Everything is wrong," Joe muttered. He was torn between telling Nelker to go back to Miami and continuing to Summer Island. There was a slight chance that there was a phone malfunction, and Eve would not forgive him if he didn't get to Jane as soon as possible.

But he didn't think there was a phone or tower malfunction. He didn't know what was happening, but he had a hunch it was all bad. Hell, he knew it was bad. He was on his way to Jane, who might not even be alive when he got there.

Eve . . .

He couldn't think of Eve right now. Emotion always got in the way when he thought of Eve, and he had to make choices.

Eve was the choice, always and forever.

Even if he had Nelker turn around, he couldn't get to Eve for another two hours minimum.

Okay, find a way to give Eve her best chance considering all the circumstances.

Venable.

He quickly dialed Venable's number.

Voice mail.

"Listen, you bastard. You've been avoiding my calls since yesterday. I'm not taking it any longer. Call me back, or I'll be coming for you."

He hung up the phone and waited.

Three minutes later, the phone rang.

"I don't take kindly to threats, Quinn," Venable said sourly. "I was tempted to ignore you."

"Like you've been ignoring me since you called me yesterday. It wouldn't have been a wise move if you'd done it now. I'm a little tense."

Silence. "I noticed."

"That's because you know me well, and you're very observant. You're also a conniving, ruthless son of a bitch when it suits you. I'm beginning to think it may be suiting you right now."

"I don't know what you mean."

"You called me yesterday and made polite inquiries about me, Eve, Jane . . . and how the world was treating us. Very suspicious, Venable."

"You're paranoid."

"Why did you call?"

"I hadn't talked to you for a while. It's not so unusual. Sometimes I think we're friends."

"Sometimes I think so, too. But not if it concerns the CIA. Then I think you're a manipulator on the grand scale. Talk to me. Why did you call?"

Venable didn't answer.

"Answer me." Joe's voice was low and tense. "Do you know where I am right now? I'm on a plane flying down to Summer Island in the Caribbean. I'm going there because Jane's been shot, and I have to get to her. What a coincidence that you called and inquired about her only yesterday. You wouldn't happen to know anything about this, would you?"

"Shot? Hell, no. How is Eve?"

"Strange you went straight from Jane's being shot to Eve. Or is it strange, Venable?"

"Is Eve okay?"

"I don't know. I can't get in touch with her."

Venable muttered a curse.

"Exactly how I feel," Joe said. "No voice mail. She was supposed to call me from Atlanta International and hasn't. So I'm putting it in your camp, Venable. I'm calling the police officer I had keeping an eye on her, but I want one of your people on the job, too."

"I don't know if we have any CIA agents in the area."

"No? Then get them there. Fast."

"Eve may be fine, Quinn. There could be any number of reasons why you can't reach her."

"Then find her; get her to call me."

"I'm not arguing. I'll look into it for you."

"How generous."

"It is generous. I don't have to do it. You've no proof I have any involvement in any of this. So back off, Quinn."

"I'm not backing off. First, go find Eve and keep her safe until you put her on a plane to the island. Then call me and tell me how and why you're pulling strings that caused Jane to end up with a bullet in her."

Silence. "I'm sorry about Jane, Quinn. I hope she'll be okay. If I can help, let me know."

"I've told you how you can help us. Get Eve on that plane so that she can get to Jane."

"I'll do my best. I'll call you as soon as I make contact with her." He hung up.

Venable had sounded genuinely sorry. Hell, he probably was regretting that Jane had been hurt, and Eve—No, don't think about what might be happening to Eve. He couldn't be certain that she was in danger. Keep calm. He'd call Ron, the officer who had been on patrol at the cottage, then hang tight until he heard back from both Venable and him. By that time he should have been able to find out if Jane was going to survive and take charge of what was happening there on the island.

Keep busy, he told himself. It could work out. He was doing the right thing.

No, he wasn't. There couldn't be anything right about flying away from Eve no matter what the emergency on the other end. So what if it was what she'd want him to do? Eve was the center of his being. Ignore everything but that fact and tell the pilot to turn around and go back to Miami.

Jane.

Jane was the one known victim. How could he abandon her?

He drew a deep, harsh breath and started to dial Ron's mobile phone. There was a chance the policeman had seen her leave or could reassure him she was safe.

Know something, dammit.

Tell me I'm jumping to conclusions.

Know something, anything.

Intent dark eyes staring down at her.

A faint flicker of emotion in those eyes. Relief?

Strange . . .

Jane knew those eyes. They frightened her.

Or did they? She had never admitted that fear to herself. Perhaps it wasn't fear of Caleb but wariness of the way he made her feel. He always knew too much. What would happen if she let him invade her space?

Too close. He always came too close . . .

"Stop frowning," Caleb said roughly. "Stop pushing me away. I'm trying to help you. Are you hurting? Devon gave you a sedative. You shouldn't be uncomfortable."

Why should she be hurting? Yet she was aware of a dull ache in her upper right shoulder.

An explosion of pain, then darkness.

"I'm . . . all right. Bullet?"

He nodded. "Sniper. Shooting from one of the hangars. It happened a little over three hours ago."

Sniper. It was like something from a war movie, she thought hazily. And it made no sense at all. She couldn't comprehend any of it. "Why?"

"I don't know." His lips tightened. "I haven't been able to go after the bastard. I couldn't leave you."

And it had made him angry, she realized. "Why? Am I dying?"

"No. Devon says that she thinks you're going to be okay. The bullet went through your shoulder and didn't appear to damage any organs. Devon doesn't like or trust the local village doctor, so she's arranging for an air ambulance to take you to a hospital in San Juan. But you scared us. You wouldn't stop bleeding. Devon had to give you a transfusion." He smiled crookedly. "Margaret wanted to donate her blood, but I'm universal, so Devon took mine."

"I would have preferred Margaret."

He nodded. "I know. But you have to take what's available. I'm very much available." He stood up. "I have to go and tell Devon and Margaret you're awake. They made me promise. They wanted to hover, but I told them that you'd do better to wake with someone you knew." His dark eyes were suddenly gleaming. "I told them you'd feel safer."

"You lied."

"Yes, but it worked. I got what I wanted. They don't understand the complications of our relationship. I brought you to the island, and, therefore, I'm presumably a man to trust."

"Presumably."

"But you don't trust me. You don't trust any man, do you?" He suddenly looked back and snapped his fingers. "No, there is a man you do trust, and it should comfort you to know that he should be arriving on the island at any moment."

"Joe?"

He smiled. "You see? You knew exactly whom I was talking about. Tell him I'll talk to him when I get back."

"Wait." She moistened her lips. "You're going to try to track down that sniper."

"I'm not going to try. If he's still on the island, I'm going to get the bastard within the next few hours." He added coldly, "If he's found a way off, it may take a little while longer."

"I'm not asking you to—"

"Be quiet, Jane," he said softly. "I've been thinking about my reward all the time I've been sitting here playing the sturdy, solid friend in need. This has a little to do with you but more with what and who I am. I want him."

Before she could answer, he was gone.

And she was left to remember how savage and violent Caleb could be when he went on the hunt.

Dammit, and she was wounded and too weak to go after him. Yes, Caleb had a primitive and barbaric desire for revenge, but this was really all about her. He wouldn't even be on the island if she hadn't asked him to come here.

"He upset you." Margaret was standing in the doorway, her gaze on Jane's face. "I told Devon it was taking a chance to let him stay with you. He's one of the wild ones. Even if he meant well, he is what he is." She came forward and sat down beside the bed. "What do you want me to do? Go after him and bring him back?"

"No, that's impossible. You couldn't do it. I told you about—you don't know what he is."

"Yes, I do." She shrugged. "I told you, he's one of the wild ones. I know all about them. It's true I haven't run across anyone quite like him. It would be hard, but I could bring him back to you if you want him."

"You don't know all about Caleb," Jane said dryly. "I guarantee that you don't. I didn't give you more than a hint. There's no one like him."

"I can get him." She was holding Jane's gaze. "Say the word."

"So then I'd have two people to worry about?" Jane said in exasperation. "No, I won't say the word, dammit."

"Now I'm upsetting you, too." Margaret suddenly smiled. "You're ill, we should all leave you alone to heal and deal with everything else ourselves."

"I'm not ill. I've been shot. There's a difference."

"Cause and effect."

"That should affect only me. And perhaps whoever is in charge of law and order on this island. Not Seth Caleb and not you."

"There's only a constable and his assistant in the village. Devon will probably tell him about the shooter in case he might be a danger to the locals. But I don't think he would be a danger to anyone but you, do you?"

"I don't know," she said in frustration. "Maybe. Why would I be a target?"

"Caleb may find out . . . if he doesn't decide to kill him instead of question him. I only know the shooter was stalking you. He was in the woods outside, and he was at the airfield."

Margaret had been coolly analytical about Caleb's

potential actions and apparently completely without judgment. "You have no objection to Caleb . . . going that far?"

"Why? It's his nature. Besides, it's justice. The man tried to kill you. Now he has to pay. I told you I believe in revenge."

"Yes, you did." But lying here looking at Margaret, it was difficult for Jane to accept. The young girl was so full of life and that youthful joyousness that it was hard to make the connection. "But this is a little more final than going after the man who poisoned Toby to punish him."

She shook her head. "Justice is justice."

"Yet you said that you'd go after Caleb and bring him back."

"Because I didn't want you to worry when you're not well." Her smile held a hint of mischief. "But I didn't say I wouldn't go after that man who shot you myself after I got Caleb back for you."

"Oh, for God's sake."

She laughed. "But I'd have to do it. Payback, remember? You saved my life. You took that bullet for me. I owe you a debt. Debts have to be paid."

"No, I don't remember it like that. Everything happened too fast. You don't owe me anything, Margaret."

"You're wrong. I don't know quite how I'll do it, but it will come to me." She got to her feet. "We won't argue about it right now. Maybe when Caleb comes back, he'll have some answers, and it will all become clear to us. You rest now, and I'll bring Joe Quinn in to see you as soon as he gets here. Caleb did tell you that he was on his way?"

"Yes, but he didn't mention Eve. Is she with him?"

"No, he's flying in from Miami. I think the plan is for her to arrive a little later."

"That would make sense." She couldn't wait to see Eve. Whenever Eve was on the scene, everything seemed right with the world. Though she doubted if even Eve could make all the ugliness that had happened lately seem normal or right.

And she still had that niggling feeling of uneasiness about that last phone call with Eve. "Where's my phone? I'd like to call her."

She shook her head. "Devon wants you to rest. You lost a lot of blood."

"I hear you offered a bit of your own. Thank you."

"It didn't happen. Caleb won that round." She headed for the door. "He seemed intrigued at the prospect. I didn't understand."

"That doesn't surprise me. Not many people understand Caleb. His background makes him unique."

"We're all unique." She smiled back over her shoulder. "You, me, Toby, Devon. Isn't nature wonderful? It's like a kaleidoscope that never shows the same picture twice." She opened the door. "Rest, Jane. I'll send your phone in when Joe Quinn gets here."

Jane stared after her with bewilderment. She wasn't sure exactly how wonderful nature could be, but she was beginning to believe that Margaret was a brilliant kaleidoscope of character in her own right. She would actually have gone after Caleb if Jane had asked. And it wasn't because she underestimated the danger he represented. Totally extraordinary.

But she wasn't up to analyzing Margaret right now,

she realized. She was feeling weak and exhausted, and the temporary adrenaline rush was fading rapidly.

Blank out the bewilderment, the unfathomable questions, Caleb and Margaret. She would deal with them later with Joe.

And then Eve would come, and they would be able to get through this nightmare as they got through everything else.

Together.

Venable.

Zander didn't hesitate as he saw the ID. He punched the access. "Has your agent got a report on Doane?"

"He got into the house. No disk. He snatched the computer, but all the data had been erased. We're having to restore it. We should know something by tomorrow."

"That should tell you something. He's covering his tracks." He paused. "And he doesn't want us to know where those tracks are going to lead. Are they going to lead to me? Or to Eve Duncan?"

Venable didn't answer.

Not good. "Answer me, Venable. Just why did you call?"

"There have been a few developments that have disturbed me. I thought it only fair to bring you into the loop."

"Disturbed?"

"Okay, scared the hell out of me," he said bluntly. "Jane MacGuire was shot by a sniper. We don't know whether she's going to make it or not."

"Jane MacGuire . . . Not Eve Duncan? Where? At the lake cottage?"

"No, Jane was on an island in the Caribbean. She was supposed to be with Eve at the cottage, but she flew down there to the island because of an emergency. Joe Quinn is on his way down there right now. He was in Miami giving evidence at a trial, and he took off immediately."

"He wasn't with Eve either? Curious."

"Not really. They lead independent lives."

"And so does Jane MacGuire, but both Quinn and MacGuire revolve around Eve Duncan. Do you think I haven't studied her world? MacGuire's a weakness in the armor, or that's what Doane would think, anyway." He was thinking quickly, putting the pieces together. "But why shoot Jane MacGuire? That wouldn't be necessary and Doane is smart enough to realize—" He stopped. "Quinn is going to the island and not Eve? That doesn't compute. Where's Eve Duncan?"

"She may be okay. We haven't been able to reach her after she told Quinn she'd call him from Atlanta International. Quinn is calling Atlanta PD to go out to the lake." He paused. "I sent one of my agents, Tad Dukes, out there last night to keep an eye on Eve. I'm trying to reach him now to check out if there was any problem. I can't contact him."

"Strange. And curious that you sent out an agent when you were trying to convince me that you doubted if Doane had made a connection to Eve Duncan."

"I believe in insurance. I'm on my way there myself."

"It may be too late. She may be dead. It depends on whether he wants instant gratification."

"You son of a bitch. You wouldn't care either way, would you?"

"I might care. It depends on how it would affect my having to transfer my operations. I'm finding your slipup very inconvenient, Venable."

"Screw you. I like Jane MacGuire and Eve. One woman may be dying, and the other is missing. I'm finding this mess more than inconvenient, Zander."

"Because you've never been able to erase emotion from the equations."

"And you've always been able to do that."

"Not always. I had to learn. But I was a very quick learner."

"I can imagine," Venable said sarcastically. "Fresh out of the cradle."

"Not quite that soon. I evolved. As soon as I realized that it could keep me alive if it made me think more logically. For instance, you're not thinking straight at all because you're emotionally involved. I'm rather surprised considering what I know about your background."

"And, of course, you're able to deduce exactly what's happening?"

"No, but I can stroke in the outlines. Doane wanted Eve Duncan alone and vulnerable, and that wasn't easy to manage. Their lives aren't as independent as you'd have me believe. When Quinn isn't around, Jane MacGuire is usually with Eve. It's not a conscious decision; it just happens because of their affection for her. Doane waited until he knew Quinn was going to be out of town, and he recognized that this was the time. But Jane MacGuire was going to come for a visit, so she had to be diverted. Hence, an emergency in the Caribbean."

He paused, thinking. "I don't know why he'd arrange for a sniper to take her out unless he needed more time and security to put his plans for Eve into place. Perhaps plans weren't going as smoothly as he'd hoped. Things sometimes go wrong . . ."

"Not for you."

"And I'd bet rarely for Doane. But he evidently had to rely on someone else to divert Jane MacGuire. That would be an unknown quantity with which he had to deal."

"Maybe he wanted Jane shot. It took Quinn out of the country and away from Eve."

"Maybe. Somehow, I don't think so. Judging by what I'm deducing about Doane, he's very proud of his planning ability. If he was part of his son's murky past, he'd have had it down to an art form to escape scrutiny."

"Bastard."

"You have to admire the process if not the result."

"I don't have to admire anything about him . . . or you."

"I'm getting very tired of your comparing me to Doane. I'm nothing like him. It's like comparing Satan to a minor demon." He was tired of talking to him. For some unknown reason, the news that Eve Duncan had been targeted had had an unusual effect on him. It wasn't that he hadn't expected it. The possibility had always been in the background. What he hadn't expected was that it would matter. "Someday, I may show you how different we are, Venable."

"A threat, Zander?"

"No, threats are without meaning. I never say anything without meaning. I gave that up a long time ago. Call me when you find out whether Eve Duncan is alive or dead." He hung up.

It was beginning. But now, at least, he knew how Doane was going to play his hand.

Perhaps.

He knew Doane was going to use Eve Duncan and not come straight at him. That didn't mean that Doane might not manipulate the situation to suit himself. He was a vengeful, angry man and skilled in the game they both knew so well.

It might prove interesting, and he hadn't been intrigued by a chase in a long time. That was probably why the news about Eve Duncan had aroused a response.

"I couldn't help but hear your conversation," Stang said quietly from his seat at the desk across the room. "I didn't have a chance to leave the study."

"I know." Zander smiled recklessly. "That's okay, I've decided to take you into my confidence."

Stang's eyes widened. "God, no."

"Come now. Step up to the plate. You might even find something that you can use as a weapon."

"I'm happy as I am. No one is more private than you. You'll change your mind, but it may be too late for me."

"There's always that possibility. Perhaps I'll limit your access. That way you might survive." He tilted his head. "Now what did you hear? Ah, Eve Duncan. She's the star of our little scenario. Unless she's dead. Even then, she'll have a leading part. You're not asking about her. Aren't you curious?"

"No."

"So wary . . ." He crossed to the desk and drew out his leather folio. He flipped it open. "Read all about them. That's Eve. The man is Joe Quinn, and the other woman is Jane MacGuire. The queen and her two knights. Only Doane has removed the knights, and she's alone now."

Stang was looking at the photos. "But you said she might be dead."

"Yes, it depends on what Doane wants. Shall I tell you about Doane?"

"No."

"Perhaps later. It's enough for you to know that he has the same ambition as you. He wants to kill me, and he thinks he has good reason to do it."

"I never said I wanted to kill you."

"No, you didn't say it, did you? Perhaps you haven't made up your mind yet." He shrugged. "I rather enjoy not knowing. It gives life a little zip. However, you notice I always keep you within viewing distance. Tell me, did you love your brother, Sean?"

"Yes, I loved him." He added, "I was surprised when you let me come to work for you after he died. You must have known it would be dangerous."

"You were willing to take the risk. How could I resist? Life is boring without the chance of its ending popping up now and then. And, until you decide it's time, you make me stacks of money and keep me organized." He smiled. "But now I've changed the rules, and I want to see you react. It will be amusing. Since I'm putting you at risk, you might as well know everything about Eve and the situation."

Stang was silent a moment, studying Zander's face. "You're not behaving normally."

"When have I ever been normal?"

"No, I mean you want to talk about this Eve Duncan. Something about the situation is bothering you."

Zander's brows rose. "How perceptive you are. But it doesn't take much insight to know that I wouldn't consider moving my entire operation if I weren't a little concerned."

"Consider? You told me to set about doing it."

"I've changed my mind." He hadn't realized that he was going to say those words until they came out. "Doane isn't worth my going on the run. I'll have to take him down sometime. It will be easier if I let him walk into a trap." He glanced at the mountains looming outside the window. "Such a beautiful trap. So now that's settled, there's nothing more to be worried about."

"I didn't say worried. I've never seen you worried. You're just . . . unsettled." He paused. "And I don't believe you'd risk having to dispose of me if you weren't—I don't think you're reacting as you usually do."

"Unsettled." He repeated the word. "Yes, you may be right. Though I'm not sure I like being referred to in that way. It sounds a bit weak."

Stang shook his head. "An earthquake is unsettled, so is a volcano."

Zander threw back his head and laughed. "Now I like that better. A force of nature is much better for my ego."

Stang looked back at the photo. "Is it because she might be dead?"

"No. Why should I care? I've never met her," Zander said. "I thought you didn't want to know about her."

"You want me to know. And at this point, it doesn't matter any longer. You've pulled me in too deep."

"You think I want to share?" He shook his head. "You're crazy, Stang."

"It was just a thought. So who is Eve Duncan?"

"It's all there in the dossier."

"No, who is she to you, Zander?"

Who was Eve Duncan to him? It was a question that he had been asking himself of late. He had tried to dismiss it from his consciousness, but it kept recurring like a persistent nightmare.

"Who is she to me?" Zander smiled faintly. "Why, Stang, I don't really know. Perhaps my nemesis."

"Dammit, they told me you were awake."

Jane opened her eyes to see Joe in the chair beside her bed. "Hi, Joe. I am awake. I was just dozing."

"Good. Then I'm not to blame for waking you. Though I would have done it anyway when I found out that you aren't on death's door. I have to know what's going on." He reached forward to give her a quick kiss on her forehead. "You scared us, baby. What the hell happened?"

"Didn't Devon and Margaret tell you?"

"Yes, what they could. Toby and poison and Caleb on the trail . . ." His lips tightened. "None of it adds up to a reason for shooting you."

"It's all we've got. Do you think I don't know it's crazy? That's what I told Eve when I talked to her. Okay, from the moment I found out Toby was sick, nothing was reasonable. It just kept rolling downhill, picking up speed like an avalanche." She shook her head. "And then I didn't like the way Eve sounded when I was talking to her, and I thought maybe—I don't know what I thought. Maybe that she was caught in the avalanche, too. That's why I was getting on that plane to leave the island and go to Eve." Her hand tightened on Joe's. "When will she be here?"

He didn't answer.

Her gaze narrowed on his face. "Joe?"

"I don't know, dammit. There's . . . a problem."

"With Eve? Don't tell me that." She could feel her heart pounding. "What's wrong? It's not like you to—"

"Quiet down. There may be nothing wrong. I just can't get in touch with her. She was supposed to take a flight out of Atlanta."

Her gaze was frantically raking his expression. "But you think something is wrong. I can see it." She was struggling to sit up. "So don't tell me to quiet down. I have to go and—"

"The hell you do." His hands were on her shoulders, pushing her back down. "You're wounded, dammit. Eve would kill both of us if I let you out of that bed." He frowned. "Look at you. You're pale as that sheet covering you, and we don't know what kind of internal damage that bullet might have done."

And she was weak as a kitten, Jane realized with frustration. Her head was swimming after that instant of rebellion.

Clear it. She had no option.

"Tell me about Eve," she said unsteadily.

"There's not much to tell. I just had a feeling

something was wrong before I left home to go to Miami. Nothing concrete."

"And Ben had a dream that brought him to Eve. Nothing concrete there either. What else?"

"Venable." He filled her in on his conversations with Venable. "He wouldn't admit to knowing anything about any threat to Eve . . . or you." His lips twisted. "Nothing substantial for me to grab and hold."

"Shall I tell you what's concrete?" Jane said. "Toby's being poisoned is concrete, my being shot is concrete. So everything that led up to it is concrete, too." She closed her eyes, and whispered, "And it's scaring me to death, Joe. What's happening?"

"I'll tell you what's happening. We're going to get you to that hospital in San Juan and have you examined and start having you treated. Then, if Eve hasn't shown up, and Venable hasn't got a clue, I'll leave you and go find her."

"Go now." Her eyes flew open. "I'll follow you as soon as I can. You know that's what we both want you to do. She's the only one who is important."

"Not quite." He held up his hand as she opened her lips to protest. "Though I may not show it all the time, you do have some importance to me."

"I know you love me." She added simply, "But I'm not Eve. It's not your fault that you have problems seeing anyone but her in the scheme of things. I feel the same way." She moistened her lips. "Look, I'll make a deal with you. I'll let you drop me off at that hospital in San Juan, but then you leave immediately, the minute they tell you that I'm not going to die or do anything else stupid."

He smiled faintly. "Dying isn't usually described as being stupid."

"I won't die." Her hand clenched on the sheet. "But they may not let me out of that hospital as quickly as I'd like. So you've got to go on and see what happened to Eve. Tell me you'll do it."

He was silent a moment before he shrugged. "You know I'll do it. No one can accuse me of not being callous and self-centered."

"You're not callous." She said quietly, "And if being self-centered means you're focused on Eve, then I wouldn't have you any other way. Now go away and see if you can find out anything about that air ambulance that's supposed to take me out of here. I hate lying in this bed."

"No, you want to jump up and run over all of us to get to Eve." He bent down and brushed his lips on her forehead. "I'll get you to San Juan as fast as I can. But I think after I check, I'll go after Caleb and see if he's found out anything."

"I expected that." She closed her eyes. "So much alike. You're both warriors . . ."

"We're nothing alike," he said as he headed for the door. "There's no one on earth like Seth Caleb. He's a throwback."

She couldn't deny that when she had often seen that streak of barbarism in Caleb. "He's also a hunter, and you wouldn't be a cop if that weren't in your makeup. And you're not that tame yourself, Joe."

He didn't answer, and she realized that he had left the room.

Keep calm. Relax. She was so damn weak. Emotional

and physical tension would make the healing process slower, and she must get well. She had to get to Eve.

Eve . . .

Dammit, the bastard had gotten away.

Caleb felt the anger tear through him as he looked out to sea. It was too late. He probably hadn't had a chance to get the son of a bitch. He'd made his choice to either go after the shooter or try to save Jane.

There hadn't really been a choice. He would not give up Jane.

But it didn't stop the rage. The blood was pounding through his body, and he could feel the throbbing of the vein in his temple.

Not good.

He had to regain control before he saw Jane again. She was wary of the savage thread that was an integral part of his character. Even if that savagery had been instigated by the attack on her.

Caleb lifted his head as he heard the sound of the plane coming in from the south.

The air ambulance, he thought as he whirled away from the small inlet. It was about time. It had been less than forty-five minutes since he'd left Jane, but it had seemed longer.

He started to run toward the airfield. No use going back to the animal hospital. He'd meet them at the airfield. Maybe by that time, he'd be under control.

Run.

Use every muscle, every breath.

Block out the bloodlust . . .

CHAPTER

6

The small air ambulance was taxiing toward the hangar when Caleb came over the hill.

No sign of a vehicle or van yet.

Good.

He was almost calm enough to act civilized. Just a little more time, and he would—

"Where have you been?"

Caleb stopped and slowly turned toward the man who had come out of the rain forest.

Quinn.

He stiffened and felt the familiar wariness sweep through him that any encounter with Joe Quinn ignited. Quinn was always a threat both because of his basic character and his position in Jane's life. He drew a deep breath. "I've been looking for the shooter. What do you think I've been doing?"

"There's never any way of knowing. And did you find him?"

"No." He started down the road toward the aircraft. "He had a speedboat drawn up onshore in an inlet a couple miles from the airfield. I saw where he pushed off. He didn't waste any time after he shot Jane."

"How did you know about the inlet?"

He shrugged. "I went to the hangar where he took his shot and started tracking him."

"On these hard dirt roads and the rain forest? Impressive."

"Not really. But I am good at it."

"I bet you are," Joe murmured.

"Yes, you can bet on it." He met Joe's eyes. "Just as I can bet that you chose to come here for the same reason I did. You needed a start, and you thought that the hangar would furnish you with something to go on."

"I was actually hoping to use your 'talent' to help me track him. I thought it would save time."

"Use me?"

"You don't like the word? Yes, I'll use you, Caleb. I don't like the idea of you with Jane. You're not only unstable, you're uncanny as hell. It's her choice, but I might as well get something out of this." He smiled without mirth. "Now, did you find anything at that inlet that I can use to get to the bottom of this?"

"No."

"Are you lying to me?"

He glanced back over his shoulder. "It's always a possibility, but as it happens I'm telling the truth." He suddenly smiled. "But you made the question too specific. It gave me an out."

"Specific."

"I didn't find anything at the inlet. But I found

something at the hangar. They have security cameras, Quinn."

"What?"

"I thought that would interest you." He pulled out a security video disk from his jacket pocket. "We just might get a break."

Joe took a step closer and held out his hand. "Give it to me."

Caleb stepped back. "I don't think so. You don't like to share."

"Give it to me, Caleb." Joe's voice was soft but laden with menace.

"Don't push me, Quinn." Caleb said. "You don't want to do that."

"The hell I don't. I'm mad and I'm scared and the two women I love may be targets of some creep who doesn't give a damn how wonderful they are. I'll push the world off its axis if I need to do it."

Caleb hadn't expected Quinn to admit to that vulnerability. The bastard was tough as nails. But maybe he should have expected it. Every man had a weakness, and Eve and Jane were clearly Quinn's. "I can see dire consequences if you interfere with gravity. Maybe we can work out a way to accommodate both of us."

"I don't want to accommodate you. You're interfering with a police investigation."

"That's true, but I'm sure you don't have jurisdiction down here." He added recklessly, "And I think you know I don't give a damn about your precious law if it gets in my way."

"Give me that security disk."

"I plan on doing that. You have the contacts to

identify anyone the security camera picked up. I could do it eventually, but it would take me more time."

Joe held out his hand again.

"No, a promise. You get in touch with me the minute you identify this bastard."

"You'd trust me?"

"If you gave your word. You're one of those rare individuals who actually value their word. Jane wouldn't feel as she does about you if you weren't straight." He gazed directly into Joe's eyes. "Promise me."

Joe hesitated, then shrugged. "I promise. If you don't try to kill him before I get to him."

"I never 'try' to kill anyone." He handed him the disk. "And I'm too irritated at what happened to Jane to not concentrate on finality. He shouldn't have made that clumsy attempt on someone who is mine."

"You arrogant son of a bitch. Jane doesn't belong to anyone but herself."

"Doesn't she?" He pretended to think about it. "You might be right, but then you might not. You don't really know, do you? Possession is so complicated. The nuances are—" He broke off as he saw the veterinary van come around the bend in the road. "At any rate, I won't do any permanent damage to him until I find out all the answers. Is that good enough for you?" He didn't wait for an answer as his pace increased as he walked toward the van. "But I warn you, I'm not going to wait around for you to make your move."

He heard a muttered curse from behind him, but his attention was now focused on the van that had pulled up before the air ambulance.

He started running again as the van's doors opened.

Devon jumped down and headed for the plane. A moment later, the stretcher bearing Jane was being lifted from the vehicle.

He felt the rage that he'd managed to control once more stinging him as he was again reminded of her helplessness. That sniper might not have taken her life, but he had temporarily taken her strength. From the moment he had met Jane, he had been aware of her endurance and strength, and it had struck a chord in him that was almost as powerful as the basic sexual attraction that had drawn him. He had known she could fight him in any arena, and it had excited him. He had tried to keep himself from looking beyond that excitement and that strange sense of possession that it brought with it.

Or wondering if there was anything beyond it at all. He'd had many women, and none of them had stirred him the way Jane did. He had not been able either to walk away or let her go. What he was feeling now was confusing, and he had felt not only anger but something deeper, stranger, when he had thought she might be dying. He refused to examine that emotion more closely. It was foreign and far too dangerous.

Better to embrace the rage and the possessiveness.

Yes, he could deal with those emotions. Protectiveness was a natural result of thinking of Jane as belonging to him. And rage? Rage was his brother, the impetus that had driven him, saved him, defined him.

And might someday destroy him.

But not now. He could use it and let it use him to find the enemy.

Jane's enemy. Caleb's enemy. They had become one

in his mind, as Jane was becoming inexorably interwoven with him in his thoughts.

He rejected the idea as soon as he recognized it. Too close. Veer away. Obey the boundaries.

"Jane."

She opened her eyes to see Seth Caleb bending over the stretcher. "Hi," she said drowsily. "I was wondering if you'd . . . get here."

"You shouldn't have wondered." He was smiling. "Expect it."

"Not . . . true. I can't expect . . . anything of . . . you." She tried to pull her thoughts together. "I'm blurry. Devon insisted on giving me another sedative to get me through the trip. Why weren't—that's right, you went after that sniper. Did you get him?"

"No, he had a boat hidden at an inlet near here." He took her hand. "But don't worry, I'll find him."

"I'm not worried. I think this drug is a mood elev . . . a happy pill. Even you're looking completely unthreatening."

"I'm not a threat to you."

"Yes, you are." Even now, through the warm haze, she could feel the swirling danger that was Seth Caleb. His hand holding her own was strong and could have been comforting, but it was not. She could feel the power and the magnetism drawing her, absorbing her. Ordinarily, she would have backed away or ignored it, but at this moment she was open, accepting . . . welcoming the invasion. "But that's okay. It doesn't matter."

"How complacent. You must really be out of it." His thumb was moving back and forth on her inner wrist. "I don't know if I like not mattering."

"Too bad." She had a sudden thought. "Where's Joe? He was going to find you."

"He's right behind me. I imagine he's going with you on the air ambulance."

"You're not going?"

"I'm flying my own plane. You can't get rid of me, Jane."

"I don't want to get rid of you. Or maybe I do. I'm confused right now." She was staring dreamily at him. "You're a truly beautiful man, Caleb. Do you know that? I'd like to paint you."

"It can be arranged. But I'm not cheap."

"You're joking? I'm having trouble telling . . . It probably wouldn't be a good idea anyway. I don't know if anyone could manage to do . . . the fire."

"What fire?"

"All around you . . . Flame and darkness. Mostly . . . flame." She wanted to reach out and touch those flames, the urge was almost irresistible. How would it feel? How would *he* feel?

"I see."

"But it doesn't interfere with how beautiful . . ." She couldn't keep her eyes open any longer. "Maybe I can . . . paint you . . ."

"If I don't burn you."

"Yes, but I don't think you . . ."

She was asleep.

* * *

Caleb watched the air ambulance take off before he turned and headed toward the Gulfstream parked across the tarmac.

"Wait for me."

He turned to see Margaret running toward him, her ponytail flying, her cheeks flushed, a knapsack on her back. She looked like a young girl running away from home, he thought.

His brows lifted in surprise. "I thought you were going with Jane on the air ambulance."

"I opted out at the last minute before they took off."

"Why?"

She fell into step with him. "I decided to go with you."

"And may I ask why I'm so honored?"

"It will cause me less trouble." She grinned. "And Devon less headaches. Puerto Rico has fairly strict immigration laws."

"And?"

"I have no papers." She corrected, "Well, that's not true. I have papers, but they're forged and won't bear close scrutiny. Devon wasn't about to look too closely, but I can't count on anyone in a bureaucracy being as lenient. They'd probably turn me over to Homeland Security."

"Why don't you have papers?"

She shrugged. "I just don't. You don't really care, do you?"

"I'm curious."

She just looked at him.

"And what makes you think I won't turn you over to Homeland Security?"

She met his gaze. "You don't like bureaucracies. You don't like rules. You don't like laws. You do as you like."

"But not necessarily as you like."

"That's true. But I want to help Jane, and that might sway you. You're stalking Jane, and you can never tell when you might need a diversion to—"

"Stalking?" He smiled faintly. "That's a strange phrase. It makes me sound like either a creep or an animal. Which one, Margaret?"

"You're not a creep."

His smile deepened. "Then what animal, Margaret?"

"I'm not sure. You're just not . . . the same as other people." She shrugged. "Not that it bothers me. Neither am I. We're all animals, aren't we? We've just evolved to being more civilized. Some of us are just closer to being what we were than others. I could tell you were very close when I first saw you."

"Interesting. Does that mean I whisper to you like some of your four-footed friends?"

"I don't know. If you did, I don't know if I'd want to listen. Sometimes I don't." She started to climb the stairs of the plane. "But I wouldn't be afraid like Jane."

He stiffened. "She's not afraid of me, Margaret."

"She's afraid of something when she's with you." She turned at the top of the steps to look down at him. "Maybe it's part of the mating ritual. What do you think?"

He stared at her coldly, then suddenly smiled. "I think you're bold as brass, and I'm beginning to like you. That could be very dangerous for one of us."

"I just tell the truth." She straightened. "And here's another truth. I owe Jane a debt, and I'll pay it. I won't let what you're planning on doing with her get in the way."

"And you still expect me to take you to San Juan?"

"Why not? You don't like anything easy. The hunt would be boring."

"What would you do if I told you to get off my plane?"

"Find another way to San Juan." She tilted her head. "Oh, and I might have to go to . . . where is it? Georgia later. Can you get me better documents than I have right now?"

"Why should I?"

"Because I can help find Eve Duncan, and that would make Jane happy. Happy with me, happy with you for putting me into a position to help her find Eve."

"So I'm to break the law because you think I might find you valuable later?"

"Wouldn't it be a good enough reason for you?" She was studying him, her gaze narrowed. "And you'd enjoy it. You like taking chances."

Her eyes were fixed on his face, and he found himself caught and held.

Clear eyes. Shrewd eyes. Wise eyes.

What the hell? he thought recklessly.

"You're damn right I'd enjoy it." He took the steps two at a time. "But if I'm taking the risk, I'm running the show. You do what I tell you once we land in San Juan. Deal?"

"Of course." Her cheerful smile lit her face. "I would never argue with an expert, Caleb."

"How do you know I am?"

"Stalking," she murmured. "Dodging and hiding are all a part of going after prey. You'd have to be good at it." She was heading for the cockpit. "This is exciting. I'm a pretty good sailor, but I've never had a chance to learn anything about flying. Will you teach me how to take off?"

"No. You'd probably try to steal the plane."

"I don't steal. Sometimes I borrow. That's all right. I'll watch and try to learn on my own."

When Jane woke again, she was being wheeled down a white-tiled corridor.

"It's okay, Jane." Joe was beside her. "We're getting you into the ER."

No darkness, no flames. Not that fascinating face that held and touched and drew her, she realized with relief that held an element of regret.

Just Joe. Safety. Strength. Comrade.

Green walls. White coats, teal coats. It had to be the hospital in San Juan. Her head was clearing, thank heavens. "We made a deal. You've delivered me, now get the hell out of here. Go to Eve."

"Shut up, brat." His smile belied the roughness of the words. "I'm working on it. I tried to reach Venable on the ambulance plane but couldn't get through. I'll call again while they're working on you in there. I've arranged to have a plane waiting, and I'll leave right after they give me a report. Okay?"

"I guess so." She reached out and grabbed his hand. "It's going to be all right, Joe." She tried to keep the desperation from her voice. "She's got to be okay. She's so good, Joe. Why would anyone want to hurt her?"

"Why would anyone want to hurt you?" His eyes were glittering. "It can be a nasty world. We both know that, Jane. We just have to make sure that dirt doesn't touch her." He released her hand as the nurse bustled toward her. "And you have to get well before you can help me do that. Do what they tell you, Jane."

"I will. You know I will." She called as the ER doors swung shut behind her, "Call Venable now, Joe . . . Let me know what he says."

"I'm at the lake cottage, Quinn," Venable said flatly as soon as he picked up the call. "She's not here." He paused. "There's one vehicle in the driveway. There's mud on the tires as if it had been driven. How many should be here?"

"Only one. I left the jeep at the airport."

"So she had to have had a ride if she went to the airport as she planned."

"She was planning on driving herself." He added, "I contacted the policeman I had watching the place. He took a look around the lake and went inside the house. He said that she was nowhere in the vicinity."

Venable was silent. "I sent an agent out here last night, too. I had Tad Dukes looking around the grounds. I can't get in contact with him."

Joe cursed low and vehemently. "And why did you have a man out there if, according to you, nothing was supposed to be wrong?"

"You were concerned when you called and left a

message. It seemed like a good idea." He continued quickly, "And I sent Agent Pastori out today and he said there was a FedEx notice on the front door that stated that the driver had been there and was unable to make the pickup."

"The reconstruction. Eve wouldn't have left without making arrangements for it to be sent out."

"Even if she was frantic about Jane?"

"She would have made arrangements. She's a professional. What else did your agent find? What about Ben? He was supposed to be there."

"No sign of him."

There was something in his tone that caused Joe to tense. "Are you lying to me, Venable?"

"Why would I do—Okay, I'm not lying. I'm just omitting."

"Omitting what?"

"We found traces of blood on the grass on the side of the road about a mile from the cottage."

He felt sick. "Eve?"

"No, I knew that would be your first question, and I had Pastori run a blood test before the police forensic team got there. B-negative. Eve is A-positive, right?"

"Yes. I don't know what Ben's blood type is."

"We're checking on it."

"Damn you. You weren't going to tell me."

"I'd have told you. Just a delay until you got here. I thought I'd know more by then." He added testily, "And there wasn't much use your making wild guesses and my life miserable."

"What else is there that you didn't tell me?"

"Fresh tire tracks in the mud. Truck. We're trying to

identify what kind of truck would use them. Traces of fertilizer and hay embedded in the cavities. Any farmers near you?"

"Several. I don't know any of them personally. Get on it."

"We already are. Right now, we're trying to contact Dukes. I don't like it. There's no reason why I shouldn't be able to reach him." He paused. "How is Jane?"

"Surviving. She could be worse. I'm in San Juan. She's in the ER right now." He said. "That's all? No Eve. No Ben? Just a few drops of blood?"

"That's all right now. I'll try to have something more for you by the time you get here. When will that be?"

"A few hours. Jane made me promise that I'd get out of here soon."

"That doesn't surprise me."

"And I may have a photo of her shooter. The hangars had video cameras. I need you to process and identify."

"Of course."

"And I don't want any stalling," Joe said grimly. "I want to know accurately and fast. No hesitation, no sleight of hand. If I think that you're keeping anything from me, it's not going to be pretty, Venable." He paused. "And when I see you at the cottage, you're going to tell me what's going on and what game you've been playing with us."

"No game. I'm not always the bad guy. Did it occur to you that I might only be trying to keep you all alive?"

"It occurred to me. It also occurred to me that you

could be manipulating us as you've done before. It could go either way."

"But you're willing to trust me enough to ask me to help you."

"I'm not asking, I'm telling you. I'd use the devil himself if I thought I could control him. I can control you, Venable. Whatever the nasty business you're dealing with, you like Eve, and you wouldn't hurt her if you didn't have to do it. I'll be there to make sure that doesn't become an option."

"I do like her, Quinn," he said quietly. "And I'll do everything I can to help you get her back. I'm happy as hell you managed to snag that video photo."

"I didn't snag it. Seth Caleb took it from the camera, and I took it from him."

"Caleb." Venable's tone was thoughtful. "An interesting man. I remember that he always seemed to be showing up when you least expected him."

"He hasn't changed."

"But this time he's been helpful?"

"Helpful? No, not intentionally. This time he thinks that he can use me." He added dryly, "As I'm using you. No one is exempt. I'll see you at the cottage, Venable." He hung up.

Blood on the grass.

Not Eve's blood. He had to take comfort in that fact. It might not even be Ben's blood.

There was no comfort in that stark scenario Venable had painted.

No Eve. No Ben.

Blood.

His palms were suddenly cold with sweat.

Stop thinking about it. Within a few hours, he'd be at the cottage and making his own assessment. Just sit here until Jane got out of ER, then he could start moving.

Blood on the grass.

Forty-five minutes later, they wheeled Jane out of the ER and down the corridor.

Her gaze was searching desperately until it fell on Joe standing against the wall. "Venable?" she whispered. "Eve?"

He shook his head. "She wasn't at the cottage. Neither was Ben." Don't tell her about the blood yet. "Venable and his agent are there." He looked at the dark-skinned intern with S. PEREZ on his name tag who was walking beside the gurney. "Is she okay?"

"No, but she will be." His white smile flashed. "A few stitches and another pint of blood, and she's responding beautifully. Give her a few days or so, and she'll be released."

"No way," Jane said flatly. "As soon as I can stand without falling, I'm out of here."

"Right." Dr. Perez continued, "As I said, a few days or so." He turned to Joe. "Now if you'll leave her for fifteen minutes, we'll get her settled in her room. You can visit her there."

"No, he can't," she said. "You heard him, I'm on the mend. Now get out of here, Joe."

"I'm going." He gave her a quick kiss on the cheek. "Do what they tell you."

"Go to hell. You wouldn't." She grabbed his arm and held him tight for an instant. "Take care of yourself. Take care of her."

"I will. I'll call you and let you know what's happening."

"You'd better." She let him go. "Because you're not telling me everything now. I can *feel* it."

"I don't know everything, Jane."

Her eyes closed. "Call me."

He watched them wheel her into a room at the end of the hall before he turned on his heel and headed for the front entrance.

"How is she?" Caleb entered through the glass doors before Joe reached them. "Pretty well, I take it. Or you wouldn't be leaving her."

"Another pint of blood. A few stitches. Okay in a few days," Joe said briefly. "I thought you'd be here sooner."

"I had a problem to take care of after I landed at the airport. Where's Jane now?"

"She's in the room at the end of the corridor."

Caleb nodded. "I'll let her rest a few minutes before I go in to see her. I have a habit of overstimulating her."

"Is that what you call it?"

He smiled. "Stimulation isn't bad. It makes you know you're alive."

"Or gives you a heart attack."

"You keep remembering what I did to that murderer that first time I met you and Eve." He smiled. "I just pumped a little extra blood into his heart. He did deserve it, you know."

"I know. But I dislike the idea of your being able to

do that and no one's being able to prove that it was cold-blooded murder."

"Never cold-blooded, Quinn." He opened the glass door and held it open for Joe. "I don't know the meaning of the term. It wouldn't work for me. Be sure to let me know as soon as you can about that photo. You've contacted Venable about it?"

"Yes." He went past Caleb. "We had a comprehensive discussion about using people."

"It's a common practice, isn't it? Even Jane isn't above doing it for the people or animal she loves. Any news about Eve?"

He shook his head. "And it's going to be hard to stop Jane from following me." His lips twisted. "You might try your hand at discouraging her if you want to keep her safe."

"I'm not sure I do. It might be to my advantage to let her put herself in jeopardy. Danger can be a strong bond."

"Bastard."

"I didn't say I'd let her harm herself. That would be stupid. Good-bye, Quinn. I truly hope you find Eve." His tone was sincere. "Which makes me very torn about my feelings about how the rest of this is going to play out." He shrugged. "As you know, I'm not very stable. We'll have to see which way I jump."

"And if it's the wrong way, Jane will trip you and barbecue you over hot coals." Joe's tone was grim.

Caleb threw back his head and laughed. "And that would be very stimulating, too. I'm sure you'll attend the festivities."

"I'm sure I will, too." He walked toward the street, not looking back at Caleb, his gaze searching for a taxi.

Dammit, he didn't like the idea of not leaving Jane in safe hands. Caleb had always been an unknown quantity, and what they did know was vaguely terrifying. But Jane had never been afraid of Caleb, and she was the one who had brought him back into their lives. She was going to have to take care of herself until he found out what had happened to Eve.

After that, he could concentrate on monitoring the actions of Seth Caleb and trying to keep him from harming Jane either physically or emotionally.

Blood on the grass.

He hailed a cab and jumped into the backseat. "Airport."

Caleb . . .

Jane's eyes focused on him sitting in a chair across the hospital room. It was dim in the room, and he was more shadow than substance. It didn't matter. She could never mistake Caleb for anyone else. The grace, the leanness, the explosive vitality that was present even when held in leash.

"What . . . are you doing here?" she asked drowsily.

"Being bored. You're not being very entertaining." He got to his feet and strolled across the room. "I told Quinn that I didn't want to unduly stimulate you, but I thought you'd at least be awake part of the time. You've been asleep for hours. How do you feel?"

"Like hell." There was a sharp, nagging pain in her

shoulder. But she didn't feel drugged as she had before. She'd take the pain over that fuzziness anytime. Her senses were sharp and alive. "You don't have to be here. Go . . . away."

"In a few more hours. I'm guarding you. Can't you tell?"

"No."

"I arranged for a local security company to send a couple men to watch your room, but until then, you've got me." He was close enough now for her to see his smile. "Aren't you lucky?"

"Don't need you."

"I don't think that you need watching either. If that sniper really wanted you dead, he'd have tried to do it before you started to leave the island." He reached out, and his forefinger touched her cheek. "But I can't be sure, and I'm not going to give you up because of a mistake in judgment."

"Then be quiet and let me go to sleep." There was heat beneath that finger on her flesh and she couldn't decide if that heat was pleasant or hurtful. Perhaps it was both.

But she didn't want him to take his hand away, she realized.

"You're hurting." He rubbed his finger gently over the curve of her cheekbone. "Why don't you relax, and I'll make it go away? I can do it, you know."

She didn't doubt that he could. She had experienced a little of that weird talent that Caleb seemed to possess. It was all connected with the pulsation of the blood, but that pulsation appeared to control everything from thought processes to sexual responses. "It's not necessary. If I want to get something for the pain, I'll call the nurse."

"But you won't do that. You're too spartan." His thumb touched the corner of her lips. "When I donated blood for you, I was too tense to think about it at the time, but now I'm beginning to appreciate the nuances. I believe I like the idea of having my blood running through your veins. It's rather provocative. As you know, there are all kinds of weird stories in my family about the power of our blood. It's interesting that we'll have a chance to test their truth."

And Jane was sure that she didn't like the idea at all of having Caleb's blood. Those stories were no doubt nonsense, but he could use them to make her feel uneasy. "I don't need you," she repeated.

"And you don't trust me. Not me, not Mark Trevor. No one but Joe Quinn. Actually, it makes me feel better that you didn't trust Trevor, either. It kind of puts us on an even keel. I'm usually working at a disadvantage on that score."

"Of course I don't trust you. I don't think you want me to trust you. It would shackle you."

"Wise Jane. You may be right." He chuckled. "Having you need me would be much more entertaining." He asked softly, "Shall I make you need me? I can do it, Jane." He bent forward and his lips touched her own. "Oh, how I'm tempted. But you're wounded, and you'd hold it against me."

"You bet I would."

"First, I'd take away the pain, then I'd make you feel . . . exceptional. I wouldn't even touch you, but you'd have a truly incredible experience . . . and so would I."

She could feel the curve of the smile on his lips as he brushed them back and forth on her own. "Quinn would try to kill me for doing this. Everyone would say what a complete bastard I am to even contemplate victimizing poor Jane. But then we both know that I don't have the same moral standards as other people." His tongue outlined her upper lip. "You're wary of that little talent of mine, but controlling the flow of blood can be fantastically erotic. This doesn't hurt, does it? You'd push me away if you didn't like it."

Why wasn't she pushing him away?

Because all pain was gone.

Because every gentle, light touch was hypnotically pleasurable.

Because she felt as languid and sexual as an animal in heat.

"Get away from me, Caleb."

"I don't think you mean that." He lifted his head and sighed. "But you might convince yourself you did later." He straightened. "So I'll bow to conventional morality and my own belief that it will probably be better if I wait." He went back to his chair across the room. "It was good touching you at least. I think about it all the time, you know."

"No, I didn't know."

"I believe you did. You choose to ignore it. I don't mind." He dropped down in the chair. "Go to sleep. I'll be here to make sure the pain doesn't come back."

She watched him settle in the chair, and he was once more blending into a barely defined outline in the half darkness.

A shadow figure.

She was feeling no pain at all.

But her lips were burning, tingling.

Her breath was short, her pulse rapid.

Heat was pounding through her body.

Her breasts were taut and ready.

He was no shadow.

CHAPTER

7

Bumping.
    Thunder.

The sound of the rain on the metal roof.

Eve sluggishly opened her lids. Heavy. So heavy.

Her entire body felt terribly heavy beneath the coarse red blanket.

She tried to push the blanket aside.

She couldn't move, she realized with panic.

She tried again, but her body wouldn't obey the command.

Bumping again . . .

Why?

Truck. She was on the floor of a truck, wedged between the backseat and the front.

And there was someone in an orange cap and camouflage rain gear driving the truck.

Familiar . . .

She should remember who he was, but she couldn't make any connection with her memory any more than she could with her reflexes.

He was speaking, she realized vaguely. But not to her; she could see the gleam of a computer screen through the space between the front seats. The driver was talking to a freckled, red-haired man who was staring defiantly out of that screen.

Skype? She used it sometimes when Joe was out of town. What did it matter what computer program . . .

Tense—the red-haired man staring out of the screen was tense, maybe even afraid. It was obvious in every line of his expression.

"You've failed me, Blick," the man driving the truck said regretfully. "You've failed both of us. You said that I could trust you, that you'd do what I told you. Kevin would be so disappointed in you."

"No, he wouldn't, he'd understand." Blick moistened his lips. "I had to do it. You told me I had to keep her on the island. You said it was important that she didn't get in your way."

"I didn't tell you to shoot her."

"She was going to leave the island. She was almost at the plane. I didn't know what else to do, Doane."

"So you decided to kill her. Stupid, Blick."

"She's still on the island, isn't she? You've got your delay. I bought you time, and you're yelling at me. Kevin would never do that."

"But how much time and at what price?"

"She's not dead yet. I didn't have a clear shot. She may not die. It's up to you from now on."

"It's always been up to me," Doane said wearily. "And I'll handle it. But I may still need your help. Are you still on Summer Island?"

"No, I used my speedboat to meet with a fisherman from Grand Cayman who I paid to take me somewhere I can get a plane to Miami." He paused. "I thought I'd go into hiding for a while. Joe Quinn is a detective, and he's going to be mad as hell at me for shooting his daughter."

"No, I need you. Did you ever know Kevin to hide when the heat was on? We've got to be as brave as he would be, Blick. I want you to go to that lake cottage in Atlanta and keep an eye on Duncan's family. I'll expect you to be there within a day."

"I'll try to be there by that time."

"Don't try, you've done very well except for this error. Do it."

Silence. "Do you have Eve Duncan?"

"Of course. She's with me now."

"And you wouldn't have her except for me." His tone was once again defiant. "I did what Kevin would have wanted me to do. He always said that you had to adjust actions to changing circumstances. That's what I did."

"Kevin was Kevin. You are you. You should have done what I told you. It wasn't necessary to shoot her." He broke the connection.

Summer Island. They had been talking about Jane, Eve thought hazily. Shooting. Danger. Death. Blick had said that Jane was still alive. She had to know if—

She opened her lips and tried again to talk.

Nothing.

Or maybe not.

She must have made a sound of some sort because Doane was looking back at her.

"Good afternoon, Eve." He smiled, and she remembered that she'd thought he had the kindest expression she had ever seen. That kindness was still there, but she mustn't trust it. Jane. He had been talking to someone who had deliberately hurt Jane. Evil.

"I'm sorry, you're trying to speak, but the drug I gave you is very potent. It takes quite a while to wear off. I chose it because it has very few lingering effects, and I didn't want you to be uncomfortable. You really shouldn't have stirred until I had you safe, but you clearly have a very strong will. But you'll go back to sleep soon."

No, she could feel the drowsiness closing in on her, but she had to fight it. Jane.

"You're looking at me as if you hate me," he said gently. "How much did you hear? Now what did we say . . ."

Jane. Jane. Jane.

"Your adopted daughter. Of course, you're angry and concerned. I didn't want your Jane to be hurt. You must have heard me tell Blick that he shouldn't have done it. I'm very angry with him." He reached down to touch her hair. "I don't want anyone hurt. You have to believe me, Eve." He frowned. "Now how else can I put your mind at rest and reassure you of my good intentions? Oh, the young man in the woods. Ben Hudson."

Ben, lying on the grass with the bloody gash in his forehead.

"He caught me by surprise, and I had to fight him to

protect myself. I would never have purposely hurt him. But I have to have your help, Eve. That's what this is all about."

She couldn't speak, but she closed her eyes in silent rejection.

"I know it looks bad for me, but you're a kind woman. You'll understand once I explain it to you." She could feel his hand gently stroke her hair. "I bundled that boy, Ben, up in the truck and dropped him off in the parking lot of an urgent-care facility outside Atlanta. I'm sure that he'll be fine."

Eve wasn't sure of anything. She could only pray that he was telling the truth about Ben and that the boy wasn't too badly hurt.

And Jane. She still didn't know how badly Jane was hurt. Was Joe with her by now? How much time had passed since she had run down that muddy road this morning? She opened her eyes to see if she could tell by the daylight streaming into the truck.

Cloudy. Still storming. No way to tell if it was still morning or afternoon. Everything was dimness and confusion.

She could see Doane's face above her, smiling almost tenderly, and that was the most bewildering of all.

"It will be fine," he said softly. "Go back to sleep. I'll take care of you. That's why I'm here. So that we can take care of each other."

She couldn't do what he said. None of this was right. It didn't matter that she wanted to trust him, that he seemed to have all the loving kindness of a brother or father she'd never had.

Stay awake. Concentrate. Think about Jane. Think about Ben.

But everything was blurring, and she couldn't think.

Thunder.

Rain on the metal roof.

Rhythmic. Soothing.

"That's right. Let go," Doane said. "We'll get it all straight when you wake up . . ."

"Hi." Margaret swept into the hospital room and plopped down on the chair by Jane's bed. "How do you feel?" Her eyes narrowed on Jane's face. "You look much better than you did when you left the island yesterday. You have some color in your cheeks."

"What are you doing here? I thought you were staying on the island to take care of Toby. Devon said that was probably why you jumped out of the plane at the last minute yesterday."

Margaret shook her head. "It wasn't necessary. I knew Devon was going to turn around and go right back to the island after she delivered you to San Juan. Toby was out of danger, and Devon would be there in case of an emergency. I just decided to hop a ride with Caleb." She reached out for the glass of water on the bedside table and held the straw for Jane. "It was more convenient for me."

"Caleb is never just a convenience," Jane said flatly after she took a sip. "And he didn't mention that he'd brought you when he visited me last night."

"He said that he'd let me tell you." She suddenly

chuckled. "I don't think he wanted to share the spot-light. Caleb likes to have your full attention when he's with you. It has something to do with the stalking."

"What?"

"Never mind. It's not important anyway. Caleb and I understand each other."

"Then that's something I've never been able to say about Caleb," Jane said dryly. She certainly hadn't understood what he'd done . . . and hadn't done to her in that moment of weakness. She hadn't understood what she felt either. Gratitude for giving her a pain-free night? Or resentment that he'd disturbed and made her so aware of both his power and presence? "And why was it more convenient for you to come with him?"

She shrugged. "No papers. I knew he wouldn't care."

"Why don't you have papers?"

She grinned. "See, that illustrates my point. Caleb never asked that question."

"Well, I'm asking. Are you some kind of criminal?"

"It depends on who you ask." She tilted her head consideringly. "But my opinion is the only one that matters, so no, I'm not a criminal."

"Margaret, you're dodging."

She beamed. "You noticed. I do it well, don't I?"

"No, you're lousy at it."

"Not true. I wouldn't have been able to persuade Caleb into bringing me to you if I wasn't good." Her smile faded. "I'm not going to tell you why I have no papers, Jane. It's . . . complicated and kind of a mess. I won't involve anyone else in it. Maybe someday."

"For heaven's sake, you're only a kid. It can't be too much of a mess."

"No?" A shadow flitted across her face, but it vanished in an instant. "Don't be too sure. I'm talented beyond my years." She shook her head, and said gently, "Drop it, Jane. I get along fine without stamps and visas."

"Until someone throws you into jail."

"That only happened once, and I managed to get out after a week." She changed the subject. "I called Devon this morning and checked on Toby. He was well enough to put with the other dogs, and Monty won't leave him. He's doing fine. I knew he would." She leaned back in the chair. "Has Joe Quinn called you with any more information about Eve Duncan?"

"Only that he and Venable were going to spend the night searching the woods near the lake, then visit the farms in the area and ask questions." She leaned back against the pillows. Why couldn't she get over this damnable weakness? She'd thought she'd be much stronger after a night's rest. "Still no word on Ben Hudson."

"But the search is centering on the lake cottage." Margaret's tone was thoughtful. "That's where we should start."

"We?" Jane shook her head. "I told you that you don't owe me anything. You're out of this, Margaret."

"I don't intend to intrude. I'll just sort of . . . help a little." She got to her feet. "And I can tell that it's better if I leave you right now. We're going to argue, and you'll get upset. I'll get back to you as soon as I have something to tell you." She squeezed Jane's hand and smiled. "Stop worrying. It's going to be okay. I know that you're going to go to your Joe as soon as you can bust out of here. I'm just going ahead to prepare the way for you."

"You're going to Atlanta? No, Margaret, I'm not taking you away from your work and Summer Island to do anything that—"

"Shh." Margaret was heading for the door. "It's not only for you. I'm very angry at that bastard who poisoned Toby. I'm betting it's the same person who shot you. It would make sense. I hate people who victimize the helpless."

"I'm *not* helpless."

"No you're not, but Toby was. For all I know, your Eve is helpless, too."

Jane shook her head.

"Good, then when we find her, she'll be able to help."

Margaret was so positive and upbeat that Jane felt an upsurge of hope. She hadn't realized until this moment how much she needed that hope. "Eve would not only help, she'd take over." Then she got back to the subject. "But that doesn't mean that I'm turning this over to—"

"Just going to prepare the way," Margaret repeated as she paused at the door. "I'll be in touch, Jane. You work on getting well."

Before Jane could speak, Margaret had glided out of the room. She gazed after her in helpless frustration. Yes, "helpless" was the word. She wanted to jump out of bed and go after her. It wasn't enough that Margaret was going to put herself in danger out of some mistaken sense of obligation to Jane. The girl obviously had baggage that could toss her into a volcano of trouble even if Eve's situation hadn't been front and center.

"You're frowning." Caleb was standing in the doorway. "Don't tell me. Margaret?"

"That was an easy enough guess. You must have seen her in the hall."

He nodded. "And she looked a lot happier than you do. But then, not much seems to bother her."

She had a sudden memory of that brief, shadowed expression. "I'm not so sure. Why didn't you tell me you'd brought her from the island?"

"I wasn't certain that you'd approve."

She raised her brows.

"Okay, I had to do a little juggling and hunting for her. She needed better credentials. I didn't want to make you an accessory."

"But you didn't mind doing it yourself."

"She made me an offer I couldn't refuse."

"I see."

He smiled. "No, you don't. She's not my type. Much too sunny. She offered to make herself useful to me."

"Stalking."

"What?"

"Just something that Margaret said about you."

"I can imagine."

"She also said that you didn't tell me she was here because you wanted to be the center of attention."

"Possibly."

His hand on her cheek. His tongue outlining her lip.

He was smiling, but she was relieved that he was obviously not going to pursue the details of that nocturnal visit. She moistened her lips. "She's talking about going to the lake cottage. I think she's going to ask you to take her."

"Do you want me to do it?"

"No, I want her to go back to the island."

"She won't do it. She's on a mission. But I can delay her if I refuse to take her."

"Then do it. Maybe I'll be out of here by that time."

"Of course I did manage to get her a very authentic-looking passport and driver's license last night after I arrived here."

"Why?"

"She wanted it, and it seemed a good idea at the time. She might not need me. She might decide to hitch a ride on a cruise ship to Miami. There's always that possibility. Then you'd lose track of her and what she's doing. Do you really want that?"

"No, I just want to find Eve without having to worry about anyone else," she said wearily.

"Then I'll see what I can do about stalling her." He smiled. "Now rest. I talked to Dr. Perez and he said you're doing well and he thinks that he can release you day after tomorrow."

She shook her head. "He can release me when I can get out of this bed and get dressed."

"Whatever." He tucked the sheet around her. "Whenever you call me, I'm at your disposal. Any news from Quinn today?"

"No, I'm going to call him by noon if he doesn't call me." She shivered. "They were searching the woods. I suppose it's good news he hasn't called me."

"But you don't feel as if it's good news. You feel as if you're treading water. I can—" His cell phone rang, and he glanced at the screen. His brows rose in surprise. "Your Joe Quinn."

Jane tensed. "Why would he call you?"

"You're thinking bad thoughts," Caleb said. "Relax. I assure you that he wouldn't call me to cushion bad news for you. He wouldn't trust my sensitivity." He turned up the volume before he answered the call. "Caleb."

"I'm sending you a file," Joe said briefly. "I gave Venable the disk when I got in yesterday, and he had it processed within a few hours, then checked the data banks. The shooter's name is Terence Blick, but he doesn't appear to have much of a record."

"What's his connection to Jane or Eve?"

"Not a damn thing that I can see. At least not in the file that Venable gave me."

"You think there are omissions?"

"I don't know what I think. It's possible. Venable is being entirely too enigmatic. I'm going to check some of my own sources and see if I can find out anything else. How is Jane?"

"Better. She's right here. Do you want to talk to her?"

"No, just show her the file. That's all I know right now. I'll call her later. I kept my word, Caleb. Now we're quits." He hung up.

"He sounds tired. He didn't have the strength to insult or abuse me." Caleb pressed the disconnect and brought up the file. "I'm sending the file to your phone for you to study." He dropped down in the chair beside her bed. "It will give you something to occupy you while you're stuck here."

He began to read the file.

She immediately grabbed her iPhone on the bedside table and pulled up the file.

Photo, first.

She didn't even know what the man who had shot her looked like.

Thirties, curly red hair, freckles, large nose, and blue eyes. She had never seen him before. No, that wasn't right. His curly hair and thick neck bore a resemblance to the photo of the man who had been at the dog day-care center, the man who had poisoned Toby. A slender, fragile connection that was totally baffling.

She began to quickly scan the file.

Terence Blick. Age thirty-four. Born in Chicago, lived for his first fourteen years in a suburb on the north side. Father, a bus driver, mother a waitress. Several charges of petty theft and shoplifting during that period, but he was never convicted. He had dropped out of high school and left town right after his fourteenth birthday. A few years later he had joined the Army and was sent overseas. He was honorably discharged eight years later and returned to Chicago. His mother and father died in an automobile accident shortly after he returned home. He sold the home that he'd inherited from them and began drifting around the country, taking minimum-wage jobs whenever he got low on funds.

Caleb was sitting waiting for her to finish when she looked up a few minutes later. "There's not much here." She frowned. "Nothing to tell me why he did this."

"And no significant criminal record. Just a few petty crimes when he was a boy. Then, apparently, he straightened himself out and joined the Army. No trouble while he was in the service. He made sergeant." He looked down at the file on his phone. "Evidently, even after he left the service, he didn't get into trouble. A few speeding tickets, one for drunken driving, a barroom fight that was pretty violent but not fatal."

"Then did he suddenly go crazy? He poisoned Toby. He tried to kill me."

He shook his head. "I'm leaning toward Quinn's theory and betting that we don't have the full story on Blick. I think that there would be an entirely different picture if we could read between the lines. I'd be interested to see what else Quinn comes up with." He grimaced. "But I don't think that I'll get a chance to do that unless you intercede with him. He considers me paid off and out of his way."

"I'll find out." She looked down at the file. "It takes a certain vileness to kill a helpless dog. Yet none of that shows here. He's either very clever or been very lucky."

"Or there's something in his past we're not seeing." He suddenly chuckled. "And only you would comment on the vileness of hurting an animal when you're lying there with a bullet wound."

She made a face. "Margaret would understand. She feels the same way about attacking those who can't protect themselves. I'm not helpless."

"And I'm very glad," he said softly as he rose to his feet. "It makes the game so much more interesting."

He was standing there, legs slightly parted, looking at her with that slight smile that was part sardonic, part wickedly sensual.

She felt the blood tingle through her, making her heart pound. She knew that he was capable of that kind of physical manipulation. Was he doing it?

He slowly shook his head. Dammit, he knew what she was thinking. He had always been able to read her.

No, it was just her basic physical response to him. Even her breasts felt tauter, and her breathing was shallow.

She would much have preferred it the other way.

It was just another sign of how Caleb could stir her even now, when she was so distraught and worried. The responses seemed to exist apart and on different planes from each other.

She looked away from him. "I'll let you know if I hear anything more from Joe. I'd appreciate if you'd keep an eye on Margaret."

"I told you I would." His tone was rough. "I take it I'm dismissed?" He was moving toward the door. "Okay, I'm going. I'm not going to let you close me out forever, Jane. You might remember that I didn't do anything to make you push me away. For God's sake, you'd think Margaret was right when she said that you're afraid of me."

"I'm not afraid—" She broke off as he strode out of the room.

Margaret had told Caleb that she was afraid of him?

Well, maybe she was right. She had always been uneasy and wary when she was with him. But it hadn't stopped her from being drawn to him. No, what she felt for Caleb was so complicated that it was safer to keep the walls high.

Yet Joe and Eve had never clung to safety in their relationship. They had walked the edge and thought every step worth it.

But she wasn't Eve. She didn't have her trust.

Eve.

The tension washed over Jane again.

Call, Joe. Tell me you know where she is. Tell me you at least have a place to start.

"You should get some sleep, Quinn," Venable said quietly as he came up the porch steps. "You're looking pretty ragged. I'll call you if I hear anything about Eve or that kid."

"I'm not sure you would," Joe said coldly as he put away his phone. "That would require a certain amount of trust. I'm not willing to give you that trust at the moment. I think you know more than you're telling me." He looked him in the eye. "Do you?"

Venable hesitated, then nodded. "Yes."

"At last," Joe said sarcastically. "It's about time you admitted it. Are you going to let me know how you involved Eve in this?"

"I didn't involve her. It wasn't my fault."

"And that report on Terence Blick was completely undoctored?"

He grimaced. "For the most part. Perhaps a few things were left out."

"You son of a bitch."

"Nothing that would keep you from finding Blick. Forget him, he's not important."

"I gathered that. Two-prong attack. Blick couldn't have been in two places. He was on the island shooting Jane. Who was here, Venable? Who took Eve?"

Venable didn't answer.

"You'd better tell me." Joe's voice was casual, almost

conversational. "You do know I'll kill you if anything happens to her?"

Venable nodded. "There are things I can't tell you. I made a promise, and I'll keep it. I'm in the dark, too. Nothing I can tell you is going to get you any closer to finding her. It's not as if I haven't got men looking for Eve, Quinn. I'm doing everything I can to find her."

"Except give me a better chance to do it myself." His voice harshened. "I can find her, Venable. No one can keep her from me. Just give me a name and a direction."

Venable shook his head.

Joe drew a deep breath and unclenched his hands. "I'll give you a little more time, Venable. I'm only doing that because of past history, and I'm hoping that you wouldn't let Eve be in danger. After that, you will tell me. I don't care how you have to hurt before you give me every single detail."

"I might point out that the present administration doesn't approve of torture of prisoners," Venable said sourly.

"No, they'd rather kill them. I'm not against that either. Screw the present administration. You talk to me, or you're going down." He picked up his phone. "And I've just sent that report on Blick to a friend at FBI headquarters and told him to give me anything else he has on Terence Blick. If I find out anything that will lead me to another name, your time will run out. I'm also calling the police in Chicago and asking them to trace—"

Venable's phone rang, and he picked up. "Venable." His hand tightened on the phone. "No, keep him there.

We're on our way." He hung up and turned to Joe. "They've found Ben Hudson."

"Alive?"

He nodded. "He's at an urgent-care facility in Floyd County. The staff found him behind some bushes on the grounds this afternoon. By his condition, they think he may have been there for hours. He's been in and out of consciousness since they brought him into the clinic. They're getting him ready to transport to the local hospital."

"But he's alive." Joe was halfway down the porch steps. "That's more than I hoped. We'll take my car."

"You mean I'm going to be permitted in the same vehicle?" Venable murmured. "I thought you'd have me trailing behind."

"It's not because I want your company. You can be a very slippery customer," Joe said curtly. "I don't want you more than an arm's length away from me until I get the info I want from you."

They'd already transferred Ben to the hospital in Rome by the time they were on the road thirty minutes, and they drove directly there.

Ben was just going in for X-rays when Joe got permission to see him.

"Do you mind if I go in with you?" Venable asked quietly. "It's either that, or I'll have to question him later. I know he's a special-needs kid, and you have a relationship with him."

Joe nodded. "Hell, yes, I have a relationship with him. When we were searching for Bonnie, he saved my life. He's had it rough from the time he was a kid. His father was a criminal and it's a wonder he survived the treatment he received until his father was killed. But he did survive and lives and works at a charity camp in south Georgia. He's pretty well self-sufficient and I won't have anyone looking down on him."

"Okay. Okay. No one is going to give the kid a hard time."

"I'll keep the local police off him, but I don't want your agents harassing him either."

"I'll do what I can."

"No, make it happen." He strode ahead of Venable into Ben's room.

The boy looked as pasty pale as the white bandage that encircled his head. He shook his head when he saw Joe. "You're going to be mad at me. I didn't do what I was supposed to do," he whispered. "She's gone, isn't she? I'm sorry, Joe."

"I know you did what you could."

"But she's gone. He took her."

"You say Eve's gone. She's still alive?"

Ben nodded. "I think so. The little girl says she is."

"Bonnie?"

"This morning, when I was crawling through the grass trying to get to the clinic, I kept falling asleep, and Bonnie was there. I told her I tried to do what she wanted. She said there was still time."

Joe hoped to hell he was right. Trust him. Trust Ben's connection with Bonnie. It was all he had right now. "Listen, Ben. How do you know Eve's gone? Did you see who took her? Can you tell me what happened?"

"Eve called me and told me to come back to the

house. I started back right away." He reached up and rubbed his temple. "A man jumped out of the bushes and hit me with something. I think it was a wrench. I fell down, and he hit me again. And then again, I think."

"Did you know him? Could you recognize him again?"

Ben nodded. "I never saw him before. But I'd recognize him if I saw him again." He frowned, puzzled. "He had grayish black hair and his face . . . He looked like . . ." He stopped. "He looked like Mr. Drury, one of the volunteers who helps out at the camp where I work. Well, not really. His nose was different, and so was his hair. But the way he . . . smiled. Mr. Drury smiled like him. Nice man, always smiling." His frown deepened. "The man who hit me looked like that, a nice old man."

"He was smiling?"

"No, he wasn't smiling. He looked . . . sad."

"But he hit you at least a couple times, then dumped you near that urgent-care facility but not near enough to be sure they'd find you. I don't think those were the actions of a 'nice old man,'" Joe said. "I think whoever hit you meant to stop you or use you as a decoy to trap Eve."

"Then I helped him." His eyes glistened with moisture. "I meant to help Eve, but I didn't do it."

"You tried, Ben." He gave his shoulder a brief squeeze and stepped away from the bed. "And you may still be able to do it. Suppose I get a police artist out here and have him help you remember what the man who hit you looked like?"

"I saw something like that on a TV show." He shook his head, troubled. "I don't know if I'm smart enough to do that."

"Sure you are. The artist just has to ask the right questions. Is there anything else you can tell me about the man who took Eve? Did you see his truck, maybe a license plate?"

He frowned. "Sort of. For just a second. It was an old red truck. No license plate. But I've been thinking. He didn't seem bad. If he's like Mr. Drury, maybe it's all a mistake. Maybe Eve won't be in trouble."

"I hope you're right. But sometimes people aren't what they seem," Joe said gently. "You have to not take people at face value and pay attention to their actions. He hit you and gave you a nasty concussion, Ben."

"And Bonnie was worried." His teeth sank into his lower lip. "So maybe he could hurt Eve. I have to make sure that doesn't happen, Joe."

"We will. But right now, you have to rest so that you can concentrate and remember what we need to know for the police artist."

Ben nodded. "But then I have to go with you to find her. You'll take me, won't you, Joe?"

"If it's best for Eve. I'm not going to make promises I can't keep."

"Bonnie wanted me to take care of Eve."

"You'll help. Just think about the man who attacked you. Remember everything you can." He turned toward the door. "You've already helped, Ben."

"No, I lost her," he said desperately. "I shouldn't have done that. I have to find her."

There wasn't anything else Joe could say to comfort him. He was as desperate as Ben and was feeling the same panic. He had hoped for more information from him than he had gotten. A model of the truck, a license number, a clue, dammit.

"He wasn't very helpful," Venable said as he followed him down the corridor. "But it's good that he managed to survive the attack."

"He did the best he could to give us what we wanted. It wasn't that he has a few problems. He has a concussion and suffered from—"

"You don't have to be defensive to me," Venable said. "I'm just commenting. As a witness, he did as well as 70 percent of the people I've questioned over the years."

"And he may be able to help more when I get an artist to give him something to prod his memory." He paused. "But is it necessary? Did you recognize the description? And if you did, are you going to tell me?"

Venable didn't answer directly. "It was a very vague description. It could be almost any pleasant-faced middle-age man. Of course, you could get a photo of that Mr. Drury he's supposed to resemble. However, that wouldn't be very scientific, would it?"

"No, and according to Ben there isn't any real resemblance, just an impression . . . mainly the expression." He zeroed in again. "You're not answering me, Venable."

"No, I'm not. I told you, I made a promise."

"Ben could have died," he said harshly. He tried to

rein in his temper. "Screw your promise." His pace increased as he headed across the parking lot toward his car. "Your time is running out. After that, I'll ram that promise down your throat and make you choke on it."

CHAPTER

8

"But Ben is going to be all right?" Jane's hand tightened on her cell phone. "He didn't kill him, Joe. He dropped him near that clinic. At least that's one good thing to come out of this nightmare. I was afraid that he would be—" She stopped to steady her voice. "It's a good sign, isn't it? Maybe the man who took Eve isn't—Perhaps we can reason with him."

"Providing we can find him," he added bluntly. "And don't be too encouraged. He dropped Ben in the woods a good half mile from the clinic. If Ben hadn't roused and begun to crawl toward it, he might not have been found."

That was true, but Jane had been trying desperately to cling to anything that would give her hope. "You said Venable might know something?"

"I think Venable knows a hell of a lot," he said grimly. "And soon I'll know everything he knows. One way or the other."

"Fine," she said bitterly. "All we need is for the CIA to find a way to make you disappear. Then I'd have to find you, too." She drew a shaky breath. "Venable likes Eve. I don't believe he'd use her as a pawn in one of his games. There must be some reason why he's stonewalling. We have to get him to work with us."

"I gave him his chance."

His tone was totally relentless, Jane thought. She wasn't going to be able to persuade him.

At least, not long-distance.

"What are you doing now?" she asked.

"We're on our way to see a farmer near the lake cottage who reported a truck stolen. After I hang up from you, I'm going to call headquarters and see when they can send out a sketch artist to see Ben in the hospital."

"No."

"What?"

"I'll go see Ben. I can do the sketch."

"The hell you will."

"Yes, the hell I will. You know I've worked with the police as a sketch artist when I was in college. I can do this."

"Maybe when you're not recovering from a bullet in San Juan. I need someone out here right away."

"You'll have someone right away. I'm a lot stronger than I was yesterday." But still damnably shaky. Forget it. She could rest whenever she got an opportunity. "And stop cursing. I'm going to do it, Joe."

"I'll tell the hospital staff not to let you in his room."

"No, you won't. I'm probably a lot better than your sketch artist. You need the best for Eve." She added, "*We* need the best."

Silence. "God help me, I'm going to let you do it."

"Let? You have no choice. Now let me get off the phone and call Caleb. I'll need some help getting out of here." She hung up.

She sat up and swung her legs to the side of the bed.

Dizzy . . .

Ignore it.

Her shoulder was throbbing painfully.

Ignore it.

Call Caleb.

She dialed the number.

"Jane?"

"Come and get me. I need to be in Georgia in the next few hours."

Silence. "I'll be there in thirty minutes. Am I going to have to bust you out of there?"

"Probably."

"Interesting." He hung up.

Clothes. She had to get to the closet across the room.

She waited a moment, bracing herself. Then she slipped off the bed and grabbed the bed rail.

Weakness. Her knees felt like Jell-O.

But they were getting stronger the longer she stood there.

A moment later, she took a step, then another.

And then another.

Just stay within reach of that bed rail in case she folded.

She opened the closet door. Her duffel was on the floor. Devon or Caleb must have brought it. A few clothes items were on hangers. No time to be picky. Just grab something, anything.

White button-down blouse.

Dark twill pants.

Underwear.

She might skip the latter for the time being. The prospect of getting dressed was looking increasingly formidable. She might need help, and she didn't want to ask anything that intimate of Caleb. She was never sure how he would react.

Sit down. Rest. Then start to dress after she recovered a little.

She threw the clothes on the bed and carefully sat down in the chair beside it.

Just a few minutes . . .

She leaned back and closed her eyes.

"Jane."

A deep voice, soft and yet strong.

She stiffened in shock.

Caleb?

Not Caleb.

She didn't even have to open her eyes.

She knew that voice so well. She had heard it in the darkest nights, thick with passion. She had listened to him laugh a thousand times. And how many times had she tensed when she had heard the anger sting like a whip?

"Open your eyes, Jane. I'm not going away just because you don't want me here. Not this time."

She slowly opened her eyes.

He was standing in the doorway smiling at her. It had been a few years, but he looked the same as the first time she'd seen him, when she was only seventeen. He was dressed in jeans and a blue-and-white-striped shirt with sleeves rolled up to the elbow. Short, curly, dark hair framed that incredibly good-looking face. Eve had always said he looked like a movie star, and she'd been afraid Jane would be swept away by that charm and charisma. She had been swept away, but not by his appearance. She had always had the strange feeling that somehow they were meant to be together.

And, Lord help her, she had that feeling right now.

In spite of everything that had happened between them, she could only remember the incredible passion and that sense that they belonged to each other.

Mark Trevor, her first love, perhaps her only love.

She cleared her throat, but it still felt tight. "What are you doing here?"

"Where else would I be?" He crossed the room and squatted beside her chair. "You're hurt. You're in trouble. You should have expected me."

"No, how did you get here? How did you know I was here?"

"Did you think I wouldn't keep an eye on you? Didn't I tell you I'd always be there for you? You can't get rid of me."

That wonderful smile that always wrapped her in intimacy. She couldn't look away from him.

Of course she could. She wasn't that besotted teenager she'd been when she'd first known him, nor the college kid who had taken him as her lover. She glanced away. "I didn't expect you. It's over. We don't want the same things. We parted ways, Trevor."

"You parted ways. I've been on the sidelines, biding my time." He leaned forward, kissed the tip of her nose, and said softly, "It had to end. All the time-outs are over for both of us, Jane."

She was cold.

Eve reached out to draw a blanket over her.

There was no blanket.

Or maybe it had fallen off the bed to the floor.

She opened her eyes.

Not the cottage. Not a bed. She was lying on a couch in a room she'd never seen before.

A large room. Rough pine walls. High ceilings. Exposed pipes.

A loft? Or factory?

Why would she be—

Then she remembered. She froze, her muscles contracting, ready to launch herself from the couch, her gaze darting wildly about the room.

Until it landed on the object on the chair only a few feet from the couch.

A skull, blackened, burned, its gaping orbital cavities staring at her.

Ugly. Threat. Horror.

"I didn't mean to frighten you, Eve." It was the man, Doane, from the truck, coming toward her. "Considering your profession, I'm surprised it would bother you. I just wanted you to become familiar with him as soon as possible." He stopped beside the chair, and his big hand reached out and gently caressed the skull. "This is Kevin. This is my son, Eve. We're both glad to have you with us at last."

She stared at him in shock. Was he mad? There was a distinct possibility. Think calmly about how to handle this situation and still survive.

She didn't want to think calmly. She wanted to launch herself at him and attack. He had not only kidnapped her, he had hurt both Jane and Ben, and she still wasn't sure if they had survived.

But she wouldn't find out by getting physical. She had to find out what this was all about; and then the path would be clear how she was to escape.

She forced herself to look at the skull. She was as surprised as he that she'd reacted with such revulsion when she'd seen the skull. "I wasn't bothered," she said coldly. "I wasn't expecting it. I suppose on some subliminal level that I thought someone was trying to frighten me." Yet she was still feeling that same horror now, she realized. She glanced away from the skull back to Doane's face. "That is what you're doing, isn't it?"

"I have no desire to frighten you. That would be counterproductive." He smiled gently. "I need you. We need you. I don't wish you harm."

"Bullshit," she said with precision. "You sent that man, Blick, after Jane. You struck Ben down, and I still don't know if he died from that blow. You drugged me and brought me to this place. What the hell do you call doing harm?"

He grimaced. "It doesn't sound very good, does it? It was all necessary, but I was hoping that no permanent damage would be caused by my plan."

"Is that why Jane was shot?" She lifted her shaking hand to cover her eyes. "You did enormous harm."

"You heard me tell Blick that he shouldn't have done it."

"Yes, you slapped his hands, but he'd already hurt her." Her hand dropped to her side. "Is she alive or dead?"

"Alive."

Relief followed by suspicion. "How do you know?"

"I called Blick back and had him make calls. I knew that would be one of the first things you'd ask me when you regained consciousness. Jane MacGuire is at a hospital in San Juan, Puerto Rico. She has only a minor wound and should be released within a week."

"And I'm supposed to believe you?"

"It would be easier for you if you did." He shook his head. "But I realize I may have to give you more solid assurances. You'll find it difficult to trust anything I say."

"You think?" she said scornfully. "Prove it to me. Let me call Joe Quinn and hear it from him."

"Ah, Joe Quinn. Yes, you'd believe him."

"He's the only one I'd believe. Where's my phone?"

"I have it safely put away in case I need to scatter a red herring or two. But really, Eve, do you think I'd let you call him? He's very smart, and he has technology at his disposal that I don't. There's a possibility that he could track us. I'll have to find another way to re-assure you." He held out his hand. "In the meantime, you need to have something to eat before we talk. Let me help you up. I'm sure you need to go to the bathroom and wash your face. As I told you, that drug I gave you has very few aftereffects but you may feel a little groggy."

"I don't feel groggy." She ignored his hand and got to her feet. "I feel angry."

"I can see that. You're almost rigid with rage. You'd like to attack me. From what I've learned about you, that might be done with a great deal of skill since you've been taught by your lover, who was in the SEALs." He took a step back. "Which is why I believe I'd better clarify our situation. You might decide to attack at some point. I do have a gun, but I don't wish to use it on you even as a threat. So I made a few advance preparations. Do you see those small holes in the ceiling?"

She looked up. "They look like empty light sockets."

"No." He took out a small keychain with a rectangular emblem from his pocket. "There's also one over the front door that works automatically when the door opens unless I disarm it. All I'd have to do is touch the emblem. I press the button, and it causes gas to spray down. Nothing lethal. Just enough to knock you out. But this time you'd have a giant headache. I'd hate that to happen."

"You could be bluffing."

"Yes."

"It would knock you out, too."

He shook his head. "No, I'm familiar with this gas. I'd only get a little dizzy before I got outside. My son used it when he was in the Army, and he taught me how to take little whiffs until I built up an immunity to it."

"Why would he do that?"

"He loved me as much as I loved him. He wanted me to be safe."

"Safe?" She stared at him incredulously. "So you played around with knockout gas?"

"It's difficult to explain. What you have to know is that as long as you stay inside and don't try to get away or attack me, you're free to move around as if this is your home."

She gazed up at one of the empty light sockets. "I'm tempted to call your bluff."

"Demonstration?" He smiled. "Just a little squirt. Not enough to—" He gave the emblem the tiniest pressure. "Did you hear it? And it smells like carnations, doesn't it?"

"I heard it. But I don't smell—" But her head felt suddenly light. Carnations. Definitely, carnations.

"You'll be fine in a minute. I did have to show you, didn't I?"

She shook her head to clear it. The dizziness was already dispersing. "And it made you feel all-powerful, dammit."

"Believe me, that's not why I did it."

"I don't believe you. Where is this bathroom?" She gazed around the huge room, which was sparsely furnished, with a chair, filing cabinet, desk, couch, and table. A small kitchenette occupied a corner of the area. She stiffened as her gaze fell on another corner that was very, very familiar.

It was a worktable and dais and computer, identical to her lab at the cottage.

"Yes, it's just like your lab down to the last detail," Doane said softly. "I had to tear out an old coin press anchored to the wall to give you light from the window but I wanted you to feel comfortable."

"Comfortable? Not likely. How were you able to re-produce it so exactly?"

"Not totally exact. You can access your forensic sculpting programs on the computer but nothing else. I've been watching you for a long time. As soon as I decided that Kevin needed you, I naturally had to in-vestigate everything about you."

"Investigate? Snooping? Electronic eavesdropping, maybe?"

"All of the above, I'm afraid."

"How long?"

"A little over two years."

She stared at him incredulously. It was hard to imag-ine that she had been under surveillance for that long and not become aware of it. It was even more amazing that Doane would have the patience to sit like a spi-der and weave his intricate web for over two years. "Why?"

"You were worth it," he said simply. "I had to have you."

"You don't have me. I assume that lab you've set up means that you want me to do a reconstruction." She looked him in the eye. "Screw you."

"We'll talk about it later." He gestured to a door to the left of the lab. "That's your bedroom and bathroom. I'll go and heat up a couple TV dinners. I'm afraid I'm a lousy cook. I've never learned the art. Kevin always cooked for us. He was a brilliant chef." He added sadly, "He was brilliant at almost everything."

"I'm not interested in your son. All I want is for you to let me go."

He turned away. "We'll talk over dinner. Don't feel

you have to hurry. I understand that you'll need time to compose yourself." He glanced over his shoulder. "Actually, I felt lucky that I remembered this old abandoned shack from my hunting trips with Kevin up here to the mountains. It's perfect for my purpose."

"As my prison? What was it before? You mentioned tearing out some kind of coin press."

"Back in the gold rush days it was a coin factory. There's a played out gold mine not far from here and the miners liked to turn their gold into actual money before they went to town and blew it." He smiled. "Blick and I remodeled the storage area for your bedroom and bath. It's a little dim in there, but you can turn on the overhead lights. It's pretty small, but you'll only need the bedroom for sleeping. We're not going to do much of that. I'm in a hurry to have Kevin finished. I plan on having you work nonstop with only short breaks when you feel you absolutely have to rest for a few hours. I'll lock you in the room during those rests and let you out afterward. I've put a rollaway bed in there that you can open. The walls are thin, and I can hear you very clearly. I'll be napping on the couch in here, and I sleep lightly. You might keep that in mind. There's only one door and no windows, so don't think that you'll have an opportunity to escape. I've planned this for a long time, and I wouldn't be that foolish."

Eve's hands clenched into fists at her sides as she watched him open the refrigerator in the kitchenette. Then she whirled on her heel and strode toward the door leading to the bedroom.

She slammed the door behind her and leaned against it.

Damn, she felt helpless.

Get over it.

So she was at a disadvantage. It was to be expected if what Doane had told her was true about the time he'd spent studying her.

She made a face. And there was the small item that she was his prisoner, and he might be nuts. He was most certainly violent if he'd attacked Ben.

Yet he didn't seem crazy, and he'd been almost gentle in his dealings with her personally.

Because he wanted something from her.

She had a sudden memory of the blackened skull that had been staring at her when she woke.

She was shivering, she realized.

Why? Because that skull could be that of the son of this man who had been responsible for Jane's shooting?

Stop analyzing. She didn't want to think of that skull right now.

She drew a deep breath and turned on the lights. No furniture in the bedroom but a rollaway bed that was folded up and pushed against the wall. She went to the bathroom and found it to be equally small, with a single vanity and an enclosed glass shower a few feet away. Pristine white tiles on the floor and inside the shower. No window, as Doane had told her.

But there was a small duffel resting on the closed lid of the toilet.

She slowly unfastened the case and opened the lid.

Underwear, pants, tunic tops. A plastic bag with shampoos, soaps and other personal items.

A chill went through her. And every brand was the

same as she used every day at the cottage. For the first time, the claim that Doane had made about those years of long surveillance actually hit home.

She felt . . . violated.

She zipped the duffel shut and turned and leaned against the vanity. This privacy invasion was such a small thing in the scheme of what Doane had done to her.

No, it wasn't. The very intimacy of the act loomed large indeed. It made her want to break something, anything. That's right, do something stupid just to relieve her feelings. Put things in perspective and be a grown-up. It was the only way to—

She had caught a glimpse of her reflection in the mirror over the sink.

Her face was pale and dirty, her hair tangled. Her clothes were rumpled and mud-stained. She looked like a victim, dammit.

She was not a victim.

All right, pull yourself together and show that bastard he had not done anything to you that couldn't be overcome, she thought. Use what he gave you and make it your own.

She locked the door and turned on the shower.

"I'm afraid these dinners are cold. You took longer than I thought," Doane said, when Eve came out of the room forty minutes later. "I wasn't expecting you to take a shower."

"No, you probably thought I'd hurry back out and let you make me jump through hoops." She strode toward the chrome table in front of the kitchenette. "I won't jump through hoops for you, Doane." She sat down at the table and gazed at the pot pie on the plate. "You're right, unappetizing." She began to eat. "It doesn't matter. I'm hungry."

"And you don't want to become weak," Doane said quietly as he sat down across from her. "Now I did expect that from you. You're a strong woman, mentally and physically. You'd have a horror of losing that strength. I just didn't expect you to bounce back so quickly."

"Why am I this hungry? How long was I unconscious?"

"It's been almost twenty-four hours." He took a bite of his pot pie. "We had a long way to go."

"And where am I?"

He shook his head.

She hadn't expected an answer. "I'll get away from you, Doane. Don't think you're going to get away with this."

"I will, you know." He smiled. "Things don't go wrong when you plan as precisely as I do."

"Evidently, you didn't plan on Blick's shooting Jane. That went very wrong, Doane." She added fiercely, "And you'll suffer for it, you son of a bitch."

"I'll just have to make adjustments." His smile faded. "And I do regret causing you this upset."

"Upset? Massive understatement. What adjustment can you make that would make me less upset?"

"I've been thinking about that while I waited for you." He frowned. "You won't be able to be reasonable until you know that Jane MacGuire and Ben Hudson are not permanently injured. I obviously need you to be put at ease on that score."

She tensed. "So what are you going to do?"

"It's difficult. You wouldn't really believe any hospital or law-enforcement unit, would you? You'd think I managed to rig it."

"Since you're so clever about your planning," she said sarcastically.

"I really am clever," he said soberly. "I have a talent. But in this case, I believe I'm going to have to risk having you talk to Joe Quinn."

She inhaled sharply. "Is this a trick? You said it was too dangerous."

"We can work around it. You wouldn't trust anyone but Quinn, and I have to have your mind at ease." His gaze went to the skull across the room. "But we have to come to an arrangement."

"You want me to do a reconstruction," she said flatly. "Why? You seem very sure that skull is that of your son, Kevin."

"I'm almost sure. They lied to me, but I know that he's my Kevin. I feel it."

"Then check the DNA."

"That's difficult."

"Why?"

"I'm not ready to share that with you yet."

"And I'm not ready to do a reconstruction on your son, Doane."

"But you'll do it," he said. "Because you want to talk to Joe Quinn, and I won't let you do that unless I have your word."

She was silent. "That's a high price."

"No, there's something else." His expression was troubled. "I'm having trouble with Blick. He wants to go back and finish the job he started. He said that Kevin would want him to do it. I need to tell him that you'll cooperate."

"The job he started," she repeated. A ripple of pure fear went through her. Don't let him see it. "You mean Jane."

"It's not my wish," he said gently. "Blick lacks control, and he's waited a long time. He needs hope, Eve."

"Don't give me that bullshit." She was silent. "You're saying that you'll let him kill Jane unless I do the reconstruction."

"I'm saying that your lack of cooperation might prevent me from stopping him," he corrected. "I can't control him from this distance if he gets upset. It's up to you, Eve."

His voice was soft, his expression kind . . . and regretful. It seemed impossible that those words held deadly intent.

She mustn't pay any attention to his expression. It was those words that counted, together with the actions of the past days. "And what will happen after I do the reconstruction?"

"Why, then I'm out of your life," he said. "That's all I want from you. But I must have that one service from you."

"I don't believe you."

"I can't help that, but it will be easier if you do."

She stared at him, trying to think, weigh her options. She didn't have any options but the one he was offering her. Not now. It would buy her time, and that was a gift in itself. The only gift. "I have to talk to Joe. I have to know that what you've said about Jane's being alive is true."

"And then you'll cooperate?"

"As long as I have to do it. I don't promise not to try to escape if the opportunity presents itself."

"That goes without saying. Of course, you'll have to accept that it may be a danger to Jane MacGuire if you try and fail before you finish the reconstruction."

Eve felt a streak of pure rage sear through her. "I accept the fact that you're a cowardly son of a bitch for threatening an innocent woman. This Blick may not have obeyed your orders when he shot Jane, but if he hurts her now, it will lie squarely at your door, and I will never stop until I punish you for it."

He nodded. "I understand. You're naturally protective of your daughter." He put down his fork and pushed his plate away. "I knew you'd be like this when I found you and started watching you. It's natural with your background that you'd treasure and protect the family you've created to take the place of the one you never had. It must not have been easy to be illegitimate, with a mother who didn't even know who your father was and on drugs all the time you were growing up."

"I made it through. Some people had it much rougher."

"Did they?" he asked softly. "I know all about Bonnie, the daughter you lost, and your search for her. That was very, very rough. We're a lot alike, Eve."

"The hell we are."

"Oh, but it's true. There's no stronger bond in the world than that between a father and child. We both love our children more than life itself." He added sadly, "And it's the tragedy of that life that we can't bring them back to be with us. I loved my Kevin the way you loved Bonnie. I feel your pain, Eve. I hope before this is over you can forgive me enough to feel mine."

His voice was sincere, and so was his expression. She could almost believe him. "You deserve any pain you feel, Doane. I never tried to victimize innocent people to find my daughter's remains. And you've evidently found your son. Let him go."

"I can't." He cleared his throat. "It hurts me to see him like this. I want to bring him back the way he was. He had such a handsome face. Everyone who looked at him wanted to touch him, be with him." His lips twisted. "And then they did that to him. I can't bear it."

"Who are 'they,' Doane?"

He shook his head. "You're not ready to hear about Kevin. You'd only say you didn't believe me. We have to become closer."

"Closer." She stared at him in amazement. "That's not going to happen."

"Yes, it will. I knew when I found it was you that it was meant to be. You're going to give me back my Kevin the way he was, and I'm going to give you what you want most in the world."

"I want Jane, Joe, and my friends safe."

"Yes, you wish that, too."

"Too?"

He smiled. "You're much more complicated than that, Eve. I told you that you're like me."

"Stop saying that."

"Of course. I'm disturbing you, and that's the last

thing I want to do." He pushed his chair back. "It's time to take your mind off it for a bit. Are you finished eating?"

"Yes." She leaned back in her chair. "But I'm not doing anything about your reconstruction until I talk to Joe."

Doane's brows rose. "But that's what I'm trying to help you do." He reached in his pocket and brought out a pair of handcuffs. "But I have to ask you to wear these for a while."

She instinctively recoiled. "The hell I will."

"Shh. I don't have any dire intentions. You can see I have to protect myself if I let you call Quinn. I'm going to allow you less than a minute of conversation. And you can't call him from here. We're going to take a little drive on the slim chance that he can trace the call even for such a limited time. I can't let him trace it back to this place. I'm afraid I can't trust you once we leave here, so you have to be secured. I'll fasten the cuffs to the seat belt of the truck and as soon as I get you back here, I'll take the cuffs off. Isn't that reasonable?"

She was silent a moment. "Yes."

"Then your wrists please."

She reluctantly extended her hands.

"Excellent." He quickly slipped the cuffs on and snapped them shut. "Now we'll get this over with so that we can clear the decks, and you can get to work. Shall we go, Eve?"

She got to her feet. "Where is my phone?"

"I've put it safely away with that gun I found in your jacket pocket. I have one that I made sure couldn't be traced in the glove compartment of the truck." He was leading her toward the door. "It's a shame we can't use your cell phone. I want this call over quickly, and he'd recognize your ID and pick up immediately. We can only hope he does that with my phone." He opened the door. "You don't mention where you are or give him any hint that he might guess. You ask your questions, tell him you're safe, then good-bye. One minute, Eve."

"I don't know where I am, dammit. How could I tell him anything?" But she had to find a way to give Joe something to go on, she thought desperately as she followed Doane from the factory. Where was she? Was there anything distinctive?

Oh, yes. The mountains in the distance. Not soft, old mountains. New, sharp, craggy, reaching for the sky. Probably the Rockies. That meant she was somewhere in the West as she'd already suspected. The coin factory looked more like a large log cabin and appeared to be nestled in a hollow of some sort, no other houses were nearby. The ancient red truck was parked to the side of the factory beside a utility shed of some sort.

"Wait." Doane stopped her as she was getting into the truck. "One other safeguard." He pulled a scarf from his pocket and blindfolded her. "We'll be passing a few landmarks and signs."

"Aren't you afraid that I'll look a little strange to anyone who even casually glances at us?"

"Not much danger. I'll take the back roads. I know all of them."

Then this was Doane's home stomping grounds. It wasn't much, but she'd take it. She had to gather as much information as she could. She might not be able to use it in this conversation with Joe, but there might be another time, another opportunity.

"I know the blindfold probably makes you feel helpless." He was lifting her into the truck and fastening the cuffs to the seat belt. "I'd hate it. We'll take it off as soon as I get where we're going."

She did feel helpless, but she wasn't going to admit it to Doane. He was once again pointing out how similar they were, and she wouldn't admit that either.

Kevin? Bonnie?

Not the same. Never the same.

Or were they?

CHAPTER

9

"It may be the right truck," Venable said to Joe as he came out of the farmhouse. "It was an old red Ford, parked down by the barn, and Mrs. Hallet, the farmer's wife, thought she saw a late-model blue Chevy parked in the woods. It looks like he changed vehicles, but he didn't leave the Chevy. He must have come back for it for some reason. I got the license-plate number of Hallet's truck from her." He handed Joe a slip of paper. "Call your headquarters and put an APB out on it."

"If he hasn't already changed cars again." Joe reached for his phone. "And why ditch a late-model car for a truck that's much older? All he'd have to do would be to change the license plates."

"Which he probably did."

"It doesn't make sense. Unless he wanted to fit into the background of the countryside at the lake house. He appears to be very careful of details. And what about

Hallet, the farmer who is missing? Did his wife hear anything about him yet?"

Venable shook his head. "The neighbors and a couple deputies are searching the woods now."

"No one saw the thief?"

"I would have told you if they had."

"Would you?" Joe asked bitterly as he started to dial the precinct. "I'm not sure that—" His phone signaled an incoming call. He glanced impatiently down at the ID.

Unknown.

He punched the access. "Quinn."

"Joe."

"Eve." He froze. "My God."

"Yes, listen, Joe, he's only giving me a minute." Eve was talking softly, urgently. "And I'm having to pay for that."

"Where are you?"

"I can't talk about that now. Jane. He says Jane is still alive? Is it true?"

"Yes, she's at a hospital in San Juan. The wound wasn't serious. How are you? Did he hurt you?"

"No. Drugs. He appears to be good at drugs. Ben? He said he dropped Ben at an urgent-care clinic. How is he?"

"Concussion. He's as good as can be expected considering that he also suffered from exposure because the clinic didn't find him for several hours."

"But he'll live?"

"He'll live. What can you tell me about that bastard? Is he going to—Tell him if he hurts you, I'll kill him . . . slowly."

"He can hear you. I'm not in immediate danger, Joe. He wants something from me."

"What?"

"The usual. What most people want from me. He's trying to convince me that he has a heart of gold. I'm not buying it. But he made me an offer I couldn't refuse. I can't talk about that right now. If you want to keep me safe, make sure that there's no way anyone can touch Jane. Because my cozy little deal with the bastard is off if they do. I'd kill him myself."

"No, you won't. My privilege. I'll hunt him down and castrate him before I cut him into small pieces. Do you hear me, you son of a bitch?"

"He hears you. And he's not pleased," Eve said quickly. "I have to go now."

"Listen, Eve. Don't let him use us to make you do anything. I'll take care of Jane and myself. You do what you have to do to get away from him."

"And he didn't like that either. My time is up. I love you."

"And I love—" But she had already hung up. He pressed the disconnect and turned to Venable. "Call up one of your whiz-kid satellite units and see if you can trace that call."

"I'm already on it," Venable said. "I started when you picked up the call. I've just gotten through to the department. I don't know if we can do it. She didn't give us much time."

"She didn't have any choice," Joe said. "Try, dammit." He turned and started back toward the car.

She was alive.

Relief was zinging through him with a force that was

making him dizzy. Why? He had been certain she was alive. He would have somehow known, felt it, if she had been taken from him. But what if fate had played one of her macabre tricks? Life wasn't always kind, and all he knew was that he had wanted to fall to his knees when he heard her voice.

Now the certainty was confirmed, and all he had to do was find her.

He felt a sudden explosion of hope and ferocity.

And he *would* find her. He would pull out all the stops, bring in all the help he needed, tap every source.

Nothing would keep her from him.

He started dialing headquarters again to set up that APB on the truck.

"Quinn's angry with me," Doane said. **"That threat** was both crude and violent."

"And heartfelt," Eve said. "Joe always keeps his word."

"So do I. You were hoping to disarm any threat to Jane MacGuire by having Quinn set up extra protection around her. That would free you from the obligation of doing Kevin's reconstruction."

"It would help to push away that gun you have pressed to my head."

He smiled. "But I've no gun aimed at you, Eve. I've handled you in the gentlest way possible. Anything else would be totally unreasonable. I want you to be free to express yourself without coercion."

She shook her head. "You actually sound as if you believed that lie."

"No lie." He stepped forward with the blindfold he'd taken off her when he'd stopped the truck and given the telephone to her. "It's important that you and Kevin become one with each other. I've heard that's how you turn out such wonderful sculptures."

"I'm not going to become one with your son. The idea appalls me."

"But how will you help yourself?" he asked quietly. "It's part of your particular magic."

"Not magic. I'm a professional." Yet she felt a frisson of unease. She couldn't deny in the last stages of a reconstruction that she felt as if the soul of the skull on which she was working was whispering, helping her bring that vision to life again. "And I'll behave as a professional."

"We'll see. Give me that phone."

She reluctantly handed it back to him.

"Time to bid good-bye to this one." He dropped the phone on the ground, stomped on it with his boot, then ground it into the earth. "That should take care of any signal. I hear those things are real spy machines. I'm not real good with all those fancy gadgets. I don't like all that technology. I don't think that Kevin would like it either. Things have changed a lot in the world since I lost him." His expression was suddenly full of pain. "He made life exciting and right. They shouldn't have taken him."

"Who?"

He ignored the question. "Time to put the blindfold back on you."

She took a quick last look at her surroundings. She hadn't been able to give Joe a hint other than that vague reference to Doane's heart of gold, which Joe probably had not caught, but there might be another time. Waterfall cascading to the rocks below. Mountains in the distance. An observation area enclosed in gray rails across the chasm.

Then everything went dark as he replaced the blindfold.

"There we are." He lifted her back in the truck. "Now we go back and start the reconstruction." The next moment, she heard the truck engine ignite. "Kevin is waiting for you."

SAN JUAN, PUERTO RICO

"Go away, Trevor," Jane said. "I don't need you. We tried a few times to make it work, and it never did. Now you pop up and ignore everything that's gone before?"

"Now that would make me a fool. I've always made a practice of building on the past." He reached out and touched her cheek. "And we have quite a past to build on. Sometimes I'd lie in bed and think about it. Did you?"

"No." He was looking at her, and she changed the answer. She had always been honest with him, and she wouldn't change now. "Yes. So we were fantastic in bed together. In the end, it didn't matter. Sex isn't why we couldn't make it together. It was more complicated than that."

"You were more complicated. I'm just a simple man with all the usual instincts."

"The hell you are."

He smiled. "You're right, I have my own complexities, but I fought to keep them in check when you came into my life. I wanted you enough to do anything to get you. For the first time, I thought that I'd found a woman I wanted to spend my life with. For a while I thought that I'd managed to pull it off." He stroked her cheek. "Oh, how good we were together. Remember?"

"Yes." She couldn't help but remember. Whenever he touched her, spoke to her, it brought back a thousand memories that were both fiery and seductive. He had always held that power over her emotions. Even when she'd been angry with him, she'd known they were only a shade away from passion. "But we agreed to disagree. I haven't seen you for a long time. I don't even know why you're here. How did you know I was hurt?"

"I'd heard you left London with one Seth Caleb." His smile faded. "That stirred me to action. I didn't like it."

"Who told you? We didn't exactly publish it."

He shrugged. "I've a few friends who have been keeping an eye on you."

"What? You, too?" Almost the same answer Caleb had given her, and it struck a nerve.

"Oh, I knew that Caleb had you in his sights. But it was okay as long as he kept his distance. But I had to know where he was taking you, so I checked the flight plan he filed. Then contacted some people I know in this area to make sure you were okay."

"And to find out what I was doing?"

"Well, that, too."

"And you found out that I'd been shot."

He nodded. "And I jumped on the next plane."

"And now you can jump on the next one and fly back to Paris."

"I'm not living in Paris any longer. I'm in Barcelona."

"Wherever." She had never been sure where Trevor would be at any given time. He'd flown in to see her several times a year and usually from a different home base. His restlessness had caused him to become a jack of all trades. He'd dabbled in gambling, smuggling of precious artifacts, and a dozen other professions, both legal and slightly illegal. Not that he needed the money now. Whatever he touched turned golden.

And he had made her think for a while that their relationship was golden, too.

"I don't need you. Go back to Barcelona."

He shook his head. "I've been asking questions. They haven't found the man who shot you."

"Joe is working on it." She paused. "It's a mess, Trevor. I don't know what's happening. I don't think it's about me at all. Eve has disappeared. She's been kidnapped, and we don't know—I have to find her."

"Eve." He gave a low whistle. "Not good. But not exactly surprising. She deals with some pretty macabre types."

"Thanks," she said sarcastically. "That's really going to make me feel better."

"You don't want me to coddle you," he said quietly. "We've gone way past that in our relationship. You'd sock me if I weren't dead honest with you."

He was right. She had been grateful that she could always be open and expect the same from him. "I'm just scared," she said wearily. "Eve deals with serial killers, child abusers, and scum of the Earth. You just put it into words. I guess I didn't want to hear it."

"We'll find her. We'll keep away all the bad guys." He reached down and took her hand. "She's smart, she'll survive until we can get her back."

She felt a sudden rush of warmth as she looked down at their joined hands. Comfort. Tenderness. Not passion. Not sex. So much more important in this moment than any other response. "This isn't your battle, Trevor. Joe and I will find her."

"You're closing me out again." His lips tightened. "When I get too near to that core that shelters who and what you are, you spin away." His hand tightened on her own. "But I'm following this time, Jane. I'm following and searching, and you're never going to get away from me again."

"I don't want to hear this, Trevor. I'm searching, too, and it's only for Eve," she said shakily. "You picked the wrong time and the wrong woman to—"

"My, my, do we have a visitor?" Caleb was standing in the doorway, his gaze on their joined hands. "You didn't tell me, Jane. Introduce me."

There was no expression on Caleb's face, but she could feel the tension.

No, anger, searing, possessive anger.

She instinctively tried to pull away from Trevor, then stopped. Why should she give in to this subtle intimidation? "He was a surprise guest. Seth Caleb, Mark Trevor."

"Delighted." Caleb came toward him with hand outstretched. "I've been thinking that I should meet you.

I just didn't think it would be this soon. Let me guess, you heard Jane was wounded and decided to come and see if you could help."

"That about covers it." He took Caleb's hand and shook it. "On the surface level."

"Oh, yes, I imagine there was much more to explore since you haven't seen each other for a while." He smiled. "But I'm sure she told you that you're not needed here."

"Yes, but I'm not discouraged. Jane knows that I'm a valuable man to have around in an emergency. This couldn't be more of an emergency for her. Eve is everything to her. Jane won't refuse my help once I'm in a position to offer it."

Jane found herself staring in fascination at the two men with hands clasped in traditional greeting. There was nothing traditional in what was going on beneath that gesture. They were like two sleek, powerful cats, backs arched, ready for the fray. No, much more dangerous than cats, and the only thing similar about them was that air of lethal purpose.

Lightness. Darkness.

Trevor was radiating those brilliant movie-star good looks and charm that had first drawn Jane to him so long ago.

Caleb was all darkness and power and magnetism that held you even while you struggled to get free.

She tore her gaze from them and grabbed the arm of the chair to lever herself to her feet. "I've had enough. Stop talking about me as if I weren't here. Both of you get out of here and let me get dressed." She looked at Caleb. "You'll still take me to Atlanta?"

"Of course, nothing has changed." He glanced at Trevor. "Has it?"

"Everything has changed." Trevor smiled. "You're going to the lake cottage?"

"I don't know. I have to do a sketch rendering of the suspect at Rome hospital."

"Then I'll be in touch. Would you like me to smooth the way to get you sprung from this place? You don't look like you're a candidate for the discharge list."

"I could arrange—" Why fight him over such a small thing? She needed her strength for the trip. "If you like, it would be a help."

"I like." He didn't move. "And would you let me help you dress? It would be quicker."

"I can manage."

"Sure?" he said softly. "It's not as if I haven't done it before. Though I'm better at taking them off."

She could have slapped him.

She was sure that he had a double purpose in that remark. He wanted to stir intimate memories, which he'd done, and he wanted to score off Caleb.

Which he'd also done. She wasn't looking at Caleb, but she could sense the stiffening, the animal tension.

She turned her back on both of them and took a step closer to the bed and reached for her bra. "Really? I always thought you were a little clumsy. I guess I forgot to tell you."

She heard Caleb chuckle as he left the room.

But Trevor was laughing, too. "Oh, Jane, how I've missed you, my love."

She kept her eyes on the bra. "I'm not your love."

"Yes, you are. I've dodged the word, and so have

you, but it's time to come to terms with it." She heard him move toward the door. "Don't sleep with Caleb. I thought I could be civilized about it if you decided to do it, but that was before I met him. He's different, he wouldn't let go. I'd end up by having to kill him."

"For heaven's sake, I'm only interested in finding Eve. I've no desire to sleep with either of you. But if I were, it would be my choice."

"Theoretically. But I'm not good at theory. See you in Atlanta . . ."

"Just be patient, Eve. I'll have that blindfold off you in just a minute. I know it's uncomfortable."

Eve heard Doane close and lock the front door behind them.

"It's like coming home, isn't it?" He unlocked her handcuffs and took them off. "Just the three of us."

"You're crazy, you know," she said, as he took the blindfold off her. "You can't get away with this. Joe will find us."

He chuckled. "For a moment I thought you meant I was crazy because I think Kevin is part of our little family. But then you wouldn't find that unusual. You think of all your reconstructions as having a certain life of their own." He added softly, "A life you give them. I regard that as a wonderful gift."

"I don't give them life. I'd have to be God to be able to do that. I give them a chance to bring solace to the people they've left behind and perhaps to get vengeance for what's been done to them."

"Vengeance. Yes, that's an important part of what

you're able to do." His expression was suddenly shadowed. "It's sad that those victims all cry out for vengeance. It causes me pain."

She stared at him skeptically. "And you're saying you don't want some form of vengeance for the death of your Kevin? I find that hard to believe."

"And rightly so. But I prefer to call it justice." He turned away. "Let me make you a cup of coffee while you examine the lab I created for you. You take it black, don't you?"

"Yes." She again felt that chill at the evidence of the extent of his knowledge about her. "How did you find out so much about me?"

"Articles. TV documentaries. You're very famous, Eve. I collected an entire scrapbook devoted to you. I like scrapbooks. They bring back memories that warm the heart."

"Touching. But that's not all, is it? What else did you do?"

He put coffee in the coffeemaker. "No, that's not all. When I found out about you, I had an insatiable thirst for information. I managed to put a few bugs in your cottage when you were away searching for your Bonnie. They're still there."

Her eyes widened. "How did you get around the security alarm?"

"With great difficulty—it's a fine system. Blick knew a few experts. I felt it necessary to have more details than those I could gather from public means." He took down a large mug from the cabinet. "I found out a great deal about you." He added soberly, "I did try to ignore the more intimate transmissions between you and Quinn. It really had nothing to do with what I needed to know and wouldn't be fair to you."

Eve felt the heat rise to her face at the thought of him eavesdropping while she and Joe made love. Not embarrassment. Sheer rage. "You're damn right it wasn't fair," she said through clenched teeth. "Nothing you've done is fair or right, you sick Peeping Tom."

"You're perfectly right to be indignant." He looked over his shoulder. "I could have lied to you. It would have been easier for me. I admit I was tempted. But that would have been wrong when I want our relationship to be as open and aboveboard as possible."

"Why?" Her fists clenched at her sides. "Why did you have to know so much about me?"

"It's part of my character, part of how I guide my life. I plan every move." He held out his palms. "See how rough and scarred my hands are? Every line and crease could tell you how hard I've worked. I'm not real smart, but I learned that if I worked hard and always planned the next step, I could make a living. I was a farmer most of my life until Kevin was born. Then I got work in the city as a carpenter so that Kevin could have a better chance for an education. Planning helped me there, too."

"Are you trying to make me feel sorry for you? No way."

"I'm trying to make you understand that I won't do anything to hurt you. Why would I want to do that when I've gone to so much trouble to make sure you were the right one to help my Kevin?" He nodded at the dais. "Would you like me to put the skull on your worktable?"

"What if I won't do it? You say you don't want me hurt. You'd hurt me terribly if anything happened to Jane. You're holding that out as a threat, which makes you a liar."

He flinched. "I try not to lie. But I want this for Kevin so badly that I might bend the truth. You have to do this, Eve."

She stared at him in anger and frustration. That face was so kind and troubled that it was difficult not to believe him. One moment, she thought his kindness and concern were actually genuine, and the next she was sure it had to be a sort of bizarre masquerade.

"Just do it," he said softly. "We both know that you won't take a chance that Jane might pay for your stubbornness."

He might seem rough and simple, but he read her very well. Why not, she thought bitterly. He had been studying her for a long time.

"Bastard." She turned on her heel and strode toward the worktable in the corner. "Bring me the skull and set him up on the dais."

"This isn't a defeat." He went toward the chair where the skull rested. "You're just being sensible, Eve."

"Am I?" She was trying to be sensible, if not in the way he meant. If she was going to do this reconstruction, she had to use it as a barrier behind which she could explore everything about Doane and this place. He was very big on finding out all about his targets so that his damned plans would work. Since she had no weapons, it might be possible to turn those methods against him. At any rate, she seemed to have no other option. She glanced at the window by the worktable.

She could see the mountains in the distance and pine trees.

And above the window sash one of those empty sockets that were also in the ceiling.

Of course, in case she tried to open that window.

Doane was standing beside her, his gaze following Eve's. "Enough light?"

"Plenty," she said curtly. "Set him on the dais."

She watched him carefully set the skull with loving hands.

Love. She couldn't deny the affection she could see in Doane's expression, in his touch. She was unable to determine if anything else about him was genuine, but he had truly loved this son who was staring back at them like a blackened, ugly skull from a horror movie.

She felt a ripple of shock at the thought. There it was again. Why couldn't she feel the usual empathy with this lost one? The threat to Jane? The terrible lengths to which Doane had gone in order to force her to do this reconstruction?

"You're looking at him with revulsion." Doane frowned. "Don't take it out on him. You have to give him a chance. Once you start work, it will be like all the others."

And it wasn't wise to antagonize Doane by revealing that revulsion. Kevin was the center of Doane's life. Eve would have to circle and avoid any direct confrontation. "Perhaps you're right." She hoped she was telling the truth. She didn't want to think she was shallow enough to blame a son for the sins of the father. "Go away. I want to get to work. The sooner I'm done, the sooner this is over. Isn't that what you said?"

"That's what I said." His frown had deepened. "I don't want to go away. I want to watch you."

"No." She began to go through the measuring tools. "You'll bother me. You want a good job, don't you?"

"You're a professional. You'll give me a good job regardless if I distract you or not."

"But you're not sure if your presence will bother me. Why do you want to be here?"

"I've always been with him during the important events in his life. You're bringing him back to me. That's very important."

She turned away from the skull to look at Doane. "Then it's important that I not be distracted. Suppose we make a deal."

"Deal?" he repeated warily.

"What do you know about forensic sculpting?"

"What I've read in those articles."

"But that's not always how I work. First, I take precise measurements, then I set depth markers, then I begin the actual sculpting. The measuring would be very boring for you. It's essential to the process, but it might even be painful for you. There's one point when Kevin would look like a voodoo doll stuck with pins. Not pretty. Let me do that by myself. Then when the actual sculpting begins, you can watch, and I won't argue."

"That won't bother you?"

"Not in the first stages." She paused. "And not if you furnish me with a little distraction, too."

"And that's your deal? What distraction?"

Her gaze swung back to the skull. "I want you to tell me how he got this way. You know, don't you?"

"Yes." He paused. "But why do you want to know? Curiosity?"

"Curiosity?" She looked at him in astonishment. "He's the reason why all this is happening. I want to know why I'm being forced to do this reconstruction. Who knows? It might even make the sculpting go smoother and faster."

He didn't speak for a long moment. "I'm not going to promise to tell you everything."

"That doesn't surprise me, and it may be more than you think." Her gaze narrowed on his face. "And I believe you'll tell me what you feel is safe. You want to tell someone about Kevin."

"How smart you are, Eve." He paused again. "I don't want to tell just anyone, Eve. I want to tell *you*. We share so many things that no one else could dream."

"Then tell me now."

He smiled. "No, you have to earn it." He moved back from the dais. "You start your work, and I'll start mine. I'll go outside and sit in the truck with my computer. I have a few more plans to put in place. Though I really would prefer to sit in that chair over there and watch you."

She watched him unlock a file cabinet next to the desk and take out his Dell computer. Then he locked it back up again and nodded at the empty ceiling socket. "As I said, don't waste time," he said gently. "Start to work, Eve."

She didn't move for a moment after the door shut behind him.

Okay, that file cabinet might have information. Or

perhaps the desk next to it. She probably wouldn't be able to get her hands on that computer, but she'd try.

The truck had been where he kept that phone he'd rigged to avoid tracing, he might have other electronic gadgets.

He had mentioned his fondness for albums. Who knew what else he might have collected to "warm the heart."

But the main project would have to be a way to disable those gas sockets. They were his principal weapon against her.

How was she going to do that? It would take time and opportunity that she'd have to squeeze from the reconstruction and—

Mull it over. Don't be negative. There had to be a way. Work it out.

She turned back to the skull. "I don't have to name you, do I?" she whispered. "You have a name and a history and a father who loves you. How are we going to get along, Kevin?"

No answer, of course.

The skull stared back at her with gaping eyes and bared teeth in its black visage.

He looked fierce, savage, as if he were about to attack her.

She instinctively stiffened.

Ignore it. It was only imagination. Kevin was a man, when she was accustomed to sculpting children. There were so many lost children, and she had a passion for trying to bring them home to give solace to their parents.

But she had done reconstructions of adults before without a reaction like this.

Not when she had been kidnapped and Jane shot to bring her to this point, this work.

Go to work, get it done.

She started to measure the midtherum area beneath the nasal cavity.

"There's a good chance I'm going to break my word," Venable told Zander bluntly. "Everything's gone to hell. My agent, Tad Dukes, can't be found on the property. The description Ben Hudson gave us matches Doane, and Blick was almost certainly Jane's shooter. Eve called Joe Quinn, and Doane wants her to do a reconstruction. Unless my team can pull in Doane within the next few hours, I'm going to tell Quinn what he has to contend with."

"That would be awkward for me."

"Screw you. I don't like where this is going. I'm not going to let Eve be sacrificed because of you. I won't do it for you, and I won't do it for General Tarther, whom I like as much as I dislike you." He paused. "You were right. Doane had everything planned out step by step, and he has to think that she can lead him to you."

"I could avoid him if I chose."

"And he could kill her."

"But that's your problem."

"No, it's yours, dammit." He drew a deep breath. "You're so sure that you could go after Doane and take him out if you decide to do it. If you can find Doane, you can find her."

"But if I did, I'd be playing into his hands. I won't do that, Venable."

"Why? Would it prove you're not a complete—"

"Our conversation is finished. You've told me what you wanted to say. I really don't know why you felt obligated to tell me you were going to break your promise. No one keeps their word these days."

"I do. And if I locate Eve in the next few hours, I'll still keep it. I owed you and General Tarther a warning in case that doesn't happen." He hung up.

And the odds were that they wouldn't find her, he thought. The satellite GPS trace had come back with nothing. The agents he had searching the house in Goldfork had been stymied, too.

Which meant that he'd have to betray Zander.

And Zander wasn't a man it was safe to betray.

He went out on the porch and watched as Joe came back down the road from the place where the forensic team was checking the shrubbery for trace evidence and possible DNA. Joe was hanging up his phone as he came even with the cottage. "Jane just arrived in Atlanta. I'm going to meet her at the hospital in Rome."

"Do you want me to go with you?"

"No, I don't want to see you again until I hear what I want to hear from you," he said coldly. "I'm afraid I'll break your neck before I choke it out of you."

"Just inquiring. The last I heard, you didn't want me out of your sight."

"If you disappear, I'll find you."

"I won't disappear," Venable said quietly. "Not until after we find Eve. I promise you."

Joe gazed at him a moment. "Are you weakening, Venable?"

Venable didn't reply directly. "Maybe. I'm not going to let anything happen to Eve. Since she's going to do that reconstruction, she has time. *We* have time, Joe."

"If I didn't believe that, you'd be in an even tighter spot than you are now." Joe got into the car. "I'll find out who took Eve by Jane's doing this sketch. But it will take time to identify him by going through data bases. I'm not going to take that time. Once I have a sketch, you're going to tell me who he is and how to get to him."

"If I knew how to get the man who took Eve, I would have already done it," he said wearily. "Bring me the sketch, and we'll talk."

"You're stalling."

"Yes." He turned back to go into the house. "It's all I can offer you right now, dammit."

The tiny metal jet in the sunken socket above Eve's bed gleamed in the darkness.

She was exhausted after hours of work on the reconstruction, but she was too on edge to sleep. She had been lying on this cot for the last thirty minutes and gazing up at that gas jet.

So clever. Doane had boasted of his skill at planning, and this silent threat certainly added weight to his claim. It kept her immobile but still allowed him to use her skills. It was infuriating and damn frustrating and totally—

She suddenly straightened on the cot. But maybe not foolproof. Maybe she could beat it.

I was able to become accustomed to the gas by gradually exposing myself to the fumes.

If Doane had been able to do that, she might be able to do the same thing. She wouldn't be able to become totally immune, but perhaps she could make herself less sensitive to the gas.

If the gas could be triggered by hand at the source in each of those sockets. If she could find a way to get up to the socket, which must be ten feet above the cot. If she could control the flow to give her a whiff without completely knocking her out.

Lots of ifs.

Hell, she didn't have a better plan, did she? It was the one way that she had a chance of escaping. It was the only way she would be on partially even terms with Doane.

Move. Try.

She listened for Doane. He was sleeping on the couch in the living area. As he'd told her, these walls were paper-thin, and she could hear everything that was happening beyond them.

And now she could hear the steady sound of his breathing. He had claimed to be a light sleeper, but he was asleep now. If she was quiet, she might keep him that way.

She slid off the cot, and her bare feet touched the floor.

Don't squeak, she prayed. Please don't squeak.

She stood there looking up at the ceiling. It was at least ten feet above her. How could she reach it?

Stand on the cot?

Not high enough.

Or was it? The cot was one of those rollaway wire beds that folded up to store. If she folded it up, then climbed on top, it would give her at least another three feet.

No squeaks . . .

Her heart was beating hard as she slowly, carefully folded up the cot. She pushed it against the wall, then propped the nightstand against it to steady it. The next minute she was climbing up on the folded edge.

Slowly.

Painstakingly silent.

With utmost care.

The socket was right above her now.

Press on the side?

No, there was a closure in the center that she could unscrew. There might be some gas trapped in the line that she could release.

Open it just a little . . .

Carnations.

She jerked her hand back. Then she hurriedly screwed the closure shut again.

Her head was spinning.

Too much.

Get down.

No noise.

No noise.

She was off the bed.

On the floor.

Curled up in a ball.

Sick . . . Doane hadn't told her it made you sick.

Had he heard her?

He hadn't come running. She might be safe.

Carnations.

Dizzy . . . sick.

She'd be all right. As soon as she got over this first bout of sickness, she'd rest, then try it again.

Two more times during this rest period ingesting the gas should be enough to start the path toward immunity. She'd be able to judge better after she recovered a little.

Afterward, she had to get up and remake the cot. Doane mustn't know what she'd been doing when he unlocked that door.

In a few minutes. After she regained her strength.

She buried her face in her arm to avoid that smell. She was going to hate the scent of carnations for the rest of her life.

But it's worth it, you bastard. I'm going to kick your ass.

CHAPTER

10

Lord, you're pale. You should be in a wheel-chair," Joe said flatly as he watched Jane walk slowly toward him down the corridor. His glance shifted to Caleb, who was beside her. "Why didn't you keep her in San Juan?"

"The same reason you didn't try to do it. I don't like to waste my time. I compromised by making sure she didn't do herself any permanent damage." He smiled down at Jane. "She's better than she seems."

"I'm fine." Her gaze was searching for the correct room number. "He's in 1602?"

"The next one down the hall," Joe said tersely. "I'll come in and introduce you to Ben."

"I don't need you," Jane said as she opened the hospital-room door. "You have more important things to do than hold my hand, Joe. This is my job. Let me do it." She paused. "Any more news?"

"Nothing about Eve." He added, "And no firm information that there have been any homicides. Ben was assaulted, but there may not have been any attempt at killing him. Hallet, the farmer who owned the stolen truck, has disappeared, but there's no evidence that he's been murdered. Venable's agent, Dukes, hasn't shown up, but he could be in pursuit."

"Is that supposed to comfort me or you?" Jane's lips twisted. "No evidence. Disappearances. Possibilities, but no proof. What does that suggest to you?"

"That Eve may be safer than we think. You were shot, but it may be Blick who was the violent partner."

"I pray that's true," she said soberly. "But I don't believe it. Caleb thinks that everything that happened to Toby and me was meant to keep me away from Eve, so that she would be more vulnerable. He didn't want to have anyone getting in his way. I was only a secondary target." She met his gaze. "And you believe that, too, don't you, Joe?"

He slowly nodded.

"And from what you've told me, he wants Eve to do a reconstruction. It would be smarter to make her think he wasn't quite as much of a threat if the path was not strewn with bodies. Ben said he appeared very likeable and unintimidating." She grimaced. "Before he tried to break his head open."

"You have it figured out."

"So do you. The difference is that you want to soothe me and try to keep me from worrying. And maybe direct me to the sidelines. It's not going to happen, Joe."

"We'll see." He turned away. "Go do your sketch. I want to see the bastard's face."

"You will." She glanced at Caleb, who had moved

to follow her into the room. "No, stay in the waiting room or help Joe. I've never met Ben Hudson, and I don't want him to have to deal with two strangers." She hesitated. "Mark Trevor contacted me in San Juan. He may want to help find Eve."

Joe's gaze shifted speculatively to Caleb before returning to her. "And what do you want?"

"If he can do anything, let him do it. I don't care who volunteers if there's even a chance they can help, I'll be grateful."

His gaze returned to Caleb. "If I don't believe they'll get in the way."

"Oh, that won't happen." Caleb smiled. "I'll either be behind you or probably ahead of you. Never in the way." He was moving down the corridor. "I'll bring you a cup of coffee later, Jane. After you've broken the ice."

"Do that," she said absently. Her gaze was already fixed on Ben Hudson in the bed across the room. He was smiling at her. Warmth. Sweetness. Shining blue eyes that were staring curiously at her.

"Hi." She found she was smiling, too, as she walked toward the bed. "You're Ben Hudson. I'm Jane. I've come to draw a picture of the man who attacked you. Will you help me?"

"Sure." His head was tilted to one side as he looked at her. "Joe said he'd send someone, but he didn't say it would be you. You're Jane MacGuire, aren't you? You belong to her."

"Belong to Eve?" She sat down and took her sketchbook out of her briefcase. "Yes, I most definitely do belong to Eve. She adopted me when I was only ten years old."

He frowned. "No, that's not what I meant. You belong to *her*."

She stiffened, then smiled with an effort. "You're talking about Bonnie. Eve told me that you sometimes dreamed about Bonnie. I'm afraid that I can't claim to belong to Bonnie. She died long before I could get to know her."

"That doesn't matter. You still belong to her because Eve loves you." He paused. "Bonnie wants to be closer to you, but she says that you won't let her near. Why is that, Jane?"

Jane hadn't bargained for this. She instinctively started to shut him out, then stopped. There was such a pure good-hearted simplicity in the question that she couldn't hurt him. The boy had probably had too many people shut him out in his life. "I'm afraid that I'm too much the realist, Ben," she said gently. "I'm not like you and Eve. I have trouble believing in dreams."

He frowned, troubled. "You think I'm not telling the truth?"

"No, I think some people live in the real world and some people have dreams to make the reality bearable." She reached out and covered his big hand with her own. "You're one of the lucky ones, Ben."

He looked down at her hand. "You have pretty hands. You're pretty all over. It's nice to look at you. You look like Eve but you're—"

"Looks aren't important." He was clearly easily distracted, and she was relieved to get off the subject. "Except when you're trying to do a sketch. Are you ready to tell me about the man who hurt you?"

"And took Eve."

She nodded. "And took Eve. She'll be grateful that you're going to help us."

His expression clouded. "I have to find her. Bonnie trusted me to take care of her."

"We'll find her." She hoped she sounded confident. At the moment, she was closer to desperation. "Let's take the eyebrows first. Were they thick, thin?"

"Thick and kinda bushy."

"Dark, light, gray?"

"Dark . . . with gray stuff in them."

"He was older?"

"Not real old. Just not young."

This might not be easy. She hadn't signed on for easy, she told herself in self-disgust. She'd told Joe she could do the job better than his artists, and she'd do it. "Straight across or arched?" When he didn't answer, she looked up to see his gaze on her face. "Ben?"

"It's going to be okay," he said gently. "You're going to let Bonnie close to you. She told me so."

He was back on the subject of dreams and ghosts and drifting away from her. She smiled. "Just now?"

"No, I wasn't sure that I should tell you. Bonnie wasn't happy about it. She wanted there to be joy. She didn't want it that way . . ."

What way? Why would there be no happiness?

Eve?

She kept her smile firmly in place in spite of the icy tension that gripped her. Ignore it. Concentrate on reality and leave the dreams to others. "It will probably be fine. Bonnie and I haven't gotten together so far, and we've managed splendidly." She looked back down at the sketch. "Straight eyebrows or arched, Ben? I'll draw both and let you choose."

"Are you almost finished?"

Jane looked up to see Joe standing in the doorway. Something was wrong. She could see the tension that was electrifying him. "Yes. We'd have finished before this, but the nose was a little hard for us. Do you need me?"

"I can wait a few minutes."

He didn't want to disturb Ben, she guessed with relief, but he didn't want to wait, either. It must not have been anything directly threatening to Eve, or he would not have cared who would be disturbed. "I think we're done." She closed her sketchbook and smiled at Ben. "But Ben was very good. He remembered everything about the man beautifully. He has a fine memory." She made a face. "Except that this man has all the menace of Peter Pan or Santa Claus. It's hard to believe that this guy could have clobbered you, Ben."

"I didn't expect it. He looked like Mr. Drury."

She got to her feet. "You keep saying that. But when I tried to draw Mr. Drury, they didn't look a bit alike. Thanks for helping me out, Ben. If you remember anything else, call me, and I'll come back."

"I won't call you back. That's the man." He watched her move toward the door. "You'll know him when you see him."

"I'm counting on it."

"Jane."

She looked back over her shoulder.

Ben was staring at her, his blue eyes were shining, but his expression was troubled. "You mustn't let it hurt you too much. It's not the end, you know. It goes on."

She froze. What did he mean?

Eve?

She knew she wasn't going to ask him. His mind was full of dreams and ghosts and things that might not exist and probably wouldn't happen. She'd have to accept all those elements as valid, and she couldn't do that. She'd face and conquer any threat to Eve, but she wouldn't be intimidated by this boy at the mere possibility of that danger. "I'm not going to be hurt," she told him firmly. "Everything is going to turn out fine now that we have this sketch. You just rest now, Ben." She smiled and followed Joe from the room.

Her smile vanished as she whirled to face him. "What's wrong, Joe?"

"Plenty. But not anything to scare you. Venable called me, and we definitely can't trace that phone call from Eve."

She searched his expression. "That's not all."

"No," he said curtly. "Venable's agents have located what might be a grave deep in the woods. They've started to excavate it."

"He thinks it might be Tad Dukes, the CIA agent who was watching Eve?"

"He hopes not. But there's a good chance. Either him or the farmer he stole the truck from. I need to get out there right away." His lips tightened. "If it is Dukes, then it might be the straw that breaks the camel's back."

"What?"

"Venable takes care of his agents. He's not going to like the idea that he sent one to his death. I may not have to force Venable to talk." He held out his hand. "Let me see that sketch."

She flipped open the book. "I was surprised. Ben seemed remarkably certain of his choices. It was . . . odd. I thought he might be having me reproduce his friend, Mr. Drury. But the features he described are completely different."

"I don't think he'd do that." Joe was shaking his head as he looked at the sketch. "Maybe a little."

"Too nice?"

"It's hard to get around that kindly face. After all these years, you'd think I'd be able to see below the surface. That butcher, Ted Bundy, was a clean-cut, nice-looking specimen, too, but he was totally ruthless." He handed the sketch back to her. "See if you can have a couple copies made in the administration office here and bring me one to the cottage. I want to show it to Venable." His lips thinned. "Though I have a hunch that face may already be familiar."

She tucked the sketch back in her case. "Caleb and I will be right behind you. I'll deliver your copy at the cottage in an hour or less."

"Good." Joe's started to turn away, then stopped. "You're okay? I'm not working you too hard?"

"Probably." She shrugged. "I'll survive. We'll worry about me when we have a firm lead on Eve." She was careful not to show unsteadiness as she walked down the hall toward the waiting room to find Caleb. She was weaker than she had let Joe see, and she would need Caleb's help to get those copies made. She was sure the hospital wouldn't react kindly to having their equipment used by a visitor, and she wasn't in shape for a battle.

Let Caleb do it. He was always ready for battle even when you wouldn't think he was. He was like a lion lying in the sun and just waiting for prey to stroll by.

Not like Trevor. Trevor always coolly picked his battles to gain maximum benefit.

Why had Trevor suddenly popped into her mind? Don't think about him. Concentrate on what she had to do for Eve. The sketch was a step toward finding her, a step toward keeping her alive.

"You mustn't let it hurt you too much. It's not the end, you know."

Death. Ben had been talking about death.

Don't think about that, either. He was a boy caught up in his dreams, and she wouldn't believe that those dreams would foretell a fate she couldn't accept.

Death.

No, Eve was strong. Eve was smart. Even now, she was probably working to get away from that bastard and come back to them.

RIO GRANDE FOREST, COLORADO

"You're right, I don't like to see Kevin like this." Doane stared distastefully at the multitude of tiny red markers that looked like swords stabbing his son's skull. "Kevin wouldn't like it either. He'd be angry with you."

"He's not pretty at the moment, but it's necessary to complete the process. The measurements have to be exact," Eve said. "If it bothers you, go away. I certainly don't want you here. Go talk to Blick on Skype again. Tell him to stay away from my Jane."

"You're being too slow." He grimaced. "I thought you'd be farther along by now."

"It's going as fast as it can go. It's not as if you're giving me much rest." She sat back on her stool and gazed critically at the skull. Doane was right, it wasn't going as smoothly as most reconstructions. Every move she made seemed weighted and slow. "I have to be absolutely sure with the measurements before I can begin the final sculpting. I assure you that I'm not stalling."

"I don't believe you're stalling." His gaze was narrowed on her face. "I think maybe you're sick. You're pale, and you look kind of pinched. You got the flu or something?"

"No." She quickly looked back at the reconstruction. Little sleep and the nausea from breathing the gas had taken its toll, but she had hoped she could hide it from Doane. "How do you expect me to look? I'm worried about Jane, and I want out of here."

"I didn't think you'd wither away. You're tougher than that."

"I'm not withering away. I'm working on your damn skull, aren't I?"

"Not fast enough," he repeated. "Maybe you should eat more. You only ate a few bites at your last meal."

Because she'd been afraid she'd throw up as she'd done when she'd gotten up after finally napping before he'd come for her. She'd managed to get to the bathroom before he'd noticed, but she couldn't expect to be that lucky throughout the day. "I'll try to eat more later. But it won't make any difference in how quickly the reconstruction gets done." She started working again. But she had to slow as the nausea immediately returned. The red markers were blurring before her eyes.

Distract Doane. Don't let him notice.

"If you're going to sit there watching, you might as well talk to me. Tell me about Kevin and how he became this horror."

He flinched. "He's not a horror. Why are you so unfair to him, when you're not with those children you reconstruct?"

"Those children are victims."

"So is Kevin. How can you look at him and not believe that's true?"

"Tell me. The skull is terribly burned. Was he killed in a fire?"

"No. He was shot with a high-powered rifle, then his body was cremated at a funeral home outside Athens." His lips were drawn with pain. "But I was able to save his skull. I made the funeral director give it to me." His words were suddenly charged with anger. "They thought that I didn't know that my Kevin was a target after he walked out of that courtroom. I'm not stupid. Kevin told me that I had to keep myself safe and let him handle those bastards who were going to go after him."

"Target?"

He didn't answer directly. "I didn't want to hide when they arrested him. But I'd always done what

Kevin wanted me to do. He was special." His voice was hoarse. "So special. And they killed him. But they won't get away with it. *He* won't get away with it."

"He?"

"Zander."

"And who is Zander?"

"A monster. He killed my son. I didn't know that—" He shook his head as if to clear it. "I'm not going to talk about Zander. Stop trying to trick me."

"Trick you? I asked a question," she said in frustration. "The only thing I'm trying to do is fight my way through this forest of lies and get myself and Jane out safely. I don't give a damn about this Zander. How could I?"

"That's right, you can't feel anything for him. However, I feel a great deal concerning him."

"Then go after him and let me go."

His gaze went to the skull. "Sometimes I wish I could, but that's not possible."

She drew a deep breath. "Okay, let me try to sort this out. It's obvious this has to be about revenge for the death of your son by this Zander. For some reason, I'm being drawn into the mix because I have the skill to do this reconstruction. But if you have the skull, DNA can be extracted even in this damaged condition. My work has value if there's no clue as to the identity of the victim. Then I can rebuild the face and circulate photos to find out. In this case, I'm not necessary."

"No one is more necessary."

"DNA is almost foolproof."

"And can be faked if you have money and influence."

"Then demand another test. Demand a dozen tests."

He shook his head. "I need you, Eve."

Why was she arguing? It was clear that he was not going to be swayed. Yet she had to make one more attempt. "You obviously had a very close relationship with your son. Do you think that he'd want you to put yourself in danger to exact some kind of revenge? You said he wanted you to keep yourself safe."

"He'd want me to do exactly what I'm doing. Kevin believed in revenge. I can't tell you how many times that he'd say, 'We have to go after that one, Dad. The bad have to be punished. They have to learn that we're the important ones.'"

Eve felt a chill. "And what did he mean by that?"

"What he said." He sadly shook his head. "You don't understand. I'm not explaining it right. Kevin should be here to tell you. It took a little while for me to learn what he meant, but then it was very clear."

"It doesn't sound clear. It sounds sick."

"Are you trying to make me angry?" He got to his feet. "Kevin wasn't sick. He was brilliant and very special. I'm proud to have him for my son." He glared at her. "Just as you're proud to have had Bonnie in your life. You shouldn't speak badly of my son."

"If your son was shot, why wasn't the killer hunted down and captured? It doesn't sound to me as if Kevin was a victim."

"He was a victim. They all wanted him dead."

"Why?"

"Because he was special."

"You keep saying that. In what way was he special?"

"In every way."

"You mentioned him walking out of a courtroom. What was he doing in court?"

"I'm through talking about Kevin. You're not being very understanding."

"Because you're not telling me the entire story, are you?"

"I'll tell you . . . someday. Right now, it might interfere with what you're doing." He turned on his heel. "I'm going out to the truck. I need some air." He looked over his shoulder as he reached the door. His sudden smile warmed his craggy face. "You've been very hard, Eve. You mustn't make us angry. But I forgive you." The next instant, he'd deactivated the gas jet at the front door and left the house.

Eve felt herself go limp. She hadn't known how Doane would respond to that far-from-delicate probing. What she had found out was sketchy at best, but she had gotten a glimpse into a murkiness she didn't want to explore.

But she had to explore it. Just as she had to dive deep into this reconstruction, which was beginning to cause her to want to run the other way.

Okay, assimilate all he had told her and try to put them in some kind of order. It might not be possible, but at least she would have them fresh in her mind to make the connection when she could do it.

Zander. Who was he? Obviously the murderer of Kevin Doane. Why was Kevin killed? Doane insisted that Kevin was innocent of wrongdoing. But the remark about the courtroom was very suspicious.

And Doane's words describing his son's philosophy had been shocking, with shades of egotism or perhaps even schizophrenia. Doane himself was something of a split personality. One moment he appeared everything warm and kind and fatherly, and the next he was talking about revenge and acting out that revenge on the innocent. Jane, Eve, even Toby, the retriever. Which personality would take over in a crucial situation?

She looked up at the gas jets overhead. Another sign of Doane's twisted character. A method of suppression that would keep her from hurting herself and permit him to use her to do the reconstruction. It was supposed to make her think of him in as kindly a light as possible. Instead, it was casting a macabre swirling haze over his actions. That kindliness was like the painted smile of the Joker in that Batman cartoon. She could see no evil, and yet she knew it must be there.

She mustn't jump to conclusions. She had to be cool and calmly analytical.

Screw it, she couldn't be cool about that man. It's what he wanted from her. He wanted to fool her into thinking there was goodness and question every doubt she had of him. How could he even think that she would be fooled after what he had done to her?

Because he had done it so many times before.

The answer came swiftly out of nowhere. He had played the part and been accepted and smiled and thought that he could do it forever. That warm, guy next door, almost fatherly charisma had become his stock-in-trade. He used it with a skill that was totally disarming. A skill that was all the more dangerous because of what it hid beneath.

Why was she so sure that was the key to Doane when it was only a guess?

Because that guess felt . . . right.

She felt the muscles of her stomach clench. Don't be afraid, dammit. He might be more dangerous than she had thought, but he could be handled. He had wanted to talk about his son. He had answered questions. The more she got to know about him, the better chance she had to get out of here.

She glanced at the door. And this might be an opportunity to see what she could find.

She moved quickly to the file case across the room. Locked. She went to the beat-up pine desk next to it.

The middle drawer was unlocked and opened immediately. Paper, pens, nothing of any importance. The drawer on the right was totally empty.

The drawer on the left was locked.

The lock wasn't complicated. A simple tool could probably jimmy it.

What tool? Doane kept the kitchen utensil drawers locked. She'd have to jimmy that lock to jimmy this one, she thought dryly.

Find another way.

What work tools did she have? Most of them were soft, and bendable to work with the clay. But there could be—

The door of the truck slammed outside in the driveway.

He was coming!

She darted across the room, hopped on the stool, and picked up a red marker as the door opened. "You didn't stay out there very long." She lowered her head as she carefully placed the marker beneath the orbital cavity. "Did I run you out, Doane?"

"I came back to say I'm sorry. This is very difficult for you. I realize that you must feel intimidated. You can't know what a fine boy my Kevin was, and I have to understand that words are the only way you have to fight back." His voice was gentle. "Just do your work, and I'll make it easy for you."

"I am working." His voice was so sincere she could almost believe him. "And you're not intimidating me."

He smiled. "Good." He turned and headed for the kitchenette. "Now I'll make us something to eat. At least, our little discord made you a little more lively. You're not pale any longer. Your cheeks are positively rosy. I'm glad you're feeling better."

Eve reached up and touched her cheek. The flush to which he was referring had been caused by panic and running full tilt back to the reconstruction worktable from the desk across the room. She still had a touch of nausea, but she felt alive and active and on the move. "Are you? So am I, Doane." She smiled back at him. "Very glad."

LAKE COTTAGE

"Is it a grave?" Joe asked as he came toward the mound of mud by which Venable was standing. "I thought you might have an answer by the time I got here."

"You knew I'd be careful not to disturb the scene. If this is Dukes, I want to nail the son of a bitch who killed him." Venable's gaze never left the two men who were carefully digging through the mud. "And he didn't want Dukes found right away. He took his time. He covered the area with leaves and branches, and he dug deep."

One of the men stopped digging and looked at Venable. "I've hit something. I see a green tarp, and there's blood on it. Should we go on?"

"Yes, just be careful." Venable took a step closer. "Draw back the tarp. I want to make sure of his ID. After that, I'll turn this over to forensics. But I have to know." He looked down at the tarp and watched them draw back the waterproof plastic.

Joe stepped forward. The dead man was dark-haired, and his gray eyes were wide open and staring into nothingness. His throat was cut from ear to ear. "Dukes?"

Venable nodded and turned on his heel. "Dukes." He walked away from the mound. "He had a wife and a kid. I'll have to call them."

"Very fitting." Joe fell into step with him. "But it would be more fitting for you to zero in on the man who cut his throat. First things first, Venable."

"I have my own priorities." Venable gave him a cold glance. "And I do things my own way."

"Unless you do them wrong. Putting Eve in jeopardy falls into that category."

"I didn't want her hurt. There was a chance she wouldn't be in jeopardy. I had to be sure."

"You just dug up evidence that should convince you."

"Knock it off, Quinn. Nothing you can say is going to influence me more than seeing Dukes with his throat cut. I liked him. He was a good man, and I worked with him for more than four years."

Joe attacked from another angle. "Why would you think that Eve wouldn't be in danger?"

"Because he wasn't the one who—" Venable broke off. "Drop it, Quinn. I'm thinking." He raised his head as they approached the cottage. "There's Jane on the porch. She looks like hell."

"Yes, but I can't convince her to rest. She won't stop." He added deliberately. "She's not like you. She thinks Eve is in danger. She's probably going to go after you when she finds out about Dukes."

"Did she finish the sketch?"

"Yes, she brought a copy with her." He was climbing the steps. "I wanted you to see it."

"Joe?" Jane took a step forward. "What about Dukes?"

"Dead. Throat cut."

"Shit." She had turned paler. She whirled on Venable, and said fiercely, "It could have been Eve. Damn you, Venable. Joe said that you know more about this than you're telling him. You talk to us."

Venable's face was without expression. "Joe said you have a sketch."

She opened her pad and thrust the copy at him.

He gazed at the sketch for a moment and handed it back to her. "You're extraordinarily good, Jane."

"That's all you're going to say?" Her gaze was narrowed on his face. "You recognized him, didn't you?"

He walked over to the porch rail and stared out at the lake. "I hoped it wouldn't be him. Everything pointed in his direction, but there was the smallest chance that it could be someone else. Because of her profession, Eve does seem to attract a wide variety of lethal weirdos."

"Who is he?" Joe asked hoarsely.

Venable didn't answer immediately. Then he shrugged. "His name is James Doane."

"More," Jane said. "Tell us more."

Venable shook his head. "Later. I've got to call Dukes's wife, and then start trying to issue a few warnings."

"If you know his name, do you know where we can start on finding him?" Jane asked.

"Right now?" He shook his head. "The last address I have is a house in Goldfork, Colorado, where he lived until last week. There's no possibility he'd take Eve there. He'd know I'd be having it watched."

Joe tensed. "He's aware you knew his address?"

"Of course." He added simply, "I've had him under protective custody for the last five years."

"What?"

"I told you, later." He met Joe's gaze. "You're going to get what you want from me, but it's going to make waves like a tsunami. I have to warn people it's coming so I can minimize the damage. I'll talk to you as soon as I can."

There was no pushing Venable any more at the moment, Joe thought. It would be useless. Venable had already committed, and he had to give him a little more space. "Not long, Venable." He frowned thoughtfully. "Doane?"

"You're already trying to work it out for yourself. Before you get on the phone and start checking, you'd better have another name other than the one we gave him." He took out his phone. "Relling. James Herbert Relling."

RIO GRANDE FOREST, COLORADO

Doane was asleep at last.

Eve could hear the steadiness of his breathing. It had taken him over an hour to settle down on his couch and another twenty minutes before she could take the chance that he was sound enough asleep so that she could start to move. Doane must have been as charged as she had been after he had opened up the floodgates about Kevin this afternoon.

She gazed up at the socket in the ceiling over the bed.

Two more minutes, and she'd start moving. She just hoped there was still gas in that line. She had opened that nozzle four times, and the last time it had not seemed to have a very powerful effect on her. That could mean that she was not getting enough gas or that she was becoming partially immune to it. She hoped it was the latter. Perhaps this time she'd leave it open a little longer and find which was true.

It would be a risk.

Hell, everything she did was a risk. This was a way out, possibly the only way out. She had to know if it was working or if she had to search out another path. Joe would say it was reckless, and she should wait for him to come for her. He had tried to free her to make a move, but she knew he didn't want her to make that move without him.

Joe.

She closed her eyes and let the thought of him surround her. His tea-colored eyes, the way he moved, the quiet that hid all the leashed fierceness, the intelligence that was both a challenge and source of pride to her. Thinking about him soothed her, and she wanted to cling to it.

She couldn't do it. She couldn't rely on him. He was her friend and her lover, but this was her battle. She had to make her own decisions.

I'm sorry, Joe. Run toward me. I'll run toward you. One way or another, we'll come together. That's the way it's always been.

She opened her eyes.

Two minutes had passed. Doane's breathing had stayed even and perhaps had deepened. Time to move.

She slipped from the bed and began to fold it up in the middle.

No sound.

Slowly.

She knew the drill now and it took her less than a minute to climb up on the bed and reach for the nozzle to unscrew it.

She drew a deep breath and opened the line.

Carnations.

She started to close the line.

Wait. A little more. Test it.

Carnations.

Dizziness.

Blackness, closing in.

She frantically turned the screw.

Too much. Too much.

Get down.

No noise.

Hold on.

Don't black out.

Hurry. Get down. You'll ruin everything if he finds out what you've been doing.

She reached the floor, staggered, and fell to her knees.

Carnations.

Had she left that line open or was the smell just still in her nostrils?

If she'd left it open, she had to go back up and close it.

Not now. She wouldn't be able to manage yet. Too weak. Much too weak.

She curled up in a ball on the floor.

Dizzy.

Darkness . . .

Stupid. She should have been sure that gas line was closed. She could vaguely remember hurriedly turning the screw but maybe—

"Stop worrying, Mama. You closed it."

Bonnie?

She opened her eyes to see Bonnie leaning against the folded bed a few yards away. Her daughter was dressed as always in her Bugs Bunny T-shirt and jeans, and her curly red hair gleamed even in the dimness of the room. So little, so beautiful, so beloved.

Bonnie suddenly chuckled. "Don't be sappy, Mama. I was never beautiful except to you. Red hair and freckles on my nose?"

"Don't make fun of me. You were—you are beautiful. It's spirit that makes beauty."

"Then I guess I should be beautiful because I'm most certainly a spirit." Her smile faded. "You shouldn't have doubled that dose of gas, Mama. You scared me. I was worried about you. I was afraid you were going to fall."

"I had to make sure that I was—"

"I know why you were doing it," Bonnie interrupted. "But you shouldn't have done it. It was working. Your body is becoming accustomed to the gas."

"You should have come and told me that before the fact," Eve said tartly. "It would have saved me a lot of trouble."

"I couldn't come to you. I've been trying. There's too much darkness holding me away. He doesn't want me near you. Sometimes it's easier to use dreams, but that didn't work either. I wouldn't have been able to come this time if the gas hadn't knocked you out. You're deep enough so that I could slip in."

So it was a dream. Sometimes she couldn't tell the difference with Bonnie. "Ben said that he'd dreamed about you."

"I had to find a way to warn you. I was helpless. He wouldn't let me near you."

"Doane?"

"No, the other one."

"What other one?"

"Kevin."

Eve felt a chill stiffen every muscle. "Kevin is dead."

"Not as long as Doane is alive. Kevin won't let go.

There's some . . . connection. Just as there is with you and me."

"Bonnie."

"I didn't want to scare you, but you have to know." She shook her head as she looked at Eve. *"Mama, you know there are things that do go bump in the night. Not many that are evil. Occasionally, something slips, or there's a force that carries over. Those are usually taken care of by the natural order. But there's something helping from your side. Very strong, very powerful."*

"I don't know what you're talking about."

"I don't know very much myself. I learn more every day I'm here. It made me afraid when I could see all that darkness heading toward you and couldn't see any way to help you. I couldn't even reach Joe. He was too close to you."

"You might not have reached him, but you managed to make him extremely nervous, didn't you?"

"Part of that was me, but most of it was Joe's instincts. He's lived with darkness for a long time. He can sense it coming."

"Yes, he can. But neither one of us could see that Jane would be pulled into this nightmare." She met Bonnie's eyes. "Did you, baby?"

She shook her head. "Jane closes me out. I can't connect with her either."

Eve nodded slowly. Jane knew that Eve believed Bonnie came to her and had never argued or tried to dissuade her. But she had never accepted Bonnie as anything but a comforting dream that gave Eve happiness. "It's not that she has any ill feelings toward you, baby."

"Are you trying to keep me from getting my feelings hurt?" Bonnie was smiling again. "You love her, and that makes me love her. I understand Jane. Someday we'll come together." Her smile ebbed, then faded. "Though I wish it was going to be different."

Eve stiffened. "What do you mean?"

"I'm not sure. The darkness . . ."

"Listen to me; nothing is going to hurt Jane," she said fiercely. "We have to keep that from happening. She's already been hurt because of that bastard. She's not going to be hurt again."

"Sometimes you can't stop it from happening."

Panic surged through her. "Don't say that. If I try hard enough, I can do anything. Why do you think I'm working on Kevin's reconstruction? I'll stall Doane until I can either get away or Joe can find me. And I told him he had to keep Jane safe."

"Who is going to tell Jane? Do you think she's not going to try to find you? She loves you. I think she loves you as much as I do, Mama."

"Then I just have to work faster, harder."

Bonnie made a face. "Not too much faster. It's good that I was able to get to you after that last whiff of gas, but I don't know how dangerous an overdose would be."

"Some stakes are worth a little risk."

"You're willing to risk too much," Bonnie said soberly. "You've been that way since I was taken from you. I have to fight to keep you from coming to me too soon. Thank God, you have Joe and Jane as anchors."

Beloved anchors, Eve thought, but at moments like this when Bonnie was close, and she was reminded *of what she had lost, it was difficult to remember that there was a balance that must be maintained. Bonnie had been her whole life before she had lost her. She swallowed to ease her tight throat. "It's hard sometimes, baby."*

"For me, too," Bonnie said softly. "But we can do it, we can wait. They need you, Mama. And you need them."

"I'm aware of all that." She smiled with an effort. "Stop lecturing me, young lady. Just because you've passed into the great beyond doesn't guarantee that you know everything."

"I wish it did." Bonnie shook her head. "I'm learning, but it's not fast enough. There should be some way to get to you when I need to do it." She repeated soberly. "It scared me."

"Particularly since you want me to cut down on inhaling that gas. By all means, apply yourself."

"I will, but I can't be sure—" She suddenly stiffened. "The gas is wearing off. You're beginning to come up through the layers. I'll lose you soon."

"No."

"I can't help it. I can feel the darkness sweeping me away from you. He's pushing, smothering, me. Such hate . . . I can feel the terrible hate and anger Kevin has for me. He wants to be what he was when he was alive. He wants to feel the power again. Over me . . . over you. He doesn't want me near you. And he's so strong . . ."

Eve could feel it, too. Bonnie was fading away, in and out of focus. "Bonnie!"

"Hush, I have to tell you . . . Doane is—it's hard

not to believe him. But you mustn't do it. It's what he does. It was his part of that horror. No matter what he tells you, it's either a lie or twisted so out of shape that it becomes what he wants it to be."

"What horror?"

"No time. You'll find out. And don't take too much of that gas."

"I heard you the first time." She could feel Bonnie ebbing away from her, and she was trying desperately to hold on to her. "And I told you that I only wanted to be sure that it was working. It's not as if I like the stuff. It makes me sick to my stomach."

"That's not the gas, Mama."

"Of course it's the gas. What else?"

"It's him. He knows what you're doing, and he's trying to stop you." She was fading away in the distance. "It's Kevin . . ."

She was gone.

And Eve was once again fully awake.

She drew a shaky breath and slowly opened her eyes. No Bonnie.

Of course there was no red-haired little girl to lighten this darkness.

Eve felt the familiar sadness and regret and yearning that always came when Bonnie left her. She wanted her back, to see her, to feel the bittersweet joy.

But Bonnie had tried and given her what she could, and Eve was warmer and more hopeful for her attempt.

She got to her feet and started to carefully unfold the bed and rumple the covers.

No sound.

Make sure that Doane was not aware of—

Sick.

She dropped down on the bed and drew her knees up as waves of nausea hit her. She bit down hard on her lower lip.

It's Kevin.

If it was Doane's son, then he was attacking at full force and speed. Lord, she was sick.

Things do go bump in the night.

Hold it off. Think of something else.

She took several slow, deep breaths.

That was better . . .

No, it wasn't. The nausea was back.

Don't throw up. Fight it.

Whether it was the gas or some spirit from beyond the grave, it could be fought.

It was more violent than the other bouts she'd experienced, which she'd attributed to the gas. Punishment?

Or maybe it wasn't Kevin but his father who was sensing her actions and was influencing her in some psychological—

Stop analyzing. Use your will and your mind and just get over this.

It took over an hour before the sickness was gone. Even then, it subsided like a surly dragon backing into his cave.

And Eve felt wrung out and weak . . . and triumphant.

Get thee behind me, Satan. Or Kevin, or whoever you are.

She turned over in bed. Go to sleep or at least rest.

She wouldn't have much time before Doane was rousing and unlocking the door. He was growing more impatient with every hour. Sometime today, she'd try to find a way to get into that desk and see what was inside. She had to gauge Doane's strength, and only knowledge of the enemy would permit her to do that.

His part in the horror, Bonnie had said.

What horror, Bonnie?

CHAPTER

11

LAKE COTTAGE

Go to bed, Jane," Joe said as he came out on the porch. "I'll wake you as soon as I hear something."

She straightened on the porch swing. "I'm okay. I've been dozing. I had to call Devon and check on Toby, but afterward, I kind of drifted off. You haven't heard anything from your old buddies in the FBI?" She grimaced. "Don't they know that—" She stopped and wearily shook her head. "I know you're doing your best. But you've been making calls and sending e-mails for hours. Something should be breaking."

"My thought exactly," he said grimly. "But there are no records on Doane or Relling or whatever his name is. At least none that anyone can access. He doesn't exist in the FBI database."

"Is that possible? Cover-up?"

"That's my guess. But whoever did it had to be high up on the chain."

"No wonder Venable felt safe giving you the names.

He knew it probably wasn't going to do you any good."
Her lips tightened. "I'm tired of being patient with Venable and waiting for him to talk." She got to her feet.
"Where is he?"

"Not on the property. I've already checked. And he's
not answering his phone."

"So he dangled a promise to help, then took off?"

"He doesn't give his word easily. I think he'll keep
it in his own time." He muttered a curse. "But I'm not
going to let him have that time."

"And how are we going to locate him?"

"I've already started. He may be CIA, but we have a
history together, and I can track him." He paused. "But
I want to explore one other avenue first. I went back to
Blick's records and started digging for a connection
with someone, anyone, during the years he was in the
service."

"Why that period?"

"I was looking for a reason for the CIA to be involved. CIA operates outside the country. Blick was
stationed outside the country during most of his Army
years. First, in Germany, then in Turkey. It was more
likely that Venable would have made contact with Blick
and Doane at one of those places."

"Logical. Did you find out anything more about
Blick?"

"I'm waiting for a call from Army records. I pulled
every string I had with the FBI to get them to put a rush
on it. I should be hearing anytime."

"And you were going to send me off to bed so that I
wouldn't have to gnaw my nails waiting to hear." She
smiled without mirth. "You're trying to protect me

again. Don't do it. The only one you should worry about is Eve."

"No, I should protect you, too. I promised Eve when she called." He reached out and squeezed her shoulder. "Not that I wouldn't anyway. But it would help if I had a little help when I'm not around. Where the hell is Caleb? Why didn't he come back to the cottage with you?"

She shrugged. "How do I know? We're not joined at the hip. I told you that I dropped him off at the airport on my way here." She gazed at him curiously. "And why do you care? He's definitely not your favorite person."

"No, he's not. But I've never met a more lethal individual. He's self-serving and damn volatile, but he comes in handy at times." He met her eyes. "And he has a reason to keep you alive."

"I have a reason to keep myself alive. I have to get Eve away from Doane. And I don't need Caleb or anyone else standing guard over me when they could be concentrating on doing that, too." She gave him a quick kiss on the cheek. "And that goes for you, Joe. Now, I'm going inside to make us a cup of coffee while you focus on Venable. It's driving me crazy just sitting here and—" She stiffened. "Headlights." Her gaze was fastened on the car coming down the lake road. "Venable?"

"Maybe."

But as the car drew up before the cottage, the porch lights fell on the windshield, and she recognized the driver. "Not Venable. It's Caleb." She started down the steps. "Speak of the devil."

"That's too close a comparison," Joe said dryly. "But

for once I'm glad to see him. That may not happen again."

"Then be polite to him. We owe him. I've been using him as a pilot since London. He didn't have to—" She stopped on the bottom step, her eyes widening as she saw who was in the passenger seat next to Caleb. "What the hell? Margaret?"

"None other," Caleb said as he got out of the driver's seat. "If I can wake her up. She's been sleeping since she got into the car at the airport. She curled up like a kitten, and it was lights out." He shook his head. "Very rude, Margaret."

"I was tired." Margaret's hand covered a yawn. "I had to work really hard to find a safe way to get here. If you'd let me come with you, it would have been much better, Caleb."

"I promised Jane that I wouldn't encourage you. Isn't that right, Jane?"

"It doesn't look to me as if you kept that promise," Jane said grimly as she watched Margaret get out of the car. The girl's hair was tousled and her shirt and jeans rumpled, but as she came awake, her smile was just as sunny as Jane remembered. "Is that why you had me drop you off at the airport, Caleb?"

Caleb nodded. "Margaret called me from San Juan and told me she thought she had a lift to get her here and asked me to pick her up." He shrugged. "What could I do? I couldn't let her wander around a strange city alone."

"Evidently, she manages to wander around the world by herself just fine," she said. "Look how she got to Summer Island."

"That's different. You wouldn't have wanted to accept the responsibility."

He was right. The reason she had insisted he not take Margaret was so that Margaret wouldn't become involved. Now that the girl had overridden all the obstacles Jane had tried to put in her path, she couldn't just toss her out. But it didn't make Jane any less exasperated with her. "Why, Margaret? I told you that I didn't need you."

"But you don't know that." Margaret reached in the backseat and brought out her duffel. "I can be very useful. By the way, I called Devon from the airport after I landed, and she said Toby was on his feet and very spry."

"I know. I called her a few hours ago. Stop changing the subject."

"I was just reminding you that I'm a proven commodity in the useful department. I thought it couldn't hurt." Margaret smiled back over her shoulder. "And Caleb tried to do what you wanted. Don't be angry with him."

"Are you trying to protect him? Don't waste the effort. He doesn't need it."

"Sure he does. We all need a little help now and then." She made a face at Caleb. "But I could have used a little more to get me out of San Juan. If Mark Trevor hadn't put me in touch with Gadsden Canine Rescue, it would have taken me a lot longer to get here."

Jane stiffened. "Trevor. You know Mark Trevor?"

"Well, not really know him," Margaret said. "I met him in the waiting room at the hospital. He was very curious about me when I told him I was there to visit you. He already knew a lot about what had happened on the island. He said he knew quite a few people around the Caribbean, and if I needed help, to give him a call." She beamed at them. "So I did."

"You didn't tell me that Trevor was involved in getting you out of San Juan," Caleb said softly. "Why not?"

"You didn't ask me. No, that's not quite true. Trevor said that it would be better if I didn't mention him to you. He didn't care about Jane's knowing, but he said you were a bit touchy where he's concerned. Are you?"

"You could say that." He glanced at Jane. "It didn't matter to him that you didn't want her here. He wanted to remind you that he was still in your life."

Margaret nodded. "I thought that might be it." She looked beyond Jane to Joe, who was still standing on the top step. "Hi, Detective Quinn. I didn't mean to ignore you, but it's a little tense. I really think I can help find Eve Duncan. Is it all right if I stay a little while and find out what's happening? I won't get in the way."

Joe gazed at her a moment, and said, "Why not? You're here, and there's not much we can do unless we turn you over to be deported." He shook his head. "I don't want to do that. You helped save Jane's dog, and Eve and I love Toby. We can work out the legalities later."

Her smile widened to brilliance. "Thank you. I'll see that you don't get in trouble because of me." She turned to Jane. "See, everything is going to work out. Detective Quinn knows that my being here is a good thing."

"I didn't say that," Joe said dryly.

"But you're very smart, and you sense things. Of course you realize that I'll be able to help." She started up the steps. "Would you mind if I took a shower and washed the dog smell off? I don't mind it, but you all might. I was with six rescue dogs on that flight to Atlanta, and I had to be practically on top of Bruno, a German shepherd, who has nerve problems. That's why the rescue group let me come along with them. Bruno was terrified of flying and they usually had to dope him. But he'd grown almost immune over the last couple years of use. I promised that I'd keep him calm and happy." She added, "And that I'd work with him when I was finished here and make sure that he'd be okay with flying without meds."

"You can do that?" Joe's eyes were narrowed. "Jane told me some fairly amazing things about you. I found it . . . interesting."

"I can do it." She met his gaze. "And Jane doesn't really know anything about me. What she does know, she's not sure she believes. I knew I was going to have a tough time convincing her to let me do payback." She tilted her head, gazing at him. "But you're thinking that I might be useful to you. I think you've already decided on a way."

"Possibly."

"Joe," Jane said. "She's not much more than a kid."

"Let me think about it." Joe turned away. "Why don't you make that coffee while I decide whether I'm going to take her up on her offer."

"You do have something in mind," Jane said. "What?"

But Joe had already gone into the house.

"Am I invited for coffee?" Caleb asked. "Or am I to be punished for dumping Margaret on your doorstep?"

"You're invited." Jane grimaced. "She would have found some way to get out here from the airport even if she had to hitchhike."

"You're right," Margaret said. "But hitchhiking can be dangerous. I preferred to tap Caleb." She chuckled. "Though he can be sort of risky, too. But not to me."

"Don't count on that," Caleb said softly. "I don't like the idea of your juggling and pitting Trevor against me to get what you want." He held up his hand as she started to speak. "And you went after Quinn to get around Jane's objections. You're very wily, Margaret. All that sunny charm may cover something darker."

She shook her head. "I'm a survivor," she said simply. "I've had to be, Caleb. And I'm not some Pollyanna phony. I try to stay away from darkness. It's always out there, but the only way I can get through it is to let in a little light now and then. Nothing wrong with that."

"Sounds pretty saccharine to me." He shrugged. "However, no one can say I'm full of sweetness and light."

"You can say that again," Jane said. "Now stop being cynical and give her a break." She opened the door. "The bathroom is down the hall and to your left, Margaret. When you've washed the travel and dog smell off, come out, and we'll talk." She met her gaze. "But no matter what Joe says, I don't know if I'm going to let you—"

"I know. I know. But you respect Joe Quinn. That's half the battle." She was walking quickly down the hall. "And I have to have information if I'm going to help at all. He's a detective and razor-sharp. If he thinks I'll be useful, he'll share. You might ration info to keep me safe."

Very canny, Jane thought. "You might get more than you bargain for. Joe is frantic, and he'll do anything to get Eve back." Her lips twisted. "Don't trust me, either. I'm trying to remember to be civilized, but I'll probably fold at the first hint that Doane's going to hurt her. You'd be much safer if you got the hell away from both of us."

Margaret's head swiftly turned. "Doane? You have a name?" Her eyes were suddenly glittering. "See, information. It can be magic. How did you find out that—"

"Go take your shower. I may tell you later. Or I may not."

"I'll hurry." Margaret disappeared into the bathroom and slammed the door.

"Are you softening?" Caleb asked.

"If I were softening, then I'd run her away from here. The word is hardening." She wearily rubbed her temple. "I wish she hadn't come. It makes it too easy to take advantage of her."

"She wouldn't consider it taking advantage. You heard her, payback." He shrugged. "I would probably take advantage, but then I'm a callous bastard. Your decision." He glanced at the kitchen bar. "Now I believe you said you were going to give me a cup of coffee. You're the one who looks like you need one. Sit down. I'll make it for us."

"I can do it."

"I'm sure you can, but I didn't take a bullet a couple

days ago." He was already around the bar. "It's more reasonable to let—"

"For God's sake, stop arguing with him, Jane," Joe said roughly as he came out of the bedroom. "Keep what strength you have. The last thing we need is for you to collapse and have to go back in the hospital."

"Don't be ridiculous. I'm—" Jane stopped, and her heart skipped a beat. "You're upset. What's wrong? Did you hear something about Eve?"

"No, I got a report on Blick's overseas years from Army personnel. It was absolutely clear and uneventful until he reached Turkey. Then there were three instances of fights in bars and a few run-ins with the locals."

"That wasn't in the report that Venable gave us."

"And therefore very suspect. The bar episodes were very violent but not lethal. Nothing that got him thrown in jail, but the incidents were written up. The Turkish complaints were because Blick was found in a private residential area where foreign soldiers were discouraged from going. He was with another man, who ran away and left Blick to take the blame when he and Blick were spotted near a Muslim girls' school." Joe added, "Blick wouldn't reveal his identity when questioned by the Turks. Nor when he was released to the U.S. military police. He claimed he was alone, and the Turks were crazy. He said he was drunk and was wandering aimlessly when they picked him up."

"He never revealed the name of the man who was with him?"

Joe shook his head. "And the charges against him

were dropped the next day. Blick was shipped back to the States a month later."

"A cover-up? Venable?"

"Maybe. But covering up what? And why?"

"Blick seems fairly ordinary up to the time when he teamed up with that man in Turkey. And he was willing to risk being thrown into a Turkish jail to protect him. From what we've learned about Blick's background, that's unusual."

"And maybe the reason that Blick only got a slap on the wrist and was shipped back to the U.S. was to protect Blick's buddy, too," Caleb said. "It's a game of maybes and ifs, isn't it? Anything else, Quinn? The connection with Venable?"

Joe shook his head. "Only that I'm doing a scan of the newspapers of those months Blick was in Turkey. I'll keep on looking, but nothing of international importance occurred as far as I can see."

"But Venable seldom operates on the surface," Jane said.

Joe grimaced. "Almost never." He paused. "There were two Muslim clerics who were killed in rather suspicious accidents in Istanbul. They were reputedly responsible for arranging for a suicide bomber to kill four U.S. Army border guards in Iraq."

"A revenge killing." Jane frowned. "That doesn't sound like Venable. He wouldn't let emotion rule. He'd have a reason before he'd turn loose a team that might spark an international incident."

Joe nodded. "And there was also a story about the disappearance of a young student on her way from Istanbul to her parents' home in Delhi. Take your pick."

"That wouldn't involve the CIA either."

"Who the hell knows what he'd do?" Joe said. "But we're going to find out. I'm tired of making guesses." He checked his watch. "Time's up. I'm going after him." He turned to Caleb. "Stay with Jane. Don't let her out—" His cell phone rang, and he stiffened as he read the ID. "Venable."

He punched the volume and access. "Where the hell are you, Venable?"

"Not there obviously. I gather by your tone that you're frustrated. You didn't get very far with checking out Relling?"

"You knew I wouldn't. No Doane. No Relling. You were very careful about erasing his records."

"Yes, but sometimes there's a slip," Venable said. "I'm glad to know they did a good job."

"So good I may break your neck if I find out that what you did made Eve a target."

"I can understand that. I never meant it to happen, but I should have been more careful." Venable added, "But you can tell me all that in person in a couple hours. I just called to let you know that I'm at General John Tarther's house in Virginia to break the news to him about Doane, but I have a plane waiting, and I'll be on my way back as soon as it's done."

"Tarther? Another hint to dangle? That won't cut it."

"I wouldn't have mentioned his name if I hadn't intended to take you into my confidence."

"Everything, Venable."

Venable paused, then finally said, "Everything." He hung up.

"Who is Tarther?"

Jane turned to see Margaret standing at the bathroom door, fully dressed in jeans and shirt but her hair wrapped in a towel. Her eyes were sparkling with curiosity as she came forward. "General Tarther? I've never heard of him."

"I've heard of him," Jane said. "He was famous. But it was a long time ago. Iraq, Joe?"

Joe nodded as he hung up the phone. "And Afghanistan. He retired years ago."

"What's happening?" Margaret asked, removing the towel from her head. "I only got to hear the last few words. And why would this Tarther—"

"We don't know," Joe interrupted. "But it seems that we're going to find out."

"But am *I* going to find out? Are you going to let me help find Eve?" Margaret asked shrewdly.

"Why not?" Joe was suddenly smiling recklessly. "If you can prove you're able to do it." He took her arm and pulled her toward the door. "We have a couple hours before Venable gets here, and I don't want to twiddle my thumbs waiting. Jane said that you have a talent that the rest of us don't possess. Even if I believed her, I'm not sure that communing with forest creatures would be of any worth in tracking down Doane."

"I'm not sure either. It's never a certainty," Margaret said. "Where are we going?"

"Into the woods. Dukes, one of Venable's agents, had his throat cut about a mile from the lake. That's all we know. The area was pristine clean. Forensics has been all over the area and not found anything yet. I want to know how he died and if Doane left any clues that we haven't found."

Jane shook her head as she followed them out on the porch. "Joe, how can she possibly tell you anything about a murder that took place while she wasn't even in the country?"

He stared Margaret directly in the eye. "Can you?"

She was silent a moment. "Perhaps."

His smile flashed tiger bright as he pulled her out of the house. "Then let's go see, Margaret."

CHAPTER

12

You're taking those red markers out of his face," Doane said approvingly as he leaned forward in his chair. "I'm glad. He looked like a demon, and Kevin is such a handsome boy."

"He's no boy. He's a man." Eve corrected herself as she checked the final depth measurements. "He was a man. I'd judge him to be late twenties when he died."

"You're trying to hurt me by reminding me he's no longer with me." Doane smiled gently. "You can't do that when I know that you feel so deeply about your Bonnie. I'm sure you feel she's still by your side."

Bonnie sitting leaning against the rollaway bed and talking to her.

"Every now and then. Every parent who has lost a child clings to memories."

"It's more than memories. Maybe it's that way with you, but it's different with Kevin and me. Sometimes a soul is so strong, it fights free." He tilted his head as he once more leaned back in his chair. "You're working very slowly today. I thought it would go faster after you got those voodoo markers out of him."

"I have to be careful. I start the sculpting process soon, and I have to have an accurate foundation on which to build." And she was sick again, fighting the nausea. It was worse now than it had been before when she had thought it had been caused by breathing that gas.

It's not the gas, it's Kevin.

I'm beginning to believe you, baby.

She stared at the mass of clay that was the reconstruction and fought the nausea. No defined features, cavities where the eyes, nose, and lips would be, just bold swathes of clay. There should have been no hint of personality yet in this unfinished state. She seldom felt a connection with the victim until she began the final sculpting.

Dear God, but she was feeling a connection now. It was faint and dark and brimming with menace.

"I'd hate to think you were stalling," Doane said. "Kevin wouldn't like it. It's important that you finish the reconstruction as soon as possible so that we can go on with what we have to do."

"And what do you have to do?"

Doane didn't answer.

"Kill me?"

"Do I look like a man who would kill a kind, worthwhile woman like you?"

"No, but I think that appearances don't reflect the true picture where you're concerned." She paused. "Have you killed anyone before, Doane?"

"No."

She waited a moment, then asked, "Has Kevin ever killed anyone? Was that why he was in court?"

Doane didn't answer.

"You don't want to tell me the truth? I'll find out sometime. I'll keep probing until I know everything about you and your precious Kevin. Why not tell me yourself?"

"It would poison you against Kevin. It might affect the reconstruction."

"You haven't researched me very thoroughly if you believe that. I don't let anything interfere with the validity of my work." She shrugged. "Who knows? It might make it come faster. Truth can be a great clarifier. Was Kevin in that court because he killed someone?"

He slowly nodded.

"Who?"

"No one important."

She stared at him in shock. "Every human being is important. Every death diminishes us."

"That's trite nonsense." He grimaced. "I used to believe that kind of bullshit before Kevin taught me the truth."

"Kevin taught you? The father teaches the son."

"No other man had a son like my Kevin. He was . . . extraordinary." Doane's face was luminous, his eyes glittering. "It took me a long while to understand that there are special people born in this world to rule and others to follow. If Kevin had lived, he would have been a leader, no, he would have been more. He would have been a god. He told me once that Hitler would have changed the world and been worshipped as he deserved if he'd been a little smarter." He added simply, "Kevin was much smarter. He only needed a little more time before he would have been able to control himself and move up where he belonged."

"Control himself?" She moistened her lips. "Who was this 'unimportant' person that your son murdered?"

He didn't speak for a moment, and then he shrugged impatiently. "It doesn't really matter what I say, does it? I've tried so hard to do what Kevin taught me to do, but it's coming to an end. I believe he's ready for it to come to an end. I can't make you believe in me. So what difference does it make?"

"Whom did Kevin murder?"

He was silent again. "Just a child. Her name isn't important. She would have been glad to sacrifice herself if Kevin had time to explain how vital her death was to him. He needed a release to keep him functioning properly. If she'd gotten to know him, she would have loved him. Everyone loved Kevin."

She closed her eyes for an instant as the horror hit home. "I understand that Hitler had his fans, too. But I don't believe that they would have been glad to die for him."

"That's why Kevin would have been greater than Hitler. He could persuade anyone to do anything."

"Including you."

"When I understood that was my duty to him. Yes, I did anything he wanted me to do, gave him anything he wanted." He met her eyes. "I'm not ashamed. I'm proud of everything I did for Kevin."

Eve's head was spinning. Images of Hitler. Ugly

visions of a dead child. How old had that child been when Kevin had killed her? As old as Bonnie when she'd been taken? "He still has you under his spell even though he's dead. Don't you realize that he was crazy? All of that bull about his needing a release is straight out of serial-killer textbooks. He obviously had delusions of grandeur, but that isn't unusual either. He was a self-indulgent monster who was using you. He probably cared nothing for you."

"He *did* care." His face was flushed. "That's all you know. Kevin loved me. When he found out that he was going to have to go to court, he wouldn't let me come to him and made sure that I'd be protected no matter what happened to him. I didn't want to go. I wanted to stay and help him. But he said he had Blick if he needed to escape. Blick would never leave him."

"Blick was Kevin's friend?" Her lips twisted. "Or should I say follower?"

"He worshipped Kevin. They were both in the Army, but Kevin was in the Special Forces when they met in Istanbul. The Army taught Kevin to kill, and he became magnificent at it."

"Like a god? But then the Army didn't know Kevin needed his little releases, did they? Did Blick know that executing the enemy wasn't enough for your son?"

"Not at first. But Blick could see his power, and Kevin let him come close to him. Kevin showed him how exciting it was to break all the rules and take what you want. He was grooming him."

"To become a monster like your son?"

"I'm getting tired of your sarcasm." His voice was

suddenly harsh. "I knew you wouldn't understand Kevin."

"Then why did you try to explain him to me? Did you want absolution for what you did to help him?"

"Absolution? No." He got to his feet. "I told you, I'm proud to be his father, proud of everything I did to help him." His voice lowered to silky softness. "I told you because Kevin wanted you to know. I *feel* it. He doesn't like it that you don't fear him. You know he's here, but you're strong enough to resist him, like the other one."

"What other one?" she whispered.

"You know."

Bonnie.

I'm fighting to keep him away, but he's getting stronger.

"Well, you've told me, and I'm still not afraid of him." But she was struggling to keep her voice from shaking from the shock she was feeling. "Do you know they made fun of Hitler during World War II? He was a monster, but get beyond that ugliness, and he was only a cruel little man who was easy to ridicule."

"Oh, that was another age. Kevin agreed with you. He admired Hitler, but he was also critical. He told me that manipulating al-Qaeda and the terrorist groups was the way to go. He was already making great strides insinuating himself into a group in Pakistan by feeding them information, when those Army bastards caught him and threw him into jail."

"Too bad it wasn't the al-Qaeda. They would have played with him a long time before they killed him."

Doane looked as if she'd struck him. "Bitch." His hands balled into fists at his sides. "You'll pay for that." He drew a deep breath. "I've got to get out of here for a while, or I'll beat you until you can't sit upright on that stool. Kevin wouldn't like that. He has such fine plans for you."

For the first time, Doane's mask was slipping. Push him a little more. "He has no plans. He's dead and gone, Doane."

"Is he?" He was striding toward the front door. "He's not gone to me. I'm not gone to him. Sometimes I feel him near me just like when he was alive. I even dream about him. If he's gone, then why do I feel he has plans for you and your Bonnie?" He paused at the door. "Keep on working. If you don't have more done when I come back, I'll call Blick and have a talk with him about Jane MacGuire." The door slammed behind him.

Eve straightened on the stool. Get control. The gloves were off, and it might be better that way. She had goaded Doane until he had jettisoned all the games he'd been playing. Now they were out in the open and face-to-face.

Not quite. There were still blanks to be filled in, but that could come later. Doane was no longer pretending to be the warm, fatherly guy next door. It had been bizarre and horrible watching his expressions change and twist. The man who had strode out of here had been completely different from the mask he had worn since she had met him.

"I've *got* you. I can see you, Doane," she whispered. "And I'll learn how to manipulate you just the way your dear Kevin did. Neither one of you is going to beat us."

Us. The word had come naturally, instinctively. Had she been referring to Jane or Joe?

Or Bonnie.

She felt a wave of nausea abruptly wash over her, and she had to grab hard at the wood of the worktable to keep from falling off the stool.

Not the gas. Not the gas. Not the gas. Bonnie's words flying back to her.

Her gaze was blurry as she stared at the face of the reconstruction. Kevin's face.

She could feel it pulling her, smothering her.

Things that do go bump in the night. He's so strong, Mama.

We'll beat him, baby.

But not by sitting here right now. Doane had given her an opportunity, and she had to take it.

The desk. The locked drawer.

She shook her head to clear it, then reached for the steel spatula she'd been using to smooth the clay. It had no sharp edges she could use to pick the lock, but it was fine steel and might be strong enough to pry the drawer open. It didn't matter any longer that Doane remain ignorant that she was trying to rifle the desk. The conflict between them was now stark and without subterfuge on either side.

Move.

She slipped down from the stool and ran across the room toward the desk.

Damn, her knees were weak.

And she could feel a tension in the middle of her back between her shoulder blades.

As if someone was staring balefully at her.

Imagination.

That blob of clay held no life.

But could it hold death?

Ignore it.

Easy to say. The cords of her neck were so tense she could hardly breathe.

Go *away*.

She closed her mind and concentrated as she inserted the spatula in the opening of the drawer.

She carefully worked it back and forth, chiseling at the soft wood around the lock. The spatula was as strong as she'd hoped. Strong enough?

A sound from outside.

She tensed and listened.

No footstep. No slamming truck door. Just a faint sound that might be Doane's voice talking on his phone.

Good. It might keep him occupied a little longer. She started working frantically at the drawer.

A moment later, the wood splintered around the lock!

Yes.

She jerked the drawer open.

She stared at the contents of the drawer in shock and disappointment.

An old beat-up photo album?

Memories that warm the heart, Doane had said.

And beneath it was the folded jacket she had worn the morning Doane had taken her.

Where the hell was her phone and her gun?

She lifted the tan album out of the drawer and tossed it on the top of the desk. Why was it so faded and well thumbed? What was inside that album that Doane held so precious that he carried it with him?

Just a quick look . . .

She opened the heavy leather cover.

Not a quick look, she realized in shock.

Because her gaze was caught and held by a yellowed newspaper front page. She didn't understand German, but she could make out that it was a Hamburg, Germany, newspaper. And the photos on the front page told their own story. Children. Little girls of seven or eight or nine. Victims. She had seen headlines in Atlanta and Chicago and dozens of other local papers that were tragically similar.

Oh, God.

She wasn't important, Doane had said.

And these little girls?

Eve closed her eyes for an instant. Get over the horror. No time for it now.

She closed the album shut and threw it on the floor.

She hurriedly started to rifle through the deep drawer. She pulled out her jacket, checked the pockets, then tossed the jacket aside.

The gun. Find the gun.

There it was! She grabbed the .38 and checked the magazine.

Empty. Dammit, of course he'd pulled the magazine clip.

She tossed the gun on the desk and started looking for her phone.

She found it a moment later.

Dead. The batteries in the cell phone had been

pulled. Find the batteries. He wouldn't leave bullets around, but batteries weren't lethal. She started looking through the other drawers in the desk.

No battery. And she hadn't had a charger with her.

Shit.

There had to be a way to get power.

She studied the laptop computer that Doane had set up for her. A slender cable connected the mouse with one of the computer's USB ports. Could that actually work? Only one way to find out.

She ran across the room and pulled the cable from the port and wrapped it around her hands. She dropped the mouse on the floor, stepped on it and yanked with all her might until the cable finally pulled free. She picked up the frayed end and peeled back the insulation until she could see four thin wires, each a different color. Red and black were for power, the others were for data, she thought. Concentrate on the red and black.

She used her teeth to strip away the red and black casings to expose the copper wires. She picked up her phone and squinted at the copper terminals in the battery compartment. There were three, not two. One was probably for the battery capacity gauge, temperature, or some other data. But which was which?

She glanced up. A sound from outside. Had he come back?

She froze, straining to hear the sound of Doane's truck or his footsteps on the front walk.

Nothing.

She turned back to the phone.

She decided to start with the two outside terminals.

If she didn't short out the phone, she could try other combinations later. She reached over to her work-bench and took two tiny dabs of sculpting clay. She carefully applied them to each wire and affixed them to her phone's first and third battery-compartment ter-minals. She plugged the other end into the laptop's USB port.

Please, please, let it give her enough power . . .

She held her breath and pressed her mobile phone's power button.

Nothing.

Her heart sank with disappointment.

Okay. Maybe the negative and positive were re-versed. She switched terminals.

She pressed the phone's power button again.

The battery lit up!

A few seconds later the carrier name and signal strength bars appeared. She was in business.

The door of the truck slammed outside.

Hurry. Call Joe. Tell him where—

She heard the front door open as she pressed the ac-cess button on the phone.

Answer, Joe. Dear God, answer me.

No answer. She didn't even hear a ring. Was she even connecting?

She heard Doane curse.

Pain.

He'd leaped across the room, struck the side of her neck, and knocked her to the floor.

He grabbed the phone from her hand, checked the ID to make sure she hadn't been talking on it, then stomped it beneath his foot, shattering it. He ground the

broken shards of the cell phone into the floor with ferocity, cursing her all the while.

Eve rolled over, got to her knees, and launched herself at him. He staggered and brought the back of his
hand against her cheek with stinging force.

She rammed her head into his stomach and heard
him gasp with agony.

Good. Now try to get in a position to use karate . . .

"Stop, you dirty little bitch," Doane grunted. "I
should have known. You're just like him. Keep your
hands off me, or I'll blow your guts out."

Eve froze as she felt the muzzle of a revolver pressed
against her abdomen.

"Scared? Not so brave now, are you?" He pushed her
away, grabbed her hair, and pulled her head back. His
eyes were glittering with anger, the cords of his neck
standing out as he stared down at her. "I wanted to
wait, but I don't know if I can. Kevin's getting impatient." He smiled mirthlessly. "So am I."

"You won't shoot me," she said, glaring back at him.
"You want me to make that skull into some semblance
of a human being. Though I don't know if he was that
even when he was alive."

He released her hair and slapped her again. "He
was more than a human being. He was magnificent."
He pushed her down into the office chair. "You were
trying to call Quinn?"

"Who else?"

"Evidently you didn't reach him, or I would have
heard you speaking to him. What a pity." He glanced
at the pieces of phone on the floor. "You won't get that

chance again. I'll handcuff you before I leave you alone."

And Doane was discarding the possibility that even though she hadn't made the final connection, the call might be traced. He had not seemed that tech savvy, maybe he didn't realize it. For that matter, neither did she know if that second of connection could be recognized and traced. "I won't get much done on dear Kevin's reconstruction with my hands cuffed."

"You'll get it done. I'll be here beside you until it's finished." His big hand grasped her throat. "And you'll finish soon. I want it done by tomorrow."

"And what if I won't work on Kevin? It would be foolish of me to complete him when that's all you're waiting for to shoot me."

"But that's not all I'm waiting for," Doane said. "It's true that I want to see him again the way he was before he was butchered. But it's more than that."

"You wanted proof of his identity?" She shook her head. "No, you know this is your son. DNA would be the legal proof, but you wouldn't care about that." Her glance went to the photo album on the floor. "No one is going to care about bringing to justice someone who killed a monster like him."

"Oh, you've been looking at Kevin's souvenirs?" He made a clucking sound as he picked up the album and put it on the desk. "But you shouldn't have been so disrespectful. Kevin wouldn't like it."

"You mentioned one little girl. I guess I didn't want to think that a 'release' for a killer like him would have to be plural. It was too painful for me." She couldn't take her gaze off the album. It was like Pandora's box hiding all the evil of the world. "How many, Doane?"

"Kevin never kept count. I wasn't with him when he was overseas in the military. I know he started needing release when he was fourteen."

"How many?"

"I told you that—" He shrugged. "I suppose there were at least fifty or so. But they weren't all little girls. He liked them best, but there were boys and even a few women."

Eve felt sick. "But he liked the little girls best. Why?"

"He said that the release was more potent because the girls seemed to have a kind of strong purity." His lips turned up with malice. "I'm sure he would have enjoyed your Bonnie. He likes little girls. Isn't it nice that he still has one available? Perhaps since they're together he's enjoying her now."

She wanted to *kill* him. He had chosen just the right words to lacerate. "They're not together."

"How do you know?" he asked softly. "I believe there's some kind of connection."

"Then you're insane." She tried to keep her voice steady. "She was special, and he was a demon."

"I'm sure the parents of those girls in my album thought they were special, too." He flipped open the album to the first page. "Look at them. Do any of them have a resemblance to Bonnie?"

"No."

"You're not looking." He took her hair and forced her head toward the album. "Perhaps the little girl in the center. Anna Grassker. She had curly hair like your Bonnie."

But not red curls, the child was blond. Yet Anna's face was sweet and her eyes bright with joy, and it hurt Eve to look at that photo. "Why are you doing this?"

"You made me angry. I like things easy, and you're making them hard."

"Did you help Kevin kill those people?"

"Not all of them."

"Some of them?"

"When Kevin needed me. I didn't actually touch them, that would have spoiled the release for Kevin."

"And that would have been horrible, right?"

"Yes, why take a life if it provided him no value?"

"How did you help him?"

"He trusted me to scout, to bring the little girls to him. It was easy for me. People like me, they trust me. Kevin was smarter than me, but I was happy and proud that I could help him. I got really good at it."

Yes, Eve could see that he was proud. His son might have been a monster, but who was the most twisted? She could imagine a little girl looking up into that face and giving him her trust. "You're his father. You could have stopped him. At some point, you would have had the opportunity to persuade him that what he was doing was wrong."

"He wasn't wrong. He was different. It took me a little while to realize that he couldn't be held to ordinary rules. When I did, it seemed very simple and clear."

"And you became his enabler."

"I don't like that word." His hand tightened on her throat. "That's what Kevin said they'd call me if I stayed by him in that courtroom."

"Enabler," she repeated deliberately. "You're as dirty

as your son. Why did you try to tell me that the court case concerned only one child if you're so proud of helping him?"

"The court case was only about one child, Dany Cavrol. The prosecution usually chooses only one victim even if there are several."

Eve's gaze was on the photos in front of her. "Which one is she?"

"None of them. Dany lived in Marseilles." He reached out and flipped several pages of the album. "This is Dany. I think they chose her because she had a wistful appeal. The bastards wanted to make sure the jury crucified Kevin."

A newspaper from Marseilles, France, and the little girl couldn't have been more than five. Dany had tight dark curls framing her thin, solemn face. She was heartbreakingly adorable.

"You see?" Doane asked. "Kevin didn't have a chance." His voice was harsh. "Dany's father, General John Tarther, set it up. What the hell did he care about the kid? She was illegitimate and lived with her aunt. Her mother signed the kid over to Tarther and left for London. Tarther made payments for Dany's upkeep but rarely came to see her. Kevin thought it was safe to take a chance on punishing Tarther for getting in his way while he was working with the al-Qaeda in Pakistan. And it *should* have been safe for Kevin. Who would know that Tarther would go crazy? But Tarther stirred everyone up. He hired detectives to find out who had killed Dany. Then he flooded the media with photos and stories, bribed politicians."

"How inconvenient," she said unevenly. "Love isn't

necessarily governed by legalities." She couldn't look at the picture of Dany Cavrol any longer. She was too beautiful. The thought of that ugliness touching her was too painful. "You skipped a lot of pages to get to Dany. What's on the other pages?"

"Oh, much the same. Naples, Istanbul, Liverpool. Do you want to see them?" Doane said. "This is the only one that's at all important. The only case where they charged Kevin."

"And they executed him?"

"No, Blick managed to bribe a witness, and the case was declared a mistrial. Kevin escaped when they were taking him back to jail. I was so happy. I'd arranged a place for him where he'd be safe until he was ready to take charge of his life again." His lips twisted. "But I never saw him again. Tarther sent his bloodhound after him."

"Bloodhound?"

"Zander."

"A detective?"

"Detective?" His laugh was harsh. "A killer. Tarther called my Kevin a killer, but then he sent that snake after him and told him to make sure that Kevin never faced another judge who would let him go free." He was looking down at the album, but Eve knew he wasn't seeing it. "Kevin and I had arranged to meet in Athens. I'd hired a captain to take us to Istanbul. Kevin had contacts with a terrorist group who operated out of there. He never showed up, never met me. Blick called me and told me that Kevin had been shot in an alley near the wharf. Zander butchered him."

"How do you know who did it? A child killer has

a world of enemies. Anyone in that courtroom would have been enraged when Kevin was let loose without being punished. I probably would have killed him myself."

"Yes, you would. Because you're like Zander, aren't you? Filth. Pure filth."

Ignore insults, find out as much as you can. The more she learned, the more weapons she had against him. "Blick knew who killed Kevin?"

"No, Kevin was picked off by a shot from a shop across the alley. It was an excellent shot. Straight to the heart. Zander's so good he didn't bother with a safe head shot. Blick ran like a scared rabbit, but he crept back later and saw Kevin being picked up by Nalaro Crematorium." His lips twisted. "I didn't get there before the funeral director, Guido Nalaro, threw Kevin into his damn furnace, but I saved Kevin's skull." He paused before he added with grim malice, "And I threw Nalaro into the furnace to keep Kevin company and burn with him." He shrugged. "I shouldn't have done it. I was in a rage, and I wasn't thinking of anything but Kevin. I should have waited to kill Nalaro until after I'd questioned him about the man who murdered my son. I ransacked his office afterward, but I couldn't find any clues to who had done it."

"Then how did you find out it was this Zander?"

"It took years. I couldn't move right away. When I thought it was safe, I sent Blick back to Athens and told him to question Nalaro's family. I've always found that sometimes you can get what you want by going through the people surrounding the prey. Nalaro was a secretive bastard, and his wife and children didn't know anything about his being bribed to get rid of the body or who bribed him. But his father knew, and Blick found out. Would you like to know what Blick did to him to make him give us Zander's name?"

"No."

"Squeamish? He deserved it. I had to have that killer's name. But I knew it must have been Tarther who was behind it all. I knew I had to start there. But I couldn't make a mistake like I'd done by killing Nalaro. Tarther was a bigwig general in the Army, and he was surrounded by Army Intelligence and CIA. I had to be patient. I had to gather in Tarther and the man who'd killed Kevin and anyone else who had been involved. I had to make them suffer. I wasn't smart like Kevin, but I knew I'd find a way. Kevin had already given me the tools to do it. I thought that he just meant to keep me safe, but maybe he knew . . ."

"What tools?"

"Kevin had a disk that he'd gotten from the Taliban that proved Tarther had sent in a team of assassins to take out several Pakistan officials who were moving Bin Laden from place to place. The White House was walking a tightrope trying to keep the routes through Pakistan open to Afghanistan, but Tarther didn't care about anything but getting Bin Laden and stopping the bastards who were hiding him. He would have been kicked out of the service if Washington had found out that he'd risked the delicate balance of power. He wasn't alone in it, and all his Pakistan and CIA buddies would have come tumbling down with him. As long as I had that disk, no one would touch me."

"Blackmail?"

"Of course. Kevin always said blackmail was just another weapon. I told Tarther that that disk would be sent to three media outlets if anything happened to me. Shall I tell you how careful they were to make sure that I was kept safe and sound? They sent a CIA man named Venable around to see me, and he told me that I was going to be put under the CIA's version of the witness protection program. That was five years ago. The CIA took good care of me, and I had time to do all the digging I had to do to find out the truth about Kevin's killing. I made my plans, then I started to move."

"In my direction. Why the hell did you do that? I wasn't involved in all this. Why did you have Blick shoot Jane?" Her gaze shifted to Kevin's reconstruction across the room. "I can see why you'd want to have him look more normal. You're obviously obsessed with that gargoyle. But you can't be insane enough to go to those lengths. Or maybe you can." Why was she expecting reason or sanity when he was obviously as unbalanced as his precious son? "Why didn't you go after Tarther or this Zander instead?"

"All in good time. I had to prepare the way. *You* had to prepare the way. I had to have Kevin as close to the way he was as I could make him before I confronted those murderers. They had to know that they hadn't really destroyed what he was. Everything had to be perfect. Besides, Kevin had already punished Tarther. Why do you think he chose his daughter, Dany, to kill? Kevin was involved with that al-Qaeda group General Tarther was targeting. Butchering the little girl was revenge the terrorists understood and approved. All I have to do is administer the final coup de grâce."

"And Zander?"

"I'm working on him. He's more difficult. But I have a good grasp of his character, I think. Once Blick and I found out who Tarther had hired to kill Kevin, I researched Zander until I knew more about him and all his secrets than anyone else on Earth."

"Then why not go after him and leave my family alone?"

"He's very elusive and difficult to locate. I prefer to have him come to me."

"Why would he do that?" She had a sudden thought. "You said he was careful about destroying evidence. Do you think Kevin's skull is evidence enough to make him uneasy enough to come after it?"

"How clever you are. It's definitely a possibility, isn't it?" His hand dropped away from her throat. "But I believe I've told you enough. Aren't you curious that I decided to confide in you?"

"No, I knew it would all come out sometime. You want to talk about Kevin. He dominates your every thought. You were able to restrain yourself as long as you thought that you might deceive and soothe me as you did those little girls you lured for your son." She reached up and rubbed her throat. She could still feel the bruising imprint of his fingers. "But, as you said, it made you angry that I wouldn't be fooled when you knew how good you were at it."

"I am good. Kevin always told me what a talent I had. It's not as if I made it harder for the little girls. I actually made them feel safe for a little while longer. I tried to do the same for you."

"Liar. That's only your peculiar brand of ego."

"That's not true." His brow wrinkled in a deep frown. "If you had—" He stopped and shrugged. "If you realized that, then you're not as clever as I thought. You knew you were taking a giant risk to break into that desk."

"I could see you were near the breaking point. I was tired of pretending that I didn't know that no matter what I did, you would kill me anyway. You will, won't you?"

He nodded slowly. "I'm afraid I can't do anything else."

"Then why should I complete that reconstruction?"

"Jane MacGuire?"

"That dog won't hunt. I have to rely on Joe to make sure that Jane is safe. I told him to care for her. I'd trust Joe against your Blick any day."

"Then to buy time on the chance that someone will come to save you?" His gaze was narrowed on her face. "I hate to rely on that reason. I've noticed you don't have a healthy fear of death. But you do care about Joe Quinn and Jane MacGuire and their love for you. You wouldn't want them to suffer when they found you dead." He tilted his head consideringly. "Perhaps in the same state I found Kevin, with your skull detached and burned beyond recognition."

"No, I wouldn't want them to find me like that." It would be a memory neither of them would be able to forget for the rest of their lives.

"I didn't think you would." He made a mocking gesture toward Kevin's reconstruction. "Then by all means continue. He's waiting."

Yes, Kevin was waiting.

Eve could feel that silent waiting like the pull of a whirlpool drawing her toward him.

"Do it. I promise that they won't find you as I did Kevin." He coaxed softly. "Believe me."

She didn't believe him. He would do whatever he chose to punish everyone connected with Kevin's death no matter how distant.

But, as he said, it would buy time. She wasn't about to let either Doane or Kevin beat her. She was going to *live*.

"You're damn right that's not going to happen." She got to her feet and moved across the room. "I'll finish your damn reconstruction. I admit, I'm curious about Kevin. I've never re-created the face of a monster. I want to see if I can do it."

She slowly settled herself on her stool in front of the skull.

Here we are, together again, Kevin.

But now we're more on even footing. I know what a cowardly beast you are. I know how you used people, even that slimeball of a father. And you're so dark and full of fury that you won't let go even now. I didn't realize that evil lasted beyond the grave. I hoped with all my heart that it ended when life did.

Though Bonnie had tried to tell her.

Bonnie. Her memory was like a cool mountain breeze, lifting the oppression and darkness.

Fury. Darkness. Nausea.

She gasped, and a shudder went through her. It felt as if she'd been grabbed and squeezed, her lungs compressed until she couldn't breathe.

So you don't like me to think about Bonnie, you son of a bitch. Why? Because she gives me strength?

She had a sudden chilling thought. Or is it because our bond gives Bonnie strength?

He likes little girls. Isn't it nice that he still has one available?

Rage tore through her, burning away all weakness.

No way. You're nothing, you won't get near her. Crawl back in your cave, you slug.

"You've been naughty," Doane said maliciously from his chair. "Kevin punished you, didn't he? He didn't like it when you tried to hurt me. He's very protective. Though I'm sure he approves of your knowing how awesome he can be."

"Protective? You poor fool, the only reason he ever tried to protect you was so that he'd have someone to do his bidding. And if that black heart of his has somehow managed to escape hell, you're still only a means to an end to him."

"You lie." His cheeks flushed. "You'll see that he cares about me."

"How? You mean if I live long enough."

"You'll live long enough. Kevin would like you to see his enemies destroyed." He leaned back in his chair. "Work. You're wasting time."

That hadn't been her intention. She'd just been delaying touching the clay until she braced herself. She reached out, and her hands started moving, molding the clay.

Tingling. Shortness of breath. Nausea.

She took a deep breath and forced herself to go on.

Evidently, Kevin didn't care how difficult he made it

for her. Maybe it was only his father who wanted Kevin's image re-created. It was a good thing that she'd already decided that this couldn't go on much longer. She had to escape quickly no matter what the risk. The situation was too volatile. It was dangerous not only for her but all the people she loved. Jane, Joe . . . and Bonnie. Perhaps Bonnie most of all. Could an eternal soul be lost or destroyed?

Block it out. Block him out.

Smooth, carve.

Stop, measure.

Show me the way, Kevin. Innocence or wickedness? Were you like your father and able to fool everyone around you? Or did you look like the monster you are?

CHAPTER

13

The old man looked more frail than he had the last time Venable had seen him, the CIA agent thought as he walked down the path toward the small garden at the rear of the house. He should not have aged this quickly. It had been a steady downhill path since he had been robbed of years and vigor by one tragic blow. Yet there was no question the general was thinner, his shoulders a little more bowed.

And he looked . . . tired.

He glanced up from the strawberry bed he was weeding and stiffened when he saw Venable coming toward him. He sat back on his heels. "Hello, Venable." He forced a smile. "I won't say it's good to see you. Do we have a problem?"

Venable nodded. "I'm afraid so, General Tarther."

The general got slowly to his feet. "And it must be a considerable problem if it rates a personal visit." He grimaced as he moved toward the striped canvas chair a few feet away. "It's hell to get old. I hate all the aches and pains." He sat down. "And it's even worse when I remember how young and strong I was only yesterday. I do a lot of remembering." He gestured to the other chair. "Sit down, Venable. Don't stand there hovering like a vulture."

Venable sat down. "I was being respectful." He smiled. "As is due a general of your caliber and stature. How are you doing, sir?"

"Health-wise, a few issues. Emotionally, more than a few. I get ambushed more frequently all the time."

"Ambushed?"

"Memories. Things that have been, things that could have been. I find the older I get, the less likely I am to keep a stiff backbone and deny that against those ambushes I'm completely helpless. Very chastening for a military man." He smiled at Venable. "I'm even admitting them to you, Venable."

"You've fought your battles, sir. You've won a hell of a lot of them. You don't have to win that battle."

"That's good, because I'm not." He looked away. "Why are you here? What's the bad news?"

"Doane has left the safe house."

"And?"

"He's abducted a woman, and she may be in danger."

"You told me that Doane wasn't like his son."

"I told you as far as I could tell there was a good possibility," Venable said. "I believe I was wrong. Even if not as bad, he certainly is very dangerous. He killed one of my agents, who was protecting Eve Duncan."

"More killing." Tarther was silent. "If he's like his son, did he help Kevin Relling kill my Dany?"

"No, he wasn't in Europe at that time. We know that for certain. I told you so when we arranged protection for Doane. You wouldn't have asked me to give Doane protection if there had been any hint that was true."

"Things seem to be changing. I had to make sure that had not changed." His gaze swung back to Venable. "Did you get the disk?"

It was the question he had known was coming and one he did not want to answer. "No, sir, I did not."

"Then we have to assume he will use it. Have you protected my men?"

"I'm in the process now, sir." He paused. "My bet is that Doane is going to be occupied in the immediate future and won't make an attempt to release any information. There's still an opportunity to get the disk back. But I had to tell you that I'll have to pull out all the stops when I go after Doane. I can't have any more lives lost."

"I know. But my men's lives are at stake, too. Why do you think I sent you to shelter that monster's father? All I wanted to do was forget that he existed and brought Kevin Relling into the world. Instead, I woke every day with the knowledge we had no proof that the apple had not fallen far from the tree. I don't want it to be for nothing, Venable."

"I'll try to take him alive," Venable said grimly. "And if I do, I guarantee you'll have that disk."

"Just save my men."

"I'll do everything I can, sir."

"I know you will," Tarther leaned back and wearily closed his eyes. "You're a good man, Venable."

"If I were that good, Doane wouldn't have slipped away."

Tarther's eyes opened, and he smiled faintly. "Now you're doing it. Another ambush, Venable. What might have been? That's the cruelest ambush of all." His gaze went to the strawberry patch he'd been weeding. "Every year I put in strawberries. My Dany loved strawberries. They would make her mouth red, and she'd rub it against my cheek and laugh. I loved her, Venable."

"I know you did, General."

"She appeared in my life when I was near the end of my career and cynical and discouraged beyond belief. I never wanted a child. I was going to pay off her mother and send them both away. What would I do with a little girl? I was nearing sixty, and it would be foolish to take on that kind of responsibility. I was a hard-bitten military man who had done his duty all his life and had no wish to be anything else." He shook his head. "Yet I could see the world around me going to hell, and I couldn't seem to stop it. The last thing I wanted was for my Dany to come into that world. But when she came, she changed everything."

"I understand that children have a habit of doing that."

"You don't have any children, do you, Venable?"

"No, sir. I've never seemed to have the time to think about a family."

"Take the time. Nothing else is worth thinking about. Not a career, or ideology, or saving the world. I never realized what an empty life I had before Dany. She was a miracle." He shook his head. "But I didn't recognize how fragile a miracle could be. I should have spent more time with her. I was always too busy. I thought I'd have more time later. I should have protected her. I never dreamed . . . but it happened. I thought I'd never forgive myself." His gaze stayed on the green stems in the rich brown earth. "I pray every day that she'll forgive me."

"I'm sure she has, sir."

"How do you know? I don't." His lips tightened. "But lately, I've felt that maybe she has forgiven me. I've felt her close to me. Sometimes, I imagine I hear her laugh. Or maybe it's not imagination. What do you think, Venable?"

"I don't think it matters, General. Not if it's there for you."

"You're probably right. I feel her most when I come out here to this little patch to garden. I find myself hurrying like a young boy down the path because I know maybe she's waiting." He nodded slowly. "And I'm waiting, too. We're just waiting to be together."

Venable cleared his throat. "Then I'll go and let you get back to your gardening." He got to his feet. "I'm sorry to bring you bad news, sir. I'll let you know of any updates."

"Do that." He got up from his chair and moved the few yards to the strawberry patch. "But all I ask is that you protect my men. Find the disk."

"I'll find it, General. Oh, and I wanted you to know I've assigned an agent to the house to protect you."

The general stopped and looked over his shoulder. "I'd forgotten that I might be a target. Yes, one thing does lead to another, doesn't it?" His smile was curiously thoughtful. "Thank you, Venable. And don't worry about me. I have an idea it's all going to work out for the best." He fell to his knees and started to weed again. "Good-bye, my friend."

Venable hesitated, watching him. The general had already closed him out, his expression absorbed. There was a patience, a methodical movement, a rhythm, to every motion, as if he was devoting every cell of his body to the simple task.

But it wasn't simple at all, Venable realized. He was preparing a gift for his Dany while he waited for her.

And Venable found it too private a gift to watch the giving. "Good-bye, sir."

He turned and left the garden.

LAKE COTTAGE

"Why wouldn't you let Jane come along?" Margaret hurried to keep pace with Joe as he strode through the woods. "If I can help, it's just a matter of concentration on my part. It doesn't matter how many people are around."

"It matters that Jane would be hovering over you, trying to keep me from damaging your delicate sensibilities."

"They're not delicate." Margaret made a face. "Nothing about me is fragile or delicate. In case you haven't noticed, I'm sturdy, and I bounce. Though I can see why you'd think Jane would make that judgment. She's tough, but I seem to have that effect on her."

"You saved her Toby. Jane is very careful about giving her affection, but she loves that dog. That probably has something to do with it." He studied her coolly. "And you're . . . disarming."

She nodded. "Yeah, most people think that. I think it's because what you see is what you get." She grinned. "And do I disarm you, Detective Quinn?"

"Joe." He shook his head. "I can't afford to be disarmed by anyone or anything right now. All I'm concerned about is whether you can produce results. You may prove valuable, or you may be a bust. I have a little time before Venable gets here, and I'm using it to see if you'll be of any use to Eve. Nothing else matters."

"I'd have to be deaf and blind not to have gathered that." Her brows rose. "And you're willing to bet on a wild card."

"I'm willing to bet on anything or anyone," he said bluntly. "I've seen and experienced weirder things than a kid who is a dog whisperer. I don't expect anything. Prove me wrong."

"I'm not a kid. And I don't expect anything, either. I just hope."

"Is that how it always works?"

"Not always. Sometimes I have somewhere to start, as I did when I was trying to find out what happened to Toby. And I had support and an intelligent animal who'd had contact with people and could translate his experience for me. That's not always the case. Particularly when I may have to deal with wild, not domestic, animals. Then I have to fumble around and try to interpret."

"How long have you known you could do this?"

"All my life. But I was five years old before I realized that other people couldn't do the same thing.

The sounds and thoughts and impressions were all around me, and I thought they were there for everyone. Then one day I told my father that our neighbor's dog, Brandy, told me that she was sick and there was something hurting her stomach."

"And?"

"My father accused me of lying and beat me until I couldn't stand."

"A five-year-old kid?"

"It wasn't the first time. He drank a lot. My mother died when I was born. My father let me go to foster care because he didn't want to take care of me. But when I was four, he took me back. I didn't know until later that the only reason he kept me around was for the welfare checks. I usually tried to stay out of his way, but I didn't know how to help Brandy." She shrugged. "I should have worked it out for myself. But at least when I went to my father and he beat me, I learned what not to say. The next day I went to see Brandy's owners, the Andersons, and told them their dog was sick. I said I'd seen her throw up a couple times, and she was crying when she did it. They were nice people who liked Brandy and didn't want to take a chance even if a little kid wasn't exactly a credible witness. They took her to the vet. It was a tumor, but they got it in time." She wrinkled her nose. "But the Andersons were grateful and went to my father and told him what a fine, observant little girl he had. He agreed, thanked them, and then when they left, he beat me again for talking to the neighbors. I wasn't supposed to ever talk to anyone outside the house. He wasn't stupid. He knew DEFACS relied on interviews with neighbors to make their quarterly reports. After that, I usually did what he wanted, but I was pretty lonely. Until I realized I didn't have to rely on my father or other people to talk to me. It was much better then." She smiled. "Of course, most people would say that it was isolation and mistreatment that led to hallucinations. You're a practical, reasonable man; isn't that what your first reaction would be?"

He nodded. "Damn right. Unless you can prove first reactions are false. So this so-called gift isn't inherited?"

She shrugged. "As I said, my mother died when I was born, so I have no idea what she could or could not do. The only thing I'm sure about is that I heard she managed to put up with my father for ten years, so she must have been a saint . . . or a fool. I only made it until I was a little over eight before I ran away from home."

"Didn't they catch you and bring you back home? That's pretty young."

She shook her head. "I knew how to take care of myself, and I was ready. I didn't go near anyone who might turn me back over to him. I was used to the woods by that time, and I lived off the land. Later, I made friends who were willing to take me in and help me get an education. There are good people in the world, and some of them don't believe you have to go by every rule. You just have to find them." She paused. "The people on Summer Island are like that. So is Jane. So are you, Joe."

"I believe in rules."

"Except where it concerns your family. Then the

rules are thrown out the window. Caleb is like that, too. But he's one of the wild ones who don't have exceptions, so I can't really include him in the mix."

"By all means, let's not include Caleb," Joe said dryly. He was silent a moment. "You're not exactly reserved about your background. I admit I didn't expect such openness since—"

"I'm traveling with false documents and might be a criminal," she finished for him. "But that's another story. I told you what I could. I thought it would help you to trust me a little. Not a lot. But we all take what we can get." She raised her head and listened. "The grave is over the next hill."

"Yes. That was easy. No voices but a disturbance in the birds?"

"That's right." She nodded. "Caleb told me that you were a SEAL. You'd know the basics." They had come over the hill, and she saw the yellow tape cordoning off the area. There was a uniformed policeman standing by a pine tree, and he lifted his hand in greeting at Joe when he saw him.

Margaret's gaze was drawn to the area in the center of the taped enclosure. She felt a wave of sadness. "Poor man. Death comes so swiftly sometimes. How did he die?"

"His throat was cut. Do you want to get closer?"

"No, this is fine. What do you want from me?"

"Anything you can give me. We need to know where Dukes was killed on the property and if there's any evidence to be found there. There's a possibility that Dukes might have been trailing Doane when he stole a truck from the Hallet farm several miles from here.

We can't find the farmer or Doane's vehicle." He added grimly. "I have search teams all over the property, but there are too many damn acres, and I need to know something now."

"It's not going to be that fast," she said absently. "You're asking too much. I have to find a carrier with a reason to be concerned." She dropped down on the ground and crossed her legs tailor fashion. "You're right; the birds are disturbed. Some of them left when the grave was being dug. Some when you excavated the body. There are only a few left who were here originally, and I don't sense any who witnessed anything disturbing." She saw Joe's skeptical look, and said, "Yes, if they saw Dukes's throat being cut, they would be particularly disturbed. Death disturbs all creatures. Even if they don't understand it or empathize with it, there's a sense of loss."

"I'll take your word for it." He hesitated, then fell to his knees beside her. "What's next?"

"I cast around for an animal I can work with who has been disturbed enough to linger or come back to the grave." She was gazing down the hill at the grave. "It may take a while."

He was silent for a few minutes, his gaze on her intent face. "How long?"

He could see the effort she had to use to jerk her attention back to him. "You don't have to stay. It's hard for you to believe it's worthwhile, that *I'm* worthwhile. I'll come back to the cottage if I have anything to report."

The words surprised him with their simple maturity. She gave the impression of cheerful high energy and youthful vigor, but he was beginning to see layers beneath that façade that intrigued him. "I'll stay. God knows I don't have anything else to do right now until Venable—" He broke off as his phone signaled an incoming call. "That may be Jane. I told her to call me if Venable showed—Shit!" He was gazing at the ID. "Eve!" He punched the button.

Nothing.

A dial tone.

He was dialing Venable as he jumped to his feet. "I just got a signal that could be a missed call from Eve. It didn't even ring. What the hell is happening? Did you get a trace on her?"

"They're working on it," Venable said. "The call was cut off before it made a connection. But they may have the tower."

"May?" Joe repeated savagely. "Who the hell knows what Eve risked to make that call. And your tech guys can't trace it?"

"They're trying, Joe. If anyone can do it, they can. I'm almost at the cottage. I'll see you within an hour." Venable hung up.

Joe whirled and started down the hill toward the path to the cottage.

"Joe." Margaret called out quietly from behind him, "I know that this seems unimportant at the moment, but I think I've found what you were looking for."

She was right. When he'd gotten the call from Eve, he'd forgotten that Margaret existed, much less for what he'd asked her to search. He looked impatiently over his shoulder. "What, already? You said that it would take—"

"It's a feral cat. I got lucky."

"And that means?"

"Cats are clever, and they stalk prey. Feral cats are always looking for food, and this one scavenges the neighboring farms as well as your woods for his next meal. The wife of the farmer who Doane stole a truck from often fed the feral cats on the property."

"So?"

"The cat was familiar with the farmer as well as his wife. There was often grain in the bed of the farmer's truck, which he went after when he couldn't find any other prey."

"What does that have to do with Dukes's death?"

"Dukes watched Doane get rid of his blue car and the farmer's body. But Dukes mustn't have been too good at his job because Doane turned stalker and went after him. He cut his throat, then took the body away to bury it. Probably because he didn't want anyone to discover his car or the farmer before he took Eve."

"This cat told you all this?" Joe asked sarcastically.

"No, don't be silly. All I get is impressions for the most part. A lot of it is my interpretation of what the cat saw combined with what you told me."

"And where is Doane's car and the missing farmer?"

Her gaze went to the north side of the lake. "The lake is deep out there?"

"Very deep."

"Then you'll have trouble retrieving the car."

"We checked the entire bank of the lake for any sign of vehicle entry."

"It was raining that night, and Doane must be very good at masking his trail."

"So judged your feral friend?"

She ignored the sarcasm. "There's a huge moss-covered rock near the bank where the car went into the water. Do you know it?"

He slowly nodded his head. "I taught Jane how to dive off that rock when she was a kid."

"Then you have somewhere to start, don't you?"

"I guess I do." It could be guesswork about that moss-covered rock on the north side of the lake, but it was a peculiar coincidence she had known about it since Margaret had just arrived at the cottage. But, hell, her story was even more peculiar than the coincidence. He had to choose which one to believe.

No, he didn't. He'd accept everything and check it out later. He started back down the trail. "I'll order a new search in that area. Come on, let's get back to the cottage. We have to be there when Venable gets there."

"We? That sounds . . . companionable. You're going to let me help Jane?"

"I'm going to let you help Eve. Providing we find signs that car went into the lake."

"Eve. Jane. It's the same thing for me."

"Not for me."

"I can see that. She stands alone." Her voice was a little wistful. "You truly love Eve, and you don't try to mask it or hide it. It's . . . nice. Most people I've met are afraid to give themselves unconditionally to any emotion."

"Then they're cheating themselves. Are you coming or not?"

She didn't move. "I'll be along soon. I have something to do."

"What?"

"The cat. He was afraid and ran away and didn't see Dukes's body being removed. I have to let him know that he doesn't have any reason to stay close to the grave."

He frowned. "Why the hell should he be doing that? I've never heard of a cat's guarding a grave."

"No." She shook her head. "Go on. I'll be down soon."

"Why?" he asked again.

She was silent a moment. "He's a feral cat," she said quietly. "He scavenges for food. How do you think he knew where Dukes was buried? He was hungry and followed Doane when he hid the body. But Doane buried Dukes, and he couldn't get at him. I have to let him know that he should go look for other food."

Joe grimaced. "Pleasant thought."

"No, but it's nature. We've got to accept it and not hang our own values on other creatures. He's doing what his instincts and self-preservation tell him to do."

"And you accept it?"

"Most of the time. When my emotions don't get involved." She turned back to look at the grave. "And I like this cat. He loves lying in the sun and everything about the forest and hunting. He's tough, but that's okay, there's no malice. Maybe we can persuade that farmer's wife, Mrs. Hallet, to be a little more proactive in taking care of the ferals."

"If the cat doesn't eat anyone she knows."

She shrugged, and said again, "Nature."

* * *

"They should be back soon." Caleb had come up be-hind Jane on the porch. "You could call Quinn if you're worried."

"He just called me. They're on their way back. He thinks he just got a signal from Eve's phone." She held up her hand as he started to speak. "But Venable doubts they can trace it, dammit. She managed to try to get word to us, and we can't even take advantage of it."

"Is there a chance?"

"Not a very good one."

"At least you know Eve is alive and working to save herself. That should give you some comfort."

"It doesn't give me comfort. I'm upset and feeling pissed off. I want her back here." She rubbed the back of her neck. "I hate staying here and waiting. Eve is helping herself, but I'm not doing anything. I could at least have gone with Margaret and Joe if he hadn't dragged her off so quickly. I want to shake someone. Preferably Joe."

"Quinn still thinks of you as walking wounded. He didn't want you to exert any extra effort."

"I know all that." She crossed her arms across her chest. She felt cold. That was probably because she was tired from lack of sleep. Don't admit even to herself that it had anything to do with the wound. Ignore it. "You're defending him. That's not at all like you, Caleb."

"I'm defending you. You need all the support you can get right now." He sighed. "It appears I'm not sufficient." He sat down on the porch swing and stretched his legs out before him. "Until you realize how mistaken you are."

She turned to look at him. "Since when have you needed any other opinion but your own?" Lord, he was magnetic, she thought suddenly. It was hard not to keep on staring at him. He was leaning lazily back in the swing, and his white shirt was clinging to the powerful muscles of his abdomen. She could see a hint of the dark hair that thatched his chest. And his eyes . . . dark, sensual, knowing. Everything about him reached out, touched, stroked. She had always thought he was probably the sexiest man she had ever met, and at this moment there was no doubt of it.

But sex could be enslaving if you couldn't trust the man who wielded it. She was right to keep Caleb at a distance. Even now, when she was weary and hurt, he managed to make her feel more than she wanted to feel.

"But I value your opinion," Caleb said with a half smile. "And I'm willing to work to be thought sufficient. Sometimes you come close, then you veer away. I agree that it's safer for you to handle me that way, but so boring. Take a chance, Jane."

"Why? You don't have anything that I need except your help finding Eve."

"No, but there might be something that you want." He suddenly straightened and got up from the porch swing with one fluid movement. She tensed, foolish to feel this threatened. "A little distraction?" he offered as he came toward her. "I'm more than sufficient at that and very willing to—"

Her phone rang, and she grabbed it quickly without checking ID.

"Did you connect with Margaret?" Trevor asked. "I

contacted the head of the search-and-rescue group, and
he said that she'd been picked up in Atlanta."

"Yes, Margaret's here, Trevor." She saw Caleb stop
and go still. He obviously didn't like or appreciate Trev-
or's calling. Too bad. She was relieved to have that moment interrupted. She wasn't too pleased with Trevor
either, but she never felt threatened around him. "You
shouldn't have put her in touch with that group. It was
none of your business. I didn't want her here."

"She wanted to come," Trevor said. "And I liked
the idea of your having someone besides Caleb and
Joe Quinn beside you." He paused. "It didn't hurt that
it kept me in the picture if only on a peripheral level.
Have you found out anything more about Eve?"

"A little." She rattled off the information they'd gathered. "Venable will be here soon and tell us more."

"I'll check out the info you've given me with my
contacts and see if I can come up with anything. You
have my number. Call me if you need me." He added,
"I'm letting you have a little time and space, but I'm
going to be on my way up there in a day or two. Expect me."

"I may not be here. If Venable gives us the information we need, we'll be going after Doane."

"Expect me," he repeated, and hung up.

"He's going to come here," Caleb said flatly, as she
pressed the disconnect. "I knew it was only a matter
of time."

So had Jane. Trevor had always done exactly what
he wanted once he made up his mind. He had clearly
made a decision that their relationship was to have a
new start, and she could only hope that he stayed out

of her way while she was searching for Eve. "Yes, tomorrow or the next day maybe."

"And I'm sure he'll try to be everything that's sufficient." His lips twisted. "No, glorious."

"Glorious? What a description. Trevor would laugh at you."

"No, that he wouldn't do," Caleb said softly. "Not more than once."

"Caleb, I won't tolerate any conflict," she said through clenched teeth. "Not from either of you."

"I'm sure you won't have trouble with Trevor. He'll be everything that's civilized. Greek-god looks, sophistication, and intelligence. How could you ask for anything more?"

"Don't be flip, dammit. And I can do without sarcasm."

Caleb didn't speak for a moment, then said, "You're right. I'm having a few problems I didn't expect. I think it's because I know you were lovers."

"What?"

"I know it's none of my business." He smiled sardonically. "And it shows how very uncivilized I am that it bothers me. Bothers me? That's an understatement. I want to—" He broke off. "You don't want to know what I want to do."

"No, I don't."

His smile changed, warmed, became completely charismatic. "Then we won't discuss it. But don't you feel better that you know where you are with me? I wouldn't be able to hide it even if I tried." He added, "And I'll be careful not to antagonize Trevor because I know it would make it difficult for you. We're just men with the usual priorities, but Trevor will be civilized, and I'll be as sensitive as I can, and it will all work out. Anything else would be exceptionally stupid."

"Yes, it would." And just because Caleb stated that truth wouldn't necessarily mean that everything would be smooth and easy. She never knew which way he was going to jump. She said deliberately, "And I would never forgive either of you if you did anything that got in my way when I'm looking for Eve."

"Point taken." Caleb looked away from her to the road. "A car just came around the bend. Venable?"

"Lord, I hope so." Her gaze followed his to the light tan Camry. "Yes, that's the car he was driving." She started quickly down the steps as she dialed Joe's number to tell him. Now things would start to move. Now some of the waiting would come to an end. "Thank God."

CHAPTER

14

He's coming to life." Doane's eyes were glowing softly as he gazed at the reconstruction. "I can *see* him. The shape of his lips . . . He always had such fine, full lips. How did you do that? I can see the cheekbones and perhaps the basic structure. But how did you get the lips?"

Eve shrugged. "Maybe I used the shape of your lips as a model. Using family resemblance is one way of creating an accurate picture."

"But not your way." He smiled. "I researched you for a long time, remember? You won't even look at photos of possible victims in case it will influence you." He reached up and touched his lips. "And my mouth is thinner and not nearly as symmetrical." His gaze shifted back to the reconstruction. "No, it's something else. He's coming alive for you."

"No!"

He ignored the instant rejection. "They always come

alive for you, don't they? You said that in one of your interviews. In the final stages, you rely on pure creativity."

"That's natural in a sculptor, which is what I am. What you're talking about is something different." She met his gaze. "I'm a sculptor, not Frankenstein."

"I wish you were," he said wistfully. "And perhaps you could be, given the opportunity. You may have the potential. Those lips . . ."

"A coincidence." She was on edge, and she was tired of his insistence. She didn't want to think about the last few hours when she had been drawn deep into the work. She had intended to block out all thought, but she had gone mindless, automatic, instead.

And when she had emerged, it was to see that face beginning to form beneath her fingers.

"It frightened you, didn't it?" Doane said softly. "I told you that he wanted to come back to me. We belong together. We've waited so long to punish those bastards."

"It didn't frighten me." She repeated, "Coincidence." She put her hands on her back and arched it. "And I've had enough for right now. I'm going to get some rest."

His smile disappeared. "I told you that you were going to work until we're finished. We're so close. I want it done."

"Then do it yourself." She forced herself to glance at the face of the reconstruction. It was not even half-completed yet she felt as if Kevin were there, veiled, ready to slide from beneath the layers of clay. "Have him help you if you think he can. But I warn you that you're going to have trouble building the nose."

"I'm not joking. I don't want to waste any more time. Finish him."

"After I rest my eyes and sleep for a while." She got up from the stool. "I'm not afraid of you, Doane. If you want to hurt me or kill me, then do it. I don't give a damn at the moment. My curiosity is wavering right now, and I'm tired of working on your monster. I'll deal with him later. I told you, I'm going to rest."

He frowned, obviously disconcerted. Then he smiled. "Kevin will be disappointed, but he's waited for a long time. I'm sure he understands. Perhaps next time he'll be more careful about scaring you."

"He didn't scare me. I'm a professional doing my job. Your son is a pitiful remnant I'm trying to put back together. Not anything else, Doane."

"You protest too much."

"Whatever." She turned toward her bedroom. Escape tonight? Or did she need one more dose of the gas as insurance to make it safer? How would she know how much she needed? she thought impatiently. It was all guesswork and depended on how deep Doane slept or how alert he'd be now that he knew that she was definitely an antagonist.

"Wait."

She didn't turn around. "I'm not going to work on him any longer, Doane."

"I'm not going to insist that you do. But I can't let the time be entirely wasted. Come back here. I have a telephone call I want you to make."

She turned warily to face him. "Call?"

"I think it's time you became acquainted with one of the men whom you found so interesting in Kevin's album. I'm not sure he'll be equally interested in you, but it will be entertaining to find out."

"What are you talking about? All I saw in that album were those poor children."

"That's right, but as a result of your prying, I told you about Tarther and Zander, didn't I? Well, it's almost the same thing."

"That's irrational. You're going to make me talk to that poor child's father?"

"Oh no, that wouldn't be at all interesting for me. It's Zander. You're going to talk to Zander."

Her eyes widened. "I have no desire to talk to that murderer. Though killing your son may have been the only decent thing he's done in his life." She met his gaze. "Maybe I should talk to him. Perhaps congratulations are in order. But why do you want me to talk to him? If he's a paid hit man, he's not going to care that I'm doing this reconstruction. DNA, maybe, but not a reconstruction that could be thrown out in a court of law."

"I told you that I want everyone connected with Kevin's death to come together. This seems a good initial opportunity since you're being uncooperative in other areas." He was dialing his phone. "Why not humor me? There's a possibility that you could touch Zander's heart, and he might come to rescue you. He obviously hates me enough to want to keep me from having anything I want. I'm a loose end, and he detests loose ends." He chuckled. "Don't get your hopes up. It's not likely. You'd be amused, too, if you knew what a coldhearted son of a bitch he is." His smile faded. "If you could have seen what was left of my beautiful boy in that furnace, even you might be sickened."

"No more than if I saw a disease-carrying rat destroyed."

"Ugly. How ugly you are."

"And how did you get this Zander's phone number? If he's as smart as you say, I'd think he would make it very difficult for you."

"He did, and I had to bounce off a dozen satellites and false numbers to narrow it down. But I had time and patience and Blick to help me." He tilted his head, waiting as the phone rang. "And I've often wondered if he didn't actually want to have me hunt him down. The bastard would feel like a caged tiger not to be able to go after a target he was salivating to get his teeth into. I'm sure he detests being frustrated." He tensed. "He's picking up. I'll put him on speaker for you." He spoke into the phone. "Zander, this is Doane."

"Not Doane, Relling." Zander's deep voice was faintly mocking. "Venable gave you that new name and stowed you away for safekeeping, but you'll always be the same scum as your son to me. No, worse. Because he had the guts to be a megamonster, and you were only a leech hanging on to him. I've been waiting for you to call. Or knock on my door. It took you long enough."

"I was savoring the moment."

"No, obsession carries one only so far and brainpower has to kick in somewhere. Anyone who could talk himself into carrying the water for a sloppy, self-indulgent executioner like Kevin Relling doesn't have much upstairs."

Doane flushed. "You're trying to make me angry."

"No, I wouldn't bother. You're not important enough. Why are you calling me? My guess is that you're trying to whip up enough courage to come after me."

"I have someone who wants to talk to you. I'll bet that Venable went running to you and told you that I've left Colorado. I've enlisted the help of someone who is going to help me bring Kevin back to what he was before you sent him into those hellish fires. I thought you should get to know each other."

Silence. "You're speaking of Eve Duncan. I've no wish to get to know her. She's nothing to me. You're nothing to me."

"I will be." He thrust his phone at Eve. "Talk to him, Eve. Tell him how well you're doing with my son's reconstruction. Tell him that he couldn't really kill my boy."

"I'm not going to tell him that," Eve said coldly as she took the phone. "Your son is dead. Hallelujah and Amen." She spoke into the phone. "I don't want to talk to you either, Zander. I abhor murderers, and I don't know enough about you to know whether you're any different than the man you killed. Probably not."

Silence. "There are a few differences. I don't kill children, and I have much more talent. I'm a professional who relies on business acumen, not emotion. Kevin Relling was ordinary, and I'm superb. Other than that, you'll have to decide for yourself. Providing Kevin's father lets you stay alive long enough to make any judgment. You do know he won't let you live any longer than he has to to accomplish his purpose? Don't let him tell you anything else. It will be a lie."

"Do you think I'm stupid? I'm not one of those

children Doane lured into Kevin's trap. I've seen evil before, and Doane is evil. I don't need you to tell me that I shouldn't trust him. Any more than I should trust you. I'm on my own, and both of you can go to hell." She thrust the phone back at Doane. "And may you both burn there until it freezes over. I'm going to bed and let you two play your games and spit your poison at each other."

She heard Doane laugh as he spoke to Zander. "She's a delight and so talented. I knew you'd appreciate Eve. Kevin and I have gotten very close to her. I can't wait until you see her work on his reconstruction." He paused before adding softly, "I want him there in the room when I cut your heart out."

"Are you finished?" Zander's voice was without expression. "I believe you've accomplished what you set out to do. You wanted to let me know you can reach out and touch me, if only by phone. You wanted to dangle Eve Duncan . . . as if I'd care. Now you're just muttering threats. You're all puffed up and trying to pretend you're as mean as your son. You're beginning to bore me."

"I wouldn't want to do that. I just want you to know what's coming and anticipate it. Kevin, Eve, and I will see you soon, Zander." He hung up and glanced at Eve, who had stopped at her bedroom door. "I'm sure Zander liked you even though you weren't kind to him. I find it promising that he decided to warn you against me."

"Why? He doesn't give a damn about me. He knows you were using me as a chess piece in this dirty battleground you're playing on. You wanted him to be sure that Kevin was still alive to you and I was part of some macabre revenge plan."

"But you'll notice that Zander said I'd accomplished my aim. Now we're all on the same page. Isn't that cozy?"

She didn't answer as the door closed behind her. Her breath released shakily. She was glad that she hadn't let Doane see how upset she was after that phone call. It shouldn't have mattered, but somehow it did. Talking to Kevin's killer had pulled her deeper into the matrix that Doane had drawn about her, smothering her, making her part of it.

He was smothering her. Not Zander, Kevin.

The memory of Kevin was suddenly before her. She could see the finely shaped lips, the gaping eye cavities, the smooth blankness of the rest of the face.

Waiting. Make me come alive. Bring me back. Punish you. Punish her.

Imagination. Oh, God, but what if it wasn't?

She had to get out of here. She couldn't touch that reconstruction again. She had to get away from him.

Don't panic. Be calm. Think.

Doane had been wired when she had come in here, vibrantly alive, every sense on high alert. He had enjoyed every minute of that call to Zander. It was the wrong time to try to deceive or escape. It would be better to wait and pick a different opportunity.

But she didn't want to wait. She wanted to break free. She wanted Bonnie to know she was safe, to know that no evil had touched her.

Bonnie . . .

But Bonnie couldn't come, he was keeping her away.

She looked up at the socket on the ceiling. But perhaps she could bring her near if she tried one more time . . .

"Don't do it again, Mama. I was worried about you. It was almost too much."

Her nails bit into her palms as her hands clenched in frustration. She had told Zander that she knew she was alone, but in this moment, that loneliness was nearly too deep to bear.

Stop whining, she thought in disgust. She would just do what had to be done. She'd stay away from that gas until the minute she tried to escape, then hope that her tolerance was strong enough. The last thing she wanted was to kill herself and let that bastard, Doane, win.

She moved across the room to the bed. Rest. Try to sleep. She had to be strong once she was on the run. She would listen for a while to make sure that Doane was as keen and alert as she thought, but tomorrow was probably the day she'd make her move.

The sound of Doane's walking on the oak floor. His stride was quick, charged. He was going toward the worktable, stopping, standing in front of Kevin's reconstruction. She could almost see him, staring eagerly, hungrily, at the half-finished sculpture.

Darkness.

Reaching out from the sculpture to enfold him. He would welcome that darkness, she knew.

But it was reaching past Doane, and she could feel that darkness touching her. She tensed and drew a deep breath, bracing herself.

Nausea.

She pushed it away. No way, you son of a bitch. You don't have any power over me.

The nausea became stronger, then reluctantly ebbed and dwindled away.

She felt an instant of triumph, which vanished immediately. She had felt that darkness like a living presence. Before it had been less strong and could almost have been mistaken for imagination. But when Doane had stood before his son's reconstruction just now, that dark wave had grown enormously.

Were they merging?

A bizarre idea, but Doane's viciousness seemed to be becoming greater with every passing hour.

Every hour the reconstruction progressed . . .

So now she was blaming herself? Ridiculous.

She closed her eyes. Ridiculous or not, she still felt a chill.

And dangerous or not, tomorrow she had to leave this place.

"Wasn't that exciting?" Doane whispered, his gaze on Kevin's face. "Zander knows that time is running out for him now. It's all coming together."

Kevin stared blankly back at him from those empty cavities. Doane hated those hollow eyes. Eve had replaced the blackened bones with smooth clay, but he wanted to look into those eyes and pretend it was Kevin's soul staring at him.

Who knows? Perhaps it would be.

"What do you think, Kevin? Time to start the list?" He took out his phone. "Oh, yes, I agree. We've waited long enough." He dialed Blick. "We're moving."

"Jane MacGuire?"

"You seem to be obsessed by her. Start at the top of your list. Let me know." He hung up. "It's done, Kevin."

He turned away from the skull and strode toward the couch. Staring at those empty eyes was causing him pain. He'd lie down and close his own eyes and remember Kevin the way he was before Zander had destroyed his bright, handsome beauty.

And perhaps those memories would make Kevin come alive again for him tonight.

"It seems Doane is getting eager. I was wondering when he'd raise his head." Zander turned to Stang as he hung up the phone. "Well, he's done it, and it's a very ugly head. He has Eve Duncan just as Venable told me. He's forcing her to do a reconstruction of his son's skull."

"Will he kill her?" Stang asked.

"Undoubtedly. The question is when it will happen. He wants her to finish the reconstruction, but she may annoy him and cause him to blow." He smiled faintly. "She's not afraid of him. Nor me. You should have heard her take on both of us. It was . . . interesting. But dangerous for her if she can't handle him."

"Of course, she can't handle him," Stang said. "She's an innocent woman who's caught in the middle. I read that dossier you have on her." He was silent a moment. "She seems to be exceptional. I don't like the idea of her being butchered."

Zander gazed at him in surprise. "I can see that you don't. You never speak up and offer an opinion. She must have impressed you."

"More than she did you."

"That's not true. Courage always impresses me. But I admit to curiosity more than admiration. I'm sure that doesn't astonish you."

"No, curiosity is cold and intellectual. Is there anything else I can do for you tonight, or may I go to bed?"

"I think that was close to an insult," Zander said softly. "Am I mistaken?"

Stang shook his head. "It wasn't an insult. Not if you see nothing wrong with being either of those things. You are what you are." He started to turn away, then stopped. "Could you stop him from killing her? You were planning on going after Doane before Venable asked you to delay."

"But now Doane wants me to come after him." He shrugged. "That was the reason for the call. He wanted to taunt me to make me angry enough to come and try to get him."

"A trap."

"One that he's been planning for a number of years. He even dangled Eve Duncan as part of the bait. I actually think he believed I might be tempted to come and save her. He obviously doesn't know me as well as you do."

"Could you save her?"

"Possibly. But having him come after me is strategically more sound and less risk. Then I get to spring the trap."

"And you said she may die after she finishes sculpting that skull if he's angry enough at her."

Zander merely gazed at him.

"I know." Stang said as he went toward the door. "You don't care. Stay out of your business. Well, you told me to read those dossiers. Why? Because it makes it my business. Maybe you knew I'd react like this and for some reason you wanted me to—" He broke off. "Why did Doane think that you might want to keep him from killing Eve Duncan?"

"He was never a good judge of character. Maybe he thought the years had softened me, and I'd be as sympathetic as you toward that poor, innocent woman."

Stang frowned. "There's something strange here. You were sure he'd go after Eve Duncan."

"He rescued his son's skull. She reconstructs skulls."

"That's logical, but I—"

"You just said I had cold intellect," Zander said mockingly. "What better demonstration?"

"None. I suppose." He paused. "But you'd never shared information with me before. Why Eve Duncan and her family? Why this time?"

Zander's smile didn't waver. "I'm tired of talking about this, Stang."

"I can't let it go. It doesn't add up. I have to figure it out." He grimaced. "Because I believe that's what you want me to do. But I'll shut up about it." He strode toward the door. "Call me if you need me, Zander."

Zander's smile vanished as soon as the door closed behind him.

Was he right? Stang was very clever. What Zander had assumed as a random impulse on his own part might hide other motives.

Good God, he never questioned his own actions or

the psychology that drove them, he thought impatiently. He had accepted his character, or lack of it, a long time ago. But on this occasion had he sought to put a barrier between his innate ruthlessness and the fate of Eve Duncan?

Nonsense.

He strolled over to the desk and opened the Duncan file.

Eve Duncan's face stared up at him. Her expression was thoughtful, alert, intelligent, strong. A hint of sadness in the firmness of her lips. No wonder Stang had been defensive of her.

He suddenly smiled. But then Stang had not been in the firing line of that scorching tongue. Eve Duncan might be innocent, but she was not helpless, and she was not suffering her imprisonment meekly. He had felt an odd flash of emotion when he had been the target. He still could not determine the nature of that feeling. Surprise? Regret? No, it must have been curiosity, as he had told Stang. It was strange that Doane had believed he'd have a shot at making Zander want to interfere with his plans for Eve Duncan.

Still, it would do no harm to call Venable and tell him that Doane was definitely on the move. He dialed quickly, and when Venable answered, he said tersely, "Doane called me and identified himself and made threats. I think he wants to signal that the game's afoot. You might warn General Tarther."

"I've already done it. I went to see him in Virginia to tell him that Doane has become a loose cannon. I've assigned an agent to guard him." He paused. "I'm surprised you went to the trouble of calling to tell me Tarther is in danger. Did Doane mention Eve Duncan?"

"I talked to her. I believe the fool thought he might be able to use her for bait."

"I'm sure you made it clear that wasn't an option. She seemed well?"

"Yes, though I didn't pay much attention. I'm hanging up now." He pressed the disconnect and looked back down at the photo of Eve Duncan.

Could you save her?

It would be an interesting challenge, but not in accordance with either his work ethic or philosophy.

Sorry, Eve Duncan. As you said, you're on your own.

He flipped the file shut.

LAKE COTTAGE

Joe and Margaret arrived back at the cottage five minutes after Venable drove up to the front door.

"Talk," Joe said grimly as he took the steps two at a time to where Venable stood on the porch. "No excuses. No stalling. I'm going to know everything you know, or, by God, I'll make you pay."

"If I hadn't intended to talk to you, I would have disappeared and not come back. Stop threatening me."

"I would have found you."

"But maybe not in time." Venable turned to Jane. "You look a little pale. Why don't you sit down?"

"I'm fine," she said through her teeth. "This isn't about me. What's happening, Venable?"

He shrugged. "Okay, okay. I might be feeling a little guilty that you're—" He shook his head. "I never thought you'd be a victim. I thought I'd kept it all under control. Doane appeared much weaker than his son, and there was no evidence that he was actively involved in any of the murders. He might have just been a father grieving for his boy. Even when he took Eve, there was a chance that he only wanted to have her do the reconstruction. She might not have been in danger. Hallet, that farmer, is missing, but there's no proof of violence toward him."

"My men are dragging the lake for that farmer now. And there's a grave out there in the woods that proves differently," Joe said. "Dukes had his throat cut. He was your agent, your responsibility, Venable."

"Do you think I don't know that?" Venable said roughly. "I realized when we found Dukes that I'd been fooling myself. Doane is as bad as his son, Kevin. Perhaps he's worse, though that's hard to believe. I knew I had to put him down no matter whom it hurts."

"And whom will it hurt?" Caleb asked.

Venable glanced at him. "Why don't you take a hike, Caleb? This isn't your concern."

"The hell it's not," Jane said fiercely. "It's anyone's concern who is willing to help Eve. She's the only one who is important."

"At last," Margaret murmured as she leaned against the porch rail. "That must include me. Yes, whom will it hurt, Agent Venable?"

"You want a list? One, General John Tarther, an honorable man who spent his entire life fighting to keep the country safe. Two, several Pakistanis who will be beheaded or thrown in prison if their countrymen find out that they helped track Bin Laden." He paused. "And at least five embedded CIA agents whose cover might be jeopardized if those Pakistanis are tortured and reveal information. It will be a chain reaction."

"That chain reaction is not going to include Eve," Joe said coldly. "Because we're going to get Doane."

"I'm not arguing," Venable said wearily. "I've already started to pull our agents out of Pakistan. It will take time. I just hope that Doane is holding off on releasing that disk on the chance he can use it as a lever in case of an emergency."

"Disk?" Jane asked. "Dammit, start at the beginning, Venable."

"The beginning?" Venable gazed out at the lake. "That was probably the day that son of a bitch Kevin Relling was born." He shook his head as if to clear it. "No, that's not what you want to know. Brief and to the point, right? Okay, I was working in the Middle East several years ago when I became involved with the group that was hunting for Bin Laden. Kevin Relling had already killed Tarther's daughter as a gift to his al-Qaeda friends. He sent photos of the kill to all his terrorist group. They were both explicit and brutal." He paused. "And he also sent the photos to Tarther. It nearly killed him. The only thing that kept him going was the chance to hunt Kevin Relling down and get him convicted of murder."

"Kevin Relling," Jane said. "Joe couldn't find any record on him. You buried it, didn't you. Tell us about Kevin Relling."

"Yes, I buried it." He shrugged. "I told you the beginning started with Relling. I'll try to keep it as short as possible. It's not pretty . . ."

CHAPTER

15

"And Kevin Relling's father has this disk?" Joe asked when Venable had finished. "That house where he lived in Colorado has been searched?"

"Am I an idiot?" Venable asked sarcastically. "It was the first thing I ordered done when we realized Doane had split. Nothing has been found. The second thing was to set a team of agents to try to find him."

"Zero there, too," Joe said coldly. "And you wouldn't give me all the information I needed to go after him myself."

"You're getting it now. I couldn't justify endangering that many innocent people until I was certain that Doane actually presented a danger and that there was no way we could snare him ourselves."

"And if you'd been able to do that, would you have sent him back to his safe house and just tried to reinstate your deal?" Jane asked.

"There's a possibility if I thought Doane wasn't a

real threat and controllable." Venable saw the expression on their faces and said harshly, "I won't make excuses. My life is all about compromises and control. That disk is important. I need to take Doane alive and take it away from him. It's life or death for too many people not to try to grab it and keep it safe. It's worth taking a risk."

"Not if it's Eve's risk," Jane said jerkily. "Screw your control. And there won't be any compromises where Eve's concerned. If there are I'll—"

"Easy." Joe put his hand on her arm. "I feel the same way, but we have to work together." His glance at Venable was icy. "We have to use him for the time being. Afterward, it may be a different matter."

"So use me." Venable's lips twisted. "I never thought I'd say that. It should tell you how much I want you to find Eve."

"If it doesn't get in the way of CIA business," Jane said. She held up her hand. "I know, Joe. I'm not being cool and logical. I'm just so damn mad." She added in a whisper, "And so damn scared." She drew a shaky breath. "All right, I have to get everything straight in my head, Venable. It's all been hurled at us in bits and pieces. This Kevin Relling was a monster of the first order. He was in the Special Forces and became an expert assassin. He was also some kind of megalomaniac who was trying to grab power by joining the terrorists who were protecting Bin Laden."

"The children," Margaret whispered. It was the first words she'd spoken since Venable had begun his narrative. Her face was pale and stricken. "Those poor children."

"The fact that he was also a child killer was merely his casual entertainment," Jane said. "Venable wouldn't regard it as important as political ramifications."

Venable flinched. "Not fair, Jane."

"I don't want to be fair. It's going to take a long time for me to forgive you." She added, "But that's not important right now. General Tarther was authorizing illegal action in Pakistan to catch the terrorist group who was protecting Bin Laden. Kevin Relling killed Tarther's daughter as revenge, but the general went on the hunt and brought Relling in to face a criminal trial. When the charge was dismissed on a technicality, Tarther couldn't believe it. When Relling escaped, the general almost went crazy. He hired a contract killer to find and kill Relling. He accomplished his mission, and that was the end of Kevin Relling." She glared at Venable. "Do I have it right?"

"But it was the beginning of your dealing with Doane," Joe said. "What the hell were you doing protecting him?"

"Doane came to us and demanded we protect him from his son's former al-Qaeda buddies. He said he'd lost his son and all he wanted to do was start a new life. He wanted to be placed in a witness protection program."

"And you did it?"

"He also said that he had a disk his son had given him and told him to use it if he felt threatened. He didn't want to use it, but he had to protect himself if we couldn't do it for him."

"And you believed him?"

"I'm a cynical bastard, but there was a chance he was

telling the truth. He was very, very good. He seemed so sincere, a grieving father who'd had no idea his son was anything but a soldier serving his country." He looked at Jane. "You drew that sketch of him from Ben Hudson's description. He looks like a nice guy, sympathetic, kind. He's even more convincing in person. He strikes just the right note. It's incredible. I researched him thoroughly, and I couldn't connect any of Kevin Relling's crimes to his father. It was worth a chance if I kept him under close surveillance. I set him up in a small town in Colorado."

"Why didn't you just have someone break in and go after the disk?"

"We searched his house four times in the last five years. No disk." He lifted one shoulder in a half shrug. "And Doane appeared to be living the life he told me he wanted. Involved with the neighbors, volunteer at the local high school. Everyone liked him."

"And then he took off?" Joe said. "Where the hell was his surveillance?"

"Too complacent. For five years, he'd watched Doane being the great guy next door. I'm sure Doane knew my agent's schedule and worked around it."

"So he was lulling everyone into thinking he was something he wasn't," Jane said. "Five years is a long time to waste building up a false image. Or did he just suddenly, impulsively break out?"

"He wasn't wasting time," Venable said. "I think he must have been very busy."

"Doing what?"

"Getting ready to go after the men he blamed for killing his son."

"Five years? Why didn't he go after General Tarther right away?"

"I'd bet he wanted the whole package. He might be able to kill Tarther, but what about the hired gun who actually pulled the trigger? He didn't even know his name." He grimaced. "Though Doane did ask me if I knew who did it when we started negotiating his protection."

"And that didn't set off any alarms?"

"I told you, he was very good. There was no anger, tears were running down his cheeks. A bewildered father trying to find answers."

"And do you know who killed Kevin Relling?"

"Yes. Tarther told me." He was silent a moment. "Though I made a deal with him that I wouldn't reveal his name to anyone in exchange for his not going after Doane to tie up loose ends. I tried to keep my word, dammit."

"You told Doane?"

"Hell, no. But I'm going to tell you. I have to do it. It's too dangerous not to do it now." He paused. "Lee Zander."

Joe frowned, going over the name in his memory for any reference. "I'm familiar with the names of a lot of professional hit men. I've never heard of him."

"That doesn't surprise me. That's why Zander's lasted all these decades without being killed or captured. He's very particular about his targets, and he's as close to being the perfect killing machine as I've ever come across. He's also incredibly expensive, and he only has to emerge from seclusion occasionally. You might say he's unique."

"I might say he's a murderer. You shouldn't have worried about keeping your word to him."

"I was more worried about keeping myself alive," he said dryly. "Zander was hard to persuade not to go after Doane, and he doesn't like people who don't keep their word. As it was, he thought he was running a risk, and Doane was going to cause him trouble."

"And he was right?" Jane asked. "But he's causing more trouble for Eve than Zander. Why?"

"He spent a long time finding out who killed his son and making his plans. She's evidently part of the entire picture."

"The reconstruction?"

He was silent a moment. "I'm sure that's one of the pieces." He went on quickly, "And since he went to a good deal of trouble to get her, we have to include her in any long-range plot Doane concocted. We have to assume she'll be on his list."

"List?"

"Kill list," he said simply. "Tarther. Zander." He paused. "Eve."

"No," Jane said hoarsely. "He had reason to kill Tarther and Zander. Not Eve." She shook off Caleb's hand as he reached out to touch her shoulder. "But since when do maniacs have to have reasons?" she asked unevenly. "He killed Dukes and probably that farmer. Okay, I'll accept that it's only a matter of time before he decides to kill her. Now we have to keep him from doing it. If he's going after Tarther and Zander, then we have a chance to capture him when he shows up." She rubbed her temple. "If he keeps Eve alive that long. We'd be much safer trying to find out where he's keeping her. You have no idea, Venable? Something you haven't told us? If you had an agent watching him all those years, he should have been able to report where he went when he left the property."

"He did, and we checked them all out. That doesn't mean that he couldn't have slipped away from him some nights." He made a face. "Complacency, again. He wasn't considered a danger. He also had a computer that he'd wiped clean. We're digging into that memory."

"And Blick," Joe said. "He had Kevin's friend, Blick, on the outside, doing his research and dirty work."

"Doane drove his car into the lake," Margaret said suddenly. "Was he worried that you might find something on or in the car? He could have gotten rid of the body of the farmer anywhere."

"We'll find out soon," Joe said. "If your damn cat isn't telling you stories."

"Cat?" Venable asked.

"Never mind," Joe said.

"Blick," Jane repeated. "He must know where Doane can be found. He's not as smart as Doane, right? Can you find him?"

"I'm working on it. I have a few leads."

"Which you didn't include in the dossier on him you gave us," Joe said sarcastically. "That was very spare."

"I had to make sure that I couldn't handle this alone."

"Oh, yes, your kindly general and all those other people at risk."

"If it wasn't Eve, you'd be just as careful."

"It is Eve." He reached for his phone. "All we have

right now is that house in Goldfork. There's got to be something there that will give us a lead."

"We went over that house with a fine-tooth comb, Joe. My team didn't find anything."

"I hope that search wasn't too thorough. They might have messed up any chance—"

"Who are you calling?"

"Someone I trust more than your guys to find anything Doane might have left behind to point the way."

Jane nodded immediately. "Kendra Michaels. Eve told me about her. Said she's amazing. Can she help us, Joe?"

"I hope to God she can. I've never seen anyone more able to delve into a crime scene and pull up answers. She and Eve are friends. I know she'll try." He turned away and walked across the porch as Kendra answered. "Kendra? Joe Quinn. I need your help. Stop bitching. I know you're busy. You're always busy. You'll have to drop whatever it is. Be quiet, and let me talk."

Jane tuned him out as she turned back to Venable. "Zander. He seems to be a principal target if Doane waited five years to hunt him down. Maybe we can get him to work with us to trap Doane." Venable was shaking his head. "Why not? It's worth a try to save her."

"He won't do it. He won't care."

"Then we'll make the son of a bitch care. If I have to do it by pointing a knife in his belly."

"Not a good idea," Caleb murmured. "There are other ways to force the issue. I might be able to help."

"You won't get near him," Venable said. "He'd consider it an annoyance."

"Do you know where he lives?"

"I know where he was a few days ago. He quite probably moved out after I warned him that Doane might be coming after him."

"He's afraid?"

"No, he just moves on if there's any chance of a disturbance that might attract attention."

"Can you find out if he's still there? You have his telephone number?"

He nodded. "But it won't do any good. Listen, I don't want you getting any more hurt than you are now, Jane. He's one of the most dangerous men I've ever met. Stay away from Zander."

"I can't stay away from him. Doane wants him dead. We may be able to use him." She looked him in the eye. "You find out where he is right now. You follow up your leads and find Blick. What about Tarther? He's a target, right? At least we know where he is."

"I could run up there and keep an eye on him," Caleb said.

"He's already being guarded," Venable said. "I set a guard as soon as I knew Doane had left Goldfork."

"Good, then I can concentrate on doing a little scouting around." He looked at Jane. "Until you need me."

She was not going to refuse. No one was more expert at the hunt than Caleb. "Thank you."

"It's better if I'm out of the way when Trevor comes anyway." He smiled. "And with any luck, I may be able to lay the head of one of those snakes at your feet. That would be much more productive for me and put me in a wonderful light." He turned to Venable. "Give me the address and any other information I should have about Tarther."

Jane took a step closer to the rail and looked out at the lake as they began to speak. Joe was still talking to Kendra Michaels, and Jane was suddenly feeling very much alone.

"It's going to be okay," Margaret said softly as she moved to stand beside her. "We'll all work hard, and we'll get her back. But I'm confused about this Kendra Michaels. Can she really help?"

"I don't know," Jane said wearily. "She's supposed to be brilliant and a bit temperamental, but Eve trusted her. She's some kind of music therapist who was blind most of her life until recently and now works with law enforcement on occasion."

"Blind?"

"I know, I know. It's all crazy. But I don't care. I'll take a chance on her." She added desperately, "I'll take a chance on anyone who's willing to try to find Eve." She moistened her lips. "Even you, Margaret. You have no business being here, but I'm going to let you take your risks. God, I'm sorry."

"I'm not sorry. It's what I want. But a moment ago you were hurling orders and marshaling us all to battle. What happened?"

"Why did I fall apart? I miss her," she said unevenly. "I'm fine while I'm doing something that could get her back, but when I have moments of quiet, the panic and sadness hit home. I can't tell you how many hours Eve and I have spent on this porch talking or just sitting and looking out at the lake. There's a closeness I never knew before I came to her. She'd had her real daughter, Bonnie, and lost her. I hadn't had anyone but a long line of foster parents who didn't give a damn about me. *She* cared. I don't know why because I wasn't an easy kid. We just sort of completed each other."

"That's pretty wonderful."

"Yeah. You bet it is."

"I never had someone like that," she said quietly. "Maybe someday." She turned toward the door. "You don't want anyone right now. I was going to talk to you about what I could do to help, but I'll go make myself useful and brew us up some coffee instead."

Margaret's sensitivity extended to more than animals, Jane thought as she looked back at the lake. She suddenly tensed as she caught sight of trucks and divers pulling up on the far north bank. They were going to search for Doane's car.

And the body inside it.

It was starting. The hunt, the deaths . . .

But not Eve's death. They had made small steps, and they would make more now that they had names and an idea of Doane's agenda.

Hold on, Eve. I'll never give up. We're coming for you.

RIO GRANDE FOREST, COLORADO

We're coming for you.

Pain. Sorrow. Panic.

Jane?

A dream . . .

Eve's eyes opened, and she lay there a moment until the drowsiness left her. It had been strange to have that dream about Jane when Bonnie hadn't been able to reach her until she was in a drugged sleep. Life and death. Perhaps it made a difference in the battle with that darkness.

Or perhaps it was just Eve's own desire to reach out for the ones she loved in this place that was filled with ugliness and hate.

Forget dreams. Change the place. Escape the ugliness herself.

She got to her feet and moved toward the bathroom. The oak boards were cool on her bare feet. It was always cool, often freezing, at night in the mountains. She had to remember to dress as warmly as she could. There was no telling how long she'd have to be on the run until she could find anyone to help her. She didn't even know how close she was to a main road. It had seemed at least fifteen minutes before they had reached smooth pavement instead of rock.

She listened a moment before she turned on the shower. Doane was breathing steadily, deeply. She had tucked the spatula into her pocket, and she could try to jimmy the lock now. Lord, she didn't want to sit down in front of Kevin's reconstruction again.

No, Doane's breathing was changing. He was waking. Perhaps it was for the best. She wasn't ready. Try later.

Plan. She had to have a plan that would take care of all aspects of her escape. And what about her course when she made it outside? Not easy. Doane had set a load of complications for her to overcome. She could do it. She just had to have a plan and not try to wing it.

Today, Doane. I promise you, it will be today, you bastard.

CHAPTER

16

You've got the nose." Doane's eyes were glinting with excitement as he stared at the skull. "You said it would be so hard, but it came quickly, almost like magic." He added softly, "Kevin's magic. He's telling you what to do, isn't he?"

"No, I'm just damn good at my job." She avoided looking at the nose that had emerged beneath her fingers in an incredibly short time. "Your son is dead, and he has no magic. All that's left of him is this hideous skull."

"It's not hideous anymore. You're making him the way he was before Zander killed him." His gaze was visually caressing the skull. "But it will be better when you put in the eyes. Go ahead and do it."

She stiffened. "It's not time. There's a lot of smoothing and fine-tuning to do. The eyes are the last thing to go in."

"You could do all that stuff later. I want to see his

eyes. They were blue like mine. But his were sharper, keener, almost mesmerizing."

"You'll be disappointed. These are glass eyes, and they only reflect color, not personality."

"Maybe. Put them in."

She did not want to put those eyes into the skull. She did not want to complete this reconstruction of a monster. "Later." She pushed her stool back. "I need a cup of coffee." She walked toward the kitchenette. She could feel the tension in every muscle. It was almost time. It was late afternoon, and she needed to escape while she could still see the terrain to give herself the best chance. Doane was excited, impatient, absorbed with his son, less likely to notice anything different about her demeanor. Good. Because she felt as if her determination and nervousness were blatantly obvious.

Calm down. She had a plan, didn't she? She had worked and experimented with those gas vents. It wasn't as if she were going at this blind.

"You can't have everything your own way, Doane." She put on the coffeemaker. "You brought me here because I'm an expert, right? Now let me do my work the way it should be done."

"Yes, you're an expert." He was frowning. "And that's one of the reasons why I brought you here. Not the only one. I had no idea you'd be so difficult. I want those eyes put in."

She turned her back on him and reached for a coffee mug.

He muttered a curse. "You're a bitch who doesn't realize how helpless you are. I'm the one in charge. I'm the one who makes the calls. I have the—" His phone rang, and she saw him check his ID as she glanced over her shoulder. "Curious?" He was smiling maliciously. "I made a call to Blick last night. I wanted some-one dead. That's how much power I have. I just say the word, and someone dies. Do you know who I told him to kill?" He punched the access. "Hold on, Blick. A lesson is in progress." He looked at Eve. "You heard me send him to your lake cottage when we were in the truck. People you care about are there. Did I tell him to kill Joe Quinn? Jane MacGuire?"

She couldn't breathe, her chest painfully tight. "I don't believe you."

"Which one, Eve?" he asked softly.

She moistened her lips. "Neither. You wouldn't want to sacrifice a possible way to control me."

"Clever. But I had you for a minute, didn't I?" He pressed the speaker button on the phone. "Go ahead, Blick. Success?"

"He's dead. I killed him in his garden. It was a great shot. I was able to break into the house next door and zero in on him from one of the upper-floor windows. Kevin would have been proud of me."

"I'm sure he would have been. Any interference?"

"A guard inside the house. I was able to get away while he was checking out the old man." He paused. "You know, I think the old man knew I was there. He lifted his head as if he was listening or something. Then he just sat there as if he was waiting. Weird."

"But he's dead, that's all that counts."

"Yeah, where do you want me to go from here?"

"I'll let you know." He looked at Eve. "Maybe back to the lake cottage."

"Whatever you say, but the woods were crawling with cops. It may be chancy."

"I'll let you know," Doane repeated. He hung up.

"Who . . . is the old man?"

"I think you can guess. You're so clever. General John Tarther. He's lucky he lived to be this old. He's been on borrowed time for the last five years." He looked back at the reconstruction. "But we got him, didn't we, Kevin? I couldn't make it last as long as I wanted. I sent him to you to do whatever you want with the bastard."

She shuddered as she saw Doane's vicious intensity. "Why now?"

"I'm sure you realized that my call to Zander last night was the signal for the game to start. I was willing to let Blick take care of Tarther so that I could concentrate on Zander."

And while Eve had slept, an old man who had only sought final justice for the death of his child had breathed his last.

Rest in peace.

Help him, Bonnie.

"So you can see that I'm in charge. I make the rules. One phone call, and I can—"

"I understand you." She didn't want to hear any more. She was sad and sick at the thought of that needless death. She had to stop that obscene bragging. "I'm duly intimidated."

"No, you're not. But you will be. Put in Kevin's eyes."

"Do it yourself."

He was taken aback. "What?"

"If you won't let me finish the rest the way it should

be done, then do it yourself." She poured the hot coffee into her mug. "Placing the eyes is the simplest part of the process, and who should know better how they should look." She took a sip of coffee. "I'll open the display case for you, if you like."

"I don't know if . . ." But he was beginning to like the idea. His expression was intrigued. "You're right; I know exactly how he should look."

"And your Kevin would love having someone simpatico add the final touches. I don't think he likes me much, does he?"

"No, he liked you better before he realized how strong you made the little girl," he said absently. He was suddenly eager, excited. "Yes, Kevin would like me to do him that service. It would be the way we helped each other when we were together."

Helped each other victimizing those children, she thought, sick. "I'll get the case." She crossed the room to the worktable. "I might have to build up the under-eye area to support the eye." She set her coffee down on the worktable and reached underneath and pulled out the case. "I usually use brown eyes, but I notice you made sure I had blue."

"Of course." He watched as she opened the case. "It's not as if I didn't know exactly what he looked like."

"Why didn't you say anything about me looking at photos then?"

"You didn't do it with other reconstructions. I wanted you to get the *feel* of him." His eyes were fixed in fascination on the glass eyes she'd revealed. "And you did."

There was no doubt about that, Eve thought. Even at this moment, she felt entirely too close to that skull.

"Now it's your turn to get the feel of him." She lifted her coffee to her lips. "Pick up one of the eyeballs. Careful."

"They're not as beautiful as Kevin's." He carefully picked up the glass eye. "But they'll have to do." His head lifted to look at the empty orbital cavities. "We're so close, Kevin. Just this one more—"

Eve threw the scalding coffee into Doane's eyes!

He *screamed*. He dropped the glass eye and frantically reached for his own eyes.

Eve's hand darted out in a karate chop to his neck. He dropped to his knees. His hand reached blindly for the weapons in his pocket. "Bitch."

Hurry.

No time to try another karate blow. Even though he couldn't see right now, she knew he had a gun as well as the emblem with the gas release in that pocket.

Keep to the plan.

She dashed the short distance to the bedroom, grabbed the duffel she had set by the door.

Then she was running back toward Doane and the reconstruction.

Doane was still flailing, but he had his gun half-out of his pocket. "You think I can't see you? You're hazy, but that's all I need to shoot you. Stop where you are. I have a use for you. I'm not ready to kill you yet, bitch."

"Really? I'm ready to kill you," Eve lifted her foot in a karate kick that struck his hand and sent the gun flying. She dove for the gun, but he was suddenly there on top of her.

He was heavy. So heavy. The best she could do was

push the gun spinning across the floor to the opposite side of the room.

No chance to get across the room to retrieve it, she realized in despair.

"Kill me?" he taunted, his hands closing on her throat. "We're too strong for you. Can't you feel our power? I'll squeeze the life out of you. No, not quite. Not yet."

She was getting dizzy as her air was shut off. Move now or not at all.

She lunged upward and butted her head against his forehead with all her strength.

He grunted with pain, and his grip loosened.

She tore free and rolled to the left, punching him in the stomach.

But he was recovering quickly, reaching for her.

Get out. Get out. Get out.

But keep to the plan.

Do the one thing she dreaded the most.

She jumped to her feet and whirled toward the dais, where the reconstruction stared at her with those blind eyes.

Don't look at him. He's nothing. He's only bone and clay.

She took a deep breath.

The next instant she reached out, snatched the skull from the dais, and threw it in her open duffel.

"What are you doing?" Doane screamed. He was right behind her, his hand grabbing her shoulder. "What are you doing to my Kevin?"

She tore away from his grip and ran toward the door.

"You're insane. I told you what would happen if you

opened that front door." He was reaching for the control emblem in his pocket. "But I'm not going to wait. I'll bring you down now and have you groveling."

She was almost at the door.

Carnations.

Don't breathe.

She held her breath.

Carnation scent surrounding her.

She unlocked the front door and heard the gas release from the vent above the door.

More carnations.

Dizzy.

Oh, God, she should have taken longer to accustom herself to the gas.

Too late.

Hold your breath and pray that you can endure it.

She was outside!

Don't breathe yet. There might be lingering scent on the air issuing from the open doorway or clinging to her clothing.

She ran.

Rocks under her feet. Trees. Head for the trees. Sharp, cold air hitting her cheeks.

Lungs bursting.

The feel of the duffel striking her thigh as she ran. Was she feeling Kevin's reconstruction through the heavy canvas?

She could hear Doane shouting behind her. No shots. He must not have retrieved the gun before he came after her or he'd be firing bullets instead of ugly words. He'd probably been too stunned that she'd been able to withstand the gas.

She took a cautious breath. It seemed safe. The faintest hint of carnation probably emanating from her shirt.

Or was it coming from the duffel, caught in the open zippered fold where Kevin's skull rested?

The scent was from her shirt. Don't think of anything else.

Just bone and clay. Just bone and clay.

"Give him back to me." Doane's voice was a raw, thunderbolt of rage. "What are you doing? Give him back to me, or I'll kill everyone that you care about. And I'll tell Blick to take his time with your fine, pretty daughter. Blick knows all about suffering. He never interfered with Kevin's pleasure, but sometimes he shared."

She tried to block out his voice. He had no weapon at the moment but words, but these filled her with desperation and fear. Don't listen to him.

Keep to the plan.

Her gaze searched wildly to the right and left. This path appeared to be going straight up the mountain, with trees on either side.

She needed to be closer to the cliff edge.

"Blick was angry that I was upset when he disobeyed me and shot Jane MacGuire. He'll be happy to have my blessing to take that anger out on her."

"I told you once that you can't use that weapon against me. Jane's stronger than you, so is Joe." Please, let that be the truth. Let good be stronger than evil.

A break in the trees ahead, and she could see a glimpse of the steep cliff that sloped to the valley hundreds of feet below.

Yes.

She increased her speed, running hard, leaving Doane a good distance behind.

"You're mad. What are you doing? You know I'll punish you. *We'll* punish you."

"Stop where you are." She'd reached the break in the trees, near the edge of the cliff, and turned to face him. She was panting, perspiring, her eyes glittering. "This is the end, you bastard."

He stopped several hundred yards down the path, his expression suddenly wary. "Suicide, Eve?" He shook his head. "I know I said that you didn't have a fear of death, but I don't think you'd willingly take your own life."

"You're damn right I wouldn't." She reached in the duffel and pulled out the reconstruction. "Poor Kevin, he's a little worse for wear with all this jouncing around. His nose looks a bit askew, doesn't it?"

Doane froze, his gaze on the skull of his son. "Give him back to me."

"No way." She glanced over the cliff. "It looks a long, long way down that slope. I'm afraid he's going to have a rough trip."

"No!" He took a step forward, then stopped as she held the reconstruction over the edge. "He's so near to being back with me. You can't do that to him."

"Watch me. And then you can decide whether you want to chase after me or go after your precious son. There's no telling what kind of damage that skull will undergo skidding down that slope toward the valley. It might break on the boulders, or it might be eaten by wolves or coyotes if you don't retrieve it right away. Don't you want to save your son, Doane?"

"You won't do it. He won't let you do it." He was glaring at her from those burned red eyes. "It's happening right now. Your muscles are locking. Aren't your hands tightening around that skull to keep it from dropping?"

"No." She deliberately forced her fingers looser on the reconstruction. She wouldn't let insidious suggestion beat her now. "Do you think that I'd let you use my work in the little nightmare scenario you've drawn in that sick mind of yours? I can see you flourishing this ghastly head in Zander's face before you kill him, and I don't give a damn. But you seem to want me to be part of the kill, and you'll have to give that up."

"I won't give it up. I want Zander to see you. I want you *there*."

"Then come and get me." She looked him in the eye. "But go and get Kevin first."

She dropped the skull over the cliff.

Doane screamed as if in mortal pain.

She whirled and started dashing up the path.

Run.

And hope that she'd managed to buy the time she needed to get away from Doane. It had been the only ploy she could think of to distract Doane from the chase.

She had a good chance of Doane's going after Kevin's skull. He was completely obsessed by everything connected to that reconstruction.

She glanced back over her shoulder.

Doane was standing at the edge of the cliff, his hands clenched into fists as he looked down the long slope where she'd thrown the skull. His face . . .

And then he looked up the path at her. Darkness. Rage. Evil.

She froze. She inhaled sharply and couldn't move. She should keep running, but the force of that evil halted her in her tracks. It was as if he'd laid a hand on her shoulder and jerked her to a stop.

"You think you're so clever." It wasn't a shout; it was hoarse, low, and they were so far apart, she shouldn't have been able to hear him. But she heard every word. "You know nothing if you think I'll let you get away. I have to have you there when I kill Zander. I've been planning it for three years, ever since I found out about you. I've been seeing it before I go to sleep at night. I've been promising it to Kevin every day. Killing Zander won't be as sweet if you're not there." He paused. "He has to see you die."

"You fool." She stared at him in disbelief. "You'd be killing me for nothing. Zander won't care."

"He'll care. He thinks he won't, but he won't be able to help himself. There's nothing stronger in this world."

The sentence sounded vaguely familiar. "What are you talking about?"

"You. Zander. What I found out three years ago when I was searching for something, anything to hurt him. It worked out so beautifully for Kevin, for me. I knew it was meant to be."

She felt a chill mixed with bewilderment and a panicky foreboding as she stared down the hill at him.

"All you found out was that I'm a forensic sculptor who could put your son's face back together."

"Oh, no. That was a side bonus to my finding you. That wasn't what I was looking for. It was just a sign that what I found was true." His voice was soft, vicious. "That I'd found the one perfect weapon to use to cut Zander to the soul and cause him to bleed."

Why was she standing here talking to him? Why couldn't she move? Her lead made her safe for only a few moments.

Turn and run.

But that might make him decide to follow her instead of going after the skull. "You're talking wild. He'd turn his back and walk away."

"No, he couldn't do that any more than I could. There's nothing stronger in the world."

This time she remembered when he'd said those words. She stiffened, her eyes widening. "What are you trying to say? You're not making sense."

"Nothing stronger than the bond between a father and his child," he repeated. "My heart was broken when that bastard killed my boy. I have to take his child from him and butcher it." His eyes narrowed on her face, drinking in every expression. "I have to butcher you, Eve."

Shock. Disbelief. "What do you—"

"That I found what I was looking for when I was searching for some way to pierce Zander's armor and cause him to suffer for the little time he'll have left before I kill him." He smiled, and the malice increased. "I found his daughter."

She inhaled sharply, as if kicked in the stomach. "If

you mean what I think you mean, then you're truly insane," she said unsteadily.

"No, Zander is your father. Even if I hadn't known it, I could tell by how like him you are. You're both the same species of monster. Full of venom and ugliness." His glance shifted to look down at the valley. "Or you could never have done that to my Kevin, you bitch."

Everything she had heard was crazy, incredible.

Lies.

Impossible.

Pay no attention to those words, which were blowing her mind. Why was she still standing here, muscles locked, staring at him like a victim fascinated by a weaving cobra? Break away. Push away those lies. "Then go down that slope and try to find your son." She forced her muscles to move. "Save him. Try to salvage that broken face. Or go to hell with him." She started to run again. "I'm not going to listen to your ravings any longer."

She heard another curse behind her, and when she glanced over her shoulder, she saw that he was no longer standing on the cliff edge.

He was coming after her.

She had lost.

"Did you think that I'd let you fool me into giving you the chance to get away? Kevin will wait for me." He was putting on speed. "He wants you as much as I do."

Her heart was pounding hard as she raced up the hill. Faster.

He's your father.

Madness.

She had to go faster. Doane was big, with long legs . . .

But she was smaller, lighter, younger.

She was pulling ahead a little.

No, just holding her own.

Even her mother had no sure idea who had fathered Eve. Doane could not know.

He was getting closer.

It was getting dark, and the trees were casting long shadows on the path. Darkness was good, it would help her slip off the path into the brush and lose Doane. If she could just get a little more ahead of him . . .

Silence except for the harsh sound of Doane's breathing behind her.

Her lungs were hurting.

Ignore the pain. Keep running.

Her legs felt weak, rubbery.

Keep running.

"You can't get away." Doane's voice was laboring. "I'm stronger than you. Kevin—makes me strong. He won't—let you free. Can't you feel him—beside you?"

She felt a sharp coolness touch her body.

It was the wind, she thought desperately. To believe anything else would be to accept defeat.

She steeled herself and began to run faster. Then, incredibly, with every step, she could feel her strength increase, her muscles burn, and the pain leaving her.

No coolness, gentle warmth enfolding her.

Bonnie?

Light. Strength. Love.

Oh God, yes, Bonnie.

She felt a rush of sheer joy.

"You're done. It's over. You've lost me!" she shouted fiercely back to Doane. The blood was pounding in her veins. Exhilaration was making her heady. "Can't you see?" She was gaining distance with each breath, every step. "I *am* free, you bastard!"

Read on for an excerpt of **Iris Johansen's**
next book,

Hunting Eve

CHAPTER

1

It was Doane's mountain.

He was the hunter, she was the prey.

Was he still behind her?

Eve tore through the underbrush at the side of the trail, lost her balance, fell, then struggled to her feet again.

She mustn't give in to this weakness. She seemed to have been running through this wilderness forever. No, it couldn't have been as long as it appeared to her. It had been late afternoon when she had broken free of Doane and the house where he had been keeping her, and darkness was only now falling.

But why was Jim Doane still behind her, dammit? He was no young man, and she should have been able to lose him long before this. As a painful stitch stabbed her side, she paused and drew a deep breath, listening.

A crashing in the brush behind her!

She started running again.

"I hear you, bitch." Doane's breathing was harsh, labored. "Come back to me. If you do, I may not kill you . . . yet. But you're making me angry and I may lose control. I don't want to do that. It would spoil everything for Kevin."

Kevin, Doane's son, whose reconstructed skull Eve had hurled off this mountain, less than an hour ago, to distract Doane. Doane's obsession with his dead son was deepening with every passing moment. Did Doane actually think she'd trust him? Kevin had been a serial killer who was a monster without a hint of conscience, and his father, Doane, had been his enabler, the one who had made it possible for him to kill all those helpless children who had crossed Kevin's path. While Eve had been Doane's prisoner after he had kidnapped her, she had begun to wonder whether it was father or son who had been the true monster.

Perhaps it was both. There had been moments when she'd had the eerie feeling while working on his forensic sculpture that Kevin was trying to break through the bonds of hell and death and merge with his father.

Crazy. Imagination.

Or truth.

It was hard to tell the difference in this nightmare into which she had been drawn.

"You shouldn't have thrown his skull off into that ravine. Did you think I'd go after it and let you escape?"

It was exactly what she had hoped. That damn skull was everything to Doane, and she'd gambled that he'd go down the side of the mountain and try to retrieve it.

She'd been wrong.

She felt the twinge in her side become actual pain. How long could she keep running?

Stop whining. She'd run as long as she had to run. She was far younger than Doane. She was strong, and she was frightened. Panic was a great spur.

And did she have Bonnie helping her?

For a little while she had thought that her daughter's spirit had been there beside her, putting speed and wings to every step. It had been a comforting thought . . .

But now there only seemed to be Doane and her in this deadly race. No loving presence that might warm and save her.

It's okay, Bonnie. I know you tried. There's nothing he can do to me that will matter in the end.

The stitch in her side was easing.

She was running faster.

She should have known Bonnie would not let her falter, she thought ruefully. Not if Eve showed even a faint hint that she would not do her best to keep herself alive.

I wasn't going to opt out, Bonnie. I wouldn't do that to Joe and Jane. I was just trying to be an understanding mother. I know you can't do everything. Well, I don't really know what a ghost can or can't do, but you seem to have some limits. I'll keep going.

As long as she could. Her heart was beating so hard that it hurt. She felt sick to her stomach.

She could hear Doane cursing behind her.

Farther behind than he had been before. Was he faltering?

Yes.

He was shouting at her, each word broken and harsh. "Don't think you're going—to get away. These are my mountains. Kevin and I spent months out here when he was a boy. He particularly liked to kill the deer. How do you think he qualified to be in the Special Forces? I taught him to be a hunter."

And had he taught him to hunt down those little girls and kill them?

"Do you hear me? I'm going back to the house and get my equipment and my gun. I'll hunt you down like Kevin and I did the deer. I just hope that hypothermia doesn't get you before I do. It gets cold in these mountains at night."

She knew it was true, but it was hard to believe when her entire body was hot and perspiring from exertion.

"I can hear every move you make in that brush. Do you know how easy you're going to be to stalk?"

She was pulling more away from him with every second. Close him out. She was *winning*.

"And then we'll go get Kevin and take him to that butcher who murdered him. I'll let Zander see how it feels when I kill you in front of him. There's no greater agony than a father feels at the death of a child."

More madness. Lee Zander, the hired assassin Doane was sure had murdered his son, was not her father. How could he be? Eve's father had disappeared long before she was born, and her mother was never even sure of his identity. This particular insanity Doane had thrown at her when he'd been enraged after she had tossed Kevin's reconstruction off the cliff to distract him. He had thought it would hurt her in some way to know she was a killer's daughter and that she was to pay for Doane's son's death. It was just one other sign that Doane's cold-blooded, calculated pursuit and abduction of her was completely bizarre and totally without reason.

Forget that nonsense. She was not the child of a murderer who was probably more deadly and ruthless than Doane. It was all part of Doane's wild hallucinations. She just had to concentrate on getting out of these mountains or contacting someone to help her.

"Do you know how many people get lost in these mountains?" Doane's shout sounded still farther away. "Some don't survive the bitter cold and the animals and the mud slides. You might be glad to come back to me after a night or two."

Not bloody likely.

"Do you think your Joe Quinn or Jane MacGuire will be able to locate you out here? You could be out here a week, and no one would catch sight of you. You'd have had a better chance staying at the house. I'm the only one who knows you're here and how to find you. And I will find you, Eve."

Keep running. He might be trying to fool her into thinking he'd temporarily stopped the hunt. Don't trust his words.

It was pitch-dark now. She couldn't see anything but the shrubs directly in front of her. This was too dangerous. She'd be lucky if she didn't tumble off the mountain.

She stopped and tried to hear something besides the pounding of her heart.

No sound.

Doane?

She stood there, listening. No rustle of brush. No harsh sound of his breathing in the stillness.

Safe?

Good God, no. There was no way she was safe, but maybe she'd have a brief respite from the fear that had been with her since she'd been taken from everything she knew that was safe and good.

Joe, Jane, the cottage on the lake where they'd lived so many years.

She could still hear nothing but the flap of an occasional bird's wings and the wilderness night sounds. But they weren't the same sounds as the ones she heard in the forest on the lake. This was wild country.

Keep moving. Put distance between herself and the place where she'd last seen Doane. Providing that she didn't move in circles. She knew a little about the basics of surviving in a forest, but she wasn't an ex-SEAL like Joe. He could survive anywhere with no problem. Her profession of forensic sculpting kept her indoors most of the time, and even as a child, she had been a city girl.

So there were a few obstacles against her. She wouldn't overcome them by self-pity or remembering how good Joe was at this kind of thing.

Or remembering Joe at all. The look of him, the way he'd tilt his head and stare quizzically at her with those tea-colored eyes, the *feel* of him. There were moments when you could afford to remember the ones you loved, but this was not one of them. The thought of Joe made her painfully conscious of the loneliness of being here without him. Perhaps that was what Doane had intended by mentioning him before he'd left. He'd meant to make her more aware of her isolation. Salt in the wound. Joe Quinn, her lover, and Jane, their adopted daughter, the two people she loved most in the world.

Eve would never have wanted to have them here and in danger but it was the—

A sound in the bushes up ahead!

A large animal. A bear. A deer?

Or Doane? He might have circled around and gotten in front of her.

Damn, she had no weapon.

Freeze. Don't move. The threat might dissolve and go away.

Darkness all around her.

She tried to breathe lightly so that she wouldn't be heard.

Please, go away.

Doane wouldn't go away. She just had to hope it was another beast looking for prey.

She was not prey, she thought with sudden fierceness. She would get out of this. She would find a weapon.

To hell with Doane and this mountain he thought belonged to him.

It's not your mountain any longer, you bastard. I'm going to make it my own.

UNIVERSITY OF SOUTHERN CALIFORNIA
LOS ANGELES

Idiots!

Kendra Michaels pushed open the heavy main door of Alexander Hall and stalked down the tree-lined pathway that would take her to the parking lot.

Idiots. Narrow-minded fools.

"Dr. Michaels." The voice came from behind her.

She didn't turn around.

"Dr. Michaels, please!"

She didn't have to look back to know it was Steve Whitty, one of the conference organizers. Kendra hated these things, and her experience here, at the American Psychological Association's Conference on Autism Causes and Treatment, reminded her why.

She finally stopped. He wasn't going to be discouraged.

Whitty ran around to face her. "You were brilliant."

She pointed back toward the auditorium. "Try telling them that."

"You got a lot of people thinking in there."

". . . Thinking I'm some kind of fraud. Were you even listening to the Q&A?"

"Naturally they're going on the attack. You're on the bleeding edge in this field. Uncharted territory. Your work could make a good many of those people's life's work obsolete."

"That's not what I'm trying to do."

"Look at it from their point of view. You're telling them that music can actually help cure autism."

"It's not a cure. It's a treatment. And I never said it was the only treatment."

"But you told them that your study had results far more impressive than anything they've done. Of course you're going to ruffle some feathers. Which is exactly why I wanted you to be here." Whitty placed his hand on her forearm. "And when those researchers get over being scared and pissed off, they're going to examine your data and look at those hours of sessions you posted on the Web. They're going to see what I saw.

They're going to see how this amazing young woman was able to draw patients out of their shells and help them join the human race."

Kendra took a deep breath, angry that she had let those fools get under her skin. She always tried to tell herself that the work was its own reward, finding the right instrument, the right chord progression, the right anything that would engage the interest of her patients and help coax them into a world beyond themselves. But she needed more, dammit. She needed to know that she was able to open those educators' eyes so that they would follow her.

She looked away from Whitty. "Look, part of me understands why they're skeptical. Believe me, I know that the music-therapy field is populated with all kinds of nuts and woo-woo, and they give my profession a bad name. But I treat it like the science that it is. I got input from ten researchers in that room when I was designing the study, and I was tougher on myself than any of them were in their initial feedback."

"They're surprised at your results. Just give them a chance to digest it."

"I've found a way to help those kids, Whitty. And that study is proof of it."

"Kendra, there's a significant variable that some people feel you haven't addressed."

She looked at him in disbelief. "Impossible. I considered every variable."

"Not quite." He smiled. "The variable I'm talking about . . . is you."

"Me?" Then she realized what he meant and cursed under her breath. He could be right. She had been nervous about the presentation and several times had caught herself trying to impress the other attendees. It was completely unlike her. "Oh, you mean the dog and pony show? I knew they thought I was a little weird. I just kind of slipped into it. I didn't mean—"

"Hell of a carnival act, but there's already been some speculation that's how you get your positive results. By being so perceptive and empathetic with your subjects, giving exactly what they need in terms of body language, tone, positive reinforcement, the whole package."

Kendra's eyes narrowed on him. "That's what they're saying? If they read the study, they'll see I wasn't the only therapist. My techniques got the same results from everyone."

He smiled. "I know that because I've read the study. And they'll know it soon enough. You just need to relax."

"If I'd wanted to relax, I would never have come to this conference. I thought for once that I could make a difference."

"Kendra, come back inside." He placed his hand on her arm again. He was trying to soothe her, dammit. He wasn't a bad guy, and the mistake had probably been her own, but it didn't matter.

She wanted to deck him.

Her BlackBerry vibrated in her pocket. Thankful for the opportunity to pull away from Whitty, she stepped back, pulled out the phone, and answered it. "Hello."

"Kendra, it's Joe Quinn."

"Quinn?" She didn't like the tone in his voice. Grim. Ragged. She turned to Whitty and mouthed an apologetic "sorry." He nodded and headed back toward the auditorium. "What's wrong, Quinn?"

"You name it, everything. I need your help."

"Dammit, I'm not a detective. And I'm busy as hell. You can't pull me into—"

"You're always busy." He paused. "It's Eve."

"Eve?" Kendra's hand tightened on the phone. "What's happened? Talk to me."

Forty minutes later, Kendra was at her condo throw-ing clothes into a suitcase on her bed.

"You didn't answer the door, so I used my key. What on earth are you doing?" Kendra Michaels's mother was standing in the doorway of Kendra's bedroom watching disapprovingly as Kendra threw clothes into the suitcase on the bed. "Besides packing with no regard to neatness or order. I taught you better than that, Kendra."

"That was when I was blind, and you thought I had to be super efficient so that no one would feel sorry for me because I was handicapped." She threw another pair of jeans and a sweater into the case. "After the stem-cell operation I discarded that guideline and embraced chaos."

"In more than packing," Deanna Michaels said dryly. "I was worried about you for a number of years after those doctors performed their miracle and made you see. I never thought that you'd sow quite so many wild oats."

"That's past history." Kendra grinned. "Now I'm just a boring musical-therapy teacher. I leave all the wild oats to you." Her mother was a history professor at U.C. San Diego and was the most vibrant and young-minded woman Kendra had ever known. And the most caring. She had used that intelligence and forceful personality to raise a child blind from birth and make her as close to independent as was physically and mentally possible.

And every day Kendra blessed her for it. Though her mother could be difficult and definitely tried to manipulate Kendra and everyone around her to suit her herself.

"That would be extremely clever of you. I like the idea of your leading a semiboring life." Her mother crossed the room and started repacking Kendra's suitcase. "But there are still lingering tendrils of that less-than-wise period you went through. Go get your things from your bathroom. Now that I've rearranged your clothes, I have a place for them in this corner of the suitcase."

"Mom . . ." She stared at her a moment and turned and went to the bathroom. She had learned to pick her battles, and this one wasn't worthwhile. A few minutes later, she brought her plastic bag to Deanna and handed it to her. "Keep it handy. I'll have to pull it for security at the airport."

"You're flying? Where?"

"Atlanta."

"Why?"

"I have something I have to do there."

"That's no answer. If you were still a teenager, I'd call it rude." She frowned. "Why didn't you answer the door?"

"I was in a hurry. I have to get out of here." She smiled. "I wasn't rejecting you. I gave you a key to the condo, didn't I? That means you're welcome anytime." She paused. "Why did you decide to come today? I don't think it's a coincidence."

"I dropped by your conference. I was going to take you to dinner."

Kendra grimaced. "And you saw me almost blow my cool."

"They were idiots. They should have known you were right. You were right, weren't you?"

"Yep. But not diplomatic."

"Thank God." She paused. "I followed you out to the parking lot, and I was going to save you from that earnest young man, but you got a telephone call." She shrugged. "You hung up right away and jumped in your car and left the conference." She met Kendra's gaze. "But I saw your expression. It's happening again, isn't it?"

"Wild oats?" Kendra shook her head. "I like my life, Mom. I'm not going to fly off and leave those kids I teach."

"You know what I mean. Who is it? FBI? The local police? Say no, Kendra."

Kendra hadn't thought she'd be able to deter her, but it had been worth a try. "I can't do that, Mom," she said quietly. "Not this time."

"Why not?" Deanna asked harshly. "Those law-enforcement people don't give a damn about you. How many times have you been hurt? And I've almost lost you before when they tapped you and ask—" She drew a deep breath. "You're too valuable to waste. You're good and giving, and you've worked too hard to become a complete person." Her lips twisted. "The only problem is that you became a bit more than complete."

"No, I won't accept that. Anyone can do what I do. All they have to do is concentrate." All during her childhood, she had trained all her senses to overcompensate for her blindness. At twenty, when she'd had the operation that had given her sight, she'd been amazed that the people around her weren't able to use those senses in the same way she did. In a way, they appeared more blind to her than she had been before her operation. It had been that ability that had brought her to the attention of the law-enforcement officers against whom her mother was so bitter. "And I assure you that most of those agents at the FBI don't consider me loving and giving. They consider me a bitch, useful but not comfortable to be around."

"I never taught you to suffer fools gladly." Deanna added, "There's a possibility I might have gone slightly overboard. But deep down, you have fine instincts. The rest doesn't matter."

"And since you taught me, it must be the world and not me that's wrong." She leaned forward and gave Deanna a kiss on the cheek. "I'll sign on to that." She grabbed her computer case. "I have to go, Mom."

"Not until you tell me who you're going to see." She added grimly, "I need to know who to go to for the body if they get you killed."

Deanna wasn't going to be deterred. Kendra had hoped she would be able to avoid explanations. She didn't have time for them. "Joe Quinn. He's a detective with Atlanta PD. You may remember my mentioning him. I worked with him when he was out here chasing down a serial killer; and then later he involved me in a missing-person case."

"I remember you weren't happy to leave one of your students at a crucial time."

"It was okay. It worked out."

Deanna was frowning. "And you were working with an Eve Duncan. You had problems with her."

"We were a little too much alike. That worked out, too," she said. "I liked her, Mom. She was kind of special."

"So you're going to be working with her again? That's why you have to become involved?"

"Yes, she's the reason." She shook her head. "But I won't be working with her. Joe Quinn called me and told me that Eve has been kidnapped by some nutcase. The man's name is Jim Doane. Quinn asked me to help find her. I have to do it."

Deanna sighed. "Dammit, then I don't have a chance of talking you out of going, do I?"

"It won't be that dangerous. I'm not going to be actively working the case. I just have to try to pull up any clues as to where this Doane took her. I'll go in and do my job and get out." She added softly, "I won't tell you not to worry because that's been your modus operandi from the moment I was born twenty-eight years ago. I celebrate that you think I'm still worth it. But this time, I honestly believe that there's not going to be any reason to do it. Okay?"

"No." She stared at her a moment. "If you don't get yourself hurt physically, you'll end up an emotional wreck. I've seen it before. And this time the odds are leaning in that direction. You told me yourself, you like this Eve Duncan. You'll get hurt again." She turned and slammed the suitcase shut. "And I'll be here to pick up the pieces. Maybe someday you'll develop a sense of self-preservation."

"I already have. Things just seem to get in the way. You'd like Eve, too, Mom."

"Would I?" Deanna asked as she turned toward the door. "I'm driving you to the airport. You can tell me about her on the way." She held up her hand as Kendra opened her lips to speak. "I'm driving you," she repeated firmly. "I'm not letting you fly off into the night without having a solid hold on the situation. Grab your suitcase."

Kendra shook her head ruefully as she hurried after her out of the condo to her mother's Mercedes in the parking space in front of her condo. "We might have to go to a therapy session or two when I get back. You're being domineering again."

"Am I?" She got into the driver's seat. "Oh, well, you can take it. Talk to me. Tell me about Eve Duncan."

"She's a forensic sculptor, one of the best in the world. She does a great deal of work re-creating the faces of skulls of victims found by police departments across the country. She tries to devote most of her time to doing reconstructions of children. Perhaps you've heard of her? She's very famous."

"The name's familiar, but I tend to avoid looking at skulls unless it has to do with something of historical significance. It reminds me of my own mortality. But a person is more than a profession. You haven't told me about Duncan, just what she does for a living."

"She's illegitimate and grew up in the slums of Atlanta. Her mother was on drugs most of her childhood and didn't list any name for the father on Eve's birth certificate. Her mother wasn't sure who he was. Eve had an illegitimate child herself when she was seventeen. It was a little girl she called Bonnie. She adored her. The little girl was kidnapped and killed when she was seven years old."

"Dear God," Deanna whispered. "How could she survive a blow like that? I don't know if I could."

"Eve survived. She went back to school and became a forensic sculptor. She spent years trying to find the body of her daughter and only succeeded a short time ago. She adopted a ten-year-old street kid, Jane MacGuire, years after her daughter disappeared, and she and her lover, Joe Quinn, raised her. Jane's now an artist and temporarily living in Europe. Recently, Eve discovered she had a half sister, Beth, and they're trying to build a relationship, but Beth lives here in California. They don't see much of each other." She looked at Deanna. "Is that enough personal background for you?"

Her mother nodded. "She's no lightweight." She made a face. "Maybe I shouldn't have asked you to tell me about her. I don't have much ammunition to convince you not to go off and try to find her."

"No, you don't. She's strong, and she's real. Like you, Mom."

Deanna didn't speak as she changed lanes to get on the freeway. "If they know the name of this man who abducted her, why can't they find them without you?"

"I don't know. Joe said that Doane had been planning

this for years. His son, Kevin, had been murdered and partially cremated, and Doane only managed to salvage his blackened skull."

"Ah, and he wanted Eve Duncan to do the reconstruction on the skull?"

"Presumably. Doane let her call Quinn and check on the condition of Jane MacGuire, and she told him she'd made a deal with him to do it."

"Condition?"

She hesitated. Her mother was not going to like this. "Jane MacGuire was shot by one of Doane's accomplices, a man named Blick."

"Shit. And this isn't going to be dangerous?"

"I go in, then get out. Jane wasn't killed, only wounded."

"What a relief," Deanna said grimly. "Wonderful."

"It is wonderful." She wouldn't tell her about the CIA man who had been found with his throat cut on the lake property. "I'm not saying that Doane isn't dangerous. He's not stable, but I'm not going to have to deal with him. That's Joe Quinn's job. And he's fully capable of handling it. Before he became a detective, he was with the FBI, and before that, he was a SEAL. He only asked me to look around and see if I come up with something."

"And he wouldn't try to pull you into the case if he thought it necessary? You said he was Eve Duncan's lover. That doesn't bode well for cool professionalism."

Trust her mother to cut through everything to get to the truth. "No, Joe isn't at all professional about Eve." Kendra wouldn't lie. "He's crazy about her. They've been together for years, and it's still a love story.

Nice . . ." She added quickly, "But no one pulls me into anything if I don't want to go. I'm not reckless. You know me well enough to realize that, Mom."

"But you don't have to be reckless if you get emotional. What about that case a few years ago, where there were kidnapped children involved? That nearly made you into a basket case."

Kendra didn't answer.

"Okay." Deanna sighed. "I'll shut up right now if you promise to call and give me reports on how things are going."

"So that you can get on your white horse and come to my rescue?" she asked gently. "Mom, you have to let me go sometime. You were the best, the most extraordinary mother a child could have. You fought a thousand battles for me and taught me to fight them, too. Now you have to trust me to make good choices. And, if I don't make them, you have to trust me to make the situation work." She added softly, "Just as you did all those years. It shouldn't be so hard. After all, I am your daughter."

Deanna didn't speak for a moment. "Was that supposed to appeal to my ego? It is hard. You'll realize that when you have a child of your own." She pulled over in front of the terminal building. "And I will come to rescue you if you don't behave sensibly. I'll give you space, but I won't give you up."

"And that makes me a very lucky woman." Kendra opened the passenger door. "How could I ask for anything else?"

"You couldn't," Deanna said brusquely. "Now, have you told me everything you know about the situation?

If I have to mount that white horse, I want to know how to program this GPS."

"How convoluted can you get?" Kendra got out of the car and retrieved her suitcase from the backseat. "I think you have the bare bones. I don't have much more than that. Quinn was rattling off names and details so fast that I still have to get everything straight in my mind. I'll probably be landing in Atlanta before it becomes clear to me." She leaned back into the car and gave Deanna a quick kiss on the tip of her nose. "Now you know as much as I do. Satisfied?"

"No." Her eyes were glittering as her palm cupped Kendra's cheek. "And if you don't want me to interfere, you'll call and keep me informed. That's not too much to ask."

"Blackmail." Kendra was laughing as she straightened. "What am I going to do with you?"

"I have no idea. I taught you to make your own decisions."

"True." She slammed the car door. "And there's really only one thing I can do with you." She turned away. "I just have to love you. I'll call you when I get to Atlanta."

She could feel her mother's eyes on her as she headed for the glass doors. She lifted her hand and waved as she went through the doors into the terminal.

Her smile faded as she went toward the kiosk. She had tried to comfort her mother and wished she had been able to be more reassuring. She knew so little, and she hated it. She wanted to reach out, to see, to hear, to touch. She was going into this hunt for Eve as blind as she had been during the first twenty years of her life.

And she had a terrible feeling that she wouldn't be able to help Eve. Eve was very sharp, and if she'd been taken by this criminal, then he must be a formidable adversary. It was hard for Kendra to understand how the wary, intelligent Eve she had come to know had become a victim.

But most criminals left traces, clues that shined a light on their path. Doane surely wouldn't be different. All she needed was to go to the crime scenes and everything would come clear.

God, she hoped he wasn't different.

I'll find him, Eve. Fight him. Give me a chance. I'll do everything I can. I'll search so hard for you . . .